The Brother of Sleep

A ST. LAWRENCE SEAWAY MYSTERY

Maggie Wheeler

Author of *A Violent End*

Published by

GENERAL STORE PUBLISHING HOUSE

499 O'Brien Rd., Box 415, Renfrew, Ontario, Canada K7V 4A6
Telephone (613) 432-7697 or 1-800-465-6072

ISBN 1-894263-91-X
Printed and bound in Canada

Design, layout and printing by Custom Printers of Renfrew Ltd.

©Maggie Wheeler, 2004

Author photo - J. Milner–Image-ine Photography
Cover artwork by Hugh Malcolm

No part of this book may be reproduced, stored in a retrieval system or transmitted in any form or by any means, without the prior written permission of the publisher or, in case of photocopying or other reprographic copying, a licence from Access Copyright (Canadian Copyright Licensing Agency), 1 Yonge Street, Suite 1900, Toronto, Ontario, M5E 1E5.

While the background of this novel is based on actual history, the characters and plot lines are products of the author's imagination and are in no way intended to resemble real events or people, either living or dead.

M.W.

"Capsized"
Words and music by Sarah Harmer.
© Copyright 2000 Cold Snap Music Ltd. All Rights Reserved.

National Library of Canada Cataloguing in Publication

Wheeler, Maggie A., 1960-
    The brother of sleep / Maggie Wheeler; edited by Susan Code McDougall.

ISBN 1-894263-91-X

    I. Wheeler, Maggie II. Title.

PS8595.H3852B76 2004   C813'.6   C2004-901748-9

Dedication

For all the friends that have touched my life,
those I've loved and lost
and found again,
and even more for those who stayed.

And to my sister Catheryn,
who was my first
(and shall be my last)
best friend.

Contributors

As with the writing of *A Violent End*, this book was a community project. Once again, people in the Seaway Valley allowed me into their homes and their memories. Discussions with readers, students and former villagers continued after the publication of my first book and into the research for *The Brother of Sleep*. All questions, comments and contributions were used in stitching together another Seaway mystery. I sincerely appreciate the interest and support of my and neighbouring communities.

In particular, I would like to mention the contributions of the following people:

Ken Runions, formerly of Maple Grove;

Bill and Ruth (Johnston) Rankin, formerly of Mille Roches;

Jim Brownell, MPP for Stormont–Dundas–Charlottenburg, past president of the Lost Villages Historical Society;

Richie Warren, retired, contract demolition and salvage, 1954–58;

Lyall Manson, retired educator and historian, formerly of Mille Roches (Lyall, thank you so much for the wonderful maps and pictures);

Yvonne Flemming, formerly of Mille Roches;

Charles Wilkins Sr., former Ontario Hydro photographer and resident of Maple Grove; and Mrs. Marion Wilkins, formerly of Moulinette;

Jean McLennan, Marjorie Vance, Jack Warner, and Rita Manson—all formerly of Mille Roches (thank you for a wonderful round-table session);

And Mary Lynn (Johnston) Alguire, retired educator and Lost Villages bus-tour guide, formerly of Mille Roches (Thanks, ML, for the personal tour, the tears, and being my jogging partner down the home stretch).

A special thank you to Sarah Harmer for letting me use the words from her riveting song "Capsized" to open Part Two.

The author also gratefully acknowledges the assistance of Mr. Olaf Heinzel, Public Relations Co-ordinator for the Waterloo Regional Police Service, and the contributions of Mr. Dennis Dack, Ontario Hydro retired, former public relations assistant to the late Robert H. Saunders, Chairman of Ontario Hydro 1947–55.

I must also mention the contribution of the late Mildred Wirt Benson—the original Carolyn Keene—who, for so many of us through the years, started the whole darn thing.

Table of Contents

Author's Note — vi
Foreword — viii

PART ONE: SHADOWS
Chapter 1: Smoke — 1
Chapter 2: Mirrors — 9

PART TWO: CAMBRIDGE
Chapter 3: Phoenix — 17
Chapter 4: Ashes — 41
Chapter 5: Through a Glass Darkly — 59

PART THREE: THE SEAWAY VALLEY
Chapter 6: Homecomings — 75
Chapter 7: Long Sault — 95
Chapter 8: Mille Roches — 107
Chapter 9: Maple Grove — 133
Chapter 10: The House of Death — 145
Chapter 11: Rage — 167
Chapter 12: Forgiveness — 187

PART FOUR: LIGHT
Chapter 13: The Hard Frost — 209

Author's Note

A question I was often asked during the research and writing of this book was, "When you wrote *A Violent End*, did you plan to do a sequel?" The answer to that is both yes and no.

In the early stages of work on the first book, the matter of most importance to me was just completing it. Since my early twenties, I had held on to the idea of writing a mystery novel. I began work on The Book in 1999 to face down the issue once and for all. *A Violent End* was the result.

In the months following the launch, as people began to know me better, the question, "Do you think you might write a sequel?" became, "When is the sequel coming out?" Pressure? Absolutely—but the kind a writer dreams about. Fortunately for me, I left many loose ends in the lives of the characters because I feel life is very like that. This gave me the foundation for *The Brother of Sleep*.

The community response to my presentation of our history was overwhelming. After the death of my parents in the early 1980s, I had closed most doors to the past as a form of survival. The cards, phone calls and e-mail I received after *A Violent End* was published became a homecoming for me. Invitations to speak to various groups throughout the area about the impact of the Seaway, yesterday and today, put me in touch with people I had not seen in twenty years.

A Violent End, by its nature and content, tapped into and continued discussions about the Seaway era within my community. For some, it began the discussions for the first time. The book became for many the means to completion of the long process of healing, allowing the people of the Seaway Valley to find context and closure for a time of tremendous change in their lives. It was, in the end, their homecoming, too.

But the response from outside the Seaway Valley was a pleasant surprise. I received e-mail from readers all over Ontario and beyond who wanted to talk about loss, grief and healing; about progress versus the past; and about the fascinating history of the Lost Villages. The loss of six villages and an entire landscape is an experience unique in the Canadian awareness, yet there seems to be a common thread within it that binds us all together. Personally, I think I know what it is.

Deep inside every adult is a special memory, a place of the heart we have carried with us since childhood. For me, that place is Preston, Ontario. My maternal grandmother called it home and, through the 1960s into the early 1970s, I spent many happy holidays there. I can say that Preston is my own "Lost Village" because in 1973 the town vanished through amalgamation with the Town of Hespeler, the City of Galt and the surrounding townships to become what is now the metropolis of Cambridge. My grandmother's house is still there, as is Riverside Park, where I swam in the wading pool and fed the swans on the Speed River. But the street she lived on has a new name, and it, like the city around it, has seen tremendous growth in the past three decades. The neighbourhood I knew and loved has vanished, too.

We are, of course, looking at these places of the heart through the stereoscopic vision of time and nostalgia. The emotional landscape of Preston is my touchstone to a gentler and simpler time in my life. Yet the reality is that I'm remembering the 1960s, a time of great change and upheaval in North America.

But try to tell that to my heart.

And I believe that it is in this way we are all connected in our souls to the Lost Villages of the St. Lawrence Seaway.

Maggie Wheeler

Foreword

By MARY LYNN ALGUIRE
RETIRED EDUCATOR, LOST VILLAGES TOUR GUIDE

Dear Reader:

It was July 1, 1958, and I was ten years old. My life was in chaos, and I wasn't sure why.

Up until a year before, the only home I'd ever known had been in the village of Mille Roches about five miles west of the City of Cornwall, Ontario. My father, mother and I lived in a huge building that had once been a hotel on the curve of Highway No. 2. My brother and sister, who were much older than I was, had both gotten married and moved into Cornwall. When my parents purchased the building, they turned half of it into "Percy Johnston's General Store" and the other half into a bed and breakfast called "Better Beds For Less." We had a summer kitchen and a winter kitchen and many of the bedrooms upstairs were often closed off, and I had to ensure my "safety" by lugging one of my cats with me "for protection against the unknown" when I had to visit the second floor all by myself. I had lots of cats because we had outbuildings filled with bags of feed for the area farmers and therefore had lots of "barn" cats and their kittens. My father's hobby was harness racing, and he won lots of trophies when we travelled around to the area's various summer and fall fairs.

I remember playing hopscotch with the long bamboo fishing poles on the wood floor in the store and being fascinated when I was allowed a peek into the huge cooler where my father kept "dead animals" hanging on huge hooks; or into the pickle barrel at the magnificent pungent dark green pickles; or through the boxes of shiny bullets. I remember waiting for all the Blue Bonnet Margarine to be sold so I could inherit the doll from the display. I loved watching him sharpen his huge knives on the big, thick, leather strap, easily cutting a great wedge of cheese off a huge round cheese wheel for a customer, then wrapping it in brown paper and tying it with string that came from the ceiling.

I guess I got in the way a lot because one of my winter jobs was to take my toboggan and search for large icicles from the edges of nearby roofs and bring them back to the store when my toboggan was loaded. After each large load I was rich, for he paid me a penny each if they were big enough. He said he needed them for his cooler, but now I realize it was a great plan to get me out from under his feet for a few hours.

My mother was a great cook, and we often had "visitors" staying in one of the upstairs rooms. They were mostly salesmen who travelled from town to town and preferred the hominess of a bed and breakfast. On cold winter mornings my mother would put my clothes in the oven of the massive wood-burning kitchen stove, and I would run downstairs and have toasty-warm clothes to put on fresh out of the oven.

We often went into the big city of Cornwall. I don't remember what we shopped for, but I remember that if we had time we'd come home "the back way" on Cornwall Centre Road. At a certain spot along the road, the ditches on both sides were usually bursting with tiger lilies and we'd get out and fill the whole car with them. When we got home, every jar, crock and vase was filled with those flowers all over the house. I remember Mom and I going to a special live cooking show at one of the beautiful Cornwall theatres and me winning a whole bag of groceries. When we got home, my mother cleared out a section of the cupboard for "my groceries," and she always asked permission before she used any of "my things." I had my dolls and my cats to dress up and my little pup tent in the yard to play in. Life was good.

When school started I walked for miles, it seemed, to get to a very grand building with desks that were anchored to the floor in rows. The floor slanted down toward the stage where the teacher sat with her big ruler to slap against her desk if people talked. It was here I met my first of many bullies and my first boyfriend in grade one, and experienced my first case of head lice. That was especially fun because my hair was thick and naturally curly and my mother had to put some very stinky liquid on my head and comb every strand with an impossibly tiny-toothed comb that was excruciatingly painful. I hated school with a passion. The only fun part was turning cartwheels on the round green pipe fence that went along the edge of the sidewalk in front of the huge factory on the way to school. The best part was when I got my first male teacher in Grade Three, because he was brand new to teaching, very young and handsome, and had a huge deep dimple in his chin. Life was good.

Then, suddenly, things began to change all around me. The upper bedrooms were opened, and lots of Hydro men came to stay at our house. We had about thirty very hard-working, busy, hungry men eating in two shifts for breakfast and supper. My mother hired girls from the village to help make the meals and tidy up, and to help pack the lunch boxes. The boarders were terrific, much more interesting than my cats. They had tales to tell about what was happening at their work, they helped me with my homework, and told me stories about their families and their children who lived far away from Mille Roches. Sometimes they were lonesome for home so I'd sing songs to them or read them a story from one of my books. The day I learned to tie my shoelaces all by myself, every single one of those men got a shoelace-tying demonstration that evening. They taught me how to sing all the words to "I'll Walk the Line" by Johnny Cash.

The store started to get empty looking. I remember the day some men came with a big truck to take away the huge glass display cases. My father sold his racehorses, and once the store closed, he started going to Cornwall every day to work at City Hall as an assessor with a huge tape measure that rolled up into a round leather case. The barn and the outbuildings were cleaned out and the cats left.

One day my parents said we had to move into Cornwall because my sister's husband and my father were going to start tearing down our huge house. Houses had been going by on big movers while I walked to school, and one day the house next door was gone when I came home. After that I checked the empty foundation every morning to see if any animals had fallen in and gotten trapped. Mille Roches was starting to look very empty and lonesome. Many of my friends at school started to go to new schools on yellow school buses and the classroom was getting empty, too.

The day came when my parents announced that I was going to start at a new school in Cornwall because they'd bought a house there. I begged to be allowed to finish the school year in my familiar classroom, but I lost. So I had to start all over again to find my place with strange kids at the new school, in my new house, with the one cat I'd been allowed to bring with me.

During all this frenzied activity, we had begun to visit the top of a high hill behind a farmer's house where my parents and my sister and her husband talked about us building a cottage. I thought my world had gone totally nuts. We were a very long way from the water on the top of a farmer's field that he was working with his tractor. Near the bottom of the hill was the farmer's house, in front of it was Highway No. 2, then the canal with the huge lakers going back and forth, and then finally the St. Lawrence River. But my parents insisted that we were going to build a lovely cottage from many of the good things saved from our house in Mille Roches. We did. It had my old familiar kitchen cupboards and counters, the windows and the doors. Even some of our Mille Roches furniture was brought on the truck to fill it. The best news of all was that we would share the cottage with my sister and her husband and their two daughters who were very close in age to me, and so we became "summer sisters."

I didn't understand much of what was happening around me because everyone was so busy they didn't have time to explain why my life was turning upside down. I was happy about my new "sisters," but just couldn't figure out why the roads we travelled to get to our cottage were so high up in the air and even had bridges, and how we were ever going to enjoy swimming since we couldn't even get close to the river because of the busy highway, the canal and all the big boats. But once again there was a bright spot, and life was good.

July 1, 1958. All my family and I are standing on the highway in front of the cottage. The farmer's home and all his buildings are gone, no boats have been in the canal for a long time, the cottage is almost finished and the air is filled with excitement. I don't quite understand the tears and the sadness all around me, but it's everywhere I go and nothing in my life is the same except for my family. I'd heard people talking about a huge flood that was going to happen and the wave would kill us all if we didn't pack up all our belongings and head north out of its path. My parents didn't believe that and so here we stood on the white line of a once busy highway, everyone waiting for something to happen. I don't remember hearing the noise of the thirty tons of dynamite exploding in the distance. But it wasn't all that long before the strangest thing began to happen. Land animals of every kind came running or slithering along the road and up the hill. Raccoons, beaver, rats with very long tails, and even snakes of every size came toward us. A little while later, the water started to get higher in the river and the canal, and started to rise up toward the highway. What was happening to my world? I felt like screaming, just like the birds flying overhead who had their nests in the long grass. We stayed there until the water covered the pavement and continued up the hill, then it was time to leave and find another vantage point to see the slow-moving floodwaters. My mother was crying. My father was very quiet. I was scared.

Why didn't someone sit me down and tell me? I guess everyone's lives were upside down and things were just moving too fast. Today, when I think about it, the tears flow uncontrollably. Why didn't someone tell me to take one last look around at Mille Roches? Why didn't I burn my town and my childhood places into my memory? Why didn't I realize that my entire youthful memories of a place and a time would be lost under water forever? Why?

About ten years ago, Susan Lopez was principal where I taught at Rothwell-Osnabruck School in Ingleside, Ontario. She and I decided it was time that the students came to understand the Seaway Story, since it was literally right in their own backyard. Fran Laflamme, a retired teacher and one of the original founders of the Lost Villages

Historical Society, answered all our questions and so began the annual three-week program with Grades Seven, Eight and Nine students to study the story of our lost heritage. I planned and scouted out a bus tour for the Grade Seven classes that would show them the location of the six villages and three hamlets. I would explain, among other things, why paved roads disappear into the undergrowth and into bodies of water, why many people of the area speak of places that no longer exist except in their memories, and of the deep emotional ties, still so very powerful over forty years later, of many area residents to their former homes lost to the floodwaters.

Jim Brownell, president of the Lost Villages and an old friend, asked if I would do a bus tour for the society. Six years later, we're still going strong. Blythe Watson, bus driver "supreme," and I now do eight four-hour tours a summer from July to the end of October and we hope to expand into June in 2004. For the past three years, every tour has sold out. We've even had to turn people away.

Over the past six years, I have come to see a phenomenal growth of interest in the story of the Seaway. At first we had people from faraway places like British Columbia, Los Angeles, Switzerland and Alaska, but the last few years have seen a rise in interest of local and area people. We still have many people today, right in our midst, who don't realize they are living beside one of the largest water projects in history—comparable only to the flooding of the Nile River and the loss forever of some pyramids to the resulting floodwaters. More locals are now taking the tours, and many of the former residents of the Lost Villages share their stories with me of where their home was and where they played as a child and so on. My tour commentary is now almost four hours long, just to fit everything in, to bring the past alive, to provide a living, breathing snapshot of a lost way of life and a lost heritage.

Many area students spend hot summer days exploring the undergrowth looking for lost evidence of their grandparents' past, of a time when doors weren't locked and everyone knew their neighbour by name. A time when the family doctor made house calls and the drive through the villages from Cornwall to Morrisburg wound through orchards heavy with fruit, lush farmers' fields, and right up alongside the mighty Long Sault Rapids. The Lost Villages Museum site is fast becoming a premier tourist attraction as people are developing a growing desire to learn about the past. It's always a special joy when people leave the bus at the end of the tour and express their amazement at what we've all lost and how close to the surface, so many years later, emotions still run. The ripple we feel must be old history teachers and deceased residents of the Lost Villages turning over in their graves with knowing smiles on their faces. We learn from our past. Never again will a project of this magnitude ever be repeated with nary a voice or a placard raised in protest because the government says it's a good thing.

Maggie Wheeler did a splendid job of teaching us about our past by wrapping us in a fantastic murder mystery rooted in one of the Lost Villages. *A Violent End* left me breathless as I read and turned each page. Often I had to reread pages because I couldn't stop the tears that flowed like the flood waters, bringing to life the deep emotions of the people who drowned a little themselves as they turned and walked away from their flower gardens, their ancestral foundations and their personal histories for the final time. I certainly wasn't alone in voicing my praises of her first novel.

Now, I have been most fortunate and honoured to be the first to read her newest novel, *The Brother of Sleep*. Once again she has taken her readers back in time to a lost generation. She spins a magnificent tale of murder and deceit, of love and hate, of passion and lost loves. This second novel takes place, in part, in my village of Mille Roches and the lost hamlet of Maple Grove on the outskirts of Cornwall, a few thousand yards from the mighty Moses-Saunders Powerhouse.

After reading *The Brother of Sleep*, if you have already read *A Violent End,* you'll want to read it again. If you haven't, you'll be searching for a copy. And you'll be anxiously begging for her third novel, which will once more turn back time and take us down "The Front" for another visit.

February 2004

PART ONE: Shadows

"It is not to Egypt that I am going," said the swallow.
"I am going to the house of death.
Death is the brother of sleep, is he not?"

And he kissed the Happy Prince
on the lips and fell down dead at his feet.

Oscar Wilde
The Happy Prince

Chapter ONE: Smoke

SEPTEMBER 10, 1957
Maple Grove, Ontario

"We'll stay if you want to stay. I'm not afraid."
The young man turned to look behind him at the woman who had spoken, and gave a slow smile. He hadn't heard her come up, but still knew she was there. Always keenly aware of her presence—as he had been since the first time he'd walked into the store.
"No," he replied firmly. "It's all been enough. I want to take you away from here. We couldn't get married here after all that. I just wish . . ." His voice trailed off as he turned back to the view before him.
Though still under construction, the Robert H. Saunders-Robert M. Moses hydroelectric power dam stretched before them over half a mile across the St. Lawrence River, as far as the eye could see. It was barely dawn, but the trucks continued to move about its base far below them, using the access tunnels carved under the old Cornwall Canal. A canal boat steamed quietly by in direct contrast to the dam that seemed, even now, to pulse with energy it would not generate for almost another year.
She stood beside him now, one hand on his arm, both of them aware that even such a simple gesture would have been forbidden until last month.
"You wish you could stay until they turn the monster on, don't you? You helped build it. I suppose I understand that."
"It's not a monster," he said, placing his hand on hers. "It's a creation. It's the beginning of something new and valuable."
"If I'm not mistaken, Dr. Frankenstein felt the same way." The woman pulled her hand away and walked across the No. 2 Highway toward the river. "Nothin' is valuable," she added over her shoulder, "if you have to start buildin' by diggin' up the dead."
He sighed and followed her. She had been this way again since the old church in Moulinette had been moved to the new historical village last month. Sheila was old family here, and he was an outsider—worse yet, an Ontario Hydro engineer. Despite their feelings for each other, this was one point that would never be won. The sooner they left, the better.

"I thought Hal would have come back by now. I wanted to say goodbye. And thanks. If it weren't for Hal, we wouldn't be together now." The man put his arms around her. *"I hope he got my telegram about Harper's death. Leslie's completely alone now. But then, Hal had plenty of troubles of his own before he left."*

SEPTEMBER 10, 1973
Cambridge Preston, Ontario

Farran Mackenzie sat in her Grade Ten English class, barely listening. It was only 9:15 a.m. and she already wanted to go home. Miss Lawson was the pretty, new teacher at Preston High School and the students loved her, but this morning the lesson left Farran cold.

It had been a cold morning, both in temperature and atmosphere. After the whopping fight she'd had with her mom the night before and then slipping out to school without saying goodbye, the girl was still very upset. She'd skipped breakfast and wasn't the least bit hungry.

And Alison Perry had left without her for school. Farran sneaked a glance at her best friend sitting one up in the next row, book closed, ramrod straight and still. Not like her, the girl thought. Not good. Maybe that's what all the yelling in the Perry house was about this morning.

Behind Farran, two girls twittered about another classmate who had not returned to school in the fall. Jeanie Ross had been a little, well, wild, and the rumours about her absence were, too.

"Pregnant, you know."

"That's no surprise, considering."

On an ordinary day, Farran would have ignored the chatter and let the teacher handle it. It was her job. But Jeanie Ross had been her friend, too, and today there was just too much sand in Farran Mackenzie's shorts.

She turned around to face the girls.

"SHUT UP," she said in a clear voice.

The chatterers stopped in mid-gape. Every head in the class turned, except Alison's. Farran slowly turned back and looked at the teacher who stood, chalk in hand. Miss Lawson looked at Farran, then at the two girls behind her. But no rebuke came, only raised eyebrows before continuing the lecture.

Farran slumped down in her seat and said no more.

In a small brick house at 251 Water Street, a woman sat silently in the kitchen. Her breakfast lay untouched, a second plate unused on the table beside her. It was already 9:30, but she would not go into work today, unusual for Leslie Mackenzie. The fight with Farran last night had left her feeling hollow and dead inside.

Since her decision fifteen years ago to disappear and raise her child alone, Leslie had known this moment would come. Maybe she'd just always figured that by now she would have the answers her daughter so desperately needed and deserved. But nothing had changed as little Fan had grown, and the fear was as real now as it had been that terrible night so long ago.

"What do I do, Harp?" Leslie whispered to the empty room. "Poppa, if I ever needed your advice, I need it now."

Keep the secret, gal. Stay safe, for the child's sake.

Leslie rubbed her eyes and stirred her cold tea. The voices in her heart always told her the same thing. But maybe John Perry was right. Maybe she couldn't do it alone anymore. Maybe it was time to trust someone, a friend.

At the very least, it was probably time to tell Fan the truth. At thirty-two, it might be time to stop thinking with her heart and use her head. God knows she'd been lonely in her self-imposed exile over the years.

Dave Carlson's face came to her. No. Never. Because a man would demand to know the truth, and rightly so.

But deep inside, Leslie Mackenzie knew that the loneliness had become her life companion, wrapping her in a protective womb like a lover's arms.

"For Farran's sake," was the mantra.

Was it still true?

At 9:40, Jessica Perry snapped off the vacuum in the house at 249 Water Street and looked out the window. Funny, Leslie's car was still in the driveway. The woman had never gotten sick or missed a day's work in her memory. Still, last night something had gone on in that house. Lights on till all hours. And after such a nice birthday supper, too.

But things were not good here, either. Alison had been strange the whole evening, despite it being her fifteenth birthday party. The girl was just too young to deal with this sort of thing. And John had been strained with Dave, his best friend. Words had been exchanged last night after the Mackenzies left, in the living room with the door shut, the good solid doors in this house making it impossible for Jessica to listen in.

She chewed her lip nervously and put the vacuum cleaner in the closet. The blast she'd expected from John after that hadn't come, but he was visibly upset. She'd decided to hold her tongue.

Dave had returned this morning on his way to the police station and caught John in the driveway. But any conversation had been cut short when a call came over the radio, and the two men had jumped into John's squad car to respond. She'd barely got a kiss before they left. Someone had called in an anonymous tip about street gang members in an underground parking garage. Ever since the Simser boy's murder, people were seeing bogeymen everywhere.

Jessica straightened the pictures on the mantel. Keep busy. Don't think about what John might be walking into. After years as a police wife, she had the strategy down pat. Still, there were days when nothing would help shut out the million scenarios running through her mind. Today was one of those days. Maybe John being a Waterloo Regional Police officer seemed somehow more dangerous than being an officer on the Preston Police Force.

"Well, now what?" Jessica surveyed the pristine rooms with no sense of satisfaction. As orderly as the house was (except Alison's room), life was upside down. It was like waiting for the axe to fall. And the cold finger of worry that had poked its way into her chest as she watched them leave this morning was still there.

But John was a good cop. And he had Dave for backup.

9:55 a.m.

"Unit Three, please wait for backup. Units One and Five are in transit to you."

The radio fell silent. The two officers in the squad car sat across the street from an entrance to underground parking for the Regency Hotel on King Street. The call from the tipster had specified two men, possibly armed, in the parking garage. With the car bombings going on, every call had to be checked out.

Sergeant John Perry put his hat on and got out of the car on the driver's side, unsnapping the holster of his gun.

"I can't wait," he said to Corporal Dave Carlson through the window. "I know it's him, and I can't let him slip through our fingers again. I want him. You wait for backup," he added.

"Then I'm going with you." Carlson rubbed his eyes under his sunglasses. Damn headache, and only two beers last night. He climbed out of the car and came around to join Perry. "If you walk in there, there's no safe position. No control without help."

John turned on his friend. "You can't," he said curtly. "I'd rather go in alone. Just tell backup where I've gone."

Dave dropped his eyes to the pavement for a moment, and then watched carefully as Perry approached the entrance. The sergeant listened, nodded to Dave, then disappeared into the gloom of the underground.

Carlson grabbed the radio. "Central, Officer Perry has gone ahead into the parking garage to assess the situation. I'm still waiting for backup."

The sound of gunshots echoed into the street. Everyone on the sidewalk froze, looking around uncertainly. Sirens were in the distance, growing louder.

"Shots fired, Central. I'm going to assist." Dave threw the radio mike on the seat, and ran across the road. Waving people away, he drew his gun and stopped at the edge of the big doorway. The sirens were very close now.

He pushed his sunglasses up on his head and the sunlight angered his headache as he slipped inside the door. The sudden darkness blinded him. Dammit. Dammit. Hurry. Focus. He moved along the wall, back to it, gun up close to his chest. The way his heart was beating, you'd think he was a rookie on his first beat. Slowly, he came around the corner into the main parking area, only half filled with cars. He thought he saw something lying partially hidden behind a panel truck. It registered somewhere in him that the sirens had stopped. Backup was here.

"John," Dave called softly. "John."

Movement in the dark. The glint of something.

He fired once, twice.

Then sound, pain and . . . nothing.

10:00 a.m.

Leslie Mackenzie picked up her dishes and rose to go to the kitchen sink. She would talk to Farran tonight, but the lump in her stomach was growing instead of calming down.

Suddenly, a cold fear she had not felt in fifteen years swept through her body, shaking her violently. She grabbed the sink to keep from falling.

The plate and mug smashed into a thousand pieces across the kitchen floor.

10:10 a.m.

"We need help, Central! Officers down! Carlson and Perry. Both of them. Send help."

Constable Gail Melvin pressed the mike to her forehead and waited for the reply. She could feel tears streaming down her face and didn't give a shit. This wasn't happening, please, please.

"Melvin," came the reply, "what's your 10-20?"

Control the situation, they'd taught her at the academy. Don't let it control you.

"The Regency Hotel garage on King." She bit her lip to keep from screaming. "They're both shot. I need a 10-52 now!"

But Gail Melvin couldn't control the shaking.

10:15 a.m.

Jessica Perry decided to drop in and see if Leslie needed anything. Not that the gesture would be taken, of course. The woman had been her neighbour for years and was still a mystery in many ways. Too closed off. Too independent. Too much Betty Friedan, perhaps.

As she passed the table in the front hall, Jessica's coat caught a large framed photograph sitting there, sending it to the floor. The glass shattered, slashing the face of the smiling groom in the Perrys' wedding picture.

10:30 a.m.

"Get the goddamn reporters out of here!" Chief Brian Miller waved his arm to take in the area. "I want this whole block sealed off. No press. No gawkers. Just the ambulance when it comes. Do it now!"

The officers spread out to follow orders and it gave him a minute to breathe. His days on the street were over, but a situation like this demanded his presence. All these young faces, some still new to him since the creation of the regional police force, trying to handle this nightmare. Trying to be cops instead of human beings.

Miller's ears heard the sound of the ambulance and his mouth formed a thin line. They could help Carlson, thank God. Too young and too much promise to lose him now. But Perry. John Perry. One of his best officers.

Constable Melvin approached him. He could see she'd been crying. Ordinarily, he would have fried her for that. But she'd done her job and done it well. The one he'd have thought would stumble when the time came. Guess Perry had been right about her, after all. But neither of them had ever thought her trial by fire would be anything like this.

"Inside is secure, sir." She turned to watch the ambulance pull up.

"Let them in, then," he said grimly.

She nodded silently and walked away.

"Melvin," Miller called out. She turned back and waited. "I'm sending Armstrong and MacDonald over to the Perrys' house to see Jessica," he explained. "I want you to go straight to the high school and get Alison. Take her home to be with her mother. I don't want that child hearing this in the goddamn locker room."

Brian Miller had known Alison Perry since she was born.

Hell, he didn't want her to hear this at all.

10:50 a.m.
"What's the matter with you?"
At the question, Farran slammed her locker door and turned to glare at her best friend. "That's rich, coming from you. You didn't wait for me this morning and you haven't spoken to me since I got here."
Alison looked away, her face flushed.
"I left early for school," she explained. "Dad and Dave had to have a big talk about something." She turned back to Fan. "But you look like hell. Are you sick?"
"I don't know," Farran replied honestly. "All I know is I feel cold all over . . . and I need to talk to my mom. I'm going home." She picked her books up from the floor.
Alison shrugged. "Maybe you're starting your per—" Her voice trailed off. Farran followed her friend's eyes to where they looked far down the hall.
The principal, Mr. Chase, was coming down the centre of the hallway, the students parting before him like the Red Sea. He had an odd look on his face. Behind him came two Waterloo Regional Police officers, a man and a woman. They looked very grim, but more in a sad way than an official one. Farran's stomach suddenly made her very glad she hadn't eaten that morning.
Mr. Chase stopped beside the two girls.
"Alison," he said gently, "your mother needs you home now. These officers will drive you."
Alison seemed suddenly a statue. Farran felt a cold hand slip into hers.
"Yes," said Fan to the unspoken question, "I'll come with you."

11:15 a.m.
Leslie Mackenzie stood out on the Perrys' porch, waiting for the girls. The day was cruelly beautiful, the sun lighting up the newly changing leaves on the trees. She would cry later when it was safe. The sound of Jessica's sobbing had quieted down. The sedative from the doctor must be taking effect.
"It's like a dream, again," she said softly to herself. "Like last time. I want to wake up from the sleep, but I can't."
The squad car pulled up in the driveway. That made four around the house. She could feel the neighbours starting to stare through their windows. She'd deal with them later, for Jessica. Or maybe the news would.
Constable Melvin got out of the car on the passenger side and opened the rear door. Gently, as though handling fine china, she

helped the girls out of the back seat. Leslie came over and took Alison by the hand.

"Your mother's in the living room, dear," she said. The girl's hand was like ice, her face set like stone. But she was shaking.

As if in a dream, Farran followed them into the house where Jessica lay on the couch. Three officers stood uncertainly around the room, and another man in civilian clothes leaned over Jessica. Alison broke free from Leslie's grip and ran to her mother.

"Tell me," she demanded. "Tell me the truth." The girl started to cry. "Where's Daddy? Where's Daddy?"

Without a word, Jessica Perry took her daughter in her arms and began to rock her as though a baby. Behind Leslie, Gail Melvin covered her face with her hands. The other officers hung their heads and discretely left the room.

Against her wishes, Leslie began to cry. She had lost a good friend, and perhaps the one person who could have helped her make it safe for Fan.

Keep the secret, gal. Stay safe.

Leslie turned and led Fan out into the sunlight. Wordlessly, they held each other. The fight was over and would not be spoken of again. There would be no more discussions of the past.

You're right, Harp, Leslie thought, stroking her child's hair. It's not safe.

It will never be safe.

Chapter TWO: Mirrors

AUGUST 10, 2003

St. John's, Newfoundland

"Aren't you on vacation or something, Paul?"

The waitress poured a second coffee in the cup without asking.

"Stress leave," the man at the counter replied without looking up. "Thanks."

"Yah," she said softly. "I can see that. Being a cop is enough stress without . . . everything else. Is there anything I can do?"

At that, Paul Vaughn met her eyes with a smile. Debbie had served him breakfast for years, and the offer was sincere, without the agenda so many other women had tried to put on him. "No thanks, Deb. Nothing anyone can do except me. And time. It just all takes time, I guess."

Debbie quickly scribbled a bill and stuck it under his saucer.

"It's August," she said. "Good weather. Why don't you get out of town? Travel some. Go see some friends and family." She made a face. "If I could get out of here for a bit, Paul, you wouldn't see me for dust."

The bell rang in the kitchen and Debbie moved off to pick up her order.

Family, she'd suggested.

Paul ran his fingers through his hair and glowered down at his coffee. Family was the root of the problem. Sudden loss and secrets from the past coming out of the woodwork at him. When it rained, it poured. A box of clippings in his father's closet that chronicled a family secret, with names of places he'd never heard of—Mille Roches and Maple Grove, Ontario. And from what he understood from the articles, these places were now gone. A dam and a little flooding somewhere.

Rubbing his eyes, he threw some money on the counter. He'd opened the box and the past had blown up in his face. He didn't trust his memory of his parents anymore. Hell, these days, the cop with all the answers wasn't sure of anything.

Get married, Paul. So many times he'd heard it from his father. *Settle down, have a family. It will give you balance, a foundation.*

Instead, he'd been married to his job for over twenty years. And now on stress leave, the six months stretched before him like the yawning mouth of a new grave.

Two new graves. Side by side.

Paul stood up quickly and threw on his coat. Debbie came up to get the bill and the money.

"I'll get your change, Paul."

"Keep it," he said briefly. "You always give me good advice." He turned to leave, then stopped. "I almost forgot. You wouldn't marry me, would you, Deb?"

Debbie gave him the eyeball. "Be careful, Sergeant Vaughn, or one of these days when you ask, I'll say yes."

The August sun warmed him when he left the diner. And despite the sun, he could feel the mist from the sea on his face. It almost felt good to be alive. But that would have to come back on its own time. Right now, he was up to his neck in emotional landmines and couldn't be bothered worrying about happiness.

Paul found a mailbox on Duckworth Street, and with only a second's hesitation, popped in a stamped envelope. One issue resolved. He felt like a shit doing it in a letter. She deserved better. The way he handled his relationships, it was no wonder he'd never married. But his focus was elsewhere, so it was better not to get any more involved.

Go somewhere, Deb had told him. He knew it. He had to get away to think for a bit. But something told him he wasn't going to get the time.

Paul reached into his coat pocket and pulled out a newspaper clipping, slowly unfolding it as though it could hurt him. Maybe it could. This one hadn't been in the box. This one was recent and his father had kept it in his wallet.

WATERLOO WOMAN INJURED IN PROVINCIAL PARK SHOOTING

Names. Strauss, a cop. Leonard, dead. Murphy, previously dead, a connection. And the woman in the picture, a woman dazed with blood all over the side of her face, being taken away by paramedics.

A woman named Farran Mackenzie.

He would have to find her, ask what it all meant to his father.

Paul sighed and looked at the handwriting at the top of the clipping. It was in his father's hand, and it said one word. A name.

Hal.

Cornwall, Ontario

"Fifty years. Fifty years . . . " The elderly woman in the wheelchair gently stroked the china doll she was never without. The windows of the Glen-Stor-Dun Lodge dining room looked out at the St. Lawrence River. This was the real river, untouched by the Power Project half a century before.

On her lap lay the latest issue of the Lost Villages Historical Society newsletter containing a discussion of how to mark next year's milestone—fifty years since the official start of the St. Lawrence Seaway and Power Project. She remembered that August day clearly: the pomp and ceremony for the Prime Minister of Canada and the Governor of New York State, the turning of the sod, the people of Maple Grove not allowed close enough to see the powers that would begin the calculated destruction of the lives they knew.

Half a century since all hell had broken loose. Since Charles Vaughn had come to town with all the rest of them. Since the terrible days of the trial. Since the last time she'd seen Sheila. It was so long ago. Was it real or had it been only a dream?

"Mila? It's noon. Let me move you to a table and I'll get you some lunch." Sarah stood over her smiling. Friendly woman, and from the old families, but as bothersome as them all. Always fussing.

"Not hungry." Mila raised her chin and looked back out to the river.

"Mila," said Sarah sternly, "you have to eat. Doctor's orders. Let me get you some soup."

Mila sighed inwardly and let herself be wheeled to a nearby table. She sat parked with three other ladies who had lost their battle with the helpers. You couldn't win over them. They were determined to keep you alive. Worse yet, keep you cheerful.

The soup appeared as promised and she absentmindedly tucked the doll under the blanket on her legs. The last gift Sheila had given her, the Christmas before the murder.

Fifty years. Mila stirred her soup slowly. I felt old then, she thought grimly. Amazing I'm still alive.

Was Sheila still alive?

Ingleside, Ontario

Ruth Hoffman sat in a chair by the window, looking out unseeing at the street. Her hand lay on her lap, a letter open in it. Funny thing, since the news of contact with Steven, she took more and more comfort from sitting in Alice's chair. Although her mother had been dead a year now, Ruth left the chair untouched in its usual place in the living room.

And today, trying to write the letter to Steven, she needed to talk with her mother all the more. Her grown children had not been overly supportive when they found out they had a long-lost brother and that

Ruth wanted to find him. Alice would have had her comments, to be sure, but for once mother and daughter would have been on the same team. Family was family.

Ruth closed her eyes. She could see him yet, a baby so tiny, but with lungs that meant business. They had let her hold him for a minute before taking him away, his cries echoing down the hall. She'd been still a child herself, then. But the tears that came on that day belonged to a woman.

Tears came now, and Ruth reached for a tissue. No changing what was, and what had been for forty years. Besides, he'd made contact. Steven would come home.

She would call Farran tonight. The secret was still a secret and she needed to talk to someone who wasn't family. Maybe this would bring Farran back home, too, where she belonged. Even for a short time. It had been a year, and all that had happened seemed like a dream.

Or a nightmare.

Long Sault, Ontario

Inspector Jerry Strauss sat at his desk, tapping a pencil end over end on his blotter. The office was quiet for just a moment in the day and quiet was to be avoided. Thinking, too. Shouldn't have gone out with Dave for drinks last night. The hangover of indecision was worse than anything alcohol could produce.

"Early retirement." Dave Lewis had slapped him on the back with his usual enthusiasm for, well, everything. Strauss had replaced Lewis at the Stormont, Dundas and Glengarry OPP detachment in Long Sault two years ago, shortly after Dave had called him in from Kingston when they'd found Hal. Then Lewis had gone into municipal politics and was now mayor of South Stormont Township. "Don't be married to the job forever," he'd continued. "It'll kill you. Take retirement while you're still young enough to enjoy it."

Strauss made his way down the central hallway in the detachment, stopping in the front lobby to look out the large glass doors at the St. Lawrence River across the highway. Had he been Jerry Strauss, police officer, too long to do anything else? For some, retirement saved their health, their lives. For others, retirement was the end. It depended on what kind of cop you were. What kind of person.

On that latter account, he'd lost the reins the day Lewis had called him about the body found where Aultsville had once been. The remains that had turned out to be all that was left of Hal Leonard, the one best friend Jerry had ever had. The friend he'd let down in the end.

And then Farran Mackenzie had come, digging up old ghosts and old wounds to rub salt into. Making him go over the past he wanted to forget, and find feelings he didn't want to have again.

He should call her. Take the first step and break the silence. Go back right now and make the call from his office, door closed.

Strauss pushed the glass doors open and walked out into the sunlight.

Cambridge, Ontario

Leslie Mackenzie
Aged 58 years
Beloved Mother
Missed Forever

The woman stood in front of the tombstone, hands buried in pockets, eyes not seeing the inscription. It wasn't necessary. Farran Mackenzie knew the words by heart.

"I made you a promise last year, Mom," she said quietly. "I'm sorry. I've been a coward again."

I will come back in the spring, she had promised herself, *to bring Mother home again. I will lay her in the earth near the man who was more father to her than any flesh and blood could replace, beside her own true love, and in sight of the great river she never forgot. And then, I think, we will both have peace.*

And her cowardice had denied her that peace.

"I'll make arrangements this week," Farran told the grave. "I'll get you home very soon."

More father to her than any flesh and blood could replace.

Farran looked around to the older part of the cemetery. It had been years since she'd been to the grave, but after only a few tries she found it, stamped with the crest of the Waterloo Regional Police Force:

Sergeant John Miles Perry
Born August 6, 1933
Died September 10, 1973
In the line of duty
Officer, Husband and Father

For a long time, Farran silently listened to the summer breeze in the trees. Thirty years ago next month. She pulled a copy of *The Cambridge Daily Reporter* from her pocket and opened it to read one of the headlines.

FORMER MAYOR TO RUN IN PROVINCIAL BY-ELECTION
After a 10-year hiatus from politics
Alison Perry Standish
seeks local provincial seat

Farran folded the paper firmly and began to walk in the direction of the cemetery office, stopping only to drop the newspaper in the trash.

"You can't do this." The young man was obviously not having a good day. He pulled at his tie and ran his fingers through his hair. It now stood up like a rooster.

A woman stood at the window, arms crossed, her back to him. She did not reply and the silence was ominous. He knew about the threats she'd received, but this woman was used to having enemies. She'd never turned tail and run before. No, this was different. Aside from his own impending catastrophe, he knew her well enough to see that something was very, very wrong.

"Alison." He crossed the room briskly and came around to face her. It was like looking at stone. "Alison, they practically rolled the red carpet out for you. The party wants you. The voters want you." He desperately played his one and only ace. "I've heard whispers this week of a possible cabinet position within the year. Not front line, of course," he added, "but your foot would be in the door very quickly. You can't walk away from *that*."

Still the woman did not respond. He waited for a full minute, then lost his temper.

"I've gone to bat for you!" he yelled. "Staked my career on this move. If you don't run, I'll look like a fool. Is that what I get for supporting you?"

Finally, Alison Perry Standish turned to look at him.

"I have something to do that cannot wait," she said simply. "And until it's finished, I can't do anything else. I'm sorry."

He struggled for a minute. Her eyes disturbed him. For the first time in several years, he couldn't get to her. She had gone somewhere out of his reach and would come back only when ready. He'd lost the battle.

"Fine," the man said coldly. "I won't be back. And just remember that the decision was yours."

The silence following the slam of the office door wrapped Alison like a blanket. For several minutes, she did not move. Then slowly and deliberately, she crossed to her desk and sat down, unlocking a drawer on the right. Taking out an envelope, she pulled out the paper within and spread it flat before her. It contained one line, and one line only.

Your father died by friendly fire.

After returning the paper to the drawer and locking it up, Alison Perry walked over to a small bathroom and promptly threw up.

PART TWO: Cambridge

when I heard about the coming day
wish I could wake up from the dream
in it I see a family photographed
and there you are tucked in the scene
and there's a jealous net inside my chest
there's a hurt, a sadness there
maybe I'd tell you all about it
if I thought you'd care

heavy heart get lighter by yourself
it's been so long since you capsized
and you've been lying out there in the sun
has it begun?
has it begun?

Sarah Harmer
"Capsized"

Chapter THREE: Phoenix

I turned and there she was.

That's how it is in real life—you spend years waiting and wondering about that Hollywood moment when someone walks back into your life. You might even rehearse all those perfect lines for the added touch. And then life cheats you by being life. On one ordinary day, you turn, and there they stand in the doorway of your office.

She stood in a suit that wasn't from a catalogue, with matching purse and makeup. Totally together except for the eyes. The eyes were filled with pain. That much I recognized from memory.

Alison Perry Standish, former mayor of the City of Cambridge, former wife of Canadian diplomat and retired Lieutenant-General Martin Standish, newly announced hopeful for the provincial seat for the greater Kitchener–Waterloo area. The city's youngest mayor to date, her years in office were legendary for tough times and tough leadership to match. And in another lifetime far, far away, she'd been the only best friend I ever had.

"Hello, Farran." Alison tried a brief smile and looked at the stack of books in my arms. "I hope I didn't catch you at a busy time."

I closed my mouth and tried to wave her to a seat. No hands. No seats either, I realized. Books everywhere. "Hang on," I said, shifting the books I was carrying so I could place them on my desk. "I'll find you somewhere to sit down." I found room for another stack of books on the floor and swept a pile from the chair nearest the desk.

"Moving in or moving out?" she said, taking the seat offered.

"Moving out." I closed the door, expertly straddled the piles on the floor on the way to my desk and sat down. And then the silence hung between us.

"Well, I'm glad at least that we're not going to bother with small talk," I said after a minute. Leaning back, I used some books for a footstool, trying to appear relaxed. Then I casually tried to keep from flipping over.

Alison looked at me with those pain-filled eyes I found hard to watch. "I really don't know where to begin." She shook her head slowly as if confused. "Except here. With you. For a lot of reasons."

This wasn't going to be small talk, and it wasn't going to be good. But thankfully it wasn't going to be phony, either. I could see Alison just didn't have it in her, and my educated guess was that only something very bad would leave her spread this thin. Over the years, I had watched her at a safe distance while she stared down the likes of municipal strikes and local organized crime without blinking. I carefully got out of my relaxed professor pose and made my way to a kettle, plugging it in.

"I hope you still drink tea because I don't have coffee," I said over my shoulder. She murmured agreement and I put two bags in the pot.

"I hope you're moving to an even better office, Farran. I like this one. Books everywhere, quiet chaos. Nice view of Waterloo." I heard her get up and gamely try to make her way to the window. There was a moment's silence while she contemplated the real vision out there. "It's almost a stereotype of a history professor, but it's you."

"The view," I turned to face her, back against the wall, "keeps me out of faculty politics as much as I can be. No one wants to wrestle me to look out on pavement all day. And to be fair, it's been a long time since you've had any idea what is 'me.'"

Alison didn't reply, then nodded vaguely, still gazing out at the parking lot. "You're right, of course. I deserve that." She turned and raised her chin just enough. "But I do know what happened last year. When I caught it in the papers, I called people to find out what went wrong, if you were all right."

"You didn't call me."

"No. No, I didn't." She sighed and looked at her hands, still sporting the big wedding ring. "I was still in Asia, winding up my divorce from Martin. It was a very unsettled time for me. But," she seemed to sense my next comment, "I know it was nothing compared to what you went through. Leslie died, and then you were almost killed."

Since Alison had tapped my return fire, I said nothing. I could hear my heart beating, and the water in the kettle beginning to make ominous noises.

"You don't know how badly I wanted to call, write or . . . or something," she continued, looking somewhere over my left shoulder. "But I couldn't. Not then. Not with everything you had to deal with. It wasn't the time to barge in."

While I honestly couldn't argue with that, neither was I giving handouts that day.

"That was a year ago, Alison, and you've been home almost that long. I read the article in *The Reporter*. So that tells me you're not here today to barge in or mend fences." Unconsciously, I crossed my arms for battle. "Why the visit?"

Alison seemed to steel herself. "Because last year, for better or worse, you found your father and the truth about him. I came to ask you to help me do the same."

The kettle shrieked and we both jumped.

By the time I had finished fussing with the teapot and cups and turned around to reply, Alison was back in the doorway, hand on the knob.

"I . . . I'm going to go, Fan. I don't think this was such a good idea. I didn't mean to assume anything, and I'm sorry."

It bothered me to hear her use my old nickname, but I held up my hand like a traffic cop. "Hold it," I said, cutting her off. "If something is really wrong and it has to do with your dad, then sit down and tell me what's going on. John Perry was good to me when I was growing up. Very good to me—and Mom. He was probably the closest thing I ever had to a father." I pulled the chair she had been sitting in around and moved it forward, her purse still in it. "Besides," I added, "you can't go far without your purse."

When I had opened the newspaper last week to see Alison's name all over it, my guts told me it was the beginning of something. What, I didn't put a name to right away. But I suddenly knew the past was going to find me once again.

It was only a few months since I'd returned home from my sabbatical. It still felt odd to be back in this place, although I'd been teaching at the University of Waterloo for over a decade. The problem wasn't the place, it was me. I knew that much. But that's all I knew. I wasn't sure who Farran Mackenzie really was anymore after my "summer off" chasing sleeping murders in the valley of the St. Lawrence River.

The book on the cultural fallout of land expropriation I had used as my ticket to the Seaway Valley was still festering in my computer, barely a hundred pages along. History is a science, and I couldn't categorize or analyze the section on the Lost Villages of the St. Lawrence Seaway. Too personal, too intrinsic, too many ghosts still walking. And in many ways, the history of that era is still being written.

And I hadn't been back since that night I said goodbye. Ruth wrote letters regularly. Lynn used e-mail sporadically, but with punch. And Jerry . . . well, Strauss was still Strauss. That's one subject I'll never put in a bell jar. A man, a cop. Someone who just won't fade away.

And now the late Sergeant John Perry was coming back into my life. Another man, another police officer who wouldn't fade away even after almost decades since he was torn violently out of our lives, gunned down in the line of duty.

Alison had been the spitting image of her mother, long brown hair and a matching smile. But inside she had been both her father and her father's little girl. The publicity shot in the paper I had read that day in the cemetery made it clear that time had continued the process. It was like looking at Alison's mother—except for the eyes. The eyes belonged to John Perry, and they had looked straight into my soul.

John stood looking over the peony hedge at the girl who was struggling with her bicycle. "Having problems, Fan?"

Fan raised her head, brushing blonde hair out of her eyes. But the usual grin didn't come.

"I think it's broken, Mr. Perry. And I just got it. Mom's going to kill me."

He glanced around conspiratorially. "Where is your mom?"

"Visiting Mrs. Farcus across the road. She won't be long."

"Then we'd better work fast." He stepped easily over the hedge with long legs and squatted down beside her. "What seems to be the problem?"

They hunched over the bike in silence for several minutes. Finally, John tightened things in a few places and then stood up to wipe his hands. "That should do it, Fan. If anything else goes wrong, let me know. But," he added knowingly, "no more dirt trails with this. It isn't built for it."

"Dirt trails?" Fan tried to sound innocent. It didn't work.

"Forget it, Farran Mackenzie. Remember who you're dealing with," Perry smiled. "Besides, Alison tells me just about everything. Which brings me to a question. Alison says you aren't going to the Grade Eight father-and-daughter night. Why not go with your mom?"

The girl stared down at the grass, making circles in it with her toe. "It wouldn't be the same," she said quietly. "And all the other girls will have their dads . . . "

John nodded solemnly. "Understood. Alison tells me that one girl is going to bring both her father and her stepfather because she can't choose. How about borrowing one of them?"

Fan opened her mouth to retort but just in time saw the twinkle in his eye. Her mouth closed in a thin line.

"Thanks for helping me with my bike, Mr. Perry. I have to go now." She wheeled the bicycle firmly in the direction of the back porch.

"Hold it, Fan, hold it," John laughed as he caught her arm. "You know I can't resist teasing. I'm sorry. Listen," he added as she stood balancing the bike between them, face down to the grass again, "I have a serious question. Alison and I think that if one daughter can bring two fathers then it should be all right if I want to bring two daughters. What do you think?"

It took a minute before Farran realized the offer. She flushed pink, stammered a reply, then threw the new bike to the ground to give John Perry a hug.

The tears had come to me then, unbidden and unexpected, as I stood by his grave. When I got home from the cemetery that day, I poured myself the first brandy in months and tossed it back without waiting for ice.

Alison tossed a folded piece of paper onto my desk beside the tea mugs. Anger flushed her face.
"Maybe you can tell me what the hell that is."
I picked it up gingerly by the corners, as though we'd just unearthed it from a tomb site. Once I opened it, the game was afoot, and I still wasn't sold on the trip. I took a breath and spread it out on the desktop.
Your father was killed by friendly fire.
I stared at the words, trying to comprehend them.
Your father was killed by friendly fire.
Simple. Straightforward. Brutal. And no suggestion of anything beyond the fact. We sat like a still life for several minutes while a thousand thoughts whirled through my head.
"Of course this is ridiculous," I said finally. "We both know there was an arrest, a trial and a conviction." I thought for a moment. "Is this the only one?"
"Yes. It arrived last week," Alison spoke in almost a whisper. "It . . . it . . . upset me deeply."
"I would say so," I said grimly. "No matter how you look at it, it's bad all around. Even if it's just a prank, it's an exceptionally cruel one. And that would mean someone out there really hates you."
As I spoke, Alison pulled another piece of paper out of her purse, unfolded it and laid it on the desk beside the first. They were almost identical. The second one looked older, a little yellowed with age. And the message was slightly different.
Your husband was killed by friendly fire.
I looked up at Alison. "I thought you just said you got only one."
"I didn't get this one," she replied quietly. "I found it a couple of years ago in Mother's things after she died. That why I know the one I got is not a joke."

Somewhere in my condominium was a box of photograph albums, quietly ticking away. Memories are volatile material, and photo albums can detonate in your face if you aren't ready. I still hadn't gone through mine, what I had had in storage there at the time of the fire when Mom died two years ago. After I finished my brandy the evening of the cemetery visit, I toyed with the idea of excavating the one with my graduation from Preston Public School. John Perry would be there, with that ever-present smile and two teenyboppers on his arms.

And Mom, too. Young, beautiful, reclusive. A woman in hiding for forty years, until the day they found my father. Then her life ended and mine began.

Some life, I thought, pouring another drink. Once my nerves settled down and regular sleep returned after my visit to the St. Lawrence River last year, I had cut out the brandy to help the process along. But the story on Alison Perry had opened a door somewhere deep in me, a door I thought I'd slammed and locked forever. I'm a history professor and the past is my business, but last year the past got brutally personal. I went home for the first time in my life and spent the summer dealing with emotional landmines. In fact, it damned near killed me. I guess digging my heels in on this one was understandable.

But I am a self-professed coward, at least to my bathroom mirror. Digging my heels in has been company policy for most of my forty-plus years. Case in point—a promise not yet fulfilled. I had yet to have my mother moved from the Woodlawn Cemetery in Cambridge to her rightful place beside my father in the St. Lawrence Valley Cemetery. Should have done that this spring, but never started proceedings. Maybe another brandy and I'd have the guts to look honestly at the reason why.

"Why would anyone do this?" I shook my head. "It can't be real. How did your mother feel about it?"

"I have no idea." Alison crossed her arms and legs, sitting back in the chair. Her face was still red. "Mother never told me about it. Not a word. I have no idea when she got it. Now that the second one has come, I'm not impressed that I was kept in the dark."

I sat back for minute, too, feeling a little sick. Then I held up the day's newspaper.

"Is this the real 'personal reasons' they mention?" I asked her bluntly. "Rumour has it there've been threats on your life from some old enemies that prefer you stay safely in retirement."

This time, *The Cambridge Daily Reporter* had given Alison top billing:

FORMER MAYOR QUITS PROVINCIAL RACE
Personal Reasons Cited for Sudden Change of Mind

She looked, then looked away.

"Yes. It's true about the threats, but I've never bowed to intimidation. But this letter . . . I feel like my life has shut down until I know. I need to know if you could figure . . . " She turned those eyes on me again. "I need to know the truth."

I looked her straight in the eye.

"Sometimes, Alison," I said slowly, "the truth can be a terrible thing."

"It's better than not knowing, isn't it?"

Another long moment of silence between us. The term "comfortable silence between friends" didn't apply here. I was anything but comfortable in her presence, and I didn't like the implications of the cryptic notes. We seemed more like two boxers circling, each waiting for the other to make the first move.

I remembered the buried picture of a smiling man with two teenyboppers on his arms.

"Alright, Alison," I sighed. "I'm not sure what I can do, but I'll help you find out what's going on."

Farran suddenly found herself on her backside in the grass. Her mother stood over her in their backyard, hands on hips—which looked a little ridiculous with her boxing gloves on. Then Leslie took her gloves and headgear off, and popped out the mouth guard.

"Fan," she said impatiently, "how many times have I told you to keep your left up? You leave yourself wide open for a hit time and again. You have to pay as much attention to protecting yourself as you do to getting the punches in." She started putting the gear back on. *"And put a little fire in those hits. Make them count, gal, my father used to say."*

The girl slowly got up, and took out her mouth guard to speak.

"I can't, Mom," she complained. "You're my mom."

"Imagine me as someone else. Someone you'd like to bop once or twice if you could get away with it," Leslie grinned.

"Who do you think of?" asked her daughter.

"Des Shaler."

"Who's that?"

But her mother suddenly went quiet and got that look on her face Farran knew only too well. The look that said Don't ask about the past.

Geared up, the two began to circle once more. This time, Farran successfully warded off two punches before scoring a glancing blow to her mother's chin.

"Bravo!"

The two looked over to see Dave Carlson crossing the lawn between the two houses. His red sports car was parked on Water

Street in front of the Perrys' home, as it so often was. He'd been a family friend for years, even before joining the Preston Police Force to work under John, a man ten years his senior.

"Can't you two get along better?" he grinned. Farran thought he looked cool in his shades. Then he rapped his knuckles on Farran's helmet. "I'm here to take you and Alison to the game as promised."

"Where's John?" Leslie piled her equipment on the grass. "Wasn't he supposed to go?"

"Got called in," Dave answered briefly. "Lots going on, I'm afraid. This amalgamation thing with Galt and Hespeler has got them talking about making one large police force for the new city. Says it will save lots of money and bring in more resources. Makes sense, I guess." He shook his head. "Maybe I'm getting old. I'm not sure progress is always a good thing."

"You're not old." A head popped up over the peony hedge. "But you're slipping," Alison smiled. "This time I sneaked up on you." She turned to her best friend. "Come on, Fan. Get changed. We're going to be late."

"Changed?" Farran looked from her own jeans to Alison's clean blouse and denim skirt. Was that lipstick? "We're going to a baseball game."

Alison shrugged. "Suit yourself."

"You look fine, Fan," said Dave, patting her head and then putting his arm around her shoulder. He smiled at Leslie. "Why don't you come with us? The girls tell me you're quite the softball coach."

Leslie smiled briefly in return. "Thanks, Dave, but I think I'll get some work done around here." She scooped up the boxing gear and vanished into the house. Dave watched her go, lost in thought.

"Fan?" Alison's voice called me back over the years. The sun had vanished behind a cloud, leaving my office in a grey pallor.

"I'm sorry. What did you say?"

"That's okay," she said quietly. "I do a lot of that, too. I asked you what you thought was the first thing we should do."

"I guess we need to find out if these notes could possibly be true. I have a problem with a witness who waits thirty years to speak up. Regardless, it means talking to the people involved the day your dad died. Who was the chief of police then?"

"A man named Brian Miller. I remember him coming to the house a few times. I think he's still in the area somewhere. I can find out."

"Okay. We'll start there. I'll need to go through the old newspapers at the library at some point." None of this was I looking forward to, but I had to admit it was going to be worse for Alison. "And of course we should talk to Dave Carlson. Do you have any idea where he is now?"

"No." Alison shook her head. "No. I know he's still around here somewhere because he sent flowers to my mother's funeral. I never saw him after the . . . the shooting. He was in the hospital for some time as you might remember, and then we moved away shortly after his release."

"Yes, I remember," I said briefly. One day you were there, my friend, and the next you were gone.

Your husband was killed by friendly fire.

Fear?

Suddenly I was afraid, and I couldn't find a reason for it.

"Alison," I said standing up, "we'll have to tread lightly through this. And be careful."

"Be careful of what?" She had returned the paper to her purse and stood also.

In this situation, paranoid is a good thing to be. My friend's warning to me from last year was as clear in my mind as if she'd been in the room. This time, I would listen.

I shrugged. "Just careful. Take care of yourself."

When my home phone rang that night, I hadn't intended to pick it up. But seeing the number, I did. Lynn Holmes became a good friend to me last year. When the truth about my father's murder reared its ugly head last summer, Lynn and I both paid a high personal price for it. Although born and raised in the Lost Village of Farran's Point and a childhood friend of my mother, she had followed a global career in journalism and now had an editorial post with *The Ottawa Citizen*. In many ways because of all these things, we spoke the same language about life.

"When are you coming home?" Lynn asked, cutting to the chase in her usual fashion.

"Why? Is something wrong?"

"Physically, no. Everyone is fine, but . . . " She sighed. "Ruth would never say it, but I think she really needs you here." Ruth Hoffman had been my mother's best friend in high school, and was now the dearest person in the world to me.

"Something's happened," I stated more than asked.

"Yes. We've found Steven." Lynn let that sink in. Steven was a son Ruth gave up for adoption as a young woman. Fathered by my Uncle Gordon, Steven would be my cousin—and the only family I have left on earth. "We got a match on the national registry last month."

For a moment, I didn't know what to say. Or what to feel. "How is Ruth about this?" I said finally.

"Up and down, as you can imagine," Lynn explained. "She didn't want to get your hopes up until we tracked him down or had a reply, but I had to call you. I've been the contact point via e-mail, but I submitted Ruth's address at her request. She felt she couldn't start with a phone call."

I nodded silently. That would be Ruth, and somehow I agreed with her.

"We just got his address in return and she's writing a letter this week. But her morale is low. I can hear it in her voice." Lynn's voice got an edge. "Her children still haven't been accepting about Steven, and aside from me she has no one to hold her hand through this. I don't get down to Ingleside very often at this point, and she could use another friend in her corner right about now."

I was quiet for a minute, letting the guilt wash over me for staying away so long.

"Look, Fan," said Lynn suddenly, "Ruth is going to call you soon one way or another about Steven, and I think it would really mean a lot to her if you could say you were coming home for a bit."

Coming home. A strange but appropriate phrase for returning to the Seaway Valley, a place I'd never seen until last year. Full of family history and long fingers reaching into the past that I found only after my mother died and my last link to it was gone.

"I'll see what I can do," I said sincerely. "Maybe I can snatch a long weekend at the end of the month. I have some . . . unfinished business there anyway."

"I'm sure *he'll* be happy to see you, too," Lynn quipped, hanging up before I could reply.

I hadn't meant Jerry Strauss, but on that account Lynn was right. Whatever had started between us the previous summer was hanging like loose threads in the silence that existed now. At first I had called occasionally and kept in touch. Jerry had responded in kind. But we are both loners, without one to lead the way in the work a relationship demands. We weren't good at the game—we didn't know the rules, and I guessed we'd just run out of ideas. I just wished I could run out of memories.

I spent that evening avoiding memories. The photo albums remained buried, and I boxed files I'd brought with me from the university. Supper was fast because I had almost no appetite. After Lynn's call, I couldn't focus enough to read so I did the unthinkable. I turned on the television.

Public broadcasting was having a telethon, so I fished aimlessly through the other channels. In desperation, I switched to the oldies channel and found myself watching *The Partridge Family*. David Cassidy, young and handsome. No wonder we all fell for him like a ton of bricks. For three years, we all had it bad, but Alison was the worst of the worst. Even after the show left the air, my best friend would drive me nuts with David this and David that. It was about that time, to be honest, that the first shift in our friendship was felt. Alison began trying to dress and act more grown-up than I did. Maybe she'd just wanted to be ready if David Cassidy ever came to town.

As if on cue, the phone rang a second time. I didn't recognize the number, but I had a gut feeling who it was.

"Hi, Fan," Alison's voice came hesitantly over the line. "Are you busy?"

"No. Actually, I was just watching *The Partridge Family*. Remember him?"

There was an odd silence. Then Alison cleared her throat.

"Yes, I remember how we were all just dying for David. Would've done anything to meet him."

"Especially you." I smiled to myself. "I thought you'd never get over him. And then one day all your posters came down. The day of your birthday—"

Alison quickly changed the subject. "I'm calling to find out if you're free this Saturday. I tracked down Brian Miller and he'll see us this weekend."

"Well," I paused. "You certainly don't waste time. I guess I'm free, although to be honest, at this point I don't know what to ask him or how to approach it."

"I don't either, but we have a couple of days to think that over. He's retired, of course, and he has a hobby farm out near Kitchener. I'll pick you up around noon." She hesitated. "Listen . . . Fan . . . thank you. For everything."

"I haven't done anything," I protested, but she'd hung up. I cradled the receiver, watched the motley Partridge bus head off down the road on my screen, and wondered what kind of journey I'd just started myself.

Brian Miller, former Chief of the Waterloo Regional Police Force, wasn't happy to see us.

"I'm so happy to see you after all these years, Alison," he said gruffly, settling his elderly frame into a favourite chair that reminded me of one in Ingleside. At the time of John Perry's death, Miller had just moved from being a small-town cop running the Preston Police to chief of the new regional force. I vaguely remembered him from thirty years ago as being a tall, burly man in his late forties, a man with the commanding presence needed in such a role. But the years had taken their toll. He seemed much smaller and quite frail—and definitely uneasy that we had come.

"Brian, do you remember my next-door neighbours from the Water Street days? This is Farran Mackenzie." I took Alison's cue to shake hands. His was cold and clammy. "She lived beside us with her mother, Leslie. Farran knew my dad quite well."

"And that's what you've come to talk about, isn't it?" Miller took a swig from a coffee mug and my educated nostrils twitched. Brandy. "I figured someday you might. Hard to believe it's thirty years since John died. All that seems like yesterday."

Good, I thought. "Mr. Miller, we're here to go over what happened the day he died," I explained, following the plan Alison and I had agreed on in the car while driving up. "Alison could never talk to her mother about it. Now that Jessica is gone, Alison thought that maybe getting the facts might help to make some closure on it. I'm just here for emotional support."

"Yes, I saw the notice about Jessica in the paper." He contemplated whatever was in his mug. "She was a fine lady." Miller seemed to rouse himself. "I'm sorry. I'm being a bad host. Would you ladies like some coffee?"

We both accepted, although I politely refrained from asking to share his brandy. While he was in the kitchen, I took the opportunity to snoop at the photos on the mantel and the walls. Usual stuff—children at different ages, same children grown with offspring of their own. Many of Miller in uniform with local dignitaries. And one with a large group of police officers, including a young and smiling John Perry with Dave Carlson right beside him.

"That was the Preston Police Force, the year before we went regional." Miller had materialized at my elbow with the promised coffee held out. I took it and blew on it. "I think fondly of those days," the old man continued. "On a small force, you get to know your officers better. Have a little fun." He smiled to himself. "One time, when I was still doing the beat, I took in several cases of stolen liquor. The night before the Old Man had an early-morning meeting with the mayor, we took the booze out of the lockup and put it all over his desk. Made it look like he'd been having a private party. Boy, did he do a quick cleanup. Couldn't get away with that in the bigger forces now."

"The Waterloo Regional Police Force was formed in 1973, the same year Cambridge amalgamated, right?"

"Yes, but it didn't happen all at once. In January of '73, we put eight municipal police forces together." Miller handed a mug to Alison. "The following year, the new force took over policing the townships that had been served by the provincial police. It was quite a change. We went from working in small, local groups to a regional force of almost

400 officers and civilians responsible for a population base of a quarter million."

Next to the first group shot was a larger one. More officers, new uniforms. Perry and Carlson were in that one, too, of course. Dave had forgotten to take off his sunglasses, and looked cooler than the rest. Seeing that Miller was waiting for me to sit down first, I sat.

"And it wasn't easy at first, either," he continued. "Even though most officers had crossed paths professionally before, they hadn't actually worked together on the street. New, much larger group. Change in dynamics as well as the system. The people factor always takes the most time."

"Were there any serious conflicts between officers?" I asked. I felt Alison look at me.

"None worth mentioning." Miller took a sip of his own, refilled coffee. This time, the smell of brandy wasn't there. "John Perry was very good at dealing with that sort of thing. He was one of the officers that got a promotion with the new force. John wasn't just a good officer, he was a good person, too. People liked and respected him." He fell silent for a moment, then looked at Alison. "It always hurts to lose an officer, especially in the line of duty. Reminds everyone how vulnerable we are out there, even though we work together like brothers in arms.

"But with your dad, the sense of personal loss was even greater with the men. And John was the first Waterloo Regional police officer to be killed in the line of duty. His death, and his funeral, fused those men into a single unit for the first time. Your father was proud to be a police officer, Alison, and I think he would have been pleased to know that."

I found myself looking at Miller carefully. Something was happening to him, and not just psychologically. His physical presence was stronger now than when we'd first arrived. I'd seen this before when interviewing elderly people about historical events. They begin the talk as themselves, but once deeply into the past they revert to who they were then—even mind and body changing with it. The power of the human mind is an amazing thing.

I could see Alison tearing up. I remembered that funeral well, too. All those uniforms, the press, the official ceremony making it seem even more like a play. And Alison small and quiet, standing away from even her mother, let alone anywhere where I could reach her.

And that is where she stayed. Until now.

I cleared my throat with a little difficulty.

"Around the time of the shooting, was John having any problems at work?"

Miller gave me an X-ray look. They must learn that in the academy. But it couldn't hide the unease returning there as well.

"Nothing I recall. Why do you ask?"

"I remember passing the house that morning and he was having a very vocal argument with Dave Carlson," I explained. "I thought perhaps you might remember what that was about."

Miller looked away and shook his head. "Nothing comes to mind. Must have been personal, and I wouldn't have known anything about that. Unless you mean," he added quietly, "the Simser boy. I know he didn't sleep well for weeks after that."

"I'm driving you to school today," Leslie said firmly. "Call Alison and see if she wants to come with us."

Farran looked up from her cereal.

"Don't you have a meeting today? You'll be late."

Her mother took her dishes to the sink and did not reply. On the table between them, The Reporter had a special dose of bad news.

BOY, 8, KILLED IN BOMB BLAST
Police Blame Gang for Child's Death; Parents Want Answers After Third Attack

Underneath was the haunting picture of a laughing boy with his arm around his sister.

Dead at eight. Gone forever, just because he walked past the wrong car on the way to school. At fifteen, Farran was just beginning to understand eternity. She wondered what God was thinking this morning.

John Perry appeared at the back door, Alison in tow. She was quiet. He looked at though he'd aged a generation overnight.

"Leslie, I'm driving Ali into school today. Do you want me to take Fan, too?"

"That would be fine, John. Thank you," said Leslie quietly. "Are you all right? You don't look as though you got much sleep."

"Worked late on this Simser thing. Didn't sleep when I did get to bed." John rubbed a hand over his eyes. "I don't know when I'll be home tonight, Leslie. Can you pick up the girls this afternoon? Jess is really on edge about this, and I can't blame her. The whole city's on red alert. No one feels safe now."

"Of course. I'll be glad when summer holidays start next week." Leslie looked guiltily at John. "I . . . I'm sure it will be over soon. I know you're all doing your best to stop this—"

"But we're not doing enough. The public thinks so, anyway." Farran saw Perry's fists clench silently. "They don't understand what we're up against. Organized crime is getting stronger everywhere, and this gang from Toronto is really bad news. They have money. They have bodies. This is a business for them, and they're very good at intimidation. They saved the car bombs for those who didn't give in to extortion the first time around. But they keep slipping through our fingers, almost like they know we're coming . . . And no one's talking. Maybe they'll talk now," he added grimly. "Girls, I'll meet you at the car in ten."

When John had left, Leslie watched him through the screen for a minute.

"He blames himself, doesn't he?" she said to the room.

"He blamed himself."

Miller and Alison both turned to look at me, and it was only then I realized I had spoken aloud. The old man crossed his arms and nodded reluctantly.

"And it got personal enough to get him killed, right Mr. Miller?"

Miller rubbed his chin. "We never did lay charges in the Simser death, and that made it all the worse. Every officer on the force wanted blood for that child. Cops are people, too. They have families. But John Perry was newly in charge of that investigation. We put more bodies on it after the first bombing. He felt he'd failed to protect that boy."

"Mike Denny, the man who went to jail for killing my father, was the leader of that gang." It was the first time Alison had spoken since we'd done our hellos, and I wondered what was going on in her head. "I remember more car bombs, and then everything stopped. My dad was a different person that summer before he was killed. Almost his whole life revolved around work, and he'd never let that happen before. My mother wasn't a happy woman, either. I guess I can see why."

"I don't know if you girls remember," said Miller, "but in the years that Cambridge was becoming a city, we started having a serious problem with gangs. They were pretty active all over Central Ontario, and started trying to set up in the Kitchener–Waterloo area. We were bracing ourselves for possible gang wars.

"In this case, Denny and his people focused on Cambridge. Started working extortion on business owners and frightening those who refused with fires and car bombs. It was a bad situation to begin with. What happened to the Simser boy just turned the heat up.

"I'm afraid your father became obsessed with shutting the gang down, Alison. He put his finger on who the leader was and went after him. Thought that by pulling the leader, the brains, the rest of the group would be much easier to bring down." Miller sighed. "I don't know if you knew, Alison, but Mike Denny was threatening a law suit for police harassment against your father. Two weeks before he died, I told John to back off for a while until things cooled down."

"And then he was gunned down." I suddenly had to move around. I got up and looked out at the countryside around us. "Why would Denny kill him if you'd pulled him back?" I turned to face Miller. "Unless John didn't follow orders."

The man shrugged. "As far as I know, he did. If he kept after Denny, it was on his own time. And as for Denny killing him, we had him hands down. A genuinely nasty piece of goods. American vet with a background in munitions. Denny was there with another punk. Both were armed, but Mike Denny had the type of gun that killed Perry."

"What type was that?" I asked.

"A .38 calibre Smith and Wesson," said Miller. "Same issue as our officers used back then. We called it a police special."

"And forensics ruled out their own guns being used on them?" I followed up.

"In the seventies, ballistics couldn't confirm the identity of a gun from a bullet, only the make. Of course, we could tell if a gun had been fired." By now, the man had the wind up and the cop in him was taking over. "What bone are you chewing on about this?"

"Just trying to understand as much as possible about that day," Alison said quickly, noting I was tongue-tied. "I could never discuss this with my mother, and there is so much I still don't know."

I sat down beside her and ventured another chew at the bone.

"If John Perry had orders to back off, why was he the one who answered the call that day?"

Miller gave me another unhappy look. "He wasn't supposed to. It was the old radio system, where everyone can hear the call. John heard it and took it as officer closest to the scene. But he didn't wait for authorization. He and Dave made it first, and we sent backup immediately in case it turned out to be legitimate."

"It feels as though the shooting was premeditated," I mused, "but there was no way Mike Denny could have known that John would be the one to answer the call." Could he? "Who made the call to the station?"

"We never found out. It was an anonymous tip."

. . . almost like they know we're coming . . .

That little ember of fear began to glow in my stomach again. I suddenly wanted to get out of there, but wrestled it down for the moment.

"What about Mike Denny?" I asked, thinking of the notes Alison had shown me. "He'd be out of prison by now. Is he still alive?"

"Never made it out of prison." Miller finished his coffee and set the mug down firmly. "Died in a prison fight. Stabbed to death by an inmate. Might not be politically correct to say, but I certainly shed no tears on that one. Live by the sword, die by the sword."

"What about Dave Carlson? He was in the hospital at the time of the funeral. My mother and I visited him there. Neither of us ever saw him after that." I looked at Alison for confirmation, but she was staring at something in her mug. "Whatever happened to him?"

"Carlson was lucky," said Miller grimly. "He was shot in the head, the bullet digging a path along the side over the ear. He lived, but was permanently blinded. He's still in the area, living on disability, I hear. At the time, I think they wanted to try some new operation to restore part of his sight, but he wouldn't go for it. I know he always felt responsible for not saving John's life. Probably saw his blindness as payment for that, who knows."

"At least he's still alive and we can talk to him." I stood up again, feeling we'd taken enough of his time. My guts still wanted to get out of there.

"Barely," said Miller. "I can give you his unlisted number, but you'd better call soon." We both looked at him questioningly. "Liver cancer," he explained. "And he won't take treatment for that, either. He's dying."

The garage was dark and quiet, a direct contrast to the Saturday traffic on King Street. Above us, the Regency Apartments teemed with life. Thirty years ago, this had been the Regency Hotel—one of the finest in the old town of Preston. It was also where John Perry's life had violently ended.

From my own experience, I knew that Alison would have to come here at some point, even just to face it. Jessica had never allowed her daughter to do so, and the adult Alison had kept the emotional door closed and locked. Until now. That's the brutal truth about life: it will always find you, sooner or later. No one gets away for free.

We had left Brian Miller that morning with more questions than we'd arrived with. At least I did. I couldn't read Alison's face, and I didn't want to start connecting the dots until I was alone. After a quick return to the farm to get the purse she'd left beside her chair, Alison drove to a nice restaurant just inside the city. She hadn't been able to eat that morning, and it was time for fuel.

It felt good to see that we still had one shared priority—food. I've never had drinking buddies, only eating buddies.

Talk about Miller was deliberately avoided by both, and we did the full meal deal in silence. Drinks, appetizer, salad, main course. Partly hunger and partly nerves. When we finally slowed down over dessert and coffee, the silence had to be filled.

"I'm glad to see you're not on some kind of 'food plan' like everyone else," I ventured. "Seems like everyone around me these days has turned eating into a religion. Allergies, sensitivities, zones." I made a face. "You're afraid to have anyone over for supper anymore." Not that I would, considering my lack of culinary skills.

Alison gave me a smile. "Well, I won't say I didn't put myself through all that garbage over the years, but I think I just got tired of being afraid of food. I'm not the size I was when I was twenty, but I'm happy with it."

"You look great," I said honestly.

"And you haven't changed at all. No, I mean it," she added, sensing my protest. "You're still stick-thin like you always were. I guess it really does come down to genetics, doesn't it?"

"Genetics and stress levels." I cleared my dessert plate and put double cream in my coffee. "I lost fifteen pounds last year, with everything that went on. Ate like a pig for comfort and watched the scale go down regardless."

"Well, maybe I have that to look forward to," Alison said, but the brightness was forced. I changed the subject.

"Remember the concoctions we used to eat in high school?" I closed my eyes. "God, it's a wonder we have stomachs left."

"We were under the influence of Jeanie Ross. Whatever happened to her? Has she ever contacted you?"

"Nope. No idea where she is. Just didn't come back to school in September, remember?"

"Yes. The rumours were an unwanted pregnancy."

"But the weird thing is, Alison, that she never came back. She disappeared and then the family moved away." Just like you, I wanted to say. Why? It was a question that had waited thirty years, and it would have to wait a little longer. This wasn't the place to open that wound.

"Just think, Fan. That child would be thirty years old now. Jeanie could be a grandmother." Alison grimaced.

"So could we," I pointed out. "Do you and Martin have kids? I don't remember the paper mentioning them."

"No." She stirred her coffee meditatively. "We tell people it was because of our careers, but the truth is we tried for ten years. I can't have children. I think it was harder on Martin than he ever admitted."

"I'm sorry, Alison. I didn't mean to pry."

"You didn't. What is, is." She took a sip of her coffee and put on another smile. "What about you, Fan? Any children hidden anywhere?"

I was really glad the bill came at that moment. Talk about putting your finger right on it. I made a fuss about paying for both meals to cover my discomfort at the question, but I'm not sure it worked.

And now we stood at the entrance to the Regency garage, ready to pay another of life's bills.

"Are you sure you want to do this?" I put my hand on her arm. "Once you see the place, it will be in your heart forever. I'm sure that's why your mother forbade you to go. "Only one of us needs to see the layout," I added.

"Thanks, Fan," Alison replied, putting her hand over mine. "But this is something I need to do. It's haunted me for thirty years anyway. Maybe it will help to see the real thing. The not knowing is always worse than the knowing."

I couldn't argue with that. As we walked in the entrance, I felt her hand slip unconsciously into mine—a habit from the past—and I suddenly felt too young for all of this.

The darkness inside the garage blinded us for a second, then everything came into focus. The wall extended about ten feet down, and then stopped. We followed it. Around the corner lay the open first floor of the garage. Well lit, mostly empty, nothing special. And quiet as a tomb.

Alison let go of my hand and slowly walked around the empty car spaces. I knew what she was doing—trying to imagine where her father's body had lain. At least she could physically get to it. I hadn't been so lucky last year.

"I wanted to ask Miller who was at the scene that day, but I didn't want to get the wind up about your letter," I said to break the silence. The place was getting to me. *Alison, your mother needs you home now. These officers will drive you.* I didn't want to go back there. I selfishly wished I'd said no to this when I'd had the chance.

Still Alison didn't speak. She was standing, pale in the florescent light, looking at the exit door that led to the back of the building. "Miller said they caught Mike Denny leaving the garage. If the squad cars arrived at the street entrance, he must have gone out that way." She strode across the pavement toward the door and I followed.

The door led to two other doors. One opened into a stairwell, the other to a back alley. We returned to the garage. I took a good second look around before noticing that Alison was still again, her face telling me that her mind was somewhere far away.

It was time to get her out of there.

"We've been here long enough," I said. "We can come back again if we need to." When she didn't respond, I walked over and put my arm around her shoulder. "Hey, Al," I said, slipping into the old nickname for the first time, "are you okay?"

35

Alison looked at me with a sad smile, but said nothing. She didn't have to. With my arm guiding her to the entrance, we slowly left the shadows behind us to rejoin the brilliant summer day.

By the time I got home, it was well after four. Despite the nice summer evening, I locked the door, turned off the phone ringer and got my pyjamas on. I wanted the world to go away for a while. Aside from an impromptu murder investigation that promised to be an emotional roller coaster, I had my own issues to sort out. Work, Mother, and going east to the big river. And that would mean another issue—Jerry Strauss.

At least I had talked to the people at Woodlawn about disinterring Mother's urn, so that was in motion. It would be done early next week. Then the fat would be in the fire for me because I'd have to take her home as promised. Emotionally, I was still digging in my heels about the trip and hadn't taken the time to really look at why. If I didn't before I left, that life invoice would be waiting for me in the Seaway Valley.

The thoughts of unfinished business made me pick up the phone. I dialled an Ingleside number and she picked up almost right away.

"Fan! How good to hear your voice." Ruth Hoffman's welcoming tone made my guilt meter rise. "I was going to call you."

"Is everything okay?" I thought of Lynn's words the other night. The needle on my meter was now heading for the red zone.

"Yes, actually. Better than okay. We've found Steven." I could hear her smiling. I smiled, too.

"Ruth, that's wonderful! Have you talked to him? What's he like?"

"I . . . I don't know. I haven't spoken to him yet," she admitted. "I'm sending a letter off today. I was up most of the night trying to figure out what to say. But Fan . . ."

"Yes?"

"I hope you won't be angry, but as to Gordon, all I said was who his biological father was. I—I didn't have the nerve to tell him what happened last year."

"Of course not," I reassured her. "There is plenty of time for that. And when you tell him, I'll help you."

"I was hoping you'd say that." The relief was palpable in her voice. "The children haven't been very happy about the idea of Steven at all. We just don't talk about it now. I wish Mother were here, Fan."

I had often wondered if the Hoffman-Tremblay offspring got their bonehead streak from their father, Ruth's ex in Montreal. They hadn't been too welcoming to me, either—Ruth's daughter Carolyn, in particular. But some of that, I grudgingly admitted to myself, might have something to do with my part in Ruth's brush with death last year. That tends to leave a bad impression with people.

"I'm coming home next week," I said impulsively. "They're taking Mother out of the cemetery Monday or Tuesday, and I should be on my way after that. I still have to call the St. Lawrence Valley Cemetery to book an interment."

"Well, Farran," Ruth said feelingly, "I'm glad things are in motion. I know it's going to be very difficult for you, dear, but once it's over you'll have closure. And for what it's worth," she added, "it'll mean a lot to me to have Leslie home again. Speaking of closure, have you had any luck with your daughter?"

My daughter. Still a strange term on my lips. Last year, Ruth and I had been soul mates in starting our searches for long-lost children. In my case, as a young woman, I'd fallen for the wrong man in university. Let's leave it at that.

"No, nothing," I admitted. "But she'd only be in her twenties now. People don't usually feel the urge to find blood relatives till they have families of their own. Maybe I'll have a wait on my hands, or maybe she just never will make contact."

"Don't you dare give up hope," said Ruth sternly. "That's what you told me, remember?"

"I remember. I'm sure you won't let me forget."

"Well, it's good advice. Maybe you should talk to Lynn," she added wisely.

"Why?"

"All those years as an investigative journalist, of course. If she can't do some private digging for you herself, maybe she would know someone who could."

The idea had crossed my mind before, but to be honest, I was afraid of what else could be unearthed along the way. I promised Ruth to consider it if I'd still heard nothing by the end of the year, and accepted her offer of help at that end with getting things ready for Mother's journey home.

It felt good to hear her voice. It made me realize I needed a friend, too, and I almost babbled the whole mess with Alison to her. Luckily, I'd taken my grown-up pill that morning and realized she had enough on her plate for now.

But Lynn was another story. I decided to call her back. About Alison, not my daughter. Maybe Lynn could dig up some dirt on the shooting and the trial through her newspaper connections, something I couldn't find next week in the *Reporter*'s morgue or the library.

I was fishing around for Lynn's number when the door buzzer went. I hesitated to answer, fearing a visit from Alison, but went anyway.

The voice was unfamiliar.

"Dr. Mackenzie? My name is Gail Melvin. May I have a few moments of your time? It won't take long." She must have sensed my hesitation because she lowered her voice and added, "I want to speak to you about my former superior, Sergeant John Perry."

That did it. I pressed the buzzer and let her in. In a few minutes, she materialized at my condo door, a tall woman in her fifties with quiet eyes. My instincts told me that Gail Melvin was the kind you turned to when you wanted the real scoop and no guff.

"I'm sorry for disturbing you," she said, taking in my pyjamas. "I called a couple of times this afternoon, but there was no answer, and I didn't want to leave a message. When I got a busy tone later, I thought I'd see if I could catch you in."

"This sounds urgent." I motioned her to a chair.

"Well, it is and it isn't," she explained as she sat down. Now I was totally confused and must have looked it. Gail laughed apologetically. "I'm sorry. I'm handling this very badly. May I start over?"

"Absolutely," I said firmly and sat down.

"Dr. Mackenzie, I'm here because retired chief Brian Miller called me earlier today after you visited him with Alison Perry. He told me you two were asking about the facts surrounding John's death."

"Yes. Why would he call you about that?"

"Because he knows I'm leaving Monday for Europe. I won't be home for several months. And because I was the first backup officer on the scene the day John Perry died."

It occurred to me that I owed Miller a thank you for thinking ahead on our account. It also occurred to me that I suddenly needed a drink.

"You were one of the officers that drove us to the house from school," I said softly. She nodded. "Why come to me?" I added. "I'd think you would want to talk to Alison before you go."

"You both left your cards, and Brian said you two were old friends. I'll speak to Alison if she wants to see me. I've wondered for thirty years if she'd ever turn up on my doorstep to ask about that terrible day. But I worked closely with John . . . and . . ."

"And?"

"And I know things I'm not sure Alison should hear. I thought perhaps we could talk about it and I'd leave it with you."

Now I really needed that drink.

"If you have dirty laundry and you're not sure it should be shared, why come to me with it at all?"

"Because I need to tell someone. I've never talked about it in all these years, but John's been on my mind ever since—"

"Since the thirtieth anniversary is coming up?" I thought of my own visit to his grave last week.

Melvin nervously licked her lips and opened her purse. When she pulled out an envelope, I got a very bad feeling.

"Ever since this came in the mail." She opened the letter within, and I could see one line on the page. She handed it to me, but I barely read it. I didn't need to.

John Perry was killed by friendly fire.

There was dead silence for a moment. Finally I spoke.

"Gail, can I offer you a drink?"

"Make it a double," she said quietly.

Chapter FOUR: Ashes

There is a blue in the late summer sky that is like no other. Perhaps it is due to the unusual contrast between the early changing leaves and the purity above. I don't know.

I found myself thinking about skies a lot. Skies and many other things. Life. Death. And what is left after destruction, like fire through a home. Ashes, I guess.

My mother's urn was disinterred on Monday and waited in the mausoleum for my pickup. After leaving a message on Alison's answering machine about Gail's visit the night before, I actively avoided my home and my own phone for the day, taking a long walk through Riverside Park in Cambridge. The park was a five-minute trek from my former house, and I had spent untold hours there throughout my childhood. It was still the place I went to think.

I sat for several hours beside the spillway, watching the Speed River go under the King Street Bridge and disappear toward the old mills. The memory of another day spent on its banks came to mind—a bright May day long ago, skipping school with Alison and Jeanie Ross. To our youthful minds, it seemed like such a daring thing to do. The small lunches we brought tasted like food fit for a king, and the afternoon, with its forbidden pleasure of "unlawful" free time, seemed to go on forever.

"We should have brought fishing poles," said Jeanie, her long legs stuck out on the grass. She pulled a blade and began to chew.

"Fishing?" Alison made a face. "No way. That's gross." She picked up a stick and wandered down the bank a little, stopping to write something in the sand.

"What's up with her, Fan?" Jeanie whispered to the girl sitting beside her. "She's been Miss Hoity-Toity lately. Never wants to have any fun. I mean," she added, "look at her. Dressed up to the nines all the time. She knew we were coming here today."

Fan shrugged and flipped her long blonde hair out of her eyes. "I don't know. She likes to dress up now, I guess. It's a free country."

Jeanie got up and made her way over to Alison. "Whatcha writing?"

Alison rubbed out most of the letters before Jeanie could see, but three remained: "DAV."

"Aw, Alison." Jeanie rolled her eyes. "When are you going to give it up? David Cassidy this and David Cassidy that. Man, he isn't even on TV anymore. He's old news."

Alison threw the stick in the water, where the current quickly took it away.

"We're all going to be fifteen soon," she shot back, brushing off her hands. "Honestly, Jeanie, you can be such a child sometimes."

Alison walked down the shoreline past Jeanie and Fan, taking her dignity with her. Behind her back, Jeanie pointed to herself and made a Me? face at Fan. They both smothered giggles, then Fan turned to look pensively at the retreating figure of her best friend.

It had been a perfect afternoon, but in hindsight, it had been the beginning of the end. Jeanie had come around less and less when I was with Alison, until the day she'd disappeared from the neighbourhood just before the start of school. Another friend Missing In Action.

And Alison? To be honest, I still didn't quite believe she was back. That summer had been the final summer, before the last strands of our friendship had snapped in the wake of her father's sudden death.

I hid in the park with no intention of making my way to Water Street. I had not returned to my mother's house since I'd sold the lot after the fire. The house was gone, of course, and something new would be in its place. But the Perry house would still be there, with all the indigenous memories threatening to pull me back.

But then I was walking back, wasn't I? For the hundredth time, I wondered what I'd gotten myself into and why. This time I ruthlessly searched for an answer. Any friendship with Alison was ancient history, dust. There were no issues of loyalty or commitment.

But John Perry was another matter. His friendship had filled some important holes in my childhood, and his death had been what brought it to an end. It had all happened too early, far too soon for both of us in my view. If there was something about his death that needed the light of day, I guess I was getting involved for him. My chance to make a small part of it right, if that were still possible.

But what *was* wrong? What did it all mean? Strange notes going to God knows whom. Why? To hurt the people involved? To frighten them? I thought of Jessica Perry suddenly selling her house a few months after the funeral and leaving town. Was that in response to her note? If so, what did she fear? And why send the notes now—after all this time?

Friendly fire. What if John Perry had been killed by friendly fire? What would it mean now? If it had been an accidental shooting, it was a tragedy and nothing more—except for the murderous Mike Denny, of course. But Gail Melvin had been adamant on that point. Both officers were highly trained and too good at their job to consider that seriously.

"We received an anonymous tip that morning that another car bomb was being set in the Regency garage. That two men were there at the time of the call. Even though we were getting a lot of false leads from the public, we had to check out every one. The call went out over the car radio."

Gail was settled in my living room like an old friend.

"Miller said John took the call and went ahead without authorization." I said. "Did he do that often?"

"No. John was a by-the-books cop. I'd never known him to do that before. Now Dave Carlson," she added, "would have done something like that from time to time. Dave was the cowboy."

"So let me get this straight," I said. "An anonymous call reports another car bomb being set in the Regency garage. Within minutes, Perry and Carlson arrive. Dispatch did not authorize, but does send backup immediately because of the possible danger. Perry goes ahead before backup arrives. Carlson hears gunfire and he follows Perry. You hear two shots on your arrival as you get out of the car. You find Perry and Carlson on the ground within a few feet of each other, both guns beside them. Denny's partner is found dead, and Denny himself is captured trying to escape out the back door. He is injured and can't put up much of a fight. You find the right type of gun to have shot the officers on Mike Denny, and although he claims Perry was alive when he left the garage, Denny is tried for John's murder.

"With Denny's record and the events over the summer involving Perry, the prosecution is able to make a case against Denny. Carlson never recovers his sight and has only partial memory left of that morning. He's not much help. Denny has an ironclad alibi for involvement in the Simser boy's death, so you can't touch him for that. But Denny is convicted for the murder of John Perry and within months is himself killed in a prison riot." Convenient.

"That's basically it," Gail said.

"Did any of the responding officers fire their guns?"

"Not that I recall. Denny was trying to make tracks, but gave up without a struggle when we arrived."

"It seems pretty straightforward. So what the hell is this?" I asked bluntly, echoing Alison's words in my office days before. I handed back Gail's version of the note.

"I don't know," she said, putting it back in her purse. "But it's disturbing at the very least."

"And you do know enough that you feel the need to see me before leaving for overseas."

"Yes."

I leaned back on the couch. "You have my complete attention."

Gail finished her drink and set it on the table beside her, refusing my motion to get a refill.

"I've been with the RCMP for the past ten years now, but I started with the Waterloo Regional Police," she began. "I was a rookie straight out of the academy. Adapting to the larger force was not an issue for me. But being female was. You have to remember this was thirty years ago. Women still had to prove they could cut it as cops, and there wasn't a lot of encouragement to do so. Not that anyone stood in our way, but many felt we just shouldn't be there. That it wasn't a job for a woman."

"How did John treat you?"

"That's just it. He was great. His team was his team and everybody pulled together. Brothers in arms, he called it, while on the streets. No guff from anybody, me included. I got duty that was no better or worse than any other officer. More or less, we all got along fine.

"But sooner or later, all of us officers face our day of reckoning—the first time we deal with a critical situation. It could be a hostage-taking, an armed robbery or a murder. That's when each of us answers the question, 'Can I do this job?'"

"And your day came with the shooting."

"Yes. Our car was the first one to the scene after backup was ordered. We heard that John had gone inside, and then Dave called in moments later saying he was going to follow. One car had gone to the rear of the building; we went down King Street to the front. The shots sounded as we got out of the car and we both headed in, guns out. I saw them first." She swallowed. "It doesn't hit you right away. You're trained to keep your head and respond for your safety and that of anyone there. We secured the area and then I ran out to call in for help. That's when it hit me." She paused for a moment, then slowly shook her head. "I thought they were both dead. It was like a dream happening, a nightmare I wanted to wake up from. But I couldn't. So I just kept doing my job and waited until I was home alone that night to throw up.

She looked straight at me. "So many times John encouraged me at work, told me I had the makings of a good officer. I didn't get a chance to make him proud of me until he was dead."

There was a long moment of silence between us.

"You said there are things you're not sure Alison should hear," I said finally.

Gail nodded. "Personal observations. If she asks me about her dad professionally, I can make that pretty straightforward. But as I said, I worked closely with John over the months, and there were things I . . . noticed. Things that began to worry me."

I tried not to worry. "Such as?"

"Such as his obsession with the Simser case. Did Chief Miller tell you about that?"

"Miller said that John Perry took it too personally when the Simser boy was accidentally killed in a gangland bombing. Felt he should have stopped the gang by then and saved the boy's life. Miller finally had to tell John to back off because the gang leader, Mike Denny, was threatening legal action against the force."

"It wasn't like John to lose his grip on his work that way," said Gail firmly, "at least in my experience with him. He started to change then, become moody and silent. Sometimes he'd even snap at Dave Carlson, and they were more like brothers than friends. Dave had started having his coffee at my desk after shift while I was doing reports. I knew he was quietly getting me to help with his paperwork, but I didn't mind." She smiled briefly. "Dave was cute and had a lot of charm. I let him get away with it as long as I was done. But one day, not long before the shooting, John came in and took a strip out of Dave about it. When John left, you could have heard a pin drop. Dave said nothing, and he never sat with me again." She rubbed her hands together as though cold. "The last two weeks were the worst."

"How so?"

"Something was very wrong with John, everyone could see that," she explained. "After Miller had pulled him off Mike Denny, John was preoccupied. Short-fused. He even seemed—" Gail struggled for a word. "He even seemed suddenly unhappy with his work, unhappy to be a police officer, if you can imagine. He withdrew into himself, didn't talk much. Did his work and went home. That wasn't John Perry."

"Maybe it was because of the Simser case and what Miller had done," I suggested.

"I'm sure that added to it, but something else was going on. I got the impression it was personal."

"Why?"

"Well," Gail began, "as an officer, you're trained to notice details. Around the same time as the Simser case, I could sense that John was worried—no, sad—about something, something he never talked about at work. He was very much a champion of team playing, so we were all encouraged to speak our minds about cases. This was something he didn't share.

"Except maybe with Dave, his best friend. A few times I'd be leaving to go home, and they'd be in the office with the door closed, talking. Dave also seemed to have something on his mind in those days, and he wasn't sharing it either. I wondered if the Perrys were having marital problems."

I sat forward. *My father was a different person that summer before he was killed . . . my mother wasn't a happy person, either . . .* "Why do you say that?"

"I guess because I'm female," Gail smiled. "John loved his work and seemed happy with his life in general. If there was a problem, my first guess was his wife. Since I couldn't believe that he would have an affair, I wondered if she were."

"Would that have preoccupied him enough to make him careless on the job?"

"No," she said firmly. "His instincts as a cop were too good to let that happen. But whatever it was, it was serious enough for him to let it show."

I would have to consider this new line of thought. "Did you ever talk to Dave about it after the shooting?"

"No," said Gail quietly. "When I finally went to see him, it was terrible. He was a shell of his former self. Blind, devastated by the death of his friend, totally taking the blame for not saving John's life. He was only thirty then, but he suddenly looked twice that. Except for the sunglasses he always wore, I wouldn't have recognized him on the street."

"Miller told me Dave refused treatment for his eyesight and now is doing the same for cancer. He's dying."

"That's what I've heard. He's been a recluse all this time. But if you want the real spin on that, I'd say the Dave Carlson we all knew died thirty years ago."

Devastation. Ashes.

I left my car in the Riverside parking lot and walked the few blocks up King Street to the Regency, firmly going past the opening to what had been called Water Street in the pre-amalgamation days. Now it boasted a fancier title: Chopin Drive. I didn't have time to visit my own ghosts today; I was busy with someone else's.

At the entrance to the Regency garage, I stopped and unfolded a drawing Gail had made for me of the old crime scene. I took a deep breath and went in, pacing out the places they'd found Perry and Carlson lying, and Denny trying to escape. I couldn't help feeling in over my head. There were a lot of problems with this whole thing. If the truth was a police issue, then I was out of my league. If it were personal, I wasn't sure I wanted to know, even if Alison was.

Yet somehow I was allowing the past to wrap me up again. And this time, it really wasn't my business. So why let myself get involved? Because, whispered my tiny heart, you still haven't made a life for yourself, Farran Mackenzie. And the universe abhors a vacuum.

I left the garage feeling more nerd than Nancy Drew. Within days I would be on my way east to finish a personal promise and help a friend. By the time I reached the door to my condo, I had convinced myself that the grown-up thing to do would be to call Alison and back out. Now was not a good time for me.

I grabbed the folded newspaper up from the floor, opened the door and walked to the phone with new resolve. The message light was going crazy and I couldn't keep count. As I reached out for the receiver, the phone rang and I jumped. It was Alison, or at least what was left of her.

"How could you do that?" she screamed at me. "This was personal. Private. I trusted you!"

"You asked me to find out the truth so I talked to her," I yelled back, caught off guard. "What the hell's the problem?"

"Not Gail Melvin, Mackenzie, the newspaper! The press has been hounding me all day. How could you?"

The Waterloo Record was still folded in my hand. With serious misgiving, I flipped it open where I stood.

The headline was beside a large picture of John Perry in uniform.

MYSTERY INFORMANT SPARKS NEW LOOK AT
30-YEAR-OLD REGIONAL POLICE DEATH

"Aw, Jesus," I said and closed my eyes without a prayer.

Well, I wasn't in—but I wasn't out, either.

The score at the end of the first inning was a three-way tie for the media, Alison and me. Once we'd stopped yelling at each other and compared notes, this is what came together. Someone at the paper had received a note like ours and acted on it, digging up a complete background including Mike Denny's threatened lawsuit against the force and the tie-in to the Simser boy's death. Alison had not responded to any calls after the first one had caught her off guard, but she did place one of her own to Chief Miller. Miller was also not picking up the phone but had returned her message, filling her in on the anonymous tip to the newspaper. For some reason, Miller had fielded questions and stonewalled as best he could without mentioning our visit that week. Gail Melvin was safely on her way to Europe by now and out of reach. The reporters were on Alison, naturally, but for now it seemed that I was not a target. This would temporarily give me room to move if I needed it.

My earlier decision to walk away was sidelined for the moment by this new development. With all hell threatening to break loose, it seemed bad manners to bow out right then. I would leave at week's end, but I still had a couple of days to keep digging. I just had to move carefully if I were to remain out of range on this.

We didn't know if Dave Carlson was still out of range himself or currently beating off reporters with a stick, but my hunch was he would be a little harder for the media to track down. If we moved quickly, chances were that we'd beat the hounds to the punch.

Early Tuesday morning found us in my car, heading to a small house in a Kitchener suburb. No car in the drive and only one parked in front. So far, so good. We'd dressed in jeans and T-shirts, sunglasses and ball caps with our hair tucked up in case of ambush. It seemed more unreal than foolish, as if we were eleven again and our favourite book was *Harriet the Spy*.

A woman in a pale blue shift and a face not used to smiling answered the door.

"Is Dave Carlson home?" asked Alison.

"He is," said the woman bluntly, "but he doesn't take visitors. He's a sick man."

"I think he'll see me." Alison switched to her best mayor voice. "Please tell him that Alison Perry is here to talk to him. It's very important."

Skeptically, Blue Shift took both our names and closed the door, leaving us feeling stupid on the sidewalk. One comfort was the thought of any reporters coming there after us. She'd probably eat them for lunch.

After a long moment, the door reopened and we were allowed in to the inner sanctum. I didn't know what to expect and was relieved to see an older man fully dressed, sitting up in a chair with a footstool. Dave Carlson had been a tall, athletic and handsome man with a lady-killer grin. But time, illness and age had taken their toll and—like Gail Melvin—I would never have known him on the street.

He wore a tie and sunglasses, hair neatly brushed. As he extended his hand toward us, I noticed a small gold watch on his wrist. I wondered if we were expected.

"Alison Perry," Dave said softly. "I'm so glad you've finally come to see me."

Alison had been looking pale. She flushed red and took his hand. "I should have come years ago, Dave, and I'm sorry. Mother wouldn't let me when I was still at home, and then later I guess I . . . I just didn't know what to say to you." She guided his hand into mine. "This is Farran Mackenzie. Remember? She used to live beside us on Water Street."

I took his hand and it was a steady grip, though frail.

"Of course I remember Fan," he said quietly, adding, "How is that beautiful mother of yours?"

"I lost her two years ago, Dave," I hated to tell him. "Heart failure. It was very sudden."

The man did not reply for a few moments, then indicated two chairs. "I'm very sorry, Fan. I liked her a lot. Alison, I did hear about Jessica but I couldn't face going to the funeral. I did send flowers. Please make yourselves comfortable," he added, and called, "Hannah?"

Apparently that was Blue Shift's name as she materialized in the living room doorway. When Dave requested coffee, Hannah did not look pleased but vanished without argument. We sat down, taking off our caps.

"You'll have to excuse us," Dave explained. "We're not used to guests."

"You'd better prepare yourself, then," I remarked grimly. "You'll probably be getting some unwanted ones shortly."

"You mean the press?"

"Yes," said Alison with surprise. "How did you know?"

Dave's mouth formed a thin line. "Brian Miller called me last night to warn me about the newspaper story. I don't get the paper, of course, so I sent Hannah out to get a copy to read to me. It's only a matter of time before they track me down." He shrugged. "Not that it's going to do them any good."

"Because you don't have any memory left of the events on the day of the shooting," I said, cutting to the chase since we were past the small talk.

He turned his face toward my voice. "Who told you that?"

"Gail Melvin."

"Gail Melvin." Dave's sightless eyes turned down to the carpet, his emotions hidden behind the dark lenses. "I remember Gail. Pretty girl. Good officer, too. She came to see me after John's funeral. She's done well as a Mountie."

"Dave," I began gently, "obviously we've come to talk to you about that day. I know your memory is incomplete, but at least tell us what you do remember. It's as much for closure for Alison as it is about the story in the press."

He nodded. "I've been waiting thirty years for you to ask me. And after all this time, I still don't know what to say to you, Alison."

Alison turned pale again, shifting in her seat. I wondered how hard this visit was for her.

49

"You don't have to say anything," she countered quickly. "We're just hoping that something from that day is still in your mind. Something that might explain these terrible notes."

"Notes?"

"Well . . . note. The mystery informant of the news story."

"And others." I shot a look at Alison and continued. "There have been other notes to various people, all along the same line. Suggesting that John Perry was not killed by Mike Denny, but in fact by another officer. The term used is 'friendly fire.'"

Hannah entered with coffee on a tray, putting a mug on a side table near Dave and guiding his hand to it before passing our mugs over. As she turned to go, Dave spoke.

"Hannah, would you bring me that note you found under the mailbox last week?"

"All right," she said sullenly, giving the two of us a glare before heading down the hall leading to what were probably the bedrooms. In a moment she was back with a folded sheet of paper she put in Carlson's hand. He, in turn, held it out to us. When Alison made no move toward it, I took it and read the single line inside.

Remember John Perry.

"Do you have the envelope?" I asked.

"It's gone," said Hannah curtly. "You're lucky to have that. It was on the porch under the mailbox. Must have fallen out. Dirty, crumpled. Thought it was garbage." She vanished into the depths of the kitchen and I heard *The Price is Right* go on.

"This came last week?" I asked Dave.

"Yes. Hannah found it. It was disturbing, but I thought it was some weirdo referring to the thirtieth anniversary of his death. I had no idea there were others. Who's received one?"

"Alison. Gail Melvin. The newspaper reporter. And you." Now that the cat was out of the bag, I'd have to ask Miller if he'd gotten one, too. "That's all we know so far. Dave, why would anyone suggest this?"

He smiled grimly. "That's the irony of the one I got. I can't remember."

Alison leaned forward. "What *do* you remember?"

Dave shook his head and sighed. "What happened that morning has come back to me in pieces, hazy bits of a puzzle. But the most important piece—what happened in the garage—is still missing." His hands gripped the arms of his chair. "But as far as I'm concerned, these poison-pen notes tell the truth. Your father did die at the hands of another officer, Alison." The man's voice sunk to almost a whisper. "Me."

For a moment, neither of us said a word. Then I caught on.

"Dave," I said quietly, "Mike Denny shot John Perry in cold blood. He almost killed you, too. It wasn't your fault."

"John was my partner and my best friend, Fan." Dave's voice was flat and empty. "We answered a call together. I was his backup. He died. You can't change that." His hands curled into fists on his knees. "I let him down, Alison, and I let you down. And even after all these years, to say sorry seems so little, far too late."

I shut up, letting the two of them finish three decades of personal loose ends.

"I don't hold you responsible, Dave," said Alison finally. "I never did. I want you to know that. I should have come years ago to tell you that, and I guess I've been a coward. I'm sorry."

There was an uncomfortable silence, and I played with the idea of looking for the washroom to give them a moment alone.

"I've followed your career through the years, Ali," Dave smiled after a moment. "I know your father would be very proud of you." He didn't see Alison tear up, of course, and continued in my direction. "What about you, Fan? Where has life taken you?"

I filled him in a little, skirting a huge circle around the story of my father's murder and the hole it had torn through my life last year. "I'm sorry to hear you're ill, Dave," I finished up. "Brian Miller told us that you're battling liver cancer. Is there anything we can do to help?"

Unexpectedly, Dave sat back and chuckled. "Amazing," he said, shaking his head. "The grapevine is as healthy as ever. I've only known myself since July. I'm not 'battling' it yet like I will be soon. Just pain I've had for a couple of months, and I take something for that." He nodded toward the table where his coffee mug sat near a small medicine bottle and an Braille copy of Agatha Christie's *The Moving Finger*—a personal favourite. "They tell me a month or maybe six months. And it won't be easy, even if I do take treatment. I'm glad you came now, while I'm still feeling up to visitors. Not that I've been much help."

"You said that pieces of that morning have come back," I ventured. "Do you remember why you went to John's house on your way to work?"

He rubbed his forehead. "I think I went to get a lift with him. I had already put my car away for the winter. That beauty was my baby, remember?" A smile lit up his face and then disappeared as quickly as it came. "How I hated to sell her after."

"You and John had a big talk that morning before you left. Do you remember what it was about?"

Dave fell silent for a moment. As I waited for his answer, I realized that Alison had not spoken for some time. "It was personal, as I recall," he said finally. "Nothing to do with the job."

"Was John upset about something?" I persisted. "Gail Melvin told me that he seemed preoccupied the last two weeks of his life. Something that made him sad more than angry." I chose my words carefully in front of Alison. "Do you remember what that might have been?"

His face took on a sombre cast. "More sad than angry," he repeated and fell silent.

I felt Alison's hand on my arm. "We've been here long enough, Dave. We don't want to tire you out. Maybe we could come back next week and continue this."

Alison was right. The man was losing his steam. But I wanted an answer to my question, and I opened my mouth to continue when the front doorbell rang. The kitchen door flew open and Hannah marched past, Bob Barker's peppy voice trailing along in her wake. We heard a short conversation, followed by the slam of the front door and Hannah's return.

"Some guy from *The Record* wants to see you," she announced to the room. "Are you famous or something?"

"Oh, no," said Alison, rising from her chair. "Not already. I can't let them find me here today," she added. "That'll only add fuel to the fire."

"Should I tell him to leave?" Hannah asked her boss. Dave roused himself and shook his head.

"Not yet. We need to stall him. Where are you parked, girls?"

"Down the block some, just in case." I started stuffing my hair back into my ball cap, and Alison followed suit.

"Good," Dave smiled. "Still the Nancy Drew. I'll let you both out the back door. Hannah, once the girls are in the kitchen, open the door and chat him up. Stall for time." He got up slowly, then moved easily toward the kitchen through the familiar room. We grabbed our sunglasses and followed. No fear about leaving a purse as we both had left them in the car. Saying goodbye at the back door, we could hear Hannah out front giving the reporter the third degree, and I almost felt sorry for him. Almost.

"It was good to see you," said Alison, shaking his hand. "I should have done this long ago."

"I know it wasn't easy, Ali," Dave said. "A lot of water under the bridge. But I'm glad you came. We need to talk. And you be careful," he added. "I've heard there are some shady people not happy with your return to politics."

Impulsively, I gave Dave a hug. He patted my head, a habit from long ago. "You're a little taller than I remember, Fan," he smiled.

"Can I call you tomorrow?" I asked.

"Yes, but I hope you'll come back soon to visit."

I promised him, and he shooed us out the door. We slunk through the hedge into the neighbour's yard as ordered and casually sauntered down the driveway away from Dave's front steps where the intrepid reporter was still hanging in under Hannah's expert stonewalling.

We drove in silence for some time, each with our own ghosts entertaining us. Finally, as we turned in to her street, Alison turned to me.

"What are you going to call Dave about?"

"I don't know," I said honestly. "I still have a hundred questions for him, and there are things bugging me about this. I need a night to sleep on it and see if I can put my finger on a few things." I thought of Gail Melvin's remark about the Perrys possibly having marital problems. Maybe that was what the big talk between Dave and John was about the morning of the shooting. I remembered the sound of two men shouting as I walked past the house that morning long ago, and the little ember of fear began to glow again in my stomach.

Maybe it was a good thing that Alison stopped the conversation when she did.

"Why didn't you pick me up for school that morning?" The words came out before I had time to stop them.

"What morning?"

"The morning your father died."

Alison looked at me for a moment while I stared at the traffic. Then she turned away.

"I don't remember," she said softly to her passenger window. "I think I was late and thought you'd already gone."

Well, for me that held about as much water as a sieve, and I started to get angry.

"Listen, Alison, if you want my help with this mess, you'd better be straight with me about everything. I really don't want to be traipsing around digging up ghosts. I had enough of that last summer to do me a lifetime." I could feel myself emotionally shrinking down like Alice to the size of a twelve-year-old. "For your information, I was going to call you last night to tell you that I can't do this right now. I have some personal stuff I have to attend to, and it can't wait. I'm leaving town at the end of the week."

"Fine." Alison got her stuff together in a huff. "Leave a friend in the lurch. I don't need you. I can do this alone."

There was more anger here than necessary from both of us, I sensed, some of it quite old. But I couldn't stop myself.

"I don't leave friends in the lurch," I retorted, slamming on the brakes to let her out. "That's your specialty, as I recall. Besides, we're not friends. Haven't been for thirty years. Just because you show up at my door doesn't mean everything's back to the way it was. I only agreed to help because of your dad."

"Then I won't take your time," said Alison curtly. "You're right. He was *my* father. That makes him my problem. I'll handle this myself." She slammed the car door and stalked up the sidewalk. I slammed the gear stick into drive and took off in a cloud of self-righteous indignation and flying gravel.

For anyone interested, being right—or at least feeling that way—isn't all it's cracked up to be. I didn't sleep well that night. No big surprise there. By about three in the morning, I had admitted to myself that my friendship with Alison wasn't completely history. The friend part was over and had been for decades, but loose ends and old wounds were everywhere. I thought I'd let go. Now I saw that agreeing to her request for help would make her in my debt. And then I could make demands, like an explanation for the untimely death of a friendship that had once meant the world to me.

After I'd left Alison in the dust, I used my newly returned sense of self-responsibility to make the drive to the cemetery. My mother's urn was packed in a small wooden crate and placed in the trunk of my car. Her tombstone would be removed later, when I returned. I planned to put a joint headstone over my father and mother when they were finally together again.

It was emotional for me to think about that moment, and I wondered how I would handle it at the St. Lawrence Valley Cemetery on the weekend. Thankfully, Ruth Hoffman would be there, along with the minister from St. Matthew's Presbyterian in Ingleside. That might keep me grounded at the time. Grounded I certainly wasn't as I flipped around in bed all that night, with thoughts of people now long dead who had made up my world. Strange notes suggesting a terrible secret. A man who once had everything entombed by his own sense of guilt for thirty years. And the one person I could have talked to about it all was entombed in an urn sitting in my front hall.

No wonder people drink.

When the first rays of light hit my window and chased the monsters from my room, I dozed at last. I got up around ten, feeling somewhat rested, but skittish. My answering machine had a few calls on it, none from Alison. I thought about calling Dave to continue our talk, but the knot in the pit of my stomach changed my mind. I didn't want to go there and now had no reason to anyway. I was off the hook. Why didn't I feel better about it?

Since I had my freedom back, I decided to leave a day early on Thursday. Wednesday would be used to do errands needed before heading east. I watered all my plants (those I hadn't killed yet) and started cleaning the condominium, piling the boxes from work in the spare bedroom.

That's when Alison called.

Her voice sounded cool, but she apologized for her half of the blowup yesterday.

"Look, Fan, I know there are a lot of loose ends between us," she said, "and we need to talk it through. Can we have a truce until this thing is over? To be honest, you're the only person I can safely talk to about it. You were there, too." I heard her sigh. "If you have some personal things to do, I understand. But I need your help. I'll take whatever you can give me before you leave."

I was quiet for a moment, feeling both sulky and relieved at her words.

"Okay," I said finally. "It's a deal. What did you want to do next?"

"Actually, it's not what I want to do, it's what Dave wants to do."

"Carlson?"

"Yes. He called me this morning about going to the cemetery with him today," Alison explained. "Seems he never did go to Dad's grave all these years, and he wants to go now while he still can. Asked if we could go with him for moral support. I said yes," she finished, adding, "I don't know if I can do this alone. Can you come?"

"What time?"

"Meet me there in an hour. I'm picking Dave up."

By early afternoon, the day had become one of those chilly August ones that Ontario is famous for. Grey clouds had taken the sun, and the wind promised rain.

At the cemetery, I zipped up my jacket as I walked around the mausoleum and down the hill to John Perry's grave. They hadn't arrived yet, and I hopped a little from foot to foot to keep warm.

This entire situation was beginning to feel like an out-of-body experience. The whole idea of John being killed by another officer seemed impossible at best, thank God. Talking to Dave Carlson and spending time with Alison was dragging me back to a past I was done with—or thought I was. I didn't want to go. The notes will stop, I told myself, and the police will find the person behind it. Case closed.

The wind brought the sound of a car on the gravel, then two doors slamming. I braced myself mentally and turned to see Alison leading Dave down the hill. I met them halfway and took his hand.

"How did it go yesterday with the press?" I asked.

"Hannah worked him over pretty well," Dave grinned. I had to smile at that one, too. "He didn't get anything out of me, and there wasn't much in the paper this morning."

"I gave a statement to them today," said Alison quietly. "They were still waiting outside the house, so I spoke to them. Gave them what they wanted. I didn't want them following me here." She sighed. "I'll probably be on the six o'clock news."

"Don't let it get to you," I said briskly.

We stopped in front of the Perry tombstone, and Dave's grip tightened.

"Are we here?" he asked.

"Yes," Alison replied softly. She set her tote bag on the grass and held his white cane.

I was watching them carefully, well aware the emotional cost this moment was to both. Dave reached out and I guided his hand to the stone's face, where he slowly traced the engraving, felt the Waterloo Regional Police crest, and followed the shape of the edges. When he straightened up, I saw he was crying.

"I should have come years ago, Johnny," he whispered. "I'm sorry. Sorry for so many things." He took out a handkerchief and wiped his eyes with a shaky hand. I put my arm around his shoulder. "You don't know how many times I prayed for a second chance," he continued. "Do it all again and fix it. Make things right. Please forgive me."

"The John I remember would never have blamed you, Dave," I said awkwardly, then looked over at Alison for support. She seemed miles away, as though silence was the key to staying all in one piece. "He would have said you did your best in a bad situation. Isn't that right, Alison?"

"Yes." She roused herself and patted the hand she still held. "He would have blamed himself first, Dave. That's the way he was."

We all fell silent, each with our own thoughts of God knows what. The grey of the afternoon wrapped around my heart, the silence of the cemetery peaceful and oppressive at the same time. Dave was finding closure to this tragedy, but I realized my own grief was still shut away. In thirty years, I had never allowed myself to mourn the loss of the only father figure in my life. The thought made me cold all over, and I shivered.

"Yes," said Dave quietly. "The wind is getting colder. We should go. Thank you both for bringing me here." He held out his hand and Alison passed him the white cane. Turning to go, he gave me a quick hug. "Remember, Fan. You promised to visit again."

"I did and I will," I said. "Call me tonight, Alison," I added as she took Dave's arm.

I watched the two figures make their way slowly up the incline, like wounded vets coming home from the war. In a way, they were—and the cease-fire was over.

But it wasn't my war, I told myself. The Waterloo Regional Police will handle it, and that's the way it should be. Without a final look at the grave, I turned and strode to my own car that was parked on the other side of the cemetery. Once abreast of the mausoleum, I looked across the grass to where Alison was helping Dave into her car. She gave a last wave as she went around to the driver's side, and I waved back. Digging for my keys, I decided not to leave a day early and see what I could do for Alison tomorrow. Maybe ask Brian Miller if he got one of those notes. Fifty bucks says he did.

And then I was face down in the grass, feet torn out from under me, a terrible roar in my head. Confused, I sat up and looked around.

Confusion became horror.

The front of Alison's car was a fireball, windows blown out, driver's door hanging open. I spotted her lying motionless on the gravel road a few yards away, eyes closed. There was blood on her face.

"Alison!" I screamed. Somehow I got to my feet and stumbled toward her. It was a nightmare and my legs wouldn't run. "Help me! Please, somebody help!" I called out uselessly. The cemetery was deserted.

I reached Alison and rolled her over. One hand clutched her chest and there was a terrible gash across her forehead, but she was alive. I held her and looked around, panic washing over me.

Dave.

He'd been getting in the car.

"Alison. *Al.*" I shook her. "Wake up!" I shrieked in a voice that wasn't mine. "Where's Dave? Where is he?"

Her eyes flew open. She looked at me dully, tried to sit up and then saw the car. She started to scream.

"The car! The car! Get him out!" Alison made it to her knees, arm still wrapped around her chest. "Fan! Get him out!"

I followed her eyes in horror to where the car burned, flames shooting out from underneath the chassis.

The gas tank.

My mind gave orders and my body grabbed Alison, hauling her across the road. I threw her behind the nearest tombstone and fell on my knees beside her in the grass. Seconds later, hell opened. A blast of heat roared over us, its infernal fingers reaching . . . reaching.

I remember kneeling, screaming, hiding, praying.

Then voices, yelling, hands, sirens.

I remember terror turning to rage.

Now it *was* my war.

Chapter FIVE:
Through a Glass Darkly

A heart of lead.

By the time they let me see Alison, the rage had burned through, cooling and hardening into a mass in my chest. I was numb, probably suffering from shock. They treated me for that in the Emergency of Cambridge Memorial Hospital while Alison was rushed off on a gurney.

It was Brian Miller who brought me the news of her condition: multiple contusions, bruising, concussion, one cracked rib and a fractured wrist. There were no internal injuries or damage to the spine. She had had her back to the car when the blast occurred, and was carried several feet across the cemetery road before slamming face down on the ground. A few feet closer and she would have died.

Dave had been in the car and died instantly.

"Can I drive you home?" said Miller.

We were in my examination cubicle, waiting for the nurse to officially kick me out. The retired police chief stood stolidly in the corner, arms crossed while I sat on the bed swinging my legs impatiently.

"I'm not going anywhere until I see Alison."

"It's a miracle she's alive," he said grimly. "But you need to get out of here. The press is already buzzing around, and you don't want that right now. They probably don't know your involvement yet beyond being a passerby."

My lower lip came out. "Not until I see Alison," I repeated. I turned to face him. "Why are you here? You're retired."

"I'm also an old friend of the family." He met my gaze steadily. "And there's more bad news. There's been a formal request to reopen the case against Mike Denny—from his son."

"Is he a criminal, too?"

"Worse," Miller sighed. "A lawyer. And he's suddenly threatening lawsuits all over the place, saying his father was wrongfully convicted. The apple doesn't fall far from the tree on this one."

"Somebody mailed him something too, then," I guessed.

"Looks that way. If I ever get my hands on the guy who did . . . The service doesn't need this crap on its thirtieth anniversary." Miller opened the curtain a crack and scouted the hall.

"Did you?" I suddenly remembered to ask.

"Did I what?"

"Get a note about John's death being by friendly fire."

At that he turned to look at me. "So you and Alison did get one, then," he said after a moment. "That's why you came to see me."

"When did yours arrive?"

"About a week before your visit. I didn't know what to make of it, but it certainly threw me."

"If you're sure you know what happened thirty years ago, why should it?"

The nurse stuck her head in and I was free. With Miller's help, I was allowed to wait inside the Emergency, away from the press. Finally, they moved Alison into Observation and, after two police officers spoke with her, I was let in.

I found her partially sitting up, with a large gauze bandage on her forehead that blended with the pale cast of her skin. One wrist was wrapped and in a sling. Both eyes and one cheek were bruised and cut, as if she'd gone a few rounds with Mohammed Ali. I took it as a good sign that there was only one machine clicking and purring away beside her, and only the nasal tube was evident.

I went around to the good hand, sat down and held it. Alison's jaw on that side was swollen and purple, and she struggled to speak.

"Should see . . . other guy, right?" She closed her bruised eyes and a single tear ran down her cheek. "Purse . . . damned pur—"

"Don't talk. Rest," I said awkwardly, well aware of my uselessness at that moment and of the sharp words we'd shared the day before. "I'll be here for a while. I'm sure they told you there's an officer on guard until further notice. You're safe here."

At that she opened her eyes again, giving me an odd look. I thought perhaps she didn't understand.

"Do you remember what happened this afternoon?" I asked gently. She looked away, but nodded. "It seems those threats weren't empty, Alison. Someone doesn't want you active again. They want you dead."

"Dave . . . dead," she mumbled.

I gave her hand a squeeze. If we were to get through this in one piece, the gloves would have to come off. "It was your car," I said quietly. "That bomb was meant for you."

"No. No." Alison drew her mouth into a thin line and shook her head. "No," she repeated firmly, then started to cry. I wondered if the nurses would toss me out for my great bedside manner.

I squeezed her hand. "Don't worry, Al. I'm here, there's a police guard posted, and Brian Miller is hovering around like a nanny. We'll find who did this."

"Not scared . . . understand?" Alison gave me a stricken look. "Not me. Can't be . . . responsible." She turned her face away from me, and I understood. If the bomb was meant to kill her, then in her mind she was to blame for Dave's death.

I didn't know what to say, and so said nothing. After a bit, she seemed to doze off, her hand still in mine. I looked at the face under the wounds, at once so familiar and so strange, remembering who she had been and wondering who she had become.

SEPTEMBER 9, 1973
Sunday afternoon

"It's the new me." Alison touched her new short shag and shrugged. *"I asked Mom to take me in yesterday afternoon. It's no big deal."*

Farran stood in her best friend's bedroom. The David Cassidy posters that had papered the walls for the past three years had vanished, and the bareness was startling.

"You've given up on David, too?" she asked incredulously. *"I thought you'd be stuck on him forever."*

"I turned fifteen this morning. It's time to stop being a kid." Alison flung herself on her bed and looked pensively at her red nails. Then she looked through them at Farran. *"We'll have to do you next, Fan."*

"Do me?" The girl set her birthday gift on the desk in the corner. She was getting that funny feeling in her stomach again, as though Alison were talking from somewhere far away. A sudden urge to grab her friend by the hand and pull her back struggled up inside, and she pushed it away. That would be crazy.

"Yah, you know. Do you up. Get rid of the sloppy kid clothes. Do your nails. Do something with your hair." Alison jumped off the bed and scooped Farran's long blond hair into an upsweep. *"You have nice hair, Fan, but long and straight isn't cool anymore."* She dropped it. *"You'll be fifteen next month, remember."*

"So you keep reminding me," Fan shot back. She suddenly wasn't looking forward to the birthday supper, even though her mother and Dave Carlson were coming, too. She suddenly wanted to go home and change.

"Sor-ree. Didn't know you were so touchy." Alison picked up the gift and shook it. *"Can I open this?"*

"Not until supper. You know your mom. It's something for the trip," Farran added, referring to the big plan of a trip to Europe, one that both Alison and Farran had been saving babysitting money toward for the past few years.

Alison flushed pink and set the box down. "Oh, that. Uh, thanks. Listen, Fan, I may have to put that on hold. I'm not sure if I can make it for next summer."

"What? Why?"

Alison waved it away. "Oh nothing certain. Mom's just beating the drums about exchange student stuff again. Let's just play it by ear, okay?"

A dull silence settled between them, unlike the comfortable silences of the past. Finally, Farran sat down in the desk chair and doodled on the blotter.

"I've seen his picture," she said quietly.

"Who's picture?"

"My father's."

Alison sat up from where she had been lying on the bed again. "You did? What's he look like?"

"Like me." Farran drew a small flower. "He wasn't much older when the picture was taken. It looks like he's standing in front of a house, but you can't see much because the picture is ripped. Half is gone."

"Does your mother have the other half?"

"I don't know. She doesn't know I've seen it." Farran slapped the pen down and looked at her friend. "You can't tell anyone I've told you this."

"Of course not," said Alison. "That's the rule."

"I went through my mother's drawer yesterday when she was working late. I wanted to see if I could find anything about him before she got back."

"Did you find anything else?"

"A small gold bracelet that I've never seen her wear," Farran replied. "It's beautiful and there's a heart locket on it. My father's picture is inside. He must have given it to her." She paused. "Mom wouldn't have been much older than me."

"Then you're old enough to hear the truth," Alison said matter-of-factly. "Tell her it's time she told you about your dad."

"I've tried," Farran sighed, "but she just won't talk about it. She always gets upset and says no."

"This time, don't let that stop you. You have a right to know. Besides," added Alison, "what could be so bad? Unwed mother? It's not like she'd have been the first."

What could be so bad? But Farran wasn't so sure she wanted to know.

"First what?" Dave Carlson stuck his head in the door and grinned. "Found you fair and square. This isn't just your birthday, Al. It's mine, too. Let's get the party started. You have to come down and be with the grownups."

"We're grownups, too," Alison protested. "At least I am. Fan's got another month."

"Ah, yes. The Big One-Five." Dave winked at Farran. "And it seems only yesterday you were in diapers."

Alison threw a pillow at him and he vanished. "He's right. If everyone's here, we'd better go." She ran a comb through her hair and sniffed. "He didn't even mention my new cut."

The girls made their way to the backyard where John Perry was busy with the barbecue. Dave, ball cap and sunglasses on, was nearby filling the cooler with beer. Jessica Perry called to the girls to bring dishes out, and they went back toward the kitchen.

"That's a good idea." Dave looked over his shoulder for a moment, then straightened up. "I'll go over and see what's keeping Leslie. Maybe she needs a hand with bringing something." He crossed the lawn and stepped over the peony hedge, disappearing into the Mackenzies' kitchen door. A few minutes later he returned with Leslie Mackenzie behind him, both bearing bowls of food.

When the picnic table was fully loaded, they all sat down except Farran, who jumped up to get her camera.

"Wait!" she said. "Everybody make a birthday toast for the picture."

Alison moved in between Dave and Leslie, facing her mother across the table. "Both birthday people in the middle," she laughed.

Jessica looked up at her husband, standing silently behind. "Smile, dear."

Farran took the photo. "Another one," she ordered. "Squeeze in more."

Everyone settled down to eat. The Sunday afternoon was beautiful and warm for a September day, and the meal seemed perfect.

"Hope we get this kind of weather next weekend, right Johnny?" said Dave.

John Perry had been quiet and seemed to come back from somewhere far away. "Yes. Absolutely. The policemen's ball is a cruise this year. If it's cold, we'll all be huddled inside."

"Did you get a date yet, Dave?" teased Farran.

"Yes, Fanny, I did," he shot back with a smile. "I'm taking your mother. She finally agreed to go with me."

Farran looked at her mother, who sat quietly with a slight flush on her cheeks. "My mom's actually going out?" said the girl with amazement. "How did you manage that?"

"Fan," said Leslie warningly.

"Very simple," Dave replied. "I just wouldn't take no for answer. She had no choice."

"I believe they call that police harassment," Leslie added quietly. Everyone laughed.

Alison got up from the table and started clearing plates. "When do we do the gifts?"

"Not till after the cake," her mother said firmly.

The cake was brought out, candles lit, and set between Alison and Dave. It had "15" on it for her, and "30" for him.

"My daughter is growing up and my best friend is growing old," said John.

"Hey, speak for yourself," Dave retorted, adding, "But I know what you mean. I remember it like yesterday when you told me you and Jess were having a baby. I was in high school, but you always treated me like an adult. Told me yourself, even before you told my parents."

"Good," said Alison brightly. "Then you can treat me like I'm an adult now. Let's make a wish, Dave."

They blew out the candles and served up the cake. Presents were passed out. Dave's cards had the theme of old age, and Alison read each one out loud teasingly. Finally, the girl opened her gifts, Farran's last. A makeup travel case.

"Very nice," said her father. "Just one more year, right girls?"

Neither one answered, and he looked at them curiously.

"Dave," Alison said quickly, "you haven't opened your gifts."

After unwrapping several joke gifts, Dave opened a small box with no tag on it. It contained a man's gold watch.

"It—it's beautiful, guys. I don't know what to say." His finger felt something on the back of the watch, and he flipped it over. "Here," he said shyly, passing it to Alison, "you might as well read this, too."

Alison glanced at the watch. "Happy 30th, Dave," she read. "September 9, 1973."

Dave carefully put the watch back in its box, his eyes unreadable behind the sunglasses. Then he raised his glass.

"It's been a good thirty years," he said quietly. "Here's to the next thirty with all of you."

As everyone joined the toast, the day seemed to darken as though something had passed over the sun. Leslie looked up. When Farran followed suit, she caught John giving a dark look to Jessica who avoided his eye. Alison and Dave sat in front, cards and gifts around them, oblivious to it all.

Thirty years later, I thought, and here we are, Dave. You're dead, and Alison's life is in danger.

Wednesday evening I spent at various locations within the hospital eating and dozing. The early start to my trip east was out, of course, but the trip itself was still on. Arrangements had been made, and I couldn't cancel. I would have to leave on Friday as planned, with Alison in the care of the Waterloo Regional Police.

I had a coffee in the cafeteria and watched the sunset through the window. As the dark filled the glass pane, I remembered another evening filled with unanswered questions.

SEPTEMBER 9, 1973
Sunday evening

Farran stood in her backyard, looking up at the stars. She couldn't imagine being fifteen, let alone thirty. Fifteen sounded so grownup, and she felt anything but. Maybe Alison was right. Maybe it was time to "do" herself up. Maybe if she acted the part, she might start to feel that way.

The girl walked down the side path to the street. She could see her mother moving around inside the house, waiting for her. When Leslie had left the birthday party that evening, Farran had stayed behind for a few minutes, using Alison's gifts to unpack as an excuse. Was she avoiding her mother? Or just the discussion she knew would come. Fan knew her mother well. This "date" with Dave Carlson would have to be discussed and explained—as though Farran would ever begrudge her mother some companionship.

But that topic would lead to the other on Farran's mind. Her father.

She sighed and kicked a pebble onto the road. A streetlight lit up Water Street . . . no, Chopin Drive . . . right in front of their house. The girl stood in its glow, her back leaning on the great old elm in the front lawn as though needing some of its strength.

"Alison?"

Farran jumped at the voice. It was Dave, leaving the Perrys' house with a bag in his hand.

"Alison, you should go inside now and not make your mother worry," he said, walking toward her. "It's getting late."

Farran stepped out onto the sidewalk. "It's me, Dave. Going home?"

"Oh, yah. Nice night for a walk." He stopped beside her. "What are you doing out here this late? I thought you went home to bed."

The girl shrugged. "Just need some time to think."

Dave nodded slowly, then rubbed his eyes. "I know what you mean, Fan. Listen, I hope you're okay with me taking your mom out next weekend."

"Sure, why not?" said Farran. "She needs to get out and have some fun."

Dave smiled. "And you need to get indoors. Same advice for you. It's late. We live in a city now," he added, "and things are still unsettled around here."

Farran followed orders and went to the front door, pausing to watch Dave make his way slowly down the street. Then she slipped inside and into her room. In a few minutes, her mother came to the door.

"Ready for bed?" Leslie asked. "Good. School night." She sat on the bed. "Can we talk for a minute?"

Farran got in bed. "You mean about your date with Dave?" she said.

"That's what I wanted to explain," Leslie replied, a touch of pink in her cheeks. "It's not a date. We're just going as friends. Dave needs a date."

"Oh, come on, Mom." The girl rolled her eyes. "I'm not a kid. Dave's a good-looking, single guy with a red sports car. Why would he need a date? He likes you. What's wrong with that?"

"I'm older than he is, Fan. I'm sure he'd want someone younger." Leslie started tucking her daughter in.

"Two years. That's all. And you're beautiful, Mom. Why wouldn't he like you?"

"Are you trying to marry me off?" the woman teased.

"No, but—" Farran sat up, her face serious. "But I think it'd be great if you had someone to hang out with. And we know Dave. You told me once that Dad died the year I was born," she added. "You've been alone all this time. That's long enough, isn't it?"

As soon as the words were said, Farran could have bitten her tongue. Her mother's face lost its smile and set like cement. Tears threatened in the corners of her eyes. It was the look Farran knew the best and feared the most.

"No." Leslie's voice was lifeless. "It will never be long enough." She rose and left the room without another word—or a kiss goodnight.

"Oh, man," Farran sighed and fell back on her pillow. Problem. Another one. Problem with Alison, problem with her mom, and now she'd probably killed Dave's chances of taking her mother out next weekend.

Do the smart thing, she thought. Turn off the light and go to sleep. Leave it alone.

You're old enough to know the truth, Alison's voice countered in her head.

Farran threw off the covers, marched out the door, and headed down the hall. She could hear her mother in the kitchen. Hesitating only a moment, she pushed open the swing door and stood there, feet apart, arms crossed—looking a lot braver than she felt.

"Mom, it's time we talked woman to woman. You can't keep treating me like a child."

"Fan, go to bed." Her mother busied herself with the last of the dishes. "It's late."

"Why can't we talk about Dad?" Farran's heart was pounding. "Why can't you tell me who my father was?"

"Your father's name was Hal. I've told you that already." There was a dangerous calm in Leslie's voice.

"Hal Mackenzie," the girl continued heedlessly. "He died in a car accident the year I was born."

"Yes." Leslie pulled the drain and let the water out of the sink, still not looking up. "You know who your father was. I think you should go to bed now."

The warning was unmistakable, but not taken.

"But that's not knowing him! What about where he came from? Where did you meet? What was he like? Did he have any family? Do I have relatives out there I don't know about?"

Leslie stood ominously still with her back to Farran, a large salad bowl in her hands. She did not reply.

The girl stamped her foot with frustration. "Talk to me! Do you know how hard it is to grow up without your dad, without even being able to talk about him with your friends?"

At that, Leslie turned on her daughter, face red with fury. She hurled the bowl to the floor, smashing it to pieces.

"Do you know how hard it is to have your baby alone? To raise a child without a father? To struggle without family?" The rage shook her body. "It has taken every ounce of me to make the life we live. I did it for you, Farran Mackenzie, because you're all I have."

The girl had never seen her mother so angry, and she was suddenly afraid for them both.

"That's right, Mom," she said softly. "You have me. You're not alone anymore. I'm old enough to help now." Farran gently reached out for her mother's hand. "Whatever happened back then, I don't care. I just want to share it with you."

The fire died in Leslie's eyes, and she looked at her daughter for a long moment.

"Share the past," she said, stroking Farran's blond hair. "You look so like him. Yes, maybe it's time."

Suddenly Leslie turned her head to one side, as though listening to something. Farran's eyes unconsciously followed and saw only the silent, empty kitchen. A shiver she couldn't stop ran down her back. And when her mother looked back, the girl could see the doors inside had slammed shut once more.

"No." Leslie slowly got the broom out and began to sweep the pieces together on the floor. "It can't be done."

Farran ran from the kitchen back to her bedroom, slamming her own door. She threw herself indignantly on the bed. It was cold war, and she wouldn't speak to her mother until things changed. Leslie always came to talk after a fight, and this time Farran wouldn't budge.

But Leslie did not come. Finally, still stretched out across her bed, the girl fell into a troubled sleep.

Several hours later, the evening chill woke Farran up. She closed her window and checked the time. Past midnight. Quietly opening her door, she could see her mother's reading light still on. Hesitantly, she made her way to the room and peeked in. It was empty.

Startled, the girl went to the living room but it, too, was empty, the TV dark. From the far side of the dining room, a small strip of light showed under the kitchen's swing door. Farran tiptoed up and put her ear to the door, careful to not make it move. She could just make out the sound of muffled crying.

Slowly she pushed the door open. Leslie sat at the kitchen table, her head down on her arms. Weary sobs shook her shoulders.

"I can't do this, Hal," Farran heard her mother whisper. "I can't do this alone anymore."

Fan silently let the swing door close and returned to her room, leaving the sound of her mother's crying and the last of her childhood behind her. She sat very still in the night thinking, for a long, long time.

I sat in the hospital waiting room that night thinking, for what seemed a long, long time.

A Waterloo Regional police officer stood guard at the door to the Observation unit, paying absolutely no attention to the media representatives circling in her face. Mercifully, the Observation waiting room was part of the unit and equally safe from reporters. I would occasionally see one try to peer over the officer's shoulder through the tiny window in the door to see me, but I also paid them no attention.

Despite my sleeplessness the previous night, after a few dozes in the waiting room, I was wide awake. Alison slept on in her cocoon of linen and bandages, and I kept running everything through my mind. Just as the summer before, I was in the middle of something I could not grasp, something that had now turned deadly. All my adult life, I had relied on my education and skill to deal with things. But education does not always equal intelligence. Twice now, in as many years, I felt stupid and helpless when faced with a bad situation. Worse, all night I could not shake the feeling that I had recently seen something important, that something had happened right in front of me, and I could not see it for what it was.

I needed intelligence and ruthless assessment, and I needed it from someone I could trust absolutely.

I needed to talk to Inspector Jerry Strauss.

A hand on my shoulder around nine the next morning brought me back to where I was. Alison was off the critical list and would be moved after breakfast to a private room, uniform still at the door. Breakfast sounded like a good idea, so after successfully dodging reporters, I tracked down the hospital cafeteria to fuel up. While I was there, the investigating officers came with more questions, and the shift at the door changed. It was almost eleven before Alison, Miller and I were having a little private party in room 403.

"When I get out of here, I go back to a regular life," said Alison stubbornly, obviously feeling much more her old self. "It's bad enough with the press on my heels."

"The officer can help with that, too." Miller didn't budge. "There's been one murder. Your safety is a priority for the police until the investigation is closed."

Alison sighed and looked at me for support. She was unsuccessful.

"Just follow orders for now, Alison," I said quietly, "and don't give them a rough time. The danger out there is very real. Real enough to get you killed."

She went silent at that.

My inner voice was anything but quiet, however, and I needed a lot more answers. The feeling that haunted me all night was still there, with a new background of uneasiness about the entire situation.

"It seems that the bomb was wired into the ignition, just under your steering. Turning the key set it off. Simple but effective, especially since you had a full tank of gas." Miller took his coat off and sat down. "It had to have been put in while you were at the gravesite."

"But that's impossible," I countered. "Someone would have seen it being done."

"Not necessarily," said Alison quietly. "I had parked behind the cemetery office to get out of the wind. And Dad's grave is down the hill a little way, remember? The car was out of sight to everyone else, and we never looked up." She shrugged, then grimaced from the pain. "We were talking."

"Why take the risk of being seen in such a public place, though?" Huge pieces of this were still slipping through my fingers.

Miller cocked his head toward the door. "The press. They've been wrapped around Alison's house since the story broke in the papers. My guess is yesterday was the first chance to get at her car."

That was true. Alison had slipped away to my place in a taxi so we wouldn't be followed the day we went to Dave Carlson's house. Forty-eight hours and a lifetime ago.

"That means you're being watched." I got up and walked over to the window. "Damn right you're having security."

"We don't want to push the odds by giving them a second crack at it," Miller said bluntly. "You were lucky this time. You're under wraps until further notice."

"Simple but effective, you said." I turned and looked at Miller. "Are we talking a professional hit or a bomb someone could make at home?"

"That's hard to answer these days, Mackenzie. You can find anything on the Internet if you know where to look. So far the word is a basic explosive device, but done by someone who knows how to handle that stuff. Why?"

"I was thinking of the late Mike Denny's son. You said he was a lawyer. Did he learn the craft of handling explosives at Daddy's knee?"

"It's being looked into," Miller admitted. "He was about ten when his father went to prison. Young, but anything's possible, I guess. The police are more serious about the threats Alison received over the past few weeks. I think that's the route to go."

I came back and sat in the chair next to the bed. "Why was Dave alone in the car when the bomb went off?"

Alison went paler, if possible, and her voice sounded shaky. "I walked him to the car and helped him get in on the passenger side. I remember making a comment about how cold the weather had become so suddenly. Then I went around to get in the driver's side and I realized . . . " She stopped and picked at her blanket.

Then I understood her disjointed words from the night before.

"You realized that you had forgotten your purse. Again."

She nodded miserably.

"Where?" I continued. "At the grave?"

Alison nodded again, clearing her throat. "I remembered setting it down to hold Dave's cane."

"Then?"

"Then I got out of the car to go back for it. I must have put the keys in the ignition, first. I don't remember anything after that until I woke up here."

"Carlson must have started the engine to warm up the car," Miller said simply.

"Does Dave have any family, Brian?" Alison spoke almost in a whisper. I remembered what she'd said yesterday about being responsible.

"Only a sister somewhere," said Miller. "He never married."

A nurse came in to do nurse stuff, and everyone fell silent for a few minutes. When she left, I spoke my mind to Miller.

"I'm going to ask you a straight question, and I expect a straight answer." I looked him right in the eye. "This whole thing isn't just about nasty notes and spreading rumours. Dave Carlson is dead and Alison is lying here by sheer luck, and there may be a connection." I leaned forward. "Is there anything screwy about the way John Perry died thirty years ago? Anything at all? Because if there is, I want you to tell us right now."

We both faced Miller expectantly. He studied the floor tiles for a moment, then crossed his arms and looked at me.

"Only one thing," he began, "but it was significant. Half the ammunition from his gun was missing. Three bullets."

"Missing?" I echoed. "Well, he did exchange gunfire with Denny and his partner."

"Not fired," said Miller ominously. "Just missing. Perry did his gun like clockwork before leaving his shift. It would have been clean and fully loaded the day before. But it wasn't when we found it. He walked into that garage with his gun half empty."

I filled a suitcase with clothes and necessities, then took it to my car where the urn was packed in the trunk. I started the car with more than a knot in the pit of my stomach, but it didn't explode. Feeling like an escaping criminal, I pulled out to the main street and headed in the direction of the highway. Sitting on my dash were keys to Alison's house. I had promised to bring her some clothes to go home in.

With a sigh, I turned the car around. I headed to the upscale side of town and soon pulled into Alison's driveway. Doing an anti-media run with my hood up in case of lingerers, I breached the front door. The house was silent, of course, and impeccably decorated with style and lots of cash. I found a small overnight bag in her bedroom closet where she said it would be and put a few pieces of clothing in it. Then, nosey creature that I am, I took a look around.

The bedroom boasted two walk-in closets, but one had only a few shirts and pants dangling with an abandoned air inside. The ex-husband's closet, I guessed. There was still a picture of him on her dresser, from happier days. Another hung on the wall, showing the smiling couple years ago with Martin in his army uniform, the United Nations designation attached. Now he was an ambassador, and she was in the hospital. I wondered if there was still any contact or if he'd called her since yesterday. Alison hadn't said anything, and I wasn't about to ask.

I turned to go and saw a large photograph framed on the wall beside the door. It was an enlargement of the one I took in her backyard on Water Street the day of her birthday dinner. They were all there, young and alive: Mom, Alison beside her with her arm around Dave, John and Jessica sitting at the picnic table with the barbecue in the background. Less than twenty-four hours before absolute tragedy.

I felt a wave of sadness come over me for all the loss.

. . . almost like they know we're coming . . .

The second wave brought anger.

He walked into that garage with his gun half empty.

On the heels of anger, came fear—full-fledged, unreasonable fear.

In this situation, paranoid is a good thing to be.

I panicked and looked around the room again. In the bottom of Martin's closet sat a suitcase. I opened it and began to hurriedly fill it with more clothes and a few things from the bathroom. Punching in Brian Miller's number, I called to tell him to meet me at the hospital. I drove there with my heart pounding. Hopefully, they wouldn't throw me in jail for this one.

"Oh, thank you so much for bringing my things." Alison put away her magazine when I came in with the overnight bag. I opened it on the bed and handed her the pants.

"Can you get into these alone or do you need help?"

"I suppose the nurse will help me tomorrow."

"Not tomorrow. Now." I opened the little bathroom door. "In the bathroom. Brian Miller will be here any minute."

"Now?" Alison looked at me as if I'd lost my mind. Maybe I had. "But I'm not leaving until tomorrow afternoon, if the doctor says okay."

"We're leaving tonight, and we're getting the hell out of here for a while." I helped her off the bed, and we shuffled to the bathroom. "I'm taking you somewhere safe."

"But I'm safe here," she protested. "I promise to let the police watch me."

I said nothing, but handed her a pair of pants. She picked up on my silence and looked me in the eye.

"You're not sure I'm safe with the police, are you?" she asked quietly.

"Alison," I replied honestly, "I'm not sure of anything right now. But my guts are telling me to get out of here, and I can't leave you alone to fend for yourself the way things are." I offered the pants a second time. "At least get these on or the whole world will see your rear view when we leave. Then we'll just throw a coat around your shoulders."

While Alison was in the bathroom, Brian Miller arrived.

"What's so important that you couldn't say over the phone?" he asked. "Did something happen?"

"I'm taking Alison somewhere safe," I cut to the chase. "I need your help to get her out of here without the hounds at her back."

"She's safe here," he scowled. "She has protection at the door."

"She leaves here tomorrow," I countered. "Then it's not so easy to be safe. I'm leaving town for a bit tonight," I added, "and I'm taking her with me. Unless she's under house arrest."

"Of course not. But she *is* part of a homicide investigation," Miller pointed out. "I know they'll want her to stick around."

"Here's my cell number," I said, giving him one of my cards. "You can reach us there anytime if you need to contact Alison."

He looked at the card skeptically. Alison opened the bathroom door, and I helped her to the bed.

"Where are you going, then?" he asked her. Alison looked at me.

"Somewhere safe," I repeated. "That's all I can tell you for now. But we need to get out without the press getting wind until later. Can you help us?"

Miller looked at us both for a few moments, then sighed.

"Let me make a few calls, see what headquarters says. Maybe we can give a statement or something. That should keep their tails wagging for a while and give you a head start."

Half an hour later, Miller allowed himself to be cornered in the hospital lobby and "forced" to make a few statements.

We stuffed a few last items in the small bag. As soon as we got the signal from the officer on guard, I threw Alison's now battered coat around her shoulders and made our way to the door. I ignored the finger wagging furiously in my head. The coast was clear. When we started out the door, Alison grabbed my arm.

"My tote bag. It's on the floor in the closet. They brought it from the cemetery for me."

I retrieved it and we headed down the hallway, away from the nurses' desk. Unfortunately, the nurses stood between us and the elevators, so we had to manage the stairs for one floor. I thought we'd never make it without looking into a camera lens, but Miller gave us the time we needed.

After much shuffling, sneaking and a constant nervous urge to giggle, we made it to the outside world. Thirty minutes later we were on Highway 401 eastbound at 120 kilometres per hour, heading home to the St. Lawrence River.

PART THREE:
The Seaway Valley

Dream delivers us to dream, and there is no end to illusion.

Ralph Waldo Emerson
"Experience"

Chapter SIX: Homecomings

"'Which one of you, having a hundred sheep and losing one of them, does not leave the ninety-nine in the wilderness and go after the one that is lost until he finds it? When he has found it, he lays it on his shoulders and rejoices.'"

The reverend from St. Matthew's Presbyterian in Ingleside read from his Bible, standing to the right of the grave. He had white hair with a dark beard and kindly eyes, and a faith he wore like a favourite sweater. I think my mother would have liked him.

Ruth Hoffman and I stood arm in arm, with no bets placed as to which one was really holding the other up. I held the tears in until she no longer could and then let mine fall without a thought. Lynn Holmes quietly moved closer to place a hand on my other arm. Somewhere behind me, Detective Constable Jordan Wiley and his family stayed a respectful distance, while Inspector Jerry Strauss stolidly remained in my peripheral vision like an oak tree. Alison sat in a chair in the small crowd behind us, wearing the sunglasses I'd bought her for camouflage.

And there was a small crowd. As we had waited to start that morning, cars began to enter the cemetery and gather on the road nearby. I thought it was another funeral and hoped it wouldn't be too close, but the people came here. Some I remembered from last summer: the Legers, the Martins, the Browns, the Harrisons. But many more I did not know. Ruth had come over and put her arm around me.

"We announced the service for your mother in church last week," she explained. "I know I didn't ask you, but I thought that at least people should know. They're here to welcome Leslie home again."

I nodded, unable to speak but trying to manage a smile.

The cars had kept coming. At one point, a van pulled up and Sarah Hall, Alice Hoffman's former home-care aid, stepped out and proceeded to empty a load of church ladies from Christ Anglican Church in Long Sault onto the lawn. Then she made her way over to me with her usual energy.

"It's good to see you again, Dr. Mackenzie," she said, pumping my hand. "I mentioned this service to my mother and she told some friends, and . . . well . . . I hope you don't mind that we attend."

"No," I said simply, giving her hand a squeeze. "Not at all. How could I?"

The weather was merciful. A beautiful August Saturday with only a slight breeze coming off the river, the sun sparkling off the water where the village of Wales had once stood. And not too many visitors to the cemetery in general.

"'Rejoice with me, for I have found my sheep that was lost.'" The reverend was winding up. "She who was lost to us is again with us, and we return Leslie Mackenzie Leonard to the ground in the grace of Almighty God. She is home once more, to take her rightful place beside her husband, Hal. May their souls be joined in heaven also, finding peace at last in the arms of God."

I inadvertently looked at the inscription on my father's tombstone, the one my Uncle Gordon had placed there two years before.

Harold William Leonard
June 19, 1940
1958
Finally, at rest

I made a mental note to ask for its removal in the near future and tuned back in to the service.

"We who remember them will take strength from this day." The reverend concluded with a short prayer.

It was over.

"Thank you, Reverend," I said as he came over. He held out his hand, and I took it.

"It's been a long journey, hasn't it, Farran?" he smiled. "But it's over. And now your heavy heart will get a little lighter each day. Be patient. And please come to see me if you wish to talk about anything." He patted my hand, took Ruth's hand, then moved on to see some of his parishioners.

It's over, he'd said. But I looked over at Alison sitting quietly with her sling and her bruised face in hiding behind the big shades, and wasn't so sure it was not actually just beginning.

The reverend had been right about the journey, though. Our escape from the Cambridge Kitchener–Waterloo region had taken over six hours. I hadn't thought about timing, and we ran right into the Toronto rush hour. Alison had finally fallen asleep for a while, and I drove steadily into the evening, trying to outpace the fear that haunted me like a bad perfume.

By 8:00 p.m., I needed a bathroom break so I turned in at Brockville and Alison woke up. We powdered our noses, got a couple of coffees and some gas, and hit the road again—this time taking County Road 2 (the former No. 2 Highway) along the river communities that had once led to the villages lost in the Seaway and Power Project.

"How long till we get there?" Alison took a sip of her coffee. "And tell me again where 'there' is."

"This is Brockville," I explained. "Next comes Prescott, the westernmost community affected by the Project. Next will come Cardinal, Iroquois and Morrisburg. The village of Iroquois was moved one mile north of its location and has one of the Canadian Seaway locks. Some of the older people who live there will tell you that there are seven, not six, Lost Villages because Iroquois was never the same after its move.

"Morrisburg lost its two main streets and the waterfront canal," I continued, "but the rest of the village is intact. After that are Ingleside and Long Sault, the two villages created from the six that were destroyed to make the lake for the dam. We're headed for Ault Island, between Morrisburg and Ingleside."

She said no more after that. Darkness left little to look at, and an awkward silence fell between us. My lack of sleep was catching up with me, and despite the coffee, I fought the urge to close my eyes.

"Time for some music," I said and popped in my Sarah Harmer CD, titled appropriately *You Were Here*. We flew along the smaller highway at a good clip, keeping an eye out for patrol cars. It felt like we were skipping school again. As Jeanie Ross would have said, we were "on the lam."

"On the lam?" Alison turned to give me a tired smile. "I haven't heard that phrase since high school."

I didn't realize I'd spoken aloud. "Yes. That was one of Jeanie's favourite sayings, remember?"

"Jeanie." Alison nodded. "How I'd like to see her again," she added unexpectedly.

"Me, too." A picture came to mind, and I giggled. "Do you remember the time she brought cattails to science class? And they burst—with a little help, of course." An evil grin crossed my face. "We were knee-deep in cattail fluff, so bad it was rolling out the door and down the hall."

Alison grinned, too. "And the vice-principal came to see what was going on. She was so upset, and poor old Mr. Simpson just kept saying, 'It's the natural pollination process, my dear.'" Her voice dropped an octave and took on a British accent, before she choked on a giggle.

It must have been fatigue. I started to laugh so hard that I was crying—not great when you're driving on the highway. Every time I started to catch my breath, Alison would do her excellent Simpson imitation and off I'd go again.

"Shut up, Perry," I gasped. "I have to drive."

Alison had been smothering her laughter, but was losing the war.

"Okay," she said, gingerly putting a hand on her side. "It hurts when I breathe. I'm injured, remember?" She picked up the CD cover absently and looked at Harmer's picture. "I love her music, too. Obviously, a woman with a past."

"I don't think you can be a woman without one," I countered, then could have bitten my tongue for offering an opening like that. But the laughs seemed to have tired Alison again, and she didn't reply.

Prescott, Cardinal, Iroquois. When we passed through Morrisburg, Alison roused herself.

"What are we looking for?"

"A small green sign saying 'Ault Island Road' just inside the Stormont County line," I said briefly. Suddenly, I was the one who found it hard to breathe. Unconsciously, I stepped on the gas.

Memories from my first visit began to come at me out of the darkness. My voice in Alice Hoffman's living room.

That man . . . the one they found . . . in Aultsville last year . . . murdered . . . Hal Leonard was my father . . .

A sawmill. A scream. Red foam.

Upper Canada Village, the historical provincial park, came up on my right, and I hit the gas again.

"You'd better slow down so we don't miss it," said Alison, peering out the side window.

The bird sanctuary. A setting sun. Whispers that seemed to come from the trees that surrounded me. *Run, child, run . . . Danger . . . Go.*

Facing down those black, soulless eyes in the old house. Running. Two gunshots.

And death.

By the time we passed the sign to Ault Island Road, we were flying. I saw Alison point out the window and turn to say something. But the flashing lights behind us cut her off.

"Oh, shit." I snapped out of it and hit the brakes, coasting to a stop on the side of the road. The lights parked behind us, and someone came up to my window. I scrolled it down, looking straight into the eyes of Inspector Jerry Strauss.

For a moment, neither of us said a word. He shone his flashlight at Alison, took in her wounded face without comment, then raised his eyebrows at me.

"Welcome back, Mackenzie," he began dryly. "Do you have any idea how fast you were going?"

I returned the look, then faced front, slumping down in my seat.

"Obviously," I shot back, crossing my arms, "not fast enough."

Strauss hadn't given me a ticket that Thursday night when he pulled us over, although he could have scored a whopper from my speed. But somehow that made it worse, and I turned the car in the direction of Ault Island feeling like a teenager who just got a rap on the knuckles for fooling around with her dad's car.

When I first turned in to the island, I noted a large new Township of South Stormont sign with "Ault Island" emblazoned on it. Other than that, it was too dark to see any changes on the island—as dark as the night I'd gone to my uncle's house to find him bleeding on the kitchen floor. Alison was exhausted, and she needed her bed. As I pulled into the driveway of what had been Uncle Gordon's home, I silently prayed that the summer tenants hadn't left too much of a mess.

I almost closed my eyes when I turned on the kitchen light, but had nothing to fear. No ghosts waiting for me, and everything was spotless. We found food in the refrigerator and fresh sheets on the beds. Even the furnace was turned on low to chase out the late summer chill. Ruth, I thought to myself.

"I'll bring in your suitcase and then make us something to eat, Alison."

"I'm hungry, Fan," she said in a flat voice, "but I'm too tired to eat. I'll think I'll just go to bed, if you don't mind." I could see that it was all catching up to her and wondered when it would hit me, too.

When I returned to the house with the suitcases, I helped Alison into her pyjamas and tucked her into bed. I threw my suitcase into what had been Gordon's room and then went out to get Mom's urn. But once outside the door, I turned instead toward the river.

It was a windless night with a full moon. My mind raced, full of the fallout of the last week. I wanted peace, silence. I wanted time to think.

A year ago, I had come home for the first time to the land of the Seaway and the Lost Villages. I had searched for history but without professional distance because it was mine—unknown, ominous and full of personal landmines. And my disturbing the past had caused it to come back to life with deadly results. A sleeping murder that led to another, and almost my own.

And now I had come back to this strange place, this Seaway Valley. Where the past and present intersect with the precision of a butcher knife. Where the aesthetic and synthetic beauties are shrouded by the forces of nature and the river. Where, since the first humans touched its soil, they have called this place sacred and called it home.

As I do now.

Finally, I went in. Alison was sound asleep, so I snapped the TV on low to catch the news. Sure enough, Dave's murder and the whole Perry issue made it to the nationals, along with the death threats to

Alison. Reporters had also tracked down Mike Denny's son and his demand to reopen the investigation.

". . . naturally, I was shocked to read the headlines," he was saying, walking briskly to his car. "I never thought Dad was guilty, but also never in my wildest dreams thought about it being another officer." The newscaster added that Denny could not later be reached for comment about the death of retired Corporal Dave Carlson.

As for Alison, she too was unavailable for comment.

"He's changed his mind?"

On Friday, the morning after our arrival in the Seaway Valley, I slept in a little and got ready to see Ruth Hoffman. Lynn Holmes was invited, too, and dropped by to offer a ride. I left a note for Alison, who walked out in her pyjamas half asleep as we were heading out the door and then disappeared after a quick apology.

We sat in Ruth's living room after lunch, Ruth unconsciously taking her mother Alice's former chair that had remained in its place at the window in the year since the old woman's death. I took the letter from her, sat on the green-gold couch and read it myself. It was a short, apologetic note from the long-lost Steven Hoffman, listing reasons he wanted to wait a bit before meeting the mother he'd never known.

> *I have some family responsibilities that won't wait, and to be honest, I need more time. Please know that I'm not saying no, just not right now. I hope you understand . . .*

I handed the letter back to Ruth. "But he registered to contact you. Why change his mind now?"

"I think it might just be all too much for him," Ruth said a little unsteadily. She rose from her chair. "I'll be right back. I just need to powder my nose." She escaped to the bathroom, and I looked up at Ruth's daughter, Carolyn. She wasn't pleased with me, as usual.

"I've done it again, haven't I?" I said bluntly.

But surprisingly, Carolyn shook her head. "No, for once Mackenzie, you're not to blame. This guy is making his own choices. But I wish Mom had listened to me and left this alone."

"How could she? Steven is her son. You have a son. Could you in her shoes?"

"Not forever," the woman explained, "just not right now. Mom's been through so much in the last year, losing Nan and meeting you . . . she needs a break for a while."

"Where is Ernie?" Lynn asked, referring to Ernie Black, an old beau of Ruth that had surfaced during the uproar of last year.

"Off consulting overseas." Carolyn lit a cigarette. "He'll be back in September."

"This Steven thing could really work out," I argued, "in time."

But Carolyn looked unconvinced. "He'll be nothing but trouble. I mean, look at his father—"

I felt my cheeks grow hot. I opened my mouth to reply, but Ruth returned with suspiciously red eyes.

"We'll just give him the time he's asked for," I said as she sat down. "I'm sure he has to break this to his family as well. Your grandchildren," I reminded her brightly.

Ruth tried to smile, then Lynn suddenly slapped her hand on the coffee table and we all jumped.

"Alison Perry." She turned to me in triumph. "So you're best friends with the pit-bull mayor of the City of Cambridge? Alison Perry Standish, newest hopeful for the provincial party and rumoured to be up the premier's sleeve. Tagged for a cabinet post within the year if elected. I didn't know you travelled in those circles, Fan."

"Who?" asked Ruth, bewildered.

"Farran's friend that's staying at the house with her, the one that flashed past me in her pyjamas this morning." Lynn looked me straight in the eye. "That's her, isn't it?"

"Former mayor," I managed after a moment. "And how did you know?"

Lynn gave me a look. "For Chrissakes, Fan, I'm the *media*! Her face has been all over the wire since the attempt on her life. So this is where she's hiding out. Why with you?"

I looked at the three of them, staring at me with undisguised interest, and realized Lynn had me. I owed at least two of them the truth.

Starting with our childhood in Preston, I told the basic facts up to our escape from the hospital. It felt good to download the whole mess, and when I finished, I sat with my chin in my hands.

"I remember you saying to me last year, Ruth, how with everything that happened you began to feel that the past was not as you remembered." I sighed. "That's exactly how I feel now."

"I think you should talk to Jerry Strauss," said Lynn. "This is definitely up his alley."

"I want to," I replied, "and I will soon. But for now, you can't say anything, Lynn. Promise me. The last thing either of us needs is a swarm of reporters around the house."

Lynn looked unconvinced. "All right," she said reluctantly, "for the time being. As I recall, the heat is turning the other way since the bombing. That Denny guy who asked for an inquiry into his father's conviction has suddenly shut up, and since that retired officer was

81

killed instead of Alison, public support has swung completely behind the police. There's a headhunt starting for any old 'friends' Alison made during her years as mayor. It's a pretty open field, but with Carlson's death, the cops are out for blood."

"Lovely," I moaned. "I don't mean to sound selfish," I added. "I know Alison is in big trouble and she's asked for my help. But I'm so in over my head with this. I'm not sure I *can* help."

"Then don't," said Carolyn bluntly. "Leave it to the police."

"Alison is my friend," I said, slowly rising to leave. "You don't leave your friends in the lurch."

"You just be careful, Farran Mackenzie." Ruth broke her silence with the stern warning.

"I will," I promised meekly.

I took my leave after settling a few details about my mother's service with Ruth, with my next stop being the St. Lawrence Cemetery. When I walked out to my car, Carolyn followed. I expected another blast, but got an apology.

"Listen, Mackenzie," she said, looking off in the distance as I started my engine. "That crack I made about Steven's father. Well . . . Gordon was your uncle, too, regardless. I was out of line."

"Forget it," I said. "I know you just want to protect your mother. I do, too." I shifted into gear and started to pull away.

"Hey, Mackenzie," Carolyn called after me. "For what it's worth, that Alison *was* your friend. Now she's just someone that you knew."

He was standing in the cemetery when I arrived.

I noticed immediately for two reasons: He was very good-looking, and he was the only other human around. At least one that was moving.

I hadn't taken Lynn up on her offer of a ride that morning as I needed to deliver the urn for the service the next day. So I did. Once that was done, I wandered out to see the family, keeping the solitary figure in the corner of my eye.

They were digging beside my father's grave for tomorrow, so I bypassed that until a better time. I also passed on Gordon's grave for the time being. I just didn't want to go there. Instead, I left a rose on my grandfather Eric Leonard's grave and then made my way to my other grandfather, Harper Mackenzie. For some minutes, I stood there, remembering the stories of his temper, his cutting tongue and his fierce determination to provide for his daughter Leslie—even after his death.

"I've sure dropped the ball on that one, haven't I, Harp?" I whispered to the grave.

Keep the secret, gal. Stay safe. For the child's sake . . .

"What?" I raised my head and looked right into his eyes. He was standing behind the stone, holding a Lost Villages Museum flyer in his hand. I judged his age to be close to mine, mid-forties. The smile was self-confident, the kind that is usually attached to a handsome man's face. But the eyes, the eyes were fathomless.

"I'm sorry. I don't mean to intrude." The smile got even nicer. "I'm looking for family headstones from," he opened the flyer for a moment, "Mille Roches, I think. Would they all be here?"

Once or twice in your life, you meet someone for the first time and have an instant connection, feeling almost as if you have known this person for years. I couldn't shake the sense of having done this before, standing there with him talking about graves. I have a strange social life, I guess.

"No," I smiled back and self-consciously tucked my flyaway hair behind my ear. "Some would be here, some in Cornwall. And some," I turned to face the river, "out there. Under the water. You may find the headstones themselves at Upper Canada Village in the pioneer memorial."

He looked slightly shocked and walked a little toward the river. I followed.

"You mean they left people out there?" He turned to me incredulously. "Family and friends?"

"This area was settled by the United Empire Loyalists." I switched into my professor mode without meaning to. "Some of the graves were too old to move. For others, there was no family left. And for those who did move their people, it could be done, but it was a big procedure. Some people," I added, "like my grandfathers, felt it was against nature to dig up the dead." I didn't mention my mother's re-interment set for the following day. "Both my grandmothers are out there. One in Aultsville, one in Farran's Point."

"And that's out here?" He pointed out to the water.

"No. Those villages were west of here, on the way to Morrisburg. Here was the village of Wales, the only inland village to be flooded." I indicated the two islands in front of us. "That's what's left of the village. The smaller one in front was the site of St. David's Anglican Church."

We lapsed into a comfortable silence for a few moments. Then he shook his head.

"I didn't realize so much was done for the dam. It must seem so strange to people living here now."

"It does for many of us," I said slowly. "For those who left the villages, it must seem like a dream now." I snapped awake and looked guiltily at my watch, thinking of Alison. "I have to go. I hope

you find what you're looking for." I pointed to the flyer in his hand.
"Definitely go there if you haven't already. The Lost Villages Historical Society will be a great help."
I started back to my car.
"Thank you," he called after me. "You've been very kind."
I slowed only to wave in return. For some stupid reason, I was afraid he'd ask me for to go for a coffee and that I would say yes.

Saturday afternoon, the basement hall at St. Matthew's Church in Ingleside was full.

Lynn Homes had held the funeral for her cousin, Meredith, in that church a year ago. When I arrived for the reception after my mother's funeral service, the memory of that other funeral ambushed me on my way across the parking lot. Fortunately, I didn't have to enter the church itself. The hall was accessed by a side door. But with a sense of déjà vu, I saw Jerry Strauss waiting for me on the sidewalk, and with tacit agreement, we entered the hall together.

"Where is your friend?" he asked quietly. "Didn't I see her at the cemetery?"

"I drove Alison back to the house," I said. "She's just come out of the hospital and tires easily."

"I hope she laid charges against whoever worked her over like that."

I opened my mouth to explain, then realized it wasn't a good time. But the time would come. Whether Jerry would still want to help me was another question altogether.

We stood in an awkward silence in the doorway. People were talking and setting chairs out around the tables set with white tablecloths. A long table in front of the hall kitchen was loaded with real church-lady food (a delicacy in my world), and two men were wrestling with the large coffee urn that was already filling the hall with its fragrance. I relaxed into the order and ritual of it all, and was grateful for this effort on my mother's behalf. I wished she could have known.

"Fan!" A young girl broke from the ranks near the food and ran over to give me a hug. Pleasantly surprised, I gave her one back.

"Diana," I said holding her at arm's length, "my God you've shot up in one year."

Diana Wiley was the daughter of Detective Constable Jordan Wiley, one of the officers under Strauss's command in the SD&G detachment. She was an intelligent girl with a passion for history, and this common ground between us had started an unexpected friendship last year.

Diana rolled her eyes. "Well, I *am* almost twelve, you know. But never mind that," she added in her usual breathless fashion. "How long are you staying?"

"I'm not sure," I mused aloud. "I thought to take just the weekend, but" I watched Jerry Strauss move off toward Constable Wiley, "I might stay a little longer. Why?"

"Mum wants to have you for supper."

"She does?" I looked skeptical. "You'd better check with your mom first, Di."

"No, she's quite right," said a voice at my shoulder. I turned to meet Mrs. Wiley, and took the hand offered. "You were very kind to Diana the last time you were here, Dr. Mackenzie, but you and I barely met. I'd like to do better this time."

The smile and the handshake were genuine. Unlike her husband and daughter—both tall, slim blondes—Michelle Wiley was a softly rounded brunette with dark eyes that spoke of her French heritage. A teacher by trade, she was a successful wife, mother, and chair of several local committees. Her gardens were the talk of Long Sault, and the goodies she sent with Diana after my surgery last fall had been wonderful. Women like me have always been wary of women like her.

"That's very kind of you, Mrs. Wiley, but it's not necessary," I said honestly. "I enjoyed her visits very much." I watched Diana slink back to the food table to reload with egg-salad sandwiches on brown. "I was quite depressed after all that happened at the time and the great talks we had did a lot to cheer me up."

"You did a lot for her, too, Dr. Mackenzie." Michelle looked at her daughter pensively. "With Jordan in the OPP, we moved around quite a bit when Diana was little. By the time he was stationed in Long Sault, Diana had been in four schools. I think that's the reason why she . . . well . . . she has her friends at school, of course, but Diana has always felt more comfortable in the company of adults. Her friendship with you sort of covered both bases, if you know what I mean."

I nodded slowly. We choose our friends and our friends choose us in response to deeper needs. That may also be the reason friendships die. Alison's face flitted through my mind.

Ruth came and put her arm through mine. "I'm going to steal Farran for a little while, Michelle. Some people aren't going to stay very long, and I want to be sure we say hello."

I think now in some ways many people came because it was an occasion that made an old wrong right again. We get so few chances to do that in life. The reception turned out to be more of a receiving line, in the end, with everyone making a point to give condolences, a happy memory or two, and their welcome. I was grateful for them all, grateful that so much of the life my mother left behind lived on in their memories.

Lynn put a glass of punch in my hand and moved away again. I wondered if being here was hard for her, too. Her cousin Meredith had been the only family she'd had left.

At one point Sarah Hall came up with her mother, a petite woman with white hair.

"Dr. Mackenzie, this is my mother, Dorothy Baker."

"Nice to meet you, Mrs. Baker." I shook her hand. "Thank you for coming today."

"Well, dear," she said shyly, "I didn't know your mother well, but I remember her as a young girl. I lived next door to the Cliffords' general store in Mille Roches, and many times your grandfather Harper would stop there on his way to Cornwall. Your mother would be sittin' in the truck with him," the elderly woman added, "not sayin' a word. But such a pretty little thing. If you ever want to talk about the old days, dear, just drop by." She patted my hand and moved on.

Finally, the crowd began to disperse and I could see the food table again—bereft of egg-salad sandwiches. Ruth led me to a table where Lynn sat, a cup of coffee and a plate of egg salad on brown beside her.

"For me?" I asked, plunking down in a chair. "Bless you, Ms. Holmes."

"Don't thank me," said Lynn. "Jerry brought them for you. Are you two going to spend some time together while you're here?"

I ignored the question, but surreptitiously looked for Strauss while I inhaled the food. He had quietly vanished, and I was quietly disappointed.

"Coffee and drinks at the house?" Ruth spoke brightly as we put our coats on in the church hall cloakroom, but she looked as whipped as I felt. The service and the reception had gone very well, but we were both glad they were over.

"No, Ruth," I said, "I think you need some rest. How about I call you in the morning?"

"Mackenzie's right, for once." Carolyn, who had spent the afternoon hovering just out of range, came up to help her mother with her coat. "I think you need a hot bath and a stiff drink in bed."

"God, that sounds good," I muttered. Lynn joined us and we all walked out into the breezy late afternoon. Ingleside was quiet, clean and orderly, as usual. A few cars were leaving Rothwell-Osnabruck

School across the road, a sports meet having just finished. Kids played street hockey nearby and someone was taking his beagle for a walk around the centre square. The peace had an almost dream-like quality to it. No sign to the untrained eye of the violent and massive upheaval that had precipitated the village's birth. But that is the truth in life. Most of our reality lies under the surface, in some cases out of reach.

I walked with Ruth and Carolyn to their car. When I opened the passenger door for Ruth, I noticed that she was crying.

"Hey," I gave her a hug. "You know that drink? Make it a double. I think we've both earned it."

"Oh, I'll be fine, Fan." Ruth gave me a brave smile. "I think it's just finally hitting me that Leslie is gone. We spent years thinking she was killed in an accident, but there was no funeral, of course. Just the rumour. And in my heart I always believed I'd see her again some day." She put a hand under my chin, making me feel about ten years old. "Your mother was the only best friend I ever had. I will always miss her."

When the car was gone, I turned to Lynn.

"How about you?" I asked. "I'm sure being here wasn't easy for you, Lynn."

She shrugged. "I couldn't have stayed away, Fan. But listen," she added briskly, "I would guess within the week, I'll have to come calling with a tape recorder if the two of you are still here. Be warned—and be careful. Bombs aren't made on a whim. Someone out there means business for your friend."

When I left Lynn and the church, I headed for Ingleside's one pizza place and bought two. Then I turned the car toward Ault Island with the radio blasting so I wouldn't think. It worked until I crossed the causeway, slowing down to manoeuvre through parked cars and people fishing, staked out on either side. As I came up to the opening to the bike path in the forest, I passed a couple more cars parked off to one side. One had an athletic-looking couple strapping very expensive bicycles to the ski rack. The other had Jerry Strauss.

Instinctively, I slowed down, but didn't immediately stop. My options were three:

- Just keep going and pretend I didn't see him
- Run him down and pretend I didn't see him
- Stop and see what was up

With great reluctance, I chose the last one and parked in front of his car. I was barely out of the seat when I felt his hand on my arm. The touch felt good, but his social skills were definitely lacking.

"Lock up," Jerry said curtly. "We're going for a walk."

"I suppose you're going to ask me how I could let myself get into this mess."

I took the last sip of coffee from the cardboard cup and crumpled it. Jerry and I were standing side by side in the forest off the bike path, looking out at the shallow bay around the Ault Island causeway. With his usual self-confidence, he'd brought two take-out coffees for our little tête-à-tête, never doubting for a moment he could sideline me for a private chat. And it had been a full disclosure chat. Like Lynn, he'd finally recognized Alison from the news and confronted me with it immediately. I spilled the beans without a fight, secretly relieved to hand it over to him.

When Strauss didn't reply, I turned to face him, taking the first good look I'd had a chance to since my arrival. Not much changed since last year. Still tall, dark and ruggedly good-looking, with a physique that broke the stereotype of male middle age. The cops-and-doughnuts thing didn't hold in this case. I noticed a touch more grey in his sideburns, though, and a slightly preoccupied air that told me something was on his mind other than just my little problems with car bombs and murder. Something—or someone? I wondered for a moment.

"No," Jerry said finally, not returning my look. "I'd have to say I'd probably do the same thing in your shoes. But it certainly is a hell of a mess."

I'd been ready with a few smart defences, but that left me with nothing to say. Deflated, I walked over to shoot my cup in one of the trash cans that dot the bike path and came back. "So what do I do now?"

"Nothing." He turned and walked past me. "The murder investigation is a police matter. Stay out of it unless they call you, Mackenzie. I can personally say that the last thing the Waterloo police need is a civilian like you to trip over."

I made a face at his back.

"And as for you two Nancy Drews," Jerry continued, "stay quiet for now and keep your heads low. I'm sure you're fine here, but let's not take chances." He dropped his cup in the trash and turned back to me. "I'd rather not be scraping what's left of you off a driveway somewhere."

Inadvertently, I shuddered. I hadn't had a decent night's sleep since Dave's death. Jerry's face changed and he took a step forward.

"I'm sorry. It's nothing to joke about." He put out a hand halfway, then dropped it to his side. "I'm just glad you weren't hurt."

I crossed my arms. "What's happening? None of this makes any sense." An otter swam by in the bay with something in his mouth. "Why stir up the past? If the bombing is connected to this, then why kill Dave—or I should say why try to kill Alison? If the notes are true, why go after John Perry's daughter? Personal retribution? And who the hell would care after thirty years?"

"I can think of a number of reasons, Mackenzie, but none are good news. I also have a problem with a few things, like Brian Miller saying he wouldn't know about any personal problems John Perry might have been dealing with at the time of his death. The chief of a small force would have his finger on anything concerning his officers, any stress that might affect their performance on the job. It probably wasn't as easy once the regional force was formed, but you said Miller and Perry had worked together for years before that. Miller would have stayed in touch about those things."

I thought about Brian Miller giving us Dave Carlson's unlisted number and sending Gail Melvin my way before she left town. Still in touch thirty years later.

"I remember the shooting, though," Jerry continued, his mouth a thin line. "I was barely a constable then, in the OPP. Some of my superiors went to the funeral." He put his sunglasses on. "It rattles the younger officers even more when that happens. None of us said it but we were all thinking the same thing—if a seasoned officer like Sergeant Perry could be taken down, what chance did the rest of us have out there?"

The sunglasses reminded me of Alison and the pizzas cooling in my car.

"I have to go. Alison is going to worry if I'm too late." I started back up to the bike path, then stopped to add, "For what it's worth, I appreciate the help. I need it." I thought about all that had happened last year, and how I literally owed my life to this man. "There is absolutely not a red 'S' on my chest this time, Strauss."

Jerry walked up to me, taking his sunglasses off. He looked in my eyes for a long moment, then nodded and faced away down the bike path. "I have a lot of people I'm still in touch with from the old days," he said to the grass. "I'll make some calls and see what the grapevine says. I'll be in touch."

On that classic closing line, I took my leave and headed down the path toward my car. It looked like the "Jerry" and "Farran" days were over—we were officially back to "Strauss" and "Mackenzie." Well, at least that was cleared up. Jerry had fallen silent over time, but so had I. With my traditional flair for relationships, I had let this one slip through my fingers.

"They smell wonderful, and I'm hungry." Alison lifted the lid on one of the pizza boxes. "I think I'm starting to bounce back." She picked a piece of pepperoni off the top. "I hope you don't mind that I didn't go to the church reception, Fan. I wanted to, but I didn't have it in me. I didn't want to answer questions about my injuries, either."

"It's better that you didn't. Did you sleep?"

"For two hours. Then I sat out in the fresh air." Alison smiled. "It's very pretty here."

"Yes, it is." I opened the other pizza box. Bacon, onions and black olives—my favourite. "The old river was smaller and more rugged in its beauty. This is different, but it's still beautiful." I took out two plates. "I wish I could have seen the rapids, though. They must have been something."

"The rapids?" Alison put a piece on a plate, set it on the coffee table and walked over to the patio doors to look out.

"Yep. The reason they did the power dam at all. The Longue Sault Rapids were the largest of the rapids between Montreal and Kingston, the apple of a hydroelectric engineer's eye for half a century. They were also the thorn in the side of every canal-boat captain that sailed the old system. But they were downriver just past where Farran's Point used to be. There's an old lookout point in the Long Sault Parkway, but nothing left of the rapids now."

"What was out here?" she asked, pointing to the small, shallow bay in front of the house and the trees on the other side.

That man . . . the one they found . . . in Aultsville last year . . . buried in the basement . . .

"Aultsville," I said quietly.

Alison turned at the tone in my voice and put a hand to her mouth. "You mean that's where . . . "

"Yes." I took a deep breath and let it go. "Right out there, across the bay, is where they found my father." I kept my eyes resolutely on the scene in front of the patio doors, as though trying to stare it down. I tried not to think of Gordon spending years looking out this same window.

"Listen," I said briskly, taking a seat, "we have to talk about what's next. I had a brief chat with Jerry Strauss on the way home today. He's the inspector of the OPP detachment for this area. I asked his advice, and he said to lie low, but don't worry. And let the police handle it back home. A standard cop response." I bit into my slice, and it was heaven. Food is the best lover of all.

"You told him everything?" Alison sat down carefully in the chair facing me.

"Had to," I replied in a minute. "He'd recognized you from the news reports, so I laid it on the line. It's the best way to handle Strauss. It would take a better person than me to pull the wool over his eyes. Besides," I added firmly, "we need all the help we can get on this one."

"So he was at the funeral." Alison thought for a moment. "Middle-aged man, tall, good-looking, dark hair with a bit of grey at the sides, military posture?"

"That's him." I got up for a second piece and decided to just bring the two boxes to the coffee table, followed by two soft-drink cans.

"He's the one who pulled us over for speeding. Do OPP inspectors do that sort of road work?"

I shrugged. "Maybe that's his idea of an evening out."

"Is there something between you two?" Alison took one can and passed it to me to pop open. "I don't think his eyes left your face through the whole service."

I took this bit of news and tucked it into my optimism account. "To be honest, Al, I don't know how to answer that." I flounced down on the couch and opened my own can. "We spent some time together last year, after the dust started to settle. But we didn't keep things up for long after I left. By Christmas, it was a card exchange and that was it. It was my fault as much as his." I took a good swig of soft drink and burped. "Ah, haven't lost my touch."

Alison grinned. "Good thing for you I'm injured or I'd take your challenge. I was always the Master of Burps, remember?"

"Only because your dad taught you how," I pointed out. "I had to learn on my own. Mom said a young lady shouldn't do that."

Alison fell silent for a moment. I looked at her sitting there with me and wondered how we'd ever ended up this way. Although I took more care about my appearance than last year, I had left my hair long. That day, she'd brushed hers back into the ponytail I remembered from grade school and with no makeup on looked very much like her old self—sans the bruises, of course. It almost felt like it had in those days, and the comfort zone between us was both pleasant and vaguely disturbing to me.

"Men are strange, aren't they?" she said suddenly. I wondered whom we were really talking about.

"You mean Strauss?" I nodded. "That one's in a class of his own."

"Well, men in general. They spend so much time pretending they don't need anyone."

"Did you hear from your ex before we left?" I ventured slowly. "I only ask because now he wouldn't know where to call you."

She shook her head. "No. I'm sure he doesn't even know. He's in Chile right now. I guess that's safer than Kosovo."

"What does he do over there?" I took another piece and told my stomach it was the last one—probably.

Alison followed suit. "Ordnance removal. He's one of the United Nations reps in charge of the Chilean project. His background in the military gave him the expertise." She noticed the blank look on my face. "Landmines," she explained.

"Sounds dangerous."

"It is, but it needs to be done. Over 24,000 people are killed or injured each year by land mines, most of them women and children. It's important work . . . " Her voice trailed off.

"But?" I prompted.

She took a deep breath. "I know this will sound shallow, but it's not the kind of life I want. I stepped on a lot of big toes as mayor, and when I retired from office, I still had many enemies. Martin took the UN posting in part because it would take me away from all that. I lived that life for ten years. I wanted to come home." Alison took a nibble. "When Mother got sick, it gave me the excuse I needed. When I got back to Kosovo, we both agreed it was time to call it a day."

"And now you're in hiding on Ault Island. Also not the life you want. Alison, what if the rumour mill about your dad's death is actually part of the plan to keep you out of politics?" I asked on a hunch. "Think about it. Everyone knows intimidation won't go half a block with you. But maybe emotional blackmail would."

"Emotional blackmail?"

"Yes. It wouldn't take a rocket scientist to figure that the sudden death–murder–of your father would be a lifetime issue. Pushing that button might get better results than a full frontal attack. It made you quit, didn't it?"

"Yes, it did," she said slowly. "But then why try to kill me? All that's done is get me back on track. Once I'm a little stronger, I'm heading home and right back to my campaign office. I can't let this situation hold me hostage forever." I was gratified to see a little of the old fire in her eyes for a moment.

Alison put her pizza down and looked me straight in the eye. "I want you to know how much I appreciate what you're doing for me. I don't know what I would have done these past few days if you hadn't been there." She swallowed. "You're being a good friend, more than I deserve."

Right then, I wanted to ask her point blank—what happened to you thirty years ago? Why did my best friend go MIA? Didn't I deserve more then, too? But—have I mentioned I'm a coward?—I changed the subject.

"Nothing you wouldn't do for me, I'm sure. Listen, it's going to be a nice day tomorrow, and I agree with Strauss. We're safe here if we keep things quiet. On the news last night it just said you were unavailable for comment. Why don't I give you a little tour of the area tomorrow: fresh air, Canada geese, and Lost Villages?"

Alison took the cue from me and dropped the subject. "Sure," she shrugged. "I would like to see more. But for now, I'd love to take a hot bath if you don't need the bathroom. I'm sore all over." She picked up her leftovers and went into the kitchen, then headed toward the bathroom.

I heard the door close, the ensuing silence broken only by the sound of the bath water running. I smiled sadly to myself. Men aren't the only creatures that spend a lot of time pretending they don't need anyone.

The pizza stared back at me, and I picked up piece No. 4. Too early for the news, I thought, and for once I didn't want to read. Tomorrow, I would take Alison into the unique past of the Lost Villages. That history would be, for us, much safer than our own.

"Well, what do you think of the big beastie?"

It was a beautiful but breezy day, and I had to raise my voice over the rush of water from the Robert H. Saunders-Robert M. Moses Generating Station. The dam was huge, extending almost a mile into the distance toward the American shore, but ironically hard to see.

Alison and I had arrived at the dam about ten that following morning. I drove inside the grounds, pointing out traces of the construction still left: the section of old Highway 2 that formerly led to Mille Roches and now runs right into the dike; the huge concrete door in the dike that allowed shipping traffic through the old Cornwall Canal until the inundation of the new seaway ended the era of the canal boats; the ghostly tie-ups beside the remnant of the canal that once were the hub of river activity and now attract only gulls.

We turned around at the security gate and headed back out.

"So no chance of getting in for a closer look?" asked Alison.

"No. Not anymore. The Lost Villages Museum bus tours will take you in for a brief stop outside the admin offices to view the dam from the parking lot, but that's it. I was told that in the sixties this place was open for tours five days a week. They stopped that years ago, and since 9/11, it's been a high-security area."

I drove out of the grounds and parked down the road in front of a field. Heading down to the river, we got a full-view effect of the massive structure.

"It's amazing." Alison cupped her good hand over her eyes for shade. "How big is it?"

"The powerhouse section is actually two generating stations, one American, one Canadian. They join to form a structure 3,300 feet long."

We both turned at the sound of the voice.

Cemetery Man stood there in jeans and a T-shirt, looking as good as I remembered. I shot a glance at Alison. There was a faint flush in her cheeks, the first healthy colour I'd seen in them in over a week. Nothing better for a woman's circulation than an attractive man.

"The Canadian half of the dam is the Robert H. Saunders Generating Station, named after the former CEO of Ontario Hydro," he continued. "It has a total of sixteen units that were brought on line between July of '58 and December of '59. Total power generation for the entire dam is 2,000 megawatts daily. As part of the St. Lawrence Seaway and Power Project, it is hands down the biggest engineering project in North America for the twentieth century."

He walked up beside us and looked out at the dam. "My father was an engineer. He helped build this thing. And for forty years, he never said a word to me about it." Then he turned and looked right in my eyes, adding, "I'm hoping, Farran Mackenzie, that you can help me find out why."

Chapter SEVEN: Long Sault

I'm thinking of getting new business cards done: *Farran Mackenzie, PhD, Professional Dark Family Secret Digger-Upper. Seasonal Only. Group Rates Available.*

I looked from Cemetery Man to Alison and back.

"How do you know my name?" I asked bluntly. "I didn't give it to you in the cemetery."

"I didn't recognize you that day until after you'd left," he answered. "You look different without blood all over your face."

Well, if this was all a pick-up line, at least it was original. "Blood?" I echoed.

At that, Cemetery Man broke into a grin. "I'm really screwing this up, aren't I? Sorry." He started to dig something out of his jacket pocket. "I've been looking for you. I tried to find you in the phone book, but I guess you have an unlisted number, and the University of Waterloo wasn't very helpful. Just said you weren't there anymore." He unfolded a piece of newsprint and held it out to me. "I think our fathers knew each other years ago. My father passed away recently, and I found this in his wallet. Obviously, it meant something to him. I was hoping you could tell me what."

WATERLOO WOMAN INJURED IN PROVINCIAL PARK SHOOTING

I felt a cold rush move through me as I read the headline. The picture seemed to be of someone else. Alison read over my shoulder, a few moments later quietly placing a hand on my arm. Then I noticed the name written at the top of the paper. "Hal. That was my father's name." I looked up at Cemetery Man, and he nodded knowingly.

"I read the follow-up in the newspaper. I'm sorry you had to go through that."

I looked at the clipping again. "Your father knew my father?"

"That's just it. I don't know." He folded the paper up and shoved it back in his pocket with a sense of helplessness I recognized all too well. "My father was an engineer. He met my mother on one of his projects in Ontario, and they settled down on the East Coast. That's all I knew growing up. Turns out my mother was from the Lost Villages, from a place called Mille Roches. I guess she met my father when he came here to work on the Hydro project. Everything else is a question mark."

I gave him an encouraging smile. "That's how I started. At least you don't have a murder investigation in your way." He looked away at the river. "So much is gone," I continued, "but a lot is still here. It's just all in pieces, and you have to know where to find it. Did you go through the displays in the Lost Villages Museum? They have a lot on Mille Roches. It was the largest of the six villages lost."

"I've just started to look around, actually. I guess I don't really know where to start."

"I'm sure if you asked someone," Alison suggested, "they would help you find what you need."

I jumped guiltily at the sound of Alison's voice.

"Oh, Alison, sorry. I'm not great with the social amenities. We met in the cemetery on Friday, both looking at gravestones," I explained. "This is . . . this is . . . Who are you, anyway?"

Cemetery Man took Alison's good hand and gave her a magazine smile. I thought I might have to hold her up.

"Sorry. I guess I'm not good with that social stuff, either," he said. "It's Paul. Sergeant Paul Vaughn, St. John's Police Service." He dug in his other pocket and pulled out an ID with badge.

"Newfoundland," I read. "You're a long way from home, Sergeant Vaughn."

He shrugged. "Had some time off coming. Thought I'd look up my mother's old hometown. Didn't realize it was under fifty feet of water."

"Not all of it," I corrected him. "There are some outlying farm areas left. Was she from the rural part of the town?"

"Haven't a clue," he admitted. "She never said a word, either."

I noticed he was referring to both parents in the past tense. "And neither one of your parents is alive now?"

"No," he said quietly. "Both dead."

Something in his voice told me the wound was still new, so I dropped that line and circled back. "My friend Alison here is right. If you ask, the Lost Villages people can be a lot of help. Most of them are former villagers. They might know someone who knew your mom. You just need to get some names to start with."

Vaughn glowered down at the grass. "I . . . I couldn't bother people I don't know with a lot of questions."

"Yes, you could," I smiled again. "It happens here a lot. This is a very old part of Canada, Seaway or no Seaway. The villages were established by the United Empire Loyalists, and the family trees go back a couple of centuries. People here are used to outsiders coming to look for their roots." I remembered the day I found the Lost Villages exhibit at Upper Canada Village and the stir I caused announcing my parentage. "Have you looked at the display at Upper Canada Village? She might be in the pictures there."

"No, I haven't yet." Paul answered. "I went there yesterday and found it a little overwhelming. I'll go back tomorrow, when it's not so busy."

"Actually, I know someone who lived in Mille Roches." Dorothy Baker's face at the funeral reception came into my mind. "She's in Long Sault now. I'll have to call her first, of course. How do I contact you about seeing her?"

When Paul patted his pockets unsuccessfully, Alison whipped a pen and paper at him from her tote bag.

"This is my cell number and where I'm staying in Cornwall," he said, scribbling it down. He passed it all back to Alison, who gave him her best smile—a bit of a stretch with the bruises and sunglasses. "Thanks."

"No problem, Sergeant Vaughn," I said. "I'll call you when I've talked to Dorothy."

"I'm glad I found you . . . here," said Paul awkwardly. "I thought I was going to have the devil of a time finding you in Waterloo."

"Well," I replied shyly, "I'm sorry to be such a dead end about my father. I never knew him. He was killed before I was born."

Something strange passed over Paul's face. "I'm sorry." He cleared his throat. "And it's Paul, please. If you'd known my dad, you'd know that Hal meant something to him. My father didn't keep clippings on a whim. They must have been good friends."

"I hope so," I said. Then Alison and I took our leave and headed back to the car.

"Remind me to start hanging around cemeteries," she muttered to me.

"Really. Can I see that paper he wrote on?"

Alison passed it to me.

Sergeant Paul Vaughn
555-5100
Ramada Inn, Room 102

Call it practice. I read the words and felt my stomach do a kick. Something told me this was just the beginning of a strange and beautiful friendship.

Long Sault, like its fraternal twin Ingleside, was born during the Seaway and Power Project years. While Ingleside housed refugees from Aultsville, Wales, Dickinson's Landing and Farran's Point, Long Sault took in the villagers from Moulinette and Mille Roches.

Beginning life as New Town No. 2, it was named after the now-vanished Longue Sault Rapids—a name chosen by the Mille Roches Chamber of Commerce.

Where there had been only empty farm fields, the town quickly sprouted: two elementary schools, four churches and an arena to replace the one lost in Mille Roches. From the former villages came 130 homes on the Hartshorne house mover, the second largest number of moved structures in the new communities (Iroquois, being moved in its entirety, took first place with 151). Long Sault also received the largest Ontario Provincial Police detachment of all the new towns, which is now the central command for the newly restructured Stormont, Dundas and Glengarry OPP post.

This particular building sits like the garrison it is, facing the highway at the front of the village just east of the shopping mall. Its front entrance sports formidable glass doors and an after-hours intercom system—a far cry from the 24/7 walk-in facility it was in the 1960s. As we drove past it on the way to another stop in the tour, I noticed a line of squad cars on Mille Roches Road in front of the building. Paranoia immediately suggested a cop convention or a manhunt for Alison, but a second glance took in large machinery digging up the parking lot behind. An idea occurred to me, and I giggled.

"What?" said Alison, opening her eyes. We had postponed a visit to the Lost Villages Museum until a weekday when it wouldn't be so busy. I had also seen a grey colour under the Vaughn-induced blush on Alison's face and decided to spread the tour over several days.

"I was looking over at the police detachment with the parking lot being dug up," I said, and then grinned. "What a hoot if they found a body or two under there!"

Alison looked back and then at me. "You're evil, girl," she said, shaking her head. "But I guess it's a good sign you can make fun of something like that. Maybe someday I'll be able to do the same."

"You will," I said shortly. "It's a survival mechanism."

"Did you ever go to where they found him?" Alison asked after a minute.

"My father? Yes, once." The water, the mud, the silence. "But it wasn't much help at the time. Last year the lake levels were up and the entire area was under water. I couldn't see a thing."

"If you want to go back, Fan, I'll go with you." Alison looked at me. "You came with me. It's the least I can do."

I nodded, but did not reply. I wasn't sure what I wanted to do. Still too many ghosts. Still something burning there underneath the jokes and the surviving.

Alison closed her eyes again and we drove in silence for several minutes. I covered Hoople's Bay, the cemetery and Ingleside at a good clip. When I finally slowed down to make a turn, Alison opened her eyes. She started to ask a question, but dropped it. I turned left toward the river and drove past two signs at right angles to each other. One explained the present and one the past:

          UPPER CANADA MIGRATORY BIRD SANCTUARY
and
             LOST VILLAGES HISTORICAL SOCIETY
                       AULTSVILLE

At approximately three-quarters of a kilometre to the south, lay the village of Aultsville, population 450, founded by United Empire loyalists of the King's Royal Regiment of New York, on the crown grant of Nicholas Ault.

                Citizens of Aultsville

I followed the gravel road in for half a mile. It had been resurfaced since my last visit, and potholes were not the same problem. When the road took a sharp left, I went straight, following two ruts in the grass—the only drivable portion left of the original Aultsville Road. We parked in the little wayside and got out.

"The hump we just drove over is the old rail bed from the Grand Trunk Railway. It connected all the villages. A train called the Moccasin did the Brockville–Montreal run six days a week twice a day for over a hundred years. Mail, freight and passengers. There are still pieces of the railway crossing equipment in the grass." I indicated a flat piece of pavement just down and to our right in the field ahead. "This was the road to the industrial section of Aultsville. Right beside the railway, of course. Where those trees stand, my grandfather Eric Leonard ran a lumberyard until it was lost in a fire in 1956." In the distance, I could see the top of the huge old silver maple that had once stood in front of the lumberyard office. I made no move to go to the maple grove, but the memory of being stalked there by my father's killer made the hair on my neck stand up in reflex.

There is a legend in the Seaway Valley that the former villagers so mourned the loss of their land and their homes that their spirits returned to them after death. If the wind is right and you listen well, the story goes, some nights you can hear the voices of the spirits coming across the water from the sites of the Lost Villages.

Despite spending my professional life in the past, I don't hold to ghost stories. But I couldn't forget what I heard in the maple grove that day last year. Those voices, whispers from the trees . . .

Danger, child.

I started and shot a glance at Alison, who obviously hadn't heard a thing. Memories and my mind playing games, I told myself. The danger that was is dead and buried.

South of us was the gravel bike path that led to the river. "That way," I said, "was Aultsville." We headed down the path and in two minutes stood at the edge of the road, looking down into a small grove of weedy trees. Inside was the last vestige of the old road, a thin strip of plant-encroached pavement that ended in the mud flat beyond. Directly to our right across the little bay was Gordon's (or, I guess, my) house, the windows watching us like eyes.

I let out all my breath, realizing only then that I'd been holding it.

"Well," I said grimly, "let's do it."

Taking Alison's good hand, I helped her down the embankment and into the trees. We followed the road out, this time the river allowing us over fifty feet before cutting us off. We moved carefully over the slimy, broken surface. Unreal to think it had been a major roadway in a village once, with houses and the Leonards' General Store along its route.

In the distance, speedboats buzzed past near the shipping lane; and one ship with CANADA STEAMSHIP LINES on the side plowed through the river, its engines pulsing. Other than that, the silence hit me like last time. Generations of human labour and industry now only trees, grass and mud. You'd think in my line of work, I'd get used to it.

"A village really stood here?" Alison sounded incredulous.

"Yes. Churches, schools, stores, brick homes. All gone." I sighed. "When we get to the museum, I'll show you pictures of where we're standing now. Can you see just over there in the water a large stone square?" I pointed a few feet away from us, to the left of the road. "That's the old foundation of my grandfather's general store. A little south of that is . . . " I faltered.

"Where they found your father." Alison finished gently.

I nodded, unable to speak. We were still holding hands from our careful manoeuvres over the slimy road, and she gave mine a squeeze. For several minutes, we just stood there like the life refugees we were. I struggled with a million different emotions all threatening to surface at the same time, valiantly keeping the internal door tightly shut. The river combed her breeze through my hair, but there was no sound. No voices. Nothing but silence . . . and emptiness.

"Are you all right, Fan?" Alison finally ventured.

"Yes," I said quietly after a moment. "I'm okay."

I turned, and we started slowly back along the old road toward the bike path, both of us knowing without saying that sometimes you can be okay, but never the same again.

The phone was ringing when we walked into the house that afternoon.

"Fan," Lynn Holmes' voice got to the point, "have you listened to the news today?"

"No. Why?" I had to ask even though I immediately knew I didn't want to hear the answer.

"There's been another bombing in Cambridge. Last night. A car again, like last time."

I took the chair next to the phone, actively avoiding Alison's eyes that were trained on me.

"Anyone hurt?" I said slowly.

"No. It seems random, maybe a copycat attack. Maybe not. But the Waterloo police aren't saying anything one way or the other. Listen, Fan," she added with a sigh, "the bloodhounds are officially on the loose now in every direction. Especially for Alison Perry. No one has seen her in almost a week."

"Understood. Thanks for the warning." By this time, Alison was standing in front of me, good arm on one hip. I stared at the floor.

Lynn paused for a moment. "Have you talked to Jerry?" she asked finally.

"Yes," I could answer honestly. "We had it out yesterday after the funeral."

"Had it out? Never mind. I don't want to know. But I think you should ask for some sort of protection."

"No way." I shook my head. "We're fine. We don't need a uniformed babysitter. Just went through that back home."

"Things have changed now, and I'm sure Jerry would agree with me. But whether or not you do," she added, "I'm on my way down tomorrow—probably after lunch. And you didn't hear it from me."

"Thanks, Lynn," I said. "We appreciate the heads up."

She hung up, and I looked Alison squarely in the eye.

"There's been another bombing in Cambridge. Just like yours."

Alison went white and sat down on the couch. Her good hand worked the armrest. "Was anyone killed?" she managed after a minute.

"No. Lynn didn't give me the details, but she did make that much clear." I rubbed my eyes. "She says the police aren't talking, but word has it the bomb might have been a copycat."

"A . . . a copycat?" She seemed to grasp at it desperately. "I never thought of that."

I pulled out my cell phone and pressed the Kitchener number I'd entered on my automatic dial. Brian Miller didn't pick up so I left a message on his machine to call me as soon as he got home.

"We'll have to catch the six o'clock news," I said as I ended the call. "Are you hungry?"

Alison didn't answer. She stared out the window at the river.

"Alison?"

She turned to me. "Sorry. What did you say?"

"Are you hungry? We could fit in supper before the news."

"No." She shook her head and rose. "Not anymore."

That makes two of us, I thought. Then another thought occurred to me.

"We have to make ourselves scarce tomorrow, Al. Lynn's on her way, looking for an interview. She says the bloodhounds are officially out for you, so we have to go somewhere private." I dug out the phone book and flipped to the pages for Long Sault. Baker, D. I punched in Dorothy Baker's number and heard the phone ring. Please be there, I said to myself. People of Mrs. Baker's generation rarely bother with an answering machine, let alone voice mail. Probably why they're sane and the rest of us are nuts.

"Hello?"

"Mrs. Baker? It's Farran Mackenzie calling. How are you?"

"Well, I'm fine, dear. Are you rested up from the service and all?"

"Yes," I smiled into the phone. "Actually slept pretty well last night for a change. I was thinking just now of what you said yesterday. If I ever wanted to talk with you about the old days?"

"Oh, yes. I do a lot of that these days. I think it's a sign of age." I heard her chuckle at the other end. "Did you want to come by this week?"

"Yes, if that's okay. I hate to ask on such short notice, but would you have time tomorrow?"

"Time I have lots of, Dr. Mackenzie. But it will have to be after lunch. Monday and Wednesday mornings I have an exercise class at the church."

I admired her discipline. The last time I'd gone to an exercise class, I'd been in high school and worn a blue, one-piece gym suit with bloomer shorts. If that didn't scar you for life, nothing would.

"After lunch would be great. Thanks for seeing us on short notice, Mrs. Baker. Oh, is it all right if I bring a . . . a friend?" Didn't know how to classify Paul Vaughn at that point, but hoped I was in the right direction. "He's a police officer, and he's looking for information on . . . " I trailed off, realizing that I never did get his mother's name.

"That's fine. Sounds interestin', actually. I'll see you tomorrow."

Mrs. Baker hung up. Alison was in the kitchen, putting on the teakettle. "What have you cooked up for tomorrow, Fan?" she asked.

"An alibi," I said ominously and called up Room 102 at the Ramada Inn, Cornwall.

Paul Vaughn was standing beside an expensive-looking black sports car parked in front of the police detachment in Long Sault at one o'clock sharp the next afternoon. He had returned my message that evening, agreeing to meet us at the front of the village and follow us in to Mrs. Baker's house. I stopped behind his car and scrolled down my window. Paul walked up and took his sunglasses off.

"I'll give you this, Farran Mackenzie," he said, leaning in to my window. "You work fast. Hi, Alison."

"Mrs. Baker lives on this street," I said without looking into his eyes. He was too close for that. "Mille Roches Road. Number forty-eight. Must be farther down toward the water tower."

"I'll follow you two." He put his sunglasses on again and sauntered back to his car. Probably expected me to check out his rear view in jeans. I didn't. Not really. Pulling out to drive around him, I glanced at the impenetrable windows of the police station. I wondered if Jerry were there and had seen our little rendezvous. I wondered if I had asked Paul to meet me there for that reason. Last night, I had left a message on Jerry's machine, asking to speak with him about the situation with Alison. Uncharacteristically, he had not yet returned my call. I wondered about that, too.

We passed Bethune Avenue, which would be considered one of the main streets of Long Sault having no less than three churches and two elementary schools calling it home. I continued around the curve, past a large senior citizens' residence and up to the Long Sault Volunteer Fire Department building, which also houses the village branch of the Stormont, Dundas and Glengarry County Library. As with Ingleside, the houses were a mix of older homes, which obviously once rode on the Hartshorne mover, and late 1950s bungalows built for those who did not choose this option. In both cases, four decades had allowed them the grace of age and establishment. The village interior had a quaint charm to it that the time-worn business strip along the highway belied.

Number forty-eight Mille Roches Road was—not surprisingly—a large, older frame house. The Bakers must have brought their home with them from Mille Roches half a century ago. Like the others of its origins, it looked finally settled and grown in. But you could tell it had been built for a much bigger space than the small residential lot on which it now stood.

Dorothy's daughter Sarah answered our knock.

"Come in, Dr. Mackenzie. I'm not working today, so I thought I'd join the party." She smiled and saw Paul and Alison behind me. "Come in, everyone. My mother is in the living room." Sarah shooed us down the hall and into a room on the right. I had a flashback to a late spring day last year, when I had followed Sarah into a living room in Ingleside and first met Alice Hoffman, Ruth's mother. In her, I found my role model for old age. But unlike Alice that day, Dorothy was not hooking a rug or even sitting down. She was sorting piles of paper spread across the dining room table and didn't hear us come in.

"Sarah, where is the receipt for the television?" Dorothy had glasses pushed up on her head. "We need to send that out." She picked up a paper and peered at it, then found her glasses and looked again. "It helps when you can see. That's not it." The older lady looked up and caught sight of us standing in her living room. She squinted, then impatiently took her glasses off.

"Dr. Mackenzie." Dorothy smiled and indicated the couch. "Please sit down. Church auction. Do it every year. Think I'm goin' to have to give it over to someone else next time." She put the paper on the table and joined us. "Oh, don't wait for me. Sit. Sit."

We sat. Sarah offered coffee and disappeared into the kitchen. Silence fell.

"Have you been doing the auction for many years, Mrs. Baker?" Alison asked pleasantly.

"Since we moved here," she replied. "Let's see. That was '56. I'm eighty-six in November . . . Forty-seven years," she finished triumphantly.

"Mrs. Baker, this is my friend Alison . . . uh, Standish." I stumbled through the introductions. "You may have seen her at the cemetery on Saturday."

"Yes," Dorothy nodded. "I'm so sorry about your accident, dear."

"Accident?" said Alison. I stiffened, expecting imminent exposure.

"Your cuts and bruises," the lady returned with the directness of advanced years. "Was it a car accident?"

"Of sorts," I cut in. In the corner of my eye, I saw Paul look at me curiously. I nodded in his direction. "And this is—"

"The police officer," Dorothy cut me off. "Of course. How do you do? Dr. Mackenzie tells me you're lookin' for information about . . . who was it, dear?" She looked at me.

"Sheila," said Paul slowly. "A woman named Sheila Pierce."

Dorothy's eyebrows rose. "Sheila Pierce. Sheila Pierce Monroe. Now that's a name I haven't heard in years. She left in '57, with that engineer man. Still just in her twenties. Could still be alive, I guess. But you must want just the history. Can't be reopenin' the case after all these years."

"Case?" I said, shooting a glance at Alison. Paul remained silent.

"Oh, yes!" The elderly lady warmed to her subject. "The talk of Mille Roches for a year, even over all the hubbub of the construction." She turned to Vaughn. "But there is no statute of limitations on murder, is there, young man?"

"Murder?" I echoed. I was starting to feel like a parrot.

"Murder. Adultery. Theft. It was the biggest scandal we ever had, even though they actually lived in Maple Grove." Dorothy looked out the window. "Old Mrs. Monroe was dead by that time, thank goodness. I would have felt sorry for her, as stuck up as she'd been when she was alive. It was the end of her family line."

"What was?" said Alison. She and I seemed to be doing all the talking. The silence from Paul's corner was growing ominous.

"Why, the murder of her only son," Dorothy turned to explain. "Sheila Pierce killed her husband Garnet Monroe to be with her lover. An engineer on the Project. Now what was his name . . . Vaughn. Vaughn. Charles Vaughn. That was it."

I froze. Alison didn't make a sound. Sarah came in with coffee, clinking cups and spoons happily in the dead quiet of the room.

"What do you take in your coffee, Officer . . . " said Dorothy. "I'm sorry, I didn't quite catch your name."

Finally Paul spoke. "Vaughn," he replied slowly. "Sergeant Paul Charles Vaughn, St. John's Police Service."

The elderly lady stopped in mid-pour, the creamer suspended over the cup. She looked up, eyes round. "Oh." Her free hand went unconsciously over her mouth. "Oh, my."

It was awful. I had to do something. Feeling like the Tin Man after a good rain, I slowly turned my head to face Paul. He sat chin up, eyes on the carpet.

For a small eternity, we stayed a still life. Then Paul reluctantly returned my horrified gaze.

"It's okay, Farran," he said quietly. "I already knew."

Chapter EIGHT: Mille Roches

POWER PROJECT LAUNCHED AT IMPRESSIVE CEREMONIES
Power Job To Take Six Years
St. Laurent And Dewey Key Figures At
Rites Near City, Massena, NY

Prime Minister Turns Sod At Maple Grove

Fifty years of planners' dreams and across-the-border discussions reached fruition early this afternoon when first ground was broken at Maple Grove for North America's second largest hydro-electric power development project. With the rushing blue waters of the mighty St. Lawrence River in the background, the prime minister of Canada, the premier of Ontario and the governor of New York state each wielded white-handled silver spades to turn the first three sods of the $600,000,000 St. Lawrence power scheme. The blistering heat of the August afternoon was shattered by the thunder of exploding rockets on the riverbank as the ground slid from the shining silver blades. The symbolic sod-turning by Prime Minister St. Laurent, Premier Frost and Gov. Thomas Dewey was preceded by addresses by the visiting dignitaries.

Dynamite Blasts Touched Off By Governor

POLLEY'S BAY, N.Y.—A dynamite blast you could feel in the pit of your stomach heralded the start of New York State's share of the St. Lawrence power project shortly before noon today. Governor Thomas L. Dewey of New York pressed the button that climaxed the colorful ceremonies, held on a site that overlooked the tumbling rapids of the Long Sault. With Governor Dewey on the platform was a group of American and Canadian citizens, including Ontario Premier Leslie M. Frost, Hydro Chairman Robert H. Saunders, Gen. A.G.L. MacNaughton, and J.L. Dansereau, representing the Canadian wing of the International Joint Commission, Mayor Aaron Horovitz and Warden A.L. Davies of the United Counties. Among the American dignitaries present were New York State Power Authority Chairman Robert Moses, Lewis G. Castle, administrator of the St. Lawrence Seaway Development Corporation, members of the New York State Power Authority, Mayor Stowell P. Fournia of Massena, R.B. McWhorter, acting chairman of the U.S. section of the I.J.C., and many others.

AUGUST 10, 1954
The Cornwall *Standard Freeholder*

The front of Clifford's General Store in Mille Roches was full of thirsty people, dropping nickels into the Coca-Cola machine for a small bottle of relief from the heat. It was almost like a party, Dorothy Baker thought to herself, but there wasn't anything to celebrate. The locals were staying inside to talk while the out-of-towners kept to themselves on the porch or in front of their cars parked along the No. 2 Highway.

The highway itself had been full since early morning, with all the excitement over the ceremony down the road in Maple Grove. Dorothy had to admit it was the reason she'd walked to the store today, more for news than for shopping. And she wasn't the only one. Even the Leonard boy, Hal, had driven down from Aultsville and was chatting Frank up for details. Not that he was getting any. The big ceremony had been for dignitaries and the press only. The residents of Maple Grove itself had not been invited, let alone anyone from neighbouring Mille Roches.

"Afternoon, Mrs. Baker." Frank turned to give her a smile as she made her way into the store. Somehow, despite all the people and the chatting, the tall and lanky youth was able to finish packing the orders of groceries due for delivery later that day. The boxes surrounded the centre counter right up to the door. It was a big job, but necessary. By offering the service, the Cliffords were able to hold their own against the shiny new supermarkets sprouting up in nearby Cornwall.

"Afternoon, Frank." Dorothy pulled out a handkerchief and patted her face. "Terrible heat. All this to-do doesn't help." She turned to Hal Leonard, the young man from Aultsville, and nodded. "Hal. I haven't seen your father since your mother's funeral in the spring. How is he doin' on his own?"

"Fine, ma'am," said the boy. "Gordy and I are pickin' up the slack as best we can. I'll tell my dad you were askin' after him."

"You do that." Dorothy winked at him. "You also tell him if that house full of men has clothes that need mendin', I'm still takin' work."

"We have the new fall patterns in you were lookin' for, Mrs. Baker." Frank stood up from the boxes, face flushed from the heat. He brushed his hands off. "As soon as things slow down here, I can show you . . . " His voice trailed off as he looked over her shoulder toward the door.

Two women stood just inside the store. A slight physical resemblance between them spoke of family connection, but beyond that Dorothy knew they were poles apart. Mila Pierce dressed as plain as she spoke. She wore the eternal bun that had made her look old long before she'd turned forty, a few streaks of grey now showing in the mousy brown colour. Behind her stood her cousin, Sheila

Monroe, her junior by over ten years. She was well dressed, her golden-brown hair gathered in an old-fashioned roll around the back of her neck, one small bracelet on her wrist. The young woman looked around the store shyly, a small smile on her face. When she caught sight of Frank coming to greet her, she held out her hand.

"Frank. It's good to see you," Sheila gave his hand a squeeze.

"It's been at least a couple of years, Sheila," he replied. "Hello, Mila. What can I do for you ladies today?"

"We're here to order some groceries," Sheila said softly. "We have to come ourselves now because we've lost all our help to Hydro. Garnet's livid, but I don't mind. It feels good to have real work to do again."

"And you'd better get to it, Sheila, or you-know-who will be in here with his knickers in a twist," added Mila tartly.

As if on cue, the door opened again and Garnet Monroe swept into the store, slamming the door behind him. Everyone stopped talking and turned to look.

"Damned sightseers," he boomed. "Everywhere you go, they're in your way. Can't get a moment's peace. Damned Hydro," he added. "Can't match their wages. Lost all my help. Have to do everything myself." Dorothy saw Mila cringe. Sheila seemed unperturbed.

"Good to see you, Mr. Monroe." Frank held out his hand. After a moment's hesitation, Garnet shook it quickly. "We take orders by telephone," the young man continued. "Next time you want groceries, just call in your order and we'll deliver it that afternoon."

"Don't have a telephone," said the man curtly. "Don't need one. Don't want one. Hurry along, Sheila," he added, "and give Frank your list. I don't want to be here all day."

Don't want to be mingling with the likes of us, Dorothy said to herself. The Monroes were the oldest family in Maple Grove and made sure everyone remembered. At least Garnet and his mother did. She wondered what life was like for Sheila in that stuffy old house.

Frank took Sheila's list and began to box the items. Sheila browsed a bit while Mila chatted with a few familiar faces. The excitement of the day was dwindling, along with the crowd in the store. A man Dorothy had never seen before came in hesitantly, followed by someone she knew on sight.

Harper Mackenzie was a giant of a man, with coal-black hair and beard. The trader from Farran's Point was renowned for his temper, but saved it for those who usually deserved it. Garnet Monroe looked at the man, dressed in shabby but clean clothes, and turned away. Mackenzie took no notice of him, or anyone else for that matter—except Frank.

"Nails, lad," said Mackenzie in a thick Scottish accent. "Two pound of them out on the porch."

"Yes, sir." Frank got two paper bags out from behind the counter, leaving the Monroe order half filled on the floor. Dorothy saw Garnet flush red and wondered if he were arrogant or foolish enough to take on Harper Mackenzie. Now this, she thought, could be some real entertainment.

Hal Leonard must have seen the same thing because he stepped forward and took the bags out of Frank's hands. "I'll do it, Mr. Mackenzie. I've done it often enough in my dad's store." The boy moved out, passing the stranger who stood quietly by the door, his eyes on Sheila Monroe. Frank finally seemed to notice him.

"Can I help you with something, sir?"

"I'm looking for a room," said the man. "I saw the sign 'Clifford's Rooming House' next door. Do I see you about it?"

"No, you'd have to see my ma. She runs that part of the business. But I think she's full right now," Frank added. "Lots of men here already for the Project. How long would you be needin' it for?"

"About four years," the stranger grinned. "I work for Hydro, too. Engineer. Charles Vaughn." He held out his hand and Frank shook it.

"Engineer?" Hal was back with the bags full and he handed them to Frank for weighing. "You buildin' that big dam?"

Vaughn turned to him. "Three dams, actually. We have to put a control dam at Iroquois Point to watch the water flow from the west, and a second dam on Barnhart Island to be the spillway for the headpond we need for the generating station at the main dam by Maple Grove."

"Spillway?" asked Hal.

"Yes. A spillway directs the water into the area of the headpond, and any extra will go around the powerhouse. That way we control the head or the difference in water levels around the generators. The drop through there is almost a hundred feet so we have to be able to control it at all times." Vaughn smiled. "It's quite the project, but we're all excited to finally have a go at it."

"I'll bet," said Hal. "The talk's been goin' round for almost fifty years now."

"Well, the good thing about that is our plans have been worked on over and over for years," Vaughn replied. "We're more than ready to go. There's a billboard with the project mapped out on it where we'll start digging in Maple Grove. They had it up for the ceremonies today."

"I would say you've already started, Mr. Vaughn," Dorothy put in. "Ever since the word came the Project was goin' through, I've had nothin' but constant trucks roarin' past my house at all hours of the day and night."

"Yes, ma'am." Vaughn took his hat off, then shot a glance at Sheila who stood nearby, listening with interest. "There's a lot to be done and not a lot of time to do it in."

"How long do you think all this will take?" Sheila asked quietly.

"About four years for the construction, miss." Vaughn cleared his throat. "Then it takes time to get all the generators on line after that."

"It's Mrs." Garnet crossed over to his wife and took her arm. "Mrs. Monroe. And four years of strangers coming around to tell us what to do is nothing to look forward to. Sheila, let's wait out in the car." He led his wife out the door, stopping to give a look at Mila, who followed behind. Dead silence followed all three.

"Huh," grunted Mackenzie. "Good riddance." The trader picked up the two bags of nails, slapped some coins on the counter and strode out. Dorothy managed to watch him out the window, wondering if words would be exchanged outside. But Mackenzie ignored the man helping the two women into a large black Buick and went straight to a Ford truck that had seen better days. She noticed a young boy in a ball cap waiting in the cab. Funny, somehow she'd gotten the idea Harper had a daughter.

"Don't mind him, Mr. Vaughn," Frank was saying. "The Monroes were one of the first families to settle here and they're kind of used to havin' things their way. Monroe House will be torn down with the others," he added, "and it's almost a hundred and fifty years old. I guess it stands to reason they'd be some upset about it."

Vaughn nodded slowly. "I can see that. Problem is, this whole thing is important to the province. Ontario is growing like crazy. Hydro is running to replace hundreds of miles of old lines, and put thousands of miles of new ones in where there are none. All these places need power, and we need to be ready to supply it."

"I'm getting' along, Frank," said Hal. "Goodbye, Mrs. Baker. And it was nice to meet you, Mr. Vaughn," he turned to the man. "I'm Hal Leonard. Do you need a lift anywhere?"

"It's Charlie. And yes, to the Hydro office if you're going that way."

"I'll tell my ma you're lookin' for a room, Mr. Vaughn," said Frank. "If you stop by next week, she may have something for you."

"I'll do that, thanks." Vaughn followed Hal outside, with Dorothy on their heels. The Ford truck was gone. Garnet leaned against the Buick, smoking. He did not look up until Frank came out with his box of groceries.

"Would it be okay if I came around sometimes to see what's goin' on?" asked Hal. The door on the Buick slammed, and the motor roared to life.

"Sure, anytime." Charlie replied, his eyes on the retreating car. *"She's very pretty, isn't she?"*
They watched the Buick disappear down the No. 2 Highway toward Maple Grove. Hal gave Charlie a friendly slap on the back, looked him in the eye and slowly shook his head.

SAUNDERS, 4 OTHERS INJURED IN PLANE CRASH
HYDRO'S CHIEF SERIOUS
AMPHIBIAN CRAFT CAUGHT IN FREEZING RAIN, SNOWSTORM

SEAWAY VALLEY SHOCKED BY DEATH OF SAUNDERS

By Burns Stewart (Staff Reporter)

Seaway Valley today mourns, with the rest of Ontario, a man who became a familiar figure in St. Lawrence riverfront communities over the past two years.

Profound shock and regret were expressed on the sudden death of "Bob" Saunders, forceful chairman of Ontario Hydro since 1948. Mr. Saunders, 51, son of a Toronto fireman who began his career as a newsboy, died early Sunday at Victoria Hospital at London, Ont., from injuries suffered in a plane crash 24 hours earlier while returning from one of his many public speaking jaunts across the province.

Robert H. Saunders was probably better known throughout Eastern Ontario than any other public official in the province. He fulfilled many speaking engagements in this district, particularly since the beginning of development of the St. Lawrence River's great power potential.

People of Iroquois will remember the heavy-set man in the dark blue suit who walked the streets of their village one day last summer, stopping to chat with them about property values and their uncertain future in view of the St. Lawrence development. Many didn't know until later they had been talking with the chairman of Hydro.

4-HOUR WORK STOPPAGE IN TRIBUTE TO SAUNDERS

January 15–19, 1955
The Cornwall *Standard Freeholder*

2ND MAJOR PROJECT PHASE IS LAUNCHED

The St. Lawrence power project entered its second major phase this week when work started on the Canadian portion of the main power dam. U.S. contractors for the New York State Power Authority started their section last week.

Heavy equipment of Iroquois Constructors Ltd. moved into the works area three miles west of Cornwall Monday to begin construction of the Canadian half of the international powerhouse.

June 28, 1955
The Cornwall *Standard Freeholder*

The early summer sun felt good on Dorothy's face as she sat on her front porch, finishing a hem. As a seamstress, she'd always been busy. But with so many workers here for the Project and all of them away from their families, she had more mending and alterations than she could handle. She didn't mind, however, for as her husband Carl said these days, make hay while the sun shines. The St. Lawrence development wouldn't go on forever—and neither would the boom times.

And these were boom times—or so it seemed at first glance. Hydro paid wages no one else could match, and workers were coming from all over North America to this quiet little place, changing it forever. And it was forever changed. When the trucks and the noise and the engineers were finally gone, Mille Roches would be gone, too.

She sighed and let the garment sit in her lap. It had been almost a year since the big ceremony in Maple Grove. Everyone talked about nothing else these days. And she had gone with Carl to see the plans for the two new villages Hydro would make. Paved streets, streetlights, new schools, new shopping malls. It all sounded like a promising future, but—

But this was home. This funny little town Dorothy had moved to as a young bride. A village cut up by the river, the canal and the CNR railway line into sections that kept their distance from one another, yet remained a community. A place where most people had spent three generations putting down roots. And now those roots were to be torn out.

Last night, she'd listened to the music coming through her back windows from the Friday-night dance at the Mille Roches arena. It had taken the whole village to raise the money to build the arena only twenty years ago, and now what had quickly become the social hub of Mille Roches would soon be gone. Hydro said they would build another one in the new town, but it wouldn't be the same.

The traffic on the No. 2 Highway was steady and people seemed to be busy going places, but most of them were strangers. A lot of Dorothy's neighbours were probably swimming at Sheek's Island, the island beside Mille Roches that was connected by a bridge, or at Gillie's swimming hole just down the road in Maple Grove. The sun was warm, and for a few minutes, she dozed.

A Ford truck in need of a muffler flew past and pulled in at Cliffords' store. Dorothy snorted, opened her eyes and shot a dark look that changed when she saw who was driving.

"Well, old girl," she said to herself rising from her chair, "here goes nothin'."

Dorothy quickly went into her house, returning in moments with a large brown paper bag in hand. Her husband's warning to mind her

113

own business was playing in her mind but, as usual, she ignored it and strode up the sidewalk to Cliffords'.

Harper Mackenzie was in the store, the young boy in the ball cap sitting waiting in the truck. But Dorothy had been right last year. Under those boyish clothes was Harp's daughter, and a fine-looking girl, to boot. Mackenzie's wife had been dead a few years now, and Dorothy's maternal instincts were kicking in. After a lot of thought, she'd come up with an idea of how to possibly help the girl without Harp taking a piece out of her.

"Hello, Leslie," Dorothy said to the girl through the truck window. "Isn't it a lovely afternoon?"

Suspicious green eyes surrounded by lashes Dorothy would have killed for years ago met the woman's smile. The suspicion was understandable, she thought. The girl probably dodged well-meaning but unwanted advice from the ladies of Farran's Point on a daily basis. But Dorothy pressed on.

"I've been wantin' to ask you if you'd do me a favour, Leslie. I'm cleanin' out my sewin' room before we get moved, you know, and I have things I made and were never bought." Dorothy held up the bag. "I found a dress I think would fit you. Nothin' special now, but the material's nice. Do you think you could use it? I'd really like to get it off my hands."

The green eyes looked over Dorothy's shoulder, and she followed them to see Harper standing behind her. The look on his face wasn't good.

"Afternoon, Harp." Dorothy kept her smile though she got none in return. "How are things at the Point? I hear they've started to cut all your trees." She began to ramble on to fill the heavy silence. "They haven't come for ours yet, but I'm sure it's only a matter of time. Must look so strange to have all the trees cut down. Bad enough to have numbers on all our houses like we're in prison. I was just sayin' to Leslie that I have to clean out my things before we leave the village, and I have some clothes I made but never sold, and I found a dress I thought might fit her, and it's nothin' fancy but the material is good, and I hoped she'd do me the favour of takin' it off my hands . . . d'you see." Dorothy faltered into a silence of her own. She saw no fool in Harp's eyes but also—was it a touch of gratitude?

"Well, gal," he said slowly, looking at Leslie, "what do you say?"

The girl hesitated. Dorothy pulled out the dress, a slim shift in red and showed it to her. Leslie began to shake her head no, and then another truck pulled up to the store, a shiny new one with LEONARDS' GENERAL STORE—AULTSVILLE on the side. The older brother Gordon was driving but Hal got out of the passenger side, helping a boy out of the back before heading for the store.

"C'mon, Jerry," he said. "Gordy might not be thirsty, but we are, right?" Gordon grumbled something and joined them. When Hal looked up and saw the Mackenzies' truck there, his eyes sought out the passenger and he smiled. He, at least, received a smile in return. Gordon frowned, nodded at them and dragged Hal into the store with Jerry in pursuit.

When Leslie turned back to Dorothy, the woman saw that the girl's cheeks were flushed.

"Thank you, Mrs. Baker," she spoke at last. "It's very kind of you. I'd like very much to have the dress." She looked up at Harper, and then took the bag.

"We're obliged, Dot," he said gruffly, touching his hat. Only when they had gone did Dorothy allow herself a sigh of relief. Then Mila Pierce marched around the corner of the building and into the store, slamming the door behind her. Maybe, thought Dorothy, I should stop in myself and get some more thread.

The Leonard boys were back out on the porch pulling Coca-Colas out of the cooler. She nodded to both before entering the store itself, mentally shaking her head. Shame how Hal was making a name for himself in the rumour mill. Fights, girls, and now stories of forged cheques with his father scrambling to fix it. Hal flashed her a smile, and she couldn't help giving him one in return. Not a bad lad, she thought, but there's nothing more headed for trouble in life than a young man without a mother to keep him in line.

". . . all I can swallow from that man." In the store, Mila slapped her hand on the counter while Frank ran to fill her order. "I've put up with a lot over the years, for Sheila's sake. But this is just too much. Imagine suggestin' that I work for them!" she fumed. "A housekeeper for my own family. And what they pay . . . Hydro isn't the only reason they can't keep their help."

"Well, Mila," said the young man quietly, "you know we're not really family to the Monroes. Just to Sheila, and she married in. I'm sure they meant no harm."

"Oh, they meant it, all right." Instead of calming down, Mila picked up steam. "The old lady is bad enough, but you can chalk it up to age. His Nibs, on the other hand, is a real piece of work. I thought when he married Sheila, he'd warm up some, but he's gotten worse over the past ten years. And I never really liked him to begin with."

"Now that's not quite true, Mila." Frank spoke over his shoulder as he finished filling her bag. "I remember a time when . . . " He turned and saw Dorothy, who immediately took a special interest in the dry goods. "Here, Mila. On your tab again?"

"Yes, Frank." Mila took the bag. "You're not serious about that diggin' stuff, are you? I would think your folks need you here, especially right now." The bell over the door jingled as Hal and the boy Jerry came in.

"Well, it won't be easy to find the time, but I hope to." Frank marked some numbers down in a book. "My teacher says the Iroquois were on Sheek's Island ages ago. Must be lots of interestin' things over there. Don't have much time left to take a look." He turned to Dorothy. "Afternoon, Mrs. Baker. Can I get you something?"

"Hey, that sounds like fun," said the boy. "Can we go, too, Hal?"

"I don't think we could get time away just now, Jer," the young man replied, putting his hand on Jerry's shoulder. "We're lucky to take a peek now and then at the Project because we have to deliver lumber."

"Maybe he could take me along." The boy looked at Frank, who was showing Dorothy different colours of thread. Frank looked up and smiled.

"And who might you be?"

"This is Jerry Strauss," said Hal. "His dad helps run our lumberyard."

"Jerry, if I ever get there, I'll be sure to look you up." Frank put two spools into a small paper bag and took the coins from Dorothy's hand.

"Don't say that," Hal grinned. "He'll hold you to it, even if it takes years."

"What about goin' to the dam site?" Jerry persisted. "We never go up close, and I always have to stay in the truck."

"It's too dangerous to go wanderin' around," Hal explained. "We'd need a personal tour guide for that."

"Will I do?" said a voice. Everyone looked up to see Charles Vaughn in the doorway, with a disgruntled Gordon Leonard behind him. Charles held a large bouquet of tiger lilies in one hand. The other he extended to Hal.

"Hey, Charlie!" said Hal. "It's good to see you. This is my friend Jerry, and the gloomy guy behind you is my warden and older brother, Gordon."

Gordon nodded and looked at Hal. "If we're goin' to make the delivery, we better get goin'."

Jerry looked at Hal, who said, "Gordy's right. We have to get to the dam."

"I'm staying here at the boarding house," said Charlie to Jerry. "You have Hal bring you by some day when you've got the time and I'll take you through the main dam site myself. They'll be pouring concrete in the two control dams by the fall."

"What's takin' so long?" Jerry asked. "It's been a year. I thought they'd be done by now."

"Oh, no." Charlie smiled. "You can't build anything where there's water so we had to put up cofferdams first to divert the water away from the dam sites. And we can't cut off the Cornwall Canal in Maple Grove because of the ships, so we have to build a new canal to go around the main dam site. With tunnels underneath as well, so we can get trucks and people to the building area all the time. Everything has to be done in the right order."

"And then they'll have to stop work in the winter or the concrete'll freeze up when they pour it," Hal added.

"No, not this time," said Charlie. "We think we've found a way to pour concrete right through the winter."

"No kiddin'?" Jerry asked.

"Hal . . . " Gordon said warningly.

"C'mon, Jer." Hal nodded to the ladies. "I'll be seein' you, Charlie. Frank."

When the Leonards had gone, Charlie looked at Frank. "The brothers are very different, aren't they?"

"Gordon has a right to be sour," Mila snapped. "Since their mother died, he's had to look out for his brother, and from what I hear, he's got his hands full."

"Now, Mila," said Frank. "Don't believe all you hear. I think Hal's just had a run of bad luck."

"That's what they always say about troublemakers," she sniffed. "I always say, where's there's smoke there's fire."

"Frank, is your mother here?" Charlie changed the subject. "She's not in the boarding house, and I picked these for her. Found a whole field of them off the Cornwall Centre Road just north of the village. They need to go in water. Ladies?" He pulled two lilies out and handed one each to Dorothy and Mila.

Then Sheila Monroe burst through the door.

"Mila? Mila, you wouldn't wait for me—" She broke off as Charles Vaughn handed her a single lily. For a long moment, they simply looked at each other. Then he touched his hat and left without a word.

Sheila turned to watch him leave. When she turned back, her cheeks were as colourful as the beautiful wild flower she held in her hand.

117

POUR CONCRETE FOR BIG DAM

MASSENA, NY—First concrete for the $25,744,258 Long Sault dam was poured Monday.

In charge of the work is the combined firm of Walsh, Perint, Morrison, Knudson, Peter Kiewitt and Utah. Elwyn P. Simpson is project superintendent.

The work of preparing the site for the dam was done by the Dravo Contracting Corporation.

October 11, 1955
The Cornwall *Standard Freeholder*

BIGGEST LAKES DREDGE STARTS WORKING TUESDAY

MASSENA, NY—Largest dredge on the Great Lakes, the "Mogul" will start work Tuesday on the removal of some 2,000,000 cubic yards of material from the riverbed in the vicinity of Chimney Island.

The huge dredge is owned by the Great Lakes Dredge and Dock Company, holders of a $4,5000,000 contract for excavation of the Chimney Point channel.

Master of the leviathan is Captain Arthur L. Richard.

November 14, 1955
The Cornwall *Standard Freeholder*

POUR CONCRETE FOR IROQUOIS CONTROL DAM

MASSENA, NY—First steady pouring of concrete on the St. Lawrence development project is now under way at the Iroquois control dam.

Some 229 yards of the concrete went into "Block" 12, or one of the spillway sluice blocks of the dam.

Initial placing of concrete on the project took place at Long Sault Dam when the concrete for a retaining wall was placed. The mix, however, came from a local supplier and not from the contractor's batch plant. The placing of concrete at Long Sault has not been steady since that time.

November 17, 1955
The Cornwall *Standard Freeholder*

"You've got it easy," Charlie Vaughn grumbled from where he stood on the footstool in Dorothy Baker's living room. *"All you had to do was ask her to dance. Ow!"*

"Well, stand still, Charlie!" Dot looked up from where she was kneeling to pin the hem of his pants. *"It's like trying to pin an eel. What's botherin' you today?"*

"Easy?" Hal Leonard gave his friend a grin. *"Leslie's father is Harper Mackenzie, the meanest man in the county. He cornered me last week about my intentions with his daughter, and my life flashed before my eyes."*

"Hmph." Dot brushed her knees as she rose and gave Hal a glare. "Harper is not the meanest man in the county and you know it. Just has a temper that gets the best of him sometimes. And what father wouldn't be lookin' out for his daughter? A girl can end up in a lot of trouble with the wrong boy."

Hal's face lost its smile. "I didn't do those things I hear people sayin'. I've never stolen anything in my life."

"I didn't say you did," Dot replied firmly. "I don't give much truck to gossip, especially around here. But you be square with Leslie Mackenzie, and Harper will have nothing to say," she added, warningly.

Hal sat down on the sofa in Dot's living room, as Charlie left to change back into his other pants.

"So what's botherin' him?" Dot took out a pin box. "He's usually so easy goin'."

"Oh, he's just lovesick for the wrong girl," said Hal easily. "She's already got a fella. I've told him to find a new one, go out to the Saturday dances in Cornwall or something, but he won't listen to me."

The woman moved a pile of clothing that wobbled beside her sewing machine. "He'd better be careful," she said quietly. "He's a nice young man with a good future with Hydro. There are a lot of girls who'd get themselves into trouble just to rope in the right husband. Wouldn't be the first time I'd see it happen in this neck of the woods. Some men just leave, but I couldn't see Charlie doin' that. Of course," she added, her mouth a thin line, "some people can buy their way out if they have the money, like Garn—"

"Here, Mrs. Baker." Charlie stood in the doorway, holding out the pants. "And don't worry about me. I can take care of myself."

"I think that goes under 'famous last words,' doesn't it?" Hal teased.

"Speak for yourself," Charlie shot back, along with the pants. Hal ducked, and the pants hit a young woman coming through the front door.

"Oh, my God, I'm sorry." Charlie rushed over to pick the offending garment off the floor. "Are you all right?" He straightened up and flushed to find himself face to face with Sheila Monroe.

"I'm fine," she laughed, brushing her hair back into place. "I guess I walked into something. Are they gangin' up on you, Mr. Vaughn?"

"No," said Hal, getting up to go. "Just tryin' to knock some sense into him. Maybe you'd have better luck," he added, ignoring the look of death Charlie gave him. "He's takin' a fancy to a girl that's already taken. I say he should shop around. Mrs. Baker says he should be careful if he does. What do you say?"

For a moment, Sheila did not reply. Then she looked up at Charlie, with a hint of pink in her cheeks.

"Is she a nice girl, Mr. Vaughn?" she asked softly.
Charlie swallowed. "I think she's very nice," he managed.
"Then maybe you should talk to this girl," she said. "Maybe she's not as happy with her young man as you think."
"Do you think I'd stand a chance, Mrs. Monroe?" Charlie looked her in the eye.
Dot suddenly had the feeling the two had forgotten the others in the room. "Well," she said briskly, "Sheila, I'll get your dresses." When she returned from the back room, Charlie and Hal were gone.
Sheila sat on the sofa, looking out the window to somewhere very far away.

NORTH SECTION OF POWERHOUSE NEARS FINISH

Approximately 75,000 cubic yards (150,000 tons) of concrete now has been placed in the north end of the main dam and powerhouse structure. This represents about 80 per cent of the concrete that will be put into the U-abutment and wing wall sector of the main structure, and indicates the significant progress that has been made in the building of permanent installations for the St. Lawrence power development project, director Gordon Mitchell stated today.

In terms that can be more readily appreciated, the 75,000 cubic yards of concrete placed so far would represent the amount of concrete that would be required for a standard sidewalk four feet wide and four inches thick, stretching for 280 miles, the distance from Cornwall to Toronto.

May 10, 1956
The Cornwall *Standard Freeholder*

NEW TOWN CONSTRUCTION WORK IS WELL ADVANCED
NEW TOWN 2 REHAB MOVE SET FOR START ON JULY 16

The access road for the housemover into Hydro's New Town No. 2 has been completed and rehabilitation work will start as soon as the equipment arrives from Iroquois.

The house-moving float is expected to arrive on the job site today while the housemovers themselves have to be broken down and shipped in sections. The engineer in charge of the town, Peter Hess, said he thought they would be reassembled and ready to work on the houses in the Mille Roche-Moulinette area about July 16.

In the town itself, some 13 foundations for the houses have now been completed. Electrical, water and sewage service to the lots is complete. The water system has been tested with a pressure pump and except for some minor parts still missing the water pumping station is ready to go into action and will be ready to supply water to the home owners as soon as they are installed in the new town.

July 10, 1956
The Cornwall *Standard Freeholder*

EVICTION ORDERS ARRIVE FOR 25 SHEEK-ISLANDERS

Final orders have come for some 25 cottagers to vacate their summer homes on Sheek Island. The cottagers have been granted permission to leave their homes on what was formerly the department of transport lands, but cannot live there this summer.

After some controversy over the past few months, the summer homeowners have been allowed to leave their houses on the island for the rest of this year. However, because of the danger from the blasting work that is being carried out on the island, some 25 of the people on the southern end of the island must vacate their premises.

July 18, 1956
The Cornwall *Standard Freeholder*

NEW TOWN 2 WORK RIGHT ON SCHEDULE

New Town Number Two is beginning to take shape as more streets are laid out and more houses moved to the townsite. The first occupied dwelling, that of Cecil Antoine of Mille Roches, was laid on its new foundation yesterday afternoon by the amazing Hartshorne house mover. With two movers and a trailer now in use, two houses instead of one are being moved in a day.

The whole west and south-west sections of the town are now released for more house construction. All the roads in the south-east section are cleared, and Moulinette and Simcoe roads in the south-west section are cleared.

The water mains, having been tested and re-tested over the past two months, were sterilized yesterday, and families will be living in their new town by the end of this week. By the time the town is completed, 150 houses will have been moved and 170 lots bought and that number of new houses built. Those who don't own a house can rent from Hydro-owned dwellings in the new town.

July 27, 1956
The Cornwall *Standard Freeholder*

"We've sold, Frank. And we have our lot in the new town. We'll be leavin' sometime next month." Dot gave Frank Clifford a small smile in the empty store. "Carl says we've got one of the best lots, right near the arena. Maybe I'll have music again on Friday nights."

"Maybe you will at that, Mrs. Baker," Frank said encouragingly. "Things have been strange enough around here the past year, but now with the houses bein' moved out . . . Well, I'm sure once we're all there things will settle down. The housemover is quite the machine, isn't it?" he added. "Lifts the house up like nothin' at all."

The rumble of thunder made them both look out the front windows. The sky had gone dark for midday and wind made the door swing open with a slam. Seconds later, the rain moved in.

"My goodness," Dot gathered her things. "I better get home before it gets bad."

"I think you might stay here till it breaks up a little," said Frank, closing the door and trying to see out the rain-streaked windows. "It sure came up fast."

The sound of an engine was followed by shrieks and laughter. Then the door burst open and three bedraggled figures ran in.

"We're soaked!" Sheila Monroe laughed as she shook water from her dress. "And just from the truck to the store. I can't imagine how I'd be if you two hadn't stopped to give me a ride."

"Well, the sky was looking pretty ugly, Mrs. Monroe," said Charlie shyly. "We couldn't just leave you there."

"It shouldn't last long." Hal looked out the window at the sky. "It's already startin' to break up. I'll have to get back to Aultsville. Will you find a ride home, Mrs. Monroe?"

"I'll be fine, Hal. Thank you." She smiled at Frank. "I have to go to the bank and then I'll pay my tab with you, Frank. Hello, Dorothy," she added.

"Sheila." Dot nodded. "How is your mother-in-law doin' with all the excitement these days?"

Sheila's face lost its smile. "Not well, I'm afraid. Mother Monroe spends more and more time in her room. Some days, she won't get up at all. Says she's not feelin' well. I'm not sure how she's going to get through this."

"Are you handlin' that big house all alone now?"

"More or less. We found a girl to come in three afternoons a week, but with Mother in bed . . . " Sheila shrugged. "Mila helps sometimes. She's there now in case Mother needs anything."

Hal waved a goodbye. "It's stoppin'. I'll be off. See ya next week, Charlie." As he left, a tall man brushed past him on the way in, followed by a woman.

"Sheila!" Garnet Monroe's face was red with fury. "Have you lost your mind? How could you leave Mother alone like that?"

"She wasn't alone, Garnet," his wife said with quiet surprise. "Mila was with her. Weren't you?" she added to the woman who stood nervously behind Monroe.

"Of course I was with her." Mila looked at Garnet. "Well, I was out in the garden when Garnet came home. So many weeds. Tried to do some before the rain came. Hard for you to keep up, I'm sure . . . "

Dot began to edge for the door. She had no interest in being caught in the middle of a family blowout.

"I told you to wait for me. I'll drive you where you want to go." Garnet looked pointedly at Charlie Vaughn, "Too many strange men around. It isn't safe."

"Garnet!" Sheila said sharply. "Mind your manners. Mr. Vaughn and Hal Leonard gave me a lift to get me out of the rain. You should be thankin' him."

"Where did they pick you up? Ernie's Hotel?" Monroe's voice took on an ugly tone.

"There's no call to talk to Sheila like that." Frank came out from behind the counter. Charlie moved to stand beside him.

"This is none of your business, Frank." The warning in Monroe's voice was unmistakable, though he kept his eyes on his wife. "Get me my tab for the week, and I'll square it with you." When Frank didn't move, Garnet turned on him. "Now, boy! Or I'll take my business elsewhere."

"You'd better go," Charlie said to Frank. "I'll wait here till you get back."

Dot opened the door to leave. Out in the parking lot, she could see Hal standing beside a battered truck, in deep conversation with the driver. She heard Frank go into the office at the back.

"You wait in the car with Mila," said Monroe.

"I'm goin' to the bank," Sheila said stubbornly. "Thank you again, Mr. Vaughn, for the ride." She held out her hand to him.

"Well, it wasn't me. It was Hal." Vaughn ignored Monroe. "He was giving me a lift here to my room."

"Ah, yes," Monroe turned to his wife. "A boarding house full of strange men. No wonder you like to come here so often, my dear."

Dot was closing the door when she heard a bang and a scream. Charlie Vaughn and Garnet Monroe were struggling over the centre counter, a red mark on the side of Monroe's jaw. The taller man began to press his advantage and grabbed Vaughn around the throat, forcing him backward over the counter. Boxes hit the floor. Sheila tried to pull her husband off, but he flung her to the floor with one hand.

She got to her feet and stumbled toward the back door. "Frank!" she screamed.

Dot ran down the steps to the truck. "Help! A fight! Hal! He's goin' to kill him."

Hal sprinted past into the store, the woman on his heels.

"You're chokin' him." The young man threw himself on Monroe. "Stop it! Stop it! You'll kill him, for God's sakes." He struggled to break the man's grip.

Then a large hand grabbed Monroe easily by the shoulder, an arm encircling his neck. Slowly, Harper Mackenzie began to squeeze the man's throat and pull him back.

"Let him go, Garnet," he whispered. "Or I'll break your neck right here."

Sheila and Frank had come out of the office, Sheila standing behind him with Mila. When Monroe loosened his grip on Charlie, Hal grabbed his friend as he sank to the floor. Harper pulled Garnet all the way back and held him.

"Is he okay, lad?"

Hal looked up and nodded. "He will be. Thank you, Mr. Mackenzie."

"Well, Garnet," Mackenzie pointedly used the first name again, "are the fun and games over? Or do you have the belly for more?"

Unable to speak, Monroe shook his head. Harper let him go. The man rubbed his throat and without a glance at anyone, left the store.

"I think we'd better go, Sheila," said Mila quietly. She led the other woman to the door.

Sheila stopped and turned to them.

"You . . . you have to understand. My husband isn't himself these days. He's under so much pressure." She looked down at Vaughn, who rose to his feet. "They're losin' everything they've had for almost two hundred years. The house. The land. The creek. Everything. It's the end of the family."

Charlie started toward her, but she shook her head and went out the door. A minute later, a motor started nearby and pulled away.

Mackenzie's mouth made a grim line. "That won't come to any good," he said to himself and walked out to his truck.

For a full minute, no one spoke. Then Hal turned to Dot.

"You're right, Mrs. Baker," he said flatly. "Harper Mackenzie isn't the meanest man in the county." He looked at the closed door. "Garnet Monroe is."

"That fight blew up as suddenly as the storm that day," Dorothy recalled. She came back to us from half a century away, and stirred her cold coffee.

"I never saw Sheila Monroe again. Not many did. Rumour was that Garnet forbade her to go to Mille Roches without him after that. Carl and I moved in the summer of '56, one of the first homes in Long Sault. They pulled it up a ramp right through where the Long Sault Marina is now.

"It was hard at first. Gravel roads, boards for sidewalks, no grass on your front lawn. And not a tree in sight. Felt like an army had gone through, and I guess it did. Hydro was so organized . . . "

Dorothy looked out the front window. "We all had to cope. Some of us did better than others," she said as though to herself. "We had a neighbour here, Stan Ewing, who had moved from his family farm in Moulinette. No more farmin' after three generations. Got a job with the St. Lawrence Parks. Went fishin' by himself on Sundays. Seemed to be doin' fine." Her free hand silently crumpled the napkin it held. "Then one Sunday, my husband went out on the river and spotted him in his boat just sittin' there. Thought Stan was watchin' his lines. But when he got close, he could see that Stan didn't even have his fishin' poles out. He was just sittin' there, starin' into the water . . . right over where his farm used to be." Dorothy shook her head and turned a sad smile to us. "Some things just don't fit on a balance sheet, you see."

She looked at Paul. "I heard all the gossip about your mother, of course. And the newspaper covered the inquest. It never went to trial, which I'm sure you know. Not long after the charges were dropped, Sheila and Charlie Vaughn left the area. We always thought they left together. I guess they did."

"You mentioned theft," said Alison. "What was stolen?"

"That was another unanswered question," Dorothy replied. "A piece of family jewellery, a necklace, I think. Disappeared at the time of Garnet's death and was never recovered. It was quite valuable, I remember. Mila could tell you about that."

"Mila Pierce is still alive?" I asked. I was still furious at Paul for dropping that bomb the way he did, and had managed to ignore him for the entire conversation.

"Oh, yes," Sarah put in. "She's one of our residents at the Glen-Stor-Dun Lodge in Cornwall. In her nineties now, but still as sharp as a tack. If you want to see her, Sergeant Vaughn, I can speak to her about it for you. I think she'd be thrilled to find a long-lost relative."

"Thank you," said Paul, and he rose to his feet. "I appreciate the time you've given me, and I'm sorry for not speaking up right away. I never knew about this part of my parents' lives and it's still sinking in. I—I don't know how to talk about it sometimes, I guess. It's awkward to say the least."

We all stood up to say our goodbyes.

"Is Frank Clifford still around, too, Mrs. Baker?" I said at the door. "Maybe we should talk to him as well."

"Yes, you should. He's family, too, Sergeant Vaughn." Dorothy turned to Paul who stood behind me. "They were all first cousins, you see. Frank's family was comfortable because his father built a successful business. But none of the Pierce men were lucky. Farmers, most of them. After the Depression, Mila's people didn't have two pennies to rub together. She moved in with Sheila's family to help out after Sheila's mother died. It gave Mila a roof over her head and three meals a day. She became a mother hen to her younger cousin until Sheila's marriage to Garnet Monroe. Frank was more like a brother to them both when they were growin' up in Mille

Roches. None of the family left now, except Mila and Frank. And what's left of your mother's farm has the dike goin' through it. Bits and pieces only."

"Where would we find him, Mrs. Baker?" Paul asked.

"He's somewhere out near Newington, in an old farmhouse from his father's side of the family, I heard. Retired. Frank's parents kept a store in the Long Sault shoppin' centre for a number of years, but finally sold the business. Frank became a teacher. When you talk to Mila, ask her how to find Frank. She'll know."

"You're angry with me, aren't you?"

Paul looked me right in the eyes, and I gave him my best death glare. We were facing off beside my car in the parking lot at the end of Trillium Drive in Guindon Park just west of Cornwall. To our north was County Road 2 (formerly Highway 2). To our south was a vast stretch of water that had once been the thriving community of Mille Roches.

I had wanted to go home after all that, but Alison reminded me that Lynn was headed our way with a microphone. Paul wanted to see what was left of the old homestead, and Alison insisted we accompany him.

"Fan," she had whispered in Dorothy's driveway, linking her good arm through mine as we went to the car. "This whole thing sounds like what we would have given our right arms for in high school. A real mystery to solve. Besides," she turned back to look at Paul as he stood waiting by his car, "he wants our help. I'm sure this whole thing is very hard for him. You must remember what it felt like."

That was dirty pool and she knew it, but she was right. So we took the lead again by car and led Sergeant Vaughn to another stop in time, to another place that lived only in memory.

"I'm not happy with the fast one you pulled on us back there," I returned. "I took the time to find someone for you, and Mrs. Baker invited you into her home as a guest. You embarrassed us both, in case you're wondering. I think we deserved better than that from you."

"You're right," he said. "You did, and I apologized. I make no excuses except to say this isn't a situation where my social graces can help me out." He noted my silence and added dryly, "Tell me, Farran, did you handle your arrival here last year oozing sensitivity? Or did you just blunder in, willing to step on toes if it brought you closer to the truth?"

I had the grace to flush at that. Paul Vaughn seemed to have the knack of putting his finger on it with me, as though he could look into my soul and see all the secrets there. I found it disturbing to say the least and wondered if the connection between us would lead us anywhere. Then Strauss's face came into my mind, but I quickly shut it out.

"Fine." I said curtly, to hide my discomfort. "Let's forget it. I'll tell you what's here." I rubbed my forehead and looked around. "I took the Lost Villages bus tour last fall. Let's see what I remember."

The small parking lot was flanked by two boat ramps and a sign that read LAUNCH AREA ONLY. Miles across the water, the power dam caught the sun. The dike, made from over five million cubic yards of glacial till, bordered our view along the east. In the water of the little bay were huge rocks scattered in the shallows.

"Those rocks came from the quarries here that gave Mille Roches its name," I said. "They came here for stone during the project years, but everything was shut down after that. The village itself stretched from here almost to the dam site, where the old No. 2 Highway followed the original shoreline. The northernmost sidewalk from Mille Roches is about fifty yards that way under the water."

We all looked out at the river for a minute.

"Then," said Paul quietly, "everything is under water. There's nothing left of where my mother grew up."

"According to Dorothy Baker, there is still part of the farm near the dike. We need to take the road around its base. You drive," I added to Paul. "I'll navigate."

The three of us got into Paul's car and headed north up to the main parking lot. I directed him east back onto Trillium Drive, and we skirted the dike on the gravel road. When we approached a small picnic area on our left, I told Paul to slow down.

"Dorothy told us that the Pierce farm was not far off the old Cornwall Centre Road," I said. "That means it's somewhere around here. You see that white farmhouse on the hill over there?" I pointed to a house on the north side of County Road 2. "That's the only house from Mille Roches still in its original place. A short piece of the old Cornwall Centre Road runs beside it. It used to come straight across the field, through this driveway, and right through where the dike stands now on its way into the heart of Mille Roches." In the bush to our right, all that was left of the road was what looked like a trail cutting across to the dike.

We rolled forward slowly while I looked in both directions. "Damn this bush," I muttered. "It's hard to see with all the leaves. Too bad it wasn't spring." Then suddenly I held up my hand.

"Hold it," I ordered, and Paul hit the brakes.

"I don't see anything," said Alison.

"You have to know what to look for," I explained. "Gaps where the bush hasn't grown could mean a sidewalk or part of a road, like with the old Cornwall Centre Road. Depressions in the ground could be sunken foundations. Or that." I pointed past Paul to the trees on the far side of the road.

"What?" he asked, bewildered. "Trees? What does that mean?"

"Not just trees, Paul. Trees growing in a straight line. Trees don't naturally grow in a straight row. They have to be planted that way. This used to be someone's property, maybe the Pierce farm."

Paul and I got out, Alison staying to rest in the car. We walked into the bush to the row of trees, and sure enough, there was a decaying old farm fence running alongside it. Half buried in the ground nearby were the rusted remains of a plow halter. But other than that, there was nothing.

Nothing but the growing wind in the trees. And then a soft whisper curling around the dancing leaves . . .

. . . you have to understand . . . they're losin' everything they've had for almost two hundred years . . .

I suddenly felt as though we were the only people left alive on the planet.

"C'mon, Paul. There's nothing more to see here." I shivered. "Let's go."

He didn't seem to hear me. With a violent tug, Paul pulled the old harness out of the ground, and it broke in pieces from the force. Angrily, he threw it down again. Then he took hold of one of the old fence posts that leaned crazily and pushed it upright. Of course, the minute he let go, the old fence sagged back into its former shape. Paul just stood there for a moment looking, saying nothing.

I, too, said nothing. I saw and recognized the rage and frustration that was building in him.

Finally, he turned to me.

"There's got to be more than this, Farran. There's got to be. It can't be all gone."

I opened my mouth to reply, but he suddenly headed out of the trees to the road. I thought he was going to the car, but instead passed it and picked up speed. I followed. When I realized what was on his mind, I started to run.

"Wait! Paul! You can't go up there. That's a restricted area. It's dangerous."

He ignored me, striding through the twenty feet of bush that separated him from the looming bulk of the dike. Barely slowing down, he jumped over the barrier with the threatening KEEP OUT sign and started the climb to the top. Not sure what he'd do, I had no choice but to follow. I cursed my allergy to exercise as I fought gravity all the way up.

Paul was standing very still when I joined him. The wind came full force across the headpond, giving us very bad hair and making conversation basically impossible. But it was the view that really took my breath away. Miles of water, a few islands, tree-lined shores. And totally deserted. If it weren't for the dam apparatus sticking out downriver, the whole scene would have been almost primeval.

For some minutes, we stood taking it all in. Then I wondered if we were on surveillance camera and the Ontario Power Generation police were headed our way with handcuffs.

"We have to go," I tried to say, but the wind tore the words from my mouth. Finally, I put my hand in his. At that, he turned to face me and I could see the fire in his eyes was gone. With little protest, Paul Vaughn let me lead him away from the edge and back down into the land of the living.

"I'm sorry. I didn't know you had company."

Strauss stood in the doorway of my kitchen, large brown envelope in one hand, wine bottle in the other. I was having a rare domestic moment around the stove making supper, Alison and Paul at the table. After the way the afternoon turned out, I took pity on Vaughn and invited him for dinner. Although in view of my culinary skills, maybe the nicer gesture would have been to let him escape to a restaurant.

It wasn't like Strauss to walk in, so something was up. I also knew damn well he hadn't missed the second car in the driveway. Probably was having the license plates run through the system as we spoke.

"Not really company, Jerry." I did the introductions. "You know Alison from the funeral service. This," I turned to Paul who rose, "is Sergeant Paul Vaughn from the St. John's Police Service. Paul, this is Inspector Jerry Strauss from our local OPP."

At the mention of Jerry's name, Paul momentarily froze. I swear he almost put his hand down. Then he gave a half smile and shook Jerry's hand.

"Fellow officer," he said. "Good to meet you."

"Are you here officially, Sergeant Vaughn?" Strauss asked as Paul resumed his seat.

"No. On holidays and looking up some family history." Paul studied his coffee mug.

"Actually, Jerry, Paul's father was a friend of my dad," I explained. "And you met him when you were a boy. Charlie Vaughn, engineer with Hydro. He boarded at the Cliffords' in Mille Roches while he was here."

"Charlie Vaughn." Strauss looked at Paul. "Yes, I remember him. He took me for a tour of the dam site in Maple Grove with Hal one afternoon. Really patient with all my questions. And I had hundreds." Strauss smiled at the memory. "Your father was a good guy, Paul. I liked him."

The compliment seemed to anger Paul, though for the life of me I couldn't see why.

"Yes, you sure did," he replied grimly. After a moment, he looked up at Strauss. "Did you meet up with him around the time of Garnet Monroe's death or the inquest?"

Strauss shook his head. "No. I only went there with Hal, and he left in the fall of '56. Garnet Monroe died in the spring of the following year. I did read the papers at the time, though, when my mother would let me. It was all pretty sensational, but I never believed Charlie could have been involved with anything like that."

"Who do you think did it?" Paul asked bluntly.

I pulled out a chair for Strauss, but he shook his head. "I've never really thought about it over the years, but as a cop I'd put my money on Sheila Monroe. I didn't know her except by sight, but she had the best motive—to be free of her husband."

"Sheila Monroe was my mother." Paul turned back to his coffee. Alison and I watched the two of them like spectators at a tennis match. For brothers in arms, the first meeting was not going well at all.

"Can you stay for supper?" I asked Jerry brightly. "It's not much but I made lots. Besides, you brought wine."

"I also brought this." Strauss laid the envelope on the table. "I said I'd ask around, and I dug up the police report." He looked at Alison. "That's why I brought the wine." He set it on the table beside the report.

Alison didn't touch the envelope. "Is it bad?" she said softly.

"Always is. Even when it's cut and dried like this one. No surprises. But," Strauss added unexpectedly, "I know what it's like to read a police report on the death of a loved one. Have a drink before you do."

"I think we *all* need a drink," I said firmly, moving for the wine.

"I'm sorry," Paul turned to Alison. "I didn't realize you'd had a recent loss."

"It wasn't recent, although it feels like yesterday," she replied. I set a large wineglass in front of her, filled to the brim. "My father was a police officer. He was killed in the line of duty thirty years ago, and the case is being dragged open again."

"Why, in heaven's name?"

I spared Alison the job of going over it all again, and brought Paul up to speed as I armed everybody with wine. Can't say my dinner parties are boring.

"So I brought her here until things cool down or they get a handle on what's going on," I finished. "You can't tell anyone who Alison is or where she's staying."

"Could the notes be true?" Paul asked. "Usually, where there's smoke there's fire." Something in his words bothered my stomach. Something, my voice said, I needed to remember.

Strauss tapped the report. "If it is, we're left with Dave Carlson. He's the only officer who physically could have shot John Perry."

"Not necessarily." Paul challenged Jerry with a look. "There could have been a fifth person, another officer there unofficially."

"What do you mean?" Alison asked.

As I got up to serve the meal, I saw a dark look pass over Jerry's face.

"Something Farran remembered your father saying about never catching Denny or the others red-handed," replied Paul, leaning back and crossing his arms. "He said, 'it's as though they know we're coming.' What if they did?"

"How?" Alison didn't seem to know what was coming, even though my intestines did. Thinking food would help, I started to dish up the plates.

"An inside connection. Someone paid to leak information to the gang to help them stay one step ahead of the police."

"He means a dirty cop." Strauss got up and walked over to look out at the river.

"A Waterloo Regional officer?" Alison sounded incredulous. I studiously finished the plates with my back to her. "That's not possible. I won't believe it. That's why I don't understand the point to these letters."

"It happens," said Paul firmly. "Doesn't it, Strauss?"

"There is no record of bullets or expended cartridges unaccounted for at the scene," Jerry replied without turning around. "Read the report yourself."

"They could have been cleaned up by someone who knew how to do it," Paul volleyed back. "And Farran said that John Perry went into the garage with three bullets missing from his gun. Maybe that was the point. You're being awfully quiet, Farran," Paul added. He turned to look at me, but I avoided his eye. "Do you think it's possible? It would explain a lot."

"You do," Alison broke in. "You as much as told me that the night we left the hospital. I said I was safe under police custody, and you disagreed."

131

"I think we need to eat, put something other than booze in our stomachs." I slammed the plates down to make my point. "Supper is served."

But Paul was like a bloodhound on the scent.

"Denny and his people are well organized," he continued. "They move into the Cambridge area. New city, and the pickings look good. But also a new and larger police force with better resources. To give them an edge, they find an officer who likes the finer things in life. Maybe fast cars and big houses. Who knows. But they buy him. And successfully slip through the fingers of the police as they put the squeeze on the Cambridge business community."

After a glare from me, Jerry took his chair. Paul rattled on, with Alison's full attention. I played with my mashed potatoes, my appetite gone.

"But then the Simser boy is killed and everything changes. The heat is on, and every officer on the force is out for blood. Being an informant is suddenly accessory to murder." Paul cut into his meatloaf with zeal. "So we are left with only two possibilities."

Alison hadn't touched her food. "Which are?"

"Either John Perry found out who the dirty cop was and was killed to keep him silent, or . . . " Something suddenly registered in Paul's face and he faltered to a stop. I looked at Jerry. Jerry looked at Paul.

"Or?" he prompted dryly.

Paul didn't look up.

Strauss laced his fingers together and leaned toward him over his plate. "Well, Vaughn," he said quietly. "You started this. I think you're the one who should finish it."

Finally Paul raised his eyes to meet Jerry's.

"Or," he said slowly, "John Perry *was* the dirty cop and Denny wouldn't let him walk away alive."

Chapter NINE: Maple Grove

"Mila, your special visitors are here."

The woman in the room seemed incredibly old. She sat upright in her bed, satin bed-jacket ribbons neatly tied. Her thinning hair had been brushed and smoothly pulled back with a matching hair band. One hand nervously stroked the long black curls of a beautiful china doll tucked under the covers beside her.

Sarah led the way into the room and showed us two chairs. Then she settled Mila in her bed, introducing us as she did.

"Mila, this is Dr. Farran Mackenzie and her friend, Sergeant Paul Vaughn. These are the people I told you about that want to meet you."

At that, Mila Pierce turned to look us over, with eyes that were clear and bright. Sharp as a tack, Sarah had told us. She was right.

"Thank you for comin' to see me, Dr. Mackenzie, but I already have a doctor." The voice was as strong as the eyes.

"I'm not a medical doctor," I smiled. "I'm a professor of history. My family comes from the Lost Villages. Maybe you remember my grandfather, Harper Mackenzie. He was a trader from Farran's Point."

"Harper Mackenzie." The eyes seemed to look right through me. "Yes, of course. He wasn't a man you were likely to forget." She looked at Paul. "Is this your husband?"

I blushed a little—God knows why. "No. No, this is a friend. His family comes from the villages, too."

"Did I know them?" she asked Vaughn.

Paul looked at me, then at Sarah. He seemed unsure how to broach the topic, so he dove right in.

"Yes. Actually, Miss Pierce, we're related. You see, Sheila Vau— Sheila Pierce was my mother. I understand she was your cousin."

Mila frowned. "But that isn't p—" She sat back and gave him a hard look. "You said 'was.' Is Shelia still alive?"

"No," he answered softly. "She died late last year. Along with my father, Charles Vaughn."

At that, Mila leaned forward. "So you're *his* son. And Sheila is dead." She fingered her blanket absently. "I've been wonderin' lately about her. If she were still alive. I guess I have my answer."

Silence filled the room, and I looked around. Clean, sunny. Some pictures on the wall, all painted by Mila. No photographs, oddly enough. The few pieces of furniture were new. The only remnants of the past were some toilet articles and a jewellery box on her dresser, along with a Victorian rose-glass lamp that had seen better days. I watched its last two dingle-dangles sway in the breeze from the open window, throwing pink, yellow and blue rainbows across the wall.

"My mother didn't say much about her life here, Miss Pierce," said Paul finally. "I guess I'm hoping you can help me fill in some of the blanks."

"So you're Sheila's son." Mila gave Paul a half smile. "I guess that does make us family. I always thought of her as my daughter, in a way. I helped raise her, you see. Her mother died when she was about ten and I came to live on the farm to help out. She'd grown up wild out there, but I turned her into a young lady. Even found her a husband."

"Garnet Monroe?" I tuned back in. "We've talked to Dorothy Baker. I had the sense there was quite an age difference between Sheila and her husband."

"Fifteen years," said Mila proudly. "She married money and a good name. Her father died peacefully, thankin' me for taking good care of his little girl."

"Was the marriage a happy one?" I asked. With no family connection, I didn't have to pussyfoot around.

Mila unconsciously shot a look at Sarah, who murmured something about getting back to work. "And not too much excitement, Mila." The warning was for all of us. "Remember your heart." Then Sarah left us to fend for ourselves.

"The marriage was happy until Charlie Vaughn came along," the old woman said tartly when the door had closed. "And I don't apologize for that remark, young man. Sheila damn near got hung for murder because of him."

I felt Paul stiffen in his chair and laid a warning hand on his arm.

"Was Garnet a violent man, Miss Pierce?"

"Violent?" Mila seemed a little taken aback. "Violent, no. He had a temper. And he was used to havin' things his own way. But Sheila always seemed to be able to handle him. Why?"

"The Seaway Project was especially hard on the Monroes, wasn't it?" I came in from another direction. "Living in Maple Grove, they lost the land that had been in the family for generations. And the house, I believe. Sheila herself called it the end of the family. That must have put Garnet under quite a strain."

"The Seaway was hard for everyone livin' in Maple Grove," she replied grimly. "Construction started there first. Day and night. Diggin' and tunnellin' and hammerin'. Trucks all the time. I truly felt sorry for the people livin' there. Maple Grove had been such a quiet little place.

"But I think the worst was when they started movin' the cemetery. I lived in Mille Roches, and for weeks the hearses went by. Every day. Sometimes twice a day." She shook her head slowly. "The church put its foot down and said no machinery. All done by shovels. Still, it went against God, you know. Something like that should never be done. I think it was the cemetery that was just too much for old Mrs. Monroe. She started to go downhill after that."

MAPLE GROVE CEMETERY MOVED TO NEW LOCATION

One of the most difficult tasks attempted by Ontario Hydro in its huge rehabilitation project was completed this week when the last of 317 graves and remains from Maple Grove cemetery were moved to a new location beside relocated Highway No. 2, about three miles west of Cornwall.

In a job requiring the utmost in dignity with a minimum of publicity, the remains were moved to the new site over a period of almost two months from the old Trinity Anglican Church cemetery at Maple Grove, which will soon be excavated for the diversion of the Cornwall canal, to the new site.

The Maple Grove cemetery, established as a private cemetery around 1790, is one of the oldest in the district. Unlike other cemeteries which have to be relocated in connection with the power development, its site will be excavated rather than flooded. This factor made necessary the actual moving of remains, rather than just headstones.

August 24, 1956
The Cornwall *Standard Freeholder*

"I never thought I'd have to bury your father twice, Garnet. Once was enough."

Mrs. Monroe wiped tears from her eyes with a shaking hand. Her son sat beside her on the davenport, in the front room of the old house on the hill.

"Sheila, get Mother some tea," he said to his wife. "Put something strong in it."

"I'll do it, Sheila." Mila rose from the chair in the corner. "I daresay you need something strong, too. It's been a hell of a day."

"No, let me." Sheila waved Mila back to her seat. "I need something to do."

"Mother," Monroe turned back to his mother, "at least it's over now and Father is safely at peace in the new cemetery. The water won't cover him like some, and they can't move him again. We can still be near him."

"I was near him in this house," she returned. "Soon the house will be gone. They'll fill in the creek. The land won't look the same. All the families will be gone." She wiped her eyes again. "I don't like this new world. No values. No respect for history and tradition. I don't belong here anymore." Her voice rose an octave. "Strangers everywhere. I don't feel safe. Things missing in the house. I know people have been here when I'm gone, going through my things. I never thought I'd say this, but I want a lock on my front door. Today," she added, facing her son. "Today, Garnet. Or I won't sleep tonight."

"Here, Mrs. Monroe," Mila came over with a small glass. "Have a little sherry. It will help you feel better."

Sheila came out with the tea tray set for four. When the kettle whistled in the kitchen, she went back to make the tea. Mila poured a brandy for Garnet and one for herself.

"Sheila, brandy or sherry?" Mila asked when her cousin came out with the teapot.

"Sherry, please." Sheila poured tea for all, handing a cup to Mrs. Monroe. Then Garnet took his wife by the arm and pulled her to one side.

"Are more things missing, Sheila?" he said in low tones.

"I'm not sure, Garnet," she replied. "Maybe a few pieces of the silverware."

"Maybe?" he snapped. "It's either here or not."

Sheila pulled her arm out of his grip. "Garnet, your mother is hidin' things. I've found jewellery under her mattress when I've changed the linen. God knows what she's squirrelled away in this house. She knows hidin' places we'll never know."

"It's true, Garnet." Mila came over quietly. "I found a small silver pitcher under the garden bench where your mother sits on good days. I put it back in the cabinet and told Sheila when we were alone."

"In the garden?" Monroe's face grew dark. "It's that girl you hired. She's stealing and hiding things to take later when no one is watching."

"Jill would never do that," Sheila protested. "They're our neighbours."

"Then maybe Mother is right," he shot back. "Maybe there are people in the house when she's gone. Are you having visitors I don't know about?"

With a stony look, Sheila turned her back on her husband and went over to sit with her mother-in-law.

"Mila, I insist you move in here for the time left," whispered Monroe. "I don't like the two of them being alone in this house all day. I need someone to keep an eye on . . . Mother."

Mila opened her mouth to reply, then closed it.

"Garnet," the old lady called tremulously. "I want to lie down. Please take me to my room."

"Mother, the land agent is coming back tomorrow." He crossed over to her, avoiding Sheila's eyes. "We need to talk about where we'll be in the fall. Do we move to Cornwall or buy a lot in Long Sault?"

Mrs. Monroe rose and swept past him to the front window, to look down the hill toward the carriage house and the creek. Across the creek were the walls of sandbags that kept the cemetery disinterment from public view. And beyond all that, in a whirlwind of trucks and construction, a lone canal boat slipped by through Lock 20 of the Cornwall canal as it always had.

"You decide, Garnet," she said to her son. "I don't care anymore. As far as I'm concerned, you can take me from this house straight to the new cemetery to be with your father."

CONSTRUCTION SERVICES FOR LONG SAULT VILLAGE

First building to be erected on Island 17, off the new community of Long Sault in the post-flooding period, is a small, buff-coloured brick structure which will house the permanent pumping station for the village.

The pumping station will have a capacity of 200 gallons per minutes for the village when it is put into operation.

Meanwhile, Hydro workmen are at work on the concrete piers for the six legs of the water tower. The tower will be 125 feet high and will have a capacity of 208,000 gallons. It will be erected by Horton Steel Company of Toronto and is expected to be in operation by the end of the year.

October 20, 1956
The Cornwall *Standard Freeholder*

"Ashes to ashes. Dust to dust."

A cold autumn wind tore through the little cemetery, huddling the tiny group of mourners together for protection. Christ Anglican Church in Moulinette had been full that morning, but only family was invited to the graveside ceremony in the new Maple Grove cemetery.

Garnet Monroe stood alone near his mother's coffin. Sheila remained at a small distance, flanked by Mila Pierce and Frank Clifford. Frank quietly held Sheila's hand, head down. Mila looked at her cousin's face but found no clue to her thoughts. Hearing a murmur of voices over the reverend's words, she turned to see another burial in the far corner.

"It's the Strauss family from Aultsville." At Sheila's words, Mila turned back to see her cousin looking in the same direction. "Losin' Bill in the lumberyard fire. Such a tragedy."

"And in God, we find strength." The reverend closed the Bible and led the group in prayer.

Then Sheila laid a hand on her husband's arm. "Let's go home, Garnet."

"Have Frank drive you home," came the curt reply. "I'll be there later."

137

She waited a moment, then dropped her hand to her side. Frank and Mila joined her as she made her way to the car. As they passed the other service, Mila whispered, "I'm surprised he has the nerve to show his face at the burial."

"Who?" asked Frank.

"The Leonard boy, of course." Mila shot a look at Hal, standing beside his father and brother, hat off, head down. Next to him, she noted, was Charlie Vaughn.

"Don't be ridiculous, Mila." Frank glared at the woman. "He's known Bill Strauss his whole life. Bill ran their lumberyard. Why shouldn't he be there?"

"Talk's bad, Frank." She muttered. "I know you're friends and all, but everyone knows he's been makin' time with Mrs. Strauss. Police have been askin' about it for the inquest—"

Sheila veered off and strode over to the service that was breaking up. She leaned down to speak to a boy who stood frozen at the side of the grave.

"Jerry," she said softly. "I'm so sorry about your father." He made no response. When the blonde woman beside him turned, Sheila extended her hand. "Mrs. Strauss, I'm Sheila Monroe. My deepest sympathies on the loss of your husband." She looked down at the boy between them. "If there is anything I can do for you or your son . . ."

Emme Strauss put her arm around Jerry. "Thank you, Mrs. Monroe. We appreciate your concern. Come, Jerry."

They went to a car waiting on the gravel drive. Mila came up as Charlie Vaughn approached from the other side.

"He's a good kid." Charlie watched Jerry leave. "He doesn't deserve this." He turned to Sheila. "I'm sorry about your mother-in-law, Sheila. Hard times for everyone these days. Can I help in any way?"

"No," she sighed. "There isn't anything anyone can do for me . . . for us."

"Have you sold the house yet?"

Sheila smiled wanly. "No one wants it, Charlie. It's too old to move to a lot. Hydro wants the rest of the property. They've already built their hospital on the west end. I guess the house will go for salvage." Sheila shook her head. "I'm glad Mother Monroe didn't live to see that. It would break her heart."

"Have you thought of offering it to the pioneer village they're building in the new park?" Charlie glanced over his shoulder at the figure of Garnet Monroe in the distance. "Don't say it was my idea or your husband will never back it. But why don't you talk to the museum people? I heard part of your house was built in the 1790s. Maybe they could add it to the village."

"And have strangers walkin' through it every day?" Mila sniffed. "Mrs. Monroe would roll in her grave."

"It's better than tearin' it down, Mila." Sheila gave Charlie a real smile and her hand. "Thank you, Charlie. We'll look into it."

"My pleasure, ma'am." He put his hat back on and whispered, "It's nice to see you smile again, Sheila. Miss Pierce," he added to Mila and followed the Leonards to a waiting car, giving Frank a passing wave.

"Bold," muttered Mila.

Sheila flushed a light pink and turned away. Then she called out to Charlie, "Oh, Mr. Vaughn! Did you ever sort things out with your young lady?"

Charlie turned and looked at her a moment. "No," he said slowly, "I haven't had the nerve to, yet. But," and a grin took over his face, "I won't say I've given up on the idea."

"That Vaughn was as bold as brass from the beginnin'." Mila looked at Paul. "He had good looks, like you only different. And charm, I guess. Sheila thought so, but I never saw it. Still, she was a married woman, for better or worse, and he should have stayed away."

"How could he have spent any time with my mother when she was cloistered in that house with you?" Paul shot back. I gave him a warning look, but instead of shutting the old lady down, his antagonism seemed to wind her up.

"I never moved into Monroe House," Mila claimed. "Never wanted to get between a man and his wife. Their troubles belonged to them. Often wondered after if I had, maybe things wouldn't have gone the way they did."

SAY AGREEMENT REACHED FOR RELOCATING COTTAGES

Official sources here disclosed to the Standard Freeholder today that agreement has been reached between the cottagers on Sheek Island, Ontario Hydro and the Department of Transportation on rehabilitation.

Cottagers whose cottages cannot be moved will be compensated for their loss. Already a team of Hydro and Department of Transport assessors have looked over some 17 cottages.

Those cottages which it would pay to move will be taken this winter across the frozen river to Island No. 17 near the newly proposed parkway. This island has been set aside for Sheek Island cottagers' use.

December 8, 1956
The Cornwall *Standard Freeholder*

"If we have to tear this house apart, we will." Garnet Monroe stormed out of the sitting room and slammed the front door behind him.

Sheila stood absolutely still at the window for several minutes. Then she turned to the woman sitting on the davenport.

"Don't let him upset you, Mila," she sighed. "He's been like this since we couldn't find Mother's jade ring to bury her with. Thank God the necklace is safe. I let Jill go last week, more to protect her than anything else. I didn't really know what else to do."

Mila refilled each of their cups with tea. "Why don't I come by some day next week, and we'll give the house a real once-over. Decorate for Christmas at the same time."

"That's very kind, Mila. The house is going to the pioneer village next summer. Let's hope we find everything before then.

"But we'll leave the decorating for now." Sheila slowly stirred her tea. "I don't think there's going to be a Christmas in this house this year. First time in over 150 years." She looked around at the opulent room, with its Victorian furniture and heavy velvet drapes shrouding the light from the windows. "There's nothing left here. It's over."

"What's over?"

Sheila didn't reply.

"Come on," said Mila with a forced cheerfulness. "Let's Christmas shop." She reached for the Eaton's catalogue and flipped it open to a page filled with china dolls. "I can't believe they still make these things. Remember the one we used to go and look at in the window at Simpson's when you were a girl? I think I wanted her more than you did." She looked up from the book to where her cousin stood, staring into space.

"What about you, Sheila?" Mila persisted. "What would you like for Christmas?"

Sheila Monroe came back from somewhere far away. "What do I want?" she said to the darkened room. "Happiness . . . "

SHEEK ISLAND POWERHOUSE DISAPPEARING

Another Seaway Valley landmark is fast disappearing in the relentless march of the power project.

The Sheek Island generating station of the St. Lawrence Power Company is being dismantled and sold for scrap. The 56-year-old generating plant served Cornwall canal and surrounding area for more than 50 years and was shut down in 1954 when Hydro started to build the St. Lawrence Power project.

The plant was originally built to supply power to the canal system, which always was one of its most important customers. The editor of the old Cornwall Freeholder went into rhapsodies over the lights along the canal bank the first night they were turned on in 1901.

RAPIDS DISAPPEARING

Rocks and pebble beach are fast appearing as the cofferdam across the Long Sault Rapids reduces them to a shadow of their former power. A lot of the roar has gone out of the famous shipping barrier and the waves no longer leap 10 feet in the air.

In less than a month, the mighty surge of the Long Sault will be no more. Water is being diverted through a cut in Long Sault Island to the south channel. The rapids will be pumped dry to finish construction of the Long Sault control dam.

March 22, 1957
The Cornwall *Standard Freeholder*

"Mila! What are you doin' here?"

Sheila looked up at her cousin from where she knelt before the body of Garnet Monroe, sprawled at the bottom of the hall staircase. His eyes were open, his head crooked at an odd angle. He was very dead.

Mila stood frozen on the front threshold, a large plastic pitcher in one hand. The other covered her mouth in horror.

"S—Soap," she finally managed. "I'm tight this week, and I need soap flakes . . . My God, Sheila. What have you done?"

"He's dead, Mila," she said faintly. "What will I do?"

Mila slammed the front door shut on the early spring day and looked out the window.

"I got a ride from Frank. He's doin' deliveries. I don't think he saw anything."

"Frank." Sheila got to her feet. "Get Frank. He'll know what to do."

Mila grabbed her before she opened the front door.

"No. No. We have to think. We have to sit down and think what we'll do. Sheila," Mila looked hard at her cousin. "Did you push him down the stairs?"

"No!" Sheila looked horrified. "No! How could you ask me that? He was here when I got home."

"Where were you just now? Can anyone say they saw you?"

Sheila grew stone-faced. "No. I was alone. I went for a walk along the creek. No one saw me."

"God help us." Mila took her by the arm and dragged her along into the kitchen. "Sit down," she ordered, pushing the boxes of food off the table. "I'm goin' to get each of us a stiff drink. Then we'll think what we'll do about this."

Sheila sat as though in a dream. "We have to get the police."

"We will when we're good and ready." Mila returned with two sherry glasses full to the rim. "Drink it."

Sheila lifted the glass to her lips with a shaking hand. "He's dead." She swallowed it at one draught. "Garnet's dead, Mila. I'm all alone now."

"You still have me. I've always taken care of you, and I will now. We have to make this look like a robbery, or the police will think you did it."

"A robbery?" Sheila echoed. "Why can't we just tell the truth? Garnet must have slipped and fallen."

"On stairs he used his whole life?" The older woman shook her head firmly. "No. People will say you pushed him. They've seen how hard he's been on you lately."

"No, we have to take some things and mess up the house a little, especially upstairs. Make it look as though Garnet walked in on it, and they knocked him down the stairs. Accidentally killed him." Mila threw her own drink back in one swallow.

"I know you mean well, Mila, but we have to tell the truth. If I lie, it will only make things worse. I have nothing to hide," Sheila added. "The truth will protect me."

"Don't be a fool. I'll fill my pitcher with soap. We'll say that I met you comin' back from your walk, and we went in the kitchen door. When I was leavin', we found him together in the front hall."

Mila went upstairs. When she returned a few minutes later, Sheila was still at the kitchen table.

"Someone was here, Sheila," said Mila flatly. "Drawers are open. Mrs. Monroe's jewellery box is gone from the bottom of her wardrobe."

For a moment, Sheila said nothing.

"My God," she whispered finally. "The necklace."

"I tried to help her," Mila said. "I said that we'd found him together, but the police were so hard, so frightening . . . I—I couldn't lie in the end. I broke down and told them the truth when they questioned me. Turned out Sheila had anyway. They turned on her then. Charged her with murderin' her own husband. That woman couldn't have hurt a fly."

"Of course she didn't." Paul got up impatiently and went to the window.

"That's why I know it was Charlie Vaughn," said the woman stubbornly. "Sheila could never do that."

Paul turned to return fire so I cut him off.

"Miss Pierce, were the stolen items ever recovered?" I leaned forward. "Mrs. Baker said one piece was never found."

"They found the jewellery box not far from the road. Someone threw it into the creek, and the spring waters carried it downstream." Mila paused for a moment. "The box was empty so they dragged the creek and found some of Mrs. Monroe's things. But only the little stuff. They never found the necklace."

"So Garnet Monroe was killed for a piece of family jewellery." Paul crossed his arms. "Why would my father bother with something like that?"

"I take it the necklace was quite valuable," I said, still trying to keep the conversation on track.

"It was to the Monroe family," Mila smoothed the comforter on her bed. "Came with them after the War of Independence. They were Loyalists, of course."

"Sounds like an interesting story, Miss Pierce," I said sincerely. My professional instincts were kicking in.

"Oh, it is, I guess." At my eyeball signal, Paul came back to sit, and Mila warmed to her audience. She probably didn't have one very often. "Starts back in the days of the American colonies. The Blake family of Boston. Well-heeled. Father was a successful merchant and his father before him. Owned a large diamond the old man had brought home from the East on one of his trips. The legend goes that it was the eye of an Indian god, cursed and everything."

The breeze in the room suddenly turned cool, and I shivered. Paul gave me a look that I ignored.

"The Blakes have a daughter, Amelia. The apple of Daddy's eye. So for her social debut, Daddy gets the stone set, and she wears it in public for the first time. Quite the talk of the town, I believe."

"Amelia has her debut in the spring of 1775." Mila looked at me. "If you remember your history, Professor Mackenzie, things were warmin' up with the American Revolution." I nodded and she continued. "Right after Ameila's debut, the British reinforcements walk into Boston, along with one Lieutenant Robert Monroe. Tall and handsome, they say. He meets Amelia Blake and it's love at first sight.

"Not that the parents are happy, of course. They're Patriots and want independence. They try to keep the lovers apart, but as usual it makes it worse. It really gets sticky during George Washington's Seige of Boston that summer, but Amelia won't give up on her English soldier.

"Finally, the followin' spring, British troops evacuate Boston. It's turned nasty. Loyalist families are bein' driven from their homes by their own neighbours, attacked by mobs, tarred and feathered. Amelia runs away to marry Robert Monroe and leave with him. She takes only what she can carry—includin' the necklace. The Monroes go north to New York with other United Empire Loyalists and Robert joins the new King's Royal Regiment of New York to help fight the Patriot forces.

"When it's all over, members of the regiment get land over here to replace what they lost across the river. It's drawn by lots, and lieutenants get 500 acres. Robert and Amelia Monroe settle down in

143

Maple Grove in 1784, and build the first part of what became Monroe House on the creek."

"And the necklace?" I admit I was on the edge of my seat.

"Oh, it stayed in the family, even through some very lean times." Mila shook her head. "But after the Second World War, the Monroes were well off again. Maybe that's why they brought it out of hidin' then. The necklace was only a local story, folklore you see, until Sheila's wedding day. Mrs. Monroe had her wear it with her weddin' dress. Even the newspaper wrote it all up."

Mila suddenly went silent, and I wondered if she were tired. I remembered what Sarah had said about her heart.

"We've been here long enough for one day, Miss Pierce." I rose from my chair and Paul followed suit. "We don't want to tire you out."

"Yes," she sighed. "I do tire easily. My heart, you know. Without my pills, I'd be dead. Like all the rest of them. Everyone's dead except me." She looked at Paul. "Even my Sheila." She held out the doll. "Sheila bought me this the last Christmas we had together. Because we were too poor as children to afford one."

Surprisingly, Paul put his hand on hers.

"May I come to visit again, Miss Pierce?" he asked.

"If you're Sheila's boy," she smiled, "you'd best call me Mila."

I helped her lie down and said I would send Sarah in before we left. As we turned to go, something in her words struck me.

"Mila?"

She turned to face me, bright eyes encased in a fading body.

"You said the Monroes brought the necklace 'out of hiding' after World War II. Why did they hide the necklace? In case of theft?"

"Oh, I'm sure that was part of it," she said slowly. Her eyes began to close. "But it was the history of the necklace. The Monroes weren't too proud of that. This was Loyalist territory, after all. Still is." She pulled the sheet up to her chin and closed her eyes.

"Because of the story of the Indian god's eye? Because the diamond might have been stolen?" By this time, it was Paul who was keeping me in line, gently pulling me toward the door. But for some reason, I couldn't let it go.

"No." Her eyes snapped open for a second with the impatience the old so often feel with the young. "Not the diamond—the settin', girl. It was the settin' that was the problem."

Mila turned over in her bed, putting her back to us. But she must have seen the incomprehension in my eyes as she did so. "It was silver filigree," she said over her shoulder. "Very fine handiwork, done by a good friend of the Blakes. A Boston silversmith named Paul Revere."

Chapter TEN: The House of Death

Like me, the river woke up angry the next morning.
With the St. Lawrence, it was fairly simple: Overnight, the wind had shifted around to come now from the east, bringing warmth and damp through my window before dawn. With first light, I saw clouds scudding across the rim of the trees, breakers on my shoreline and whitecaps as far as the eye could see.
The knee I had abused to the point of reconstructive surgery last summer was starting to make its presence known—throbbing and aching as it always did now before a turn for the worse in the weather. Rain was in the air, possibly a storm.
But the clouds over my brooding head were not as easy to fathom.
It wasn't as though I didn't have a few options to choose from. After Paul dropped the bomb at my dinner table the other night, the social chatter died. By dessert it was obvious that Jerry wasn't speaking to Paul, Paul wasn't speaking to Jerry, Alison wasn't speaking to either Paul or me, and I wasn't speaking to all of the above.
I was also entertaining more than a little guilt toward Ruth Hoffman, whom I had not visited since the funeral in lieu of a stranger's personal quest and the needs of a dear friend who now was also a stranger to me.
Then a bit of leftover guilt was allotted for Alison. I didn't seem to be able to help my old friend sort things out or find out the truth. Aside from keeping her safe from gangsters, politicians and the media (temporarily), I had done nothing to help. In fact, she was worse off now emotionally since the dinner—and for once it wasn't my cooking.
And the icing on the cake was the possible existence of an original Paul Revere piece—an historical artifact that, if still in existence and I could track it down, would be the find of my career.
"You're not really buying that story, are you?" Paul almost had to scrape me off the ceiling of his car on the way back from the Glen-Stor-Dun Lodge. "You said you were a history professor. Mila is lonely and bored. She's giving you the 'full meal deal' on that one. Besides," he added as I went to protest, "I'm no history major, but didn't Revere do dishes and silverware, not jewellery?"
"Yes, as far as we know," I admitted, "but it's still more than possible. Most of the families that built the Lost Villages came here

as United Empire Loyalists after the American Revolution. God knows what they could have brought with them."

"Well, don't get too geared up," he smiled. "Even if the story is true, the necklace vanished almost fifty years ago. It's long gone."

I passed on visiting Frank Clifford until the following day. Sarah had asked Mila for his address before our visit, so we were set to go to Newington.

"I need to spend some time with Alison," I said, as he pushed on past Ingleside toward Ault Island. "She's still pretty upset."

"Do you think I should stop in for a moment?" Paul asked. "See if I can fix things up?"

"I guess it's worth a try."

When we came down the road to my house, I noticed something new: a FOR SALE sign posted at the small brown cottage I had rented last year. Despite the luxury of my uncle Gordon's home, I missed the little frame house on blocks. Not just because of the bad memories in the big house. Perhaps it was the bareness of the cottage, the lack of clutter and obligation. I suddenly wished for room to breathe.

Alison was on the phone when we walked in, the smell of coffee behind her.

"You're back." She hung up. "How did it go?"

"Mila Pierce is an interesting woman," I commented dryly.

"And a storyteller," Paul added, then said quietly taking her hand, "I hope you've forgiven me from dinner last night, Alison. I certainly never meant to insult your father's memory. It was just some deductive brainstorming on the situation."

Two pink dots appeared on Alison's cheeks. "Forget it. I know you wouldn't hurt my feelings, Paul." She didn't pull her hand away. "I would just never consider the possibility. Unlike some people who should know better," she added, glaring at me.

"I said the idea of a cop on the take had occurred to me, too." I glared back. "I never said I thought it was your dad. It's just an option we have to keep in mind." I walked briskly into the kitchen and offered coffee. In the middle of cups and creamers, my cell phone rang.

"Mackenzie?" The gruff voice didn't waste time on social chat.

"Chief Miller." My stomach tightened into a knot. Paul and Alison stopped talking and looked at me.

"You've probably seen the news on TV," he said. "There's been a second car bombing here in Cambridge."

"Yes, we know. But that's all we know," I added. "That's why I called you the other day."

I heard the older man sigh on the other end. "I'm supposed to be retired, but I'm involved with this unofficially because of the history.

This second bomb could have been just a copycat attack, but we're not sure. You two will have to keep your heads low a little longer."

"Was the bomb the same type as the one used on Alison's car?" I asked.

"Not as sophisticated," came the reply. "But close enough."

I cut to the chase. "Do you think it's connected to Alison?"

"Yes, I do," he said quietly. "The bomb was set outside her campaign office. The office was closed, of course, because she's not running, and that's why no one was hurt. I'd say it was a calling card, to remind her to stay out of the political race. Listen, Mackenzie," Miller added, "we need to know where you are."

I thought for a moment and made an executive decision.

"How about a compromise, Miller?" I looked at Alison. "We're somewhere in Eastern Ontario, along the Seaway Valley. The OPP inspector here is Jerry Strauss. He knows where we are." I gave Miller the number to call, and then passed the phone to Alison.

"A second bombing?" Paul looked grim. "What's the connection to Alison?"

"Miller says it was outside her old campaign office, the one she closed last week."

"Is Strauss giving you protection here?"

I shook my head. "We don't want it. We should be fine here if we keep a low profile."

"I disagree," said Paul firmly. "And I would suspect Strauss would be on my side, at least for that. Car bombs are nasty stuff. Someone out there is very serious about keeping Alison under wraps."

While Alison finished her conversation with Brian Miller on my cell phone, I used the house phone to call Jerry Strauss.

We skipped the warm and fuzzy stuff. I told him about the call from Cambridge and that the retired police chief would be giving him a call in the near future. I sensed Strauss was going to lecture me on having protection as Paul had, so I switched to what was really on my mind.

"Jerry, I just got back from visiting Mila Pierce. She told us about the day of Garnet Monroe's death and the loss of the heirloom silver necklace. Did the jewellery ever come to light as stolen goods or for sale on the black market?"

"Not to my memory," came the reply, "neither then nor when they restored the house at Upper Canada Village. But then I never really kept tabs on that. Why?"

"Because if it has a sizable diamond in it, and it actually was made by Paul Revere, it would be very valuable," I said grimly. "Possibly a motive for murder."

"I can check into it," he offered. "But it may take some time."

"I'd appreciate that. Thanks for your help—and for bringing the report last night," I added sincerely. Maybe if I started thinking about other people's feelings once in a while, I'd have a few friends to my name. Let alone anything more.

"Are you alone?" Jerry said unexpectedly. "There's something I need to talk to you about."

"No. We're all fine here," I added, in code. "Paul's visiting for coffee with Alison and me." Well, code and just maybe a shot to test the waters with Strauss. So much for treating other people's feelings with respect.

"Soon," he said curtly and hung up.

I deserved that. I've often wondered if my Neanderthal finesse with relationships was simply a weakness in me or a successful control mechanism. We all know the best way to have total control of your own life is to be the only one in it.

That night, Alison and I stayed away from the powder keg of her dead father's integrity, working over both her return to Cambridge and the mystery surrounding Paul Vaughn's parents.

"I'd love to stay here, Fan. It's so quiet and beautiful." Alison stood looking at the reflection of the sunset on the river. "But I've made the decision to get back on the campaign trail as soon as I'm a little stronger, threats or no threats. It's important."

"I'm sure it is."

"Not just for me." Alison turned to face me. "Our police services are always at the bottom of the food chain when it comes to government funding. Even at the federal level, they waste tax money on a useless gun registry when they should be asking the cops on the beat what they need to do their jobs better. Tougher laws. More funding to the provinces for policing services. We need more officers, and our officers need more clout to deal with crime. Scum like dealers who make their money off children. That's why I'm back in the political ring. I want to push for more support for our police here in Ontario.

"If I get to Queen's Park," Alison continued, sitting down, "my team has been told I'll be given a portfolio within twelve months. After that, who knows. There are other MPPs who feel as I do, and I've promised I'll swing some support behind them. It's the least I can do for my father."

"Well, that might explain the letters, along with the attack on your life," I said thoughtfully. "Get you out of the way, and smear the Waterloo Regional police—and police in general—at the same time." Whoever it was hadn't counted on Dave Carlson being in the car. His death had put public sympathy back behind the police right after the request for an investigation into the old killing—exactly the opposite effect desired. Unless . . .

"So where are we with the Lost Villages mystery?" Alison broke into my thoughts. "*The Murder in Mille Roches*. I can see it now." She smiled.

"Except this is for real," I reminded her.

"Oh, I know. I know. But it's all so romantic, isn't it? The beautiful woman, the older rich husband, the handsome lover and the old family house with the missing heirloom jewellery. Just the 'case' we would have died for in our Nancy Drew days."

"Well, we'll give it a go and see what we can do for Paul Vaughn, but," I added warningly, "I can tell you from experience that sleeping murders, like sleeping dogs, are dangerous things to get close to. The term 'to die for' is the thing to remember."

"When do you have to be back at the university?" Alison changed the subject. "I was talking to my office today about it and they wanted to know when I'd be back. I guess I'll just go back with you, if that's okay."

"Uh . . . I'm not sure yet when I'm leaving, but I'll let you know," I answered evasively. "Did you tell anyone where you are?"

"No. Just said I was resting somewhere safe."

"Okay," I nodded. "Will you stay for your birthday? It's coming up."

At that, Alison gave me the first real smile I'd seen since high school. "Fancy you remembering that. Yes, I'll try. We could go out somewhere and try to get into trouble," she grinned. "It would feel like old times."

And the next morning, the anger was back.

I didn't call Jerry, and he didn't call me. Paul came after lunch, and we headed for Newington. Alison begged off from fatigue and went to nap on her bed.

Twenty minutes later, we were skirting an old farmhouse with pristine grounds on County Road 12, arguing as to who was to have called ahead as neither did.

"Well, we're here now." Paul switched off the engine and we heard raindrops on the roof of the car. "Let's see if Frank Clifford is home." He put his hand on the door handle and turned to me. "Thanks for coming around with me, Farran. You know, I've spent my whole career asking other people questions, but this time it's too personal. But I'm sure I don't have to explain that to you. You seem to understand."

The car was suddenly too small and cozy.

"Been through it," I said gruffly and got out on my side.

149

The man who answered our knock was tall and slim, with a thick shock of white hair. Except for the hair, Frank Clifford seemed younger than his almost seventy years. He was energetic and smiling, with the sharp eyes of his older cousin Mila.

"We'll have to turn on a light here," said Frank as we sat down. "I think we're in for a good storm tonight." When the lamp dispelled the gloom, I took a look around.

Frank had more taste (and, to be fair, more room) for old furniture and personal touches than Mila. The pieces in the living room were probably original to the house, maybe family pieces. On every available table were pictures of smiling friends and family, married couples probably long dead, and laughing children who had since become seniors. And in every corner, on every shelf, and in piles on the floor were old newspapers carefully folded. Hundreds of them.

Frank noticed my scrutiny. "Believe it or not, I have a filing system," he smiled. "If you've been sent here about local history, you've come to the right place."

"Mila Pierce sent us," said Paul bluntly. "Mr. Clifford, my mother's name was Sheila Pierce."

This was obviously the last thing Frank Clifford had expected to hear. Paul was learning to use the tool I had last year—surprise attack. It had worked well for me—tragically so.

"You're Sheila's son?" He looked confused for a moment, then asked, "Is she still alive?"

"No."

An unnamed emotion replaced the confusion. "You said your name was Vaughn, Sergeant. Is Charlie Vaughn your father?"

"Yes, sir. He was." Paul stressed the word "was."

Frank looked at him, then nodded in understanding. "I see. You must excuse me. This is so unexpected."

"My mother never made contact with you in all these years?" Paul asked.

"No. Neither me nor Mila." Frank sighed. "I think she did that to protect us, after the scandal of her husband's death."

"My parents never spoke about their past here in the Seaway Valley," Paul explained. "Farran is helping me find people who can give me some answers."

"You knew my father, Mr. Clifford," I finally spoke. "Hal Leonard from Aultsville."

Frank's mouth became a straight line. "I heard what went on last year, Dr. Mackenzie. I'm very sorry things turned out the way they did. We had no idea . . ."

He sat in silence for a few moments, then rose and signalled us to follow. We went into the next room, the dining room. It, too, was full of newspapers on the buffet, the table, the floor. But we almost didn't notice.

"That's how I remember my Sheila," said Frank softly.

The portrait hung over the buffet, dominating the room. The young woman in it stood in evening dress with upswept hair, one hand on a marble mantelpiece. The other rested lightly on her chest to showcase the diamond pendant necklace she wore. Sheila Monroe seemed beautiful and alive, as though she had stopped for a moment to acknowledge us and would quickly move on.

"This was painted just after her marriage to Garnet Monroe," Frank explained. "Sheila would have been barely eighteen."

"Garnet would have been in his thirties," I mused.

"Yes, quite an age difference," Frank admitted. "It seemed a good thing at the time. Good for Sheila to marry into the family. Good for the family to have some new life in that old house. But as time went on, I wasn't so sure."

"Why?" I asked. Paul remained silent, staring at the image of his mother.

"It's hard to explain without sounding superstitious. The family had its share of bad luck. A lot of the Monroes died young over the years, including children. Monroe House sat on a small hill, clear of the woods, yet there always seemed to be a shadow on it. It had a certain miasma, and was never a happy place. We thought that Sheila would break the spell, so to speak. But instead, the gloom wore her down. Took away her spirit, too."

"Was Sheila happy in her marriage to Garnet Monroe?" I asked, stealing a look at Paul. He had the same presence, the same carriage as the woman in the portrait, but physically it seemed he took after his father.

"At first, I think she was. Everyone in the village was happy for her. It all seemed so romantic—the rich man marrying the beautiful but poor girl."

"Why did he, aside from the fact she was beautiful? Surely there must have been other women in the area more from his social class."

Frank shook his head. "The difference between them was purely economic. The Monroes had done well for themselves. But the Pierce family was of equal status, also of Loyalist descent. Poor, but respected. Both Sheila's father and grandfather were decorated for special service in the wars. They were in big demand as advance scouts for enemy ambush. Saved a lot of lives, they did."

"Because they were farm boys and grew up in the bush?" I guessed.

"Nope. Colour-blind. Does something to the vision. Less colour, more outlines. That's invaluable when you're looking for booby-traps in the woods. War heroes, both of them, but never wore a matched pair of socks in their lives." Frank smiled and pulled up his pant legs far enough to show us his socks—one dark red, one dark grey.

"Is family history your hobby, Mr. Clifford?" I smiled back.

"History is my life, Dr. Mackenzie," he replied. "You must know what I mean. My parents ran a successful store in Mille Roches, and I thought I would take over the business one day. But I ended up being a history teacher instead so my hobby could be my work."

We started moving back to the living room, Paul silently following us. I sensed he was feeling a little overwhelmed by the image of his mother in another life, so I moved the talk back toward our target.

"Then you must have found the Seaway and Power Project fascinating." I reclaimed my chair.

"The Seaway project showed me where my heart really was." He reached up and quickly pulled out a newspaper yellowed by age. Opening it to the front page, he handed it over, pointing to a photograph under the national headlines. It showed the picture of a young man sitting on a large anchor surrounded by what looked like round rocks.

FOUND IN LONG SAULT

Arthur Raymond, 17-year-old son of Mr. And Mrs. George Raymond, Sheek Island farmers, sits among 11 cannon ball-shaped mortar shells and an anchor which he discovered in the dried-up river bottom of the former Long Sault rapids. The find is the most important so far made by either amateur or professional museum piece hunters. Both U.S. Army officials, who believe the cannon balls are from the War of 1812 and the battle of Col. Crysler's farm, and the Ontario St. Lawrence Development Commission officials at Morrisburg would like them for their collection.

May 6, 1957
The Cornwall *Standard Freeholder*

"When Arthur Raymond found those cannonballs, I was pea-green with envy," Frank said, sitting down. "My parents had kept me from joining the dig on Sheek's Island the year before because the store had been so busy with all the new people in town. But by the summer of '57, we were moving to Long Sault and my father was setting up a new store in the mall. Business was way down with Mille Roches almost empty of people. I joined the group that summer and spent a few weekends digging with them for artifacts. Had the time of my life.

"I got to know Charlie Vaughn a little in the years before Garnet Monroe died. He boarded in my mother's boarding house. After he had a bad run-in with Garnet one day, he found lodgings elsewhere. I met up with him again during the dig."

Frank turned to Paul. "I hadn't seen him for months, not since the day of Garnet's funeral. Sheila had basically gone into seclusion after that. All I knew of how she was getting along was what Mila told me. It was hard for me to not be able to help her. We were all family. She saw no one. Not even my parents. Then, in the summer, all that changed," Frank added. "Sheila was arrested, and after a brief hearing, put on trial for the murder of her husband."

LAST SUMMER'S DIGGING AT AULT PARK

(Alex Mullin, Staff Reporter) The rumble and rattle of heavy machinery have replaced the roar of the Long Sault at Ault Park on Sheek Island, but the patient quest for artifacts that are man's only source of knowledge of the Point Peninsula Indians goes on.

The 'dig', under the direction of Dr. J Norman Emerson, supervisor of archeological studies in the University of Toronto's Department of Anthropology, has already uncovered a little more ground than last year's party, and the trenches have yielded a rich assortment of pottery and stone fragments.

The Point Peninsula people lived about 4,000 years ago, and studies now show that they use the Ault Park site as a campsite, probably for months at a time and in very large numbers. It was also a burial site. They buried some important chiefs, judging from material found in the graves, just on the brow of the hill overlooking the rapids.

July 27, 1957
The Cornwall *Standard Freeholder*

"What do you think it is?" The girl at the next box leaned closer for a better look.

Frank carefully brushed the dirt off a smooth rock as the other young people gathered around. He held it up for them to see.

"It looks like an ornament of some kind, like something you'd wear as a pendant." He looked at it closely. "Seems to be made of slate."

The find seemed to fuel the others, who returned to their marked squares with new enthusiasm. Frank placed the ornament to one side, then carefully got up from the earth he'd marked off for digging.

Brushing his hands, he picked up the artifact and started toward the main tent to hand it in. About thirty people dug patiently in the earth of Ault Park, taking off the sod with a shovel and then carefully digging in the sand with a trowel to find what the past would give them. Tents were up for the team from Toronto to stay in, and the old park pavilion was used as a dining room. Sightseers still came to watch, look over the finds, and sign the guest book.

In spite of all the activity, Frank hummed to himself as he went just to help fill the silence. The deathly silence that had reigned since the draining of the great rapids. He stopped for a moment to look out over the devastation. Where once there had been the roar of water sprays ten feet in height, there were now only rocks and wind. The cheerful summer cottages that had dotted the shoreline of the island were gone. Smoke hung in the air from the constant burning of brush and trees to clear the land to become the bottom of the headpond.

And in less than a year, that headpond would cover this ancient site forever, burying the past beyond any recovery.

"Frank! Frank Clifford!"

Jumping at the sound of his name, Frank turned to see Charlie Vaughn striding across the park to meet him.

"Charlie!" Frank offered his hand as the other came up. "It's been a long time. Has Hydro been keepin' you busy?"

Charlie shrugged absently. He ran his hand through his hair and looked around. "You know, I worked with mockups of this place for five years in Etobicoke. Waited patiently after trying things over and over on three true-scale models, just to make sure where the water would go. Now it's almost done, and I still can't believe it even though it's happening right in front of my eyes."

He shook his head. "Funny thing, though. I thought I'd be more excited about it at this point, but things haven't worked out the way they should. Started when Bob Saunders died, I think. He was one of the men that got the Americans on board. Had all of us raring to go. Loved his work and believed in what Hydro needed to do. Make power for a brave new world.

"You know, he was the chairman of Ontario Hydro, and yet he went door to door asking people what their concerns were. Always had a hello for everybody on the job. We all liked him. They're going to name the new generating station the Robert H. Saunders. Doesn't seem fair he didn't live to see it completed."

Charlie threw his hands in the air.

"Then all hell breaks loose with Hal and his family. Can't believe he'd leave like that. Leslie Mackenzie was devastated, I know. He's a good guy. He didn't do anything wrong."

Charlie looked back at Frank. "And now all this with Sheila. I'm sorry to bother you here, Frank. Looks busy. But I didn't know who else to turn to."

"We are busy. Don't have much time left." Frank held out the artifact. "We're findin' stuff like this that's thousands of years old, and thanks to your headpond, we're fast runnin' out of time."

Charlie sighed. "So is Sheila. And I don't know what to do. Will they let you in to see her? You're family."

"Let me in?" Frank looked at Charlie. "They moved Monroe House to the pioneer memorial village last month. Sheila is livin' in Cornwall until she decides where to go. What do you mean, let me in?"

Charlie's face cleared. "You don't know. Have you been staying here for the past few days?" When Frank nodded, Charlie grew grim. "Sheila's been arrested for Garnet's murder. She's in the Cornwall jail on Water Street. The trial is set for the first week of August."

Frank put the ornament in his pocket and turned away, looking out at the site of the former rapids.

"Why?" he demanded, suddenly turning back. "Garnet died in March. If they had their suspicions, why wait until now?"

"I don't know. I think they found some neighbours who heard some bad fights between Garnet and Sheila in the week leading up to his death. The police have pieced together enough that it doesn't look good for her. The robbery motive didn't hold up because the only thing missing is the necklace. And the old lady could have tucked that away somewhere. It's only Sheila's word that it was in the jewellery box when it was stolen out of Mrs. Monroe's bedroom."

"What the hell are we goin' to do?" Frank muttered.

Charlie began to pace. "I haven't seen Sheila since . . . since Garnet's death. I sent a letter after that, but no reply. I never see her out anywhere. Mila won't help me talk to her. Says Sheila doesn't want to see me." He grabbed Frank by the shoulders. "You have to go to her, Frank. Make sure she's all right. Tell her I'm here and I'm worried. Ask her what she wants me to do. I'd like to see her if she'll let me."

"You?" Frank shook his head. "You're the last person who should go near her, especially now. No, I'll tell you right here. If you go anywhere near Sheila Monroe, you'll be the final nail in her coffin."

"She told your father to stay away." Frank took the paper and smoothed it before folding and filing it away. "Whether or not they'd actually had an affair didn't matter. There was talk in Mille Roches, and as far as the police were concerned, the old saying goes. Where there's smoke, there's fire."

As Frank looked for another paper, I felt that finger of fear press quietly into my chest, just above the anger churning in my gut. He held out a newspaper to Paul. The headline read:

DRAMATIC TURN IN MONROE MURDER TRIAL

Beside the article, a picture caught my eye—the church from Upper Canada Village being moved from Moulinette. I thought of my mother burying my grandfather Harper that day.

"But he didn't," Frank continued. "Charlie went to the hearing every day. I'd see him in the back corner of the crowded courtroom. And I guess in the end, he was right. If he hadn't been there, nothing on earth would have saved her."

MOVE 125-YEAR-OLD CHURCH

Pictured above is Ontario Hydro's large house moving vehicle in the process of relocating Christ Church which was formerly situated at Moulinette. The Anglican Church is being taken down the main street of Aultsville to Upper Canada Village in Crysler's Farm Memorial Park. This was the first church moved from the area. The moving took place yesterday.

August 13, 1957
The Cornwall *Standard Freeholder*

The woman on the stand in the crowded courtroom sat chin up, eyes on no one. She was dressed in grey, her head bare. Yet, as Frank Clifford listened in his seat behind the defence table, she answered the questions clearly and without hesitation.

"Mrs. Monroe, did you have an altercation with your husband the night before his death?" The Crown attorney moved in on his prey.

"I don't remember," came the reply. "We had several fights that week. Garnet was very depressed, in a black mood over selling Monroe House."

"Did you threaten to leave him?"

"Yes, I did. Life was becoming very difficult with him."

"What did your husband say to that, Mrs. Monroe?" The lawyer looked down at a paper on his table.

"He said he would never give me a divorce. I was with him for better or worse."

"How did that make you feel?"

"Dead." The word caused a stir in the audience, and the judge had to bang his gavel before the Crown could proceed.

"That you wanted to kill your husband? That you wanted him dead?"

If the man were trying to provoke Sheila Monroe, he would have to try harder.

"No," she said quietly. "That I felt dead inside. I did not kill my husband."

"Where were you the morning of Garnet Monroe's death?"

"I told you. I was out for a walk by the creek."

"Alone?"

"Yes." She looked at the crowd for a moment, then away.

"So no one can vouch for you? Not even Mila Pierce?"

"No."

He picked up a paper and came over. "She tried, though, didn't she, Mrs. Monroe? Mila Pierce tried to lie to the police and say you were together."

"She loves me," said Sheila simply. "Mila was a second mother to me. She was trying to protect me. She has . . . " Tears welled up in Sheila's eyes. "She has a good heart."

"I think she did that because she feared you were guilty. You knew where the necklace was and threw the entire jewellery box into the creek to make it look like a robbery. The necklace is hidden for you to take later."

"Why should I take the necklace? As Garnet's wife, it's mine anyway."

"The death has been placed at between midmorning and noon. You were there when Mila Pierce walked in. I think you never left. I think you acted in a moment of rage and then, horrified by what you'd done, you stayed with him until Miss Pierce walked through the door."

"I was at the creek all morning," she repeated stubbornly.

"Your Honour," the Crown attorney turned to the judge. "The Crown has no further questions for this witness. In fact, unless the defence has anything more to add, we rest our case. Sheila Monroe had both motive and opportunity to kill her husband that morning."

"Mrs. Monroe," said the judge, "you may step down."

The defence lawyer looked behind him to the back of the courtroom and nodded, then rose.

"Actually, Your Honour, the defence respectfully requests the hearing of one last witness, a new one that came forward this morning."

The judge motioned both lawyers to approach the bench. There was a brief discussion, then the judge addressed the courtroom.

"Does the Crown wish to have due process for this new witness?" The judge looked at the Crown attorney. "If so, we'll adjourn until Monday at this time."

The Crown shook his head, and smiled at the defence. "Not really, Your Honour. The Crown is confident we have proved sufficient evidence against Mrs. Monroe. In the interest of the court's time, we'll waive due process."

"Thank you, Mr. Lalonde," the judge acknowledged. "The defence will call its last witness."

Sheila's lawyer stood up, avoiding her eye as she crossed the floor to the prisoner's box.
"The defence calls Mr. Charles Vaughn."
"No!" Scarcely heard as the crowd started up again, Sheila stopped dead in her tracks and turned on her lawyer. "I won't allow it."
"Order! I will have order in my courtroom!" The judge banged the gavel again.
Charlie Vaughn came up and stood facing Sheila.
"Charlie," she said softly. "Don't do this. It isn't necessary."
"Yes, it is, Sheila." he replied. "And we both know it."
Vaughn took the stand and was sworn in. Sheila's lawyer stepped forward.
"Mr. Vaughn, can you tell us your movements on the morning of Tuesday, March 26th?"
"Yes." Charlie took in a big breath and let it out. "It started out a regular day. I went to work, that day to the generating station. But half an hour later, I cut my hand on some steel. They sent me to the Hydro hospital for a tetanus shot and some stitches. An hour later, I was off for the day. So I went out for a walk across the field in the direction of the creek."
"What time was this?"
"I start work at 7:00 a.m." Charlie figured. "By the time I left the hospital, it would have been close to nine."
"What did you do then, Mr. Vaughn?" The lawyer walked back toward the box where Sheila sat silently as though waiting for execution.
"I went to the north end of the creek to put space between me and Monroe House. I guess I walked the length because the creek will be gone soon, when the construction is finished. It's small, but very pretty. I found a large tree and went to sit under it."
"How long did you stay?"
"Until lunchtime."
"That's all morning. Why did you stay so long?"
For a moment, Charlie hesitated. "I was talking to a friend," he said finally.
"So you found a friend already at the north end of the creek when you arrived at 9:00 a.m., and that friend stayed with you until lunchtime when you left?"
"That's correct."
By this time, Frank could have heard a pin drop in the silent courtroom. He suddenly realized he was holding his breath.
"Mr. Vaughn, could you tell the court the name of that friend?"
A long pause, then a reply barely above a whisper.
"Mrs. Sheila Monroe."

The silence in the room disappeared into the din of rising voices.

"No more questions, Your Honour." The lawyer spoke firmly above the noise.

When the judge had order again, he let the Crown cross-examine Vaughn.

"What did you and Mrs. Monroe do for three hours by the creek?" Lalonde paced in front of the witness stand like a cat by a mouse hole.

"We talked."

"Talked for three hours?"

"Yes. When I found her there, it was obvious she was crying and had been for some time. She was very upset with the way Monroe had become and needed someone to talk to. Someone who wasn't family. So we talked."

"This is very convenient, Mr. Vaughn," said Lalonde sarcastically. *Charlie said nothing.*

"We've been conducting this trial for almost ten days now," the attorney continued. *"Why is it only today you have this sudden recall?"*

"It isn't a sudden recall. I've wanted to speak up all along."

"Then why didn't you?"

"Sheila wouldn't let me." Charlie raised his head to look the man in the eye. *"I couldn't see her, but she sent word that I was to do nothing and stay away. She didn't want me dragged into this."*

"Admirable. Admirable," Lalonde agreed dryly. *"But you are willing to be dragged in anyway."*

"Yes."

"Why? To help a friend in trouble?"

"That's right, a friend." Charlie looked over at Sheila, who raised her head to meet his eyes. *"And the woman I love."*

"After that, you couldn't hear yourself think," Frank pursed his lips. "I remember the judge couldn't get order back so he stood to adjourn proceedings. Then they cleared the courtroom. The following day, the judge cited insufficient evidence against Sheila in the face of Vaughn's statement that gave her an alibi, and dismissed the jury. The charges were dropped and she was free. Garnet's death was ruled murder by person or persons unknown."

"When did they leave town?" asked Paul.

"About a month after that. Sheila finished settling Garnet's estate, gave some money to Mila to help her out. I asked for her portrait. Then one day she was gone. Vaughn disappeared at the same time. His job mysteriously dried up after the hearing, so he was out of

159

work. We all figured they had left together to get married and start over."

"They did." Paul roused himself. "That's where I can pick up the thread. They married, and my dad found work on the East Coast. I was born and they settled down in Newfoundland. Mom and Dad lived in St. John's until they died."

We all fell silent for a moment, letting the past catch up with us.

"What was she like as a child?" Paul asked suddenly. "Mila said you grew up together."

"Yes, we did. We were cousins, you know. They both grew up on farms just outside Mille Roches. My mother moved into the village when she married my father because he ran the store, so I grew up there. But," Frank added, "we stayed close for years. Back then, family was all you had. Sheila was definitely a free spirit. Mila was like Sheila's second mother. I guess you could say I was the brother she never had."

"Mille Roches was the largest of the villages lost to the Seaway, wasn't it?" I put in.

"Oh, yes, it was quite healthy. Even after the Provincial Paper Company closed its mill down just before the Seaway Project started and put several hundred people out of work. The town had almost 1,400 people. Even had a taxi service." Frank got up and pulled out a photo album. "Would you like to see some pictures?"

I found myself watching Paul closely as we flipped back in time through the pages. There were shots of his mother as a girl, skinny with long braids and a big smile. The few of Sheila after her marriage showed no braids—and no smile. I wondered what was going through Paul's head as I remembered my own pilgrimage here twelve months ago. But at least for him, it was only a piece of the puzzle that was missing, not an entire life.

The pictures of Mille Roches itself showed a rambling village spread out along the river and across to Sheek's Island. Echoing the shoreline on the north side of the river was the Cornwall canal, and several pictures showed canal boats quietly puffing past farmhouses and homes built along the old No. 2 Highway that also skirted the river. One aerial shot gave a panoramic view of the entire village.

"That's a good shot, "I said, handing it back to Frank. "Who took it from a plane?"

"Someone with a little foresight, I imagine," Frank smiled. "I don't know. I sometimes make presentations to interested groups about the Lost Villages, and a man brought this one night to ask me if I could tell him anything about it. I'm afraid I laid it on a little thick with him. After I had a good look, I told him I could say not only where it was, but also the time of year, the day of the week and the time of day."

"How did you do that?"

He pulled out a magnifying glass from a drawer beside his chair. "Take a good look. I said it was clearly Mille Roches, late March on a Monday afternoon."

I scoured the picture and found traces of snow on the ground. "Okay, I see recognizing the village and finding the last of the snow—but Monday afternoon?"

"Look among the houses. Do you see those white lines?" As Frank explained, Paul leaned over my shoulder. "I thought at first it was more snow. But look closer. It's laundry. On the line to dry. Monday was washday every week in every village along the St. Lawrence. Do the wash in the morning, hang it out in the afternoon. Like clockwork. Hence Monday afternoon." He chuckled. "I played that for all it was worth. Impressed the hell out of the audience."

"What's that big building?" Paul pointed to what looked rather like an Iroquois longhouse in the centre of the picture.

"That's the Mille Roches arena. Took the whole village working together to build it in the '30s. We were proud of it, hated to see it torn down. Hydro demolished it in April of '58. It collapsed during the salvage, damn near killed a man. The older folks said it was a bad omen."

As if on cue, we heard the first rumble of thunder.

"Then Dorothy Baker's house would have been right around here." I pointed to a cluster of houses right beside the arena.

"Ah, yes. Right there. And this long building was my parents' store and boarding house. Here was the orchard. Just at the left is the start to the bridge to Sheek's Island. That's the CNR track running right through the village, and if you look closely, you can see the Moccasin going past the arena. She went through twice a day. That little nest of cottages across the river is sitting on what we called Frying Pan Island. Most of them were pushed upriver to Island 17 on the winter ice. And up here on the right is the northern edge of the village. Today, it's the southern edge of Guindon Park. They launch boats there now."

"Unreal." Paul shook his head. "All this under fifty feet of water."

"Yes." Frank Clifford took the photo back from me. "On July 1st, 1958, they dynamited the cofferdam that was holding the water back from the work areas and formed the headpond to run the generating station. It took four days to cover the villages."

"How did my mother feel about the Seaway Project?" Paul asked.

"She was resigned to it from the start, I think, but she hated the idea of losing the village. That might be another reason she never came back. Couldn't stand the thought of seeing everything so different after the flooding." Frank suddenly stood up. "I'm sorry. I didn't even offer you coffee. Get me started on history and I can ramble for hours."

"That's not necessary." I rose, too, and held out my hand. "We've taken your afternoon, and the rain seems to be picking up speed. We should be on our way."

Paul stood beside me and shook hands. "Thanks for all your help, Mr. Clifford. It was good to meet you.'

"And you, Paul. Will you be staying long in the area?"

"Not sure at this point. It's all a lot to take in."

"I'm sure it is. If your parents didn't tell you, how did you find out?"

"My dad had a box of clippings, and I found it going through his things after he died."

Frank sighed. "Must have been rather a shock. I'm sorry."

As we moved into the front hall, I remembered the necklace.

"Mr. Clifford, the diamond necklace Sheila is wearing in the portrait—Mila told us a curious story about its history. Is it true?"

"The Paul Revere necklace?" Frank crossed his arms. "What a piece of history. There's no way to confirm the family story without having the necklace authenticated." He turned to Paul. "Unless your mother . . . "

Paul shook his head. "Can't help you with that. She never mentioned that either. I didn't know it existed until yesterday."

I braced myself to face the rain and wind and started to open the door.

"Mr. Clifford, I'm going to ask you a straight question, and I hope you'll give me a straight answer." Paul stopped and turned to face Frank. "If my mother didn't kill Garnet Monroe, who do you think did?"

But for some reason, the question seemed to have unnerved the older man. Shaken, he shook his head and murmured, "Garnet? I . . . I really don't know. Don't know."

We ran out into the pouring rain and dove into the car. Through the rain-streaked window, I watched Frank Clifford watch us drive away.

"He means he thinks it was my dad and he didn't want to say. Too polite." Paul sat at my kitchen table with his hands wrapped around a hot cup of tea.

"You're reading things into his words. Don't jump to conclusions." I sipped mine and walked to the window to see if Alison was on her way back. The note we'd found on our return to Ault Island said she'd gone for a walk.

"I'm not," he insisted. "We have two camps. Dorothy Baker votes for my mother, Mila for my father. With Frank, my father pulls ahead as the murder suspect over my mother two to one."

"Who said it has to be one of them? Why not someone else?"

"Like who? Frank was out on his rounds that morning, and Mila was with him till he dropped her off at Monroe House. Nobody else had a motive."

"We don't know that for sure. What you have to do now is keep your emotions out of it. Work strictly with the facts. Or you'll drown in it."

"Easier said than done." He looked up at me, one of those rare men who look better wet than dry. I always look like a drowned rat. "How did you handle it? Everywhere I go, I see a side of my parents I never knew. It's as though they're suddenly strangers to me."

"You're a cop," I said. "Get the job done. Be a cop first, a son later."

Paul rubbed his eyes. "But the whole thing. My mother, a beautiful but poor girl, marries a rich husband and gets to live in a spooky old house full of death and family curses because of American Revolution jewellery. And the stories come from a strange little old lady in a nursing home and a man who's going to die alone in a house with only newspapers and memories. Christ, Farran," he threw his hands up, "it sounds like a Nancy Drew story."

"Didn't know you were into Nancy Drew," I quipped. "Had you pegged more as a Hardy Boys type."

"Funny, Mackenzie." He got up and came to look out the window with me. "I hope Alison's okay. Wonder why she went for a walk in rain like this."

"Paul," I changed the subject to mask my own growing fear, "do you mind if I ask how your parents died?"

He looked back out into the rain and didn't answer. I was wishing I'd kept my big mouth shut when he quietly said, "Traffic accident. Head-on collision. Both killed instantly. Never knew what hit them."

"My God. I'm so sorry," I stumbled. "It must have been terrible."

"And then to find the box of clippings." Paul shook his head slowly. "That was the icing on the cake. That's what I mean, Farran," he turned to me. "It's enough to make you squirrelly. You had a lot on your plate last year. When I decided to look for you, I dug up all the reports from the papers. Your father's body is found. Everyone thought he just left to go shipping and never returned. Your mother dies from a heart attack on hearing the news. And you come here cold trying to piece it together when everything is under water." His mouth went grim. "Stir in your uncle and a long-lost cousin. How did you handle it all without going a bit strange?"

Deep in my chest, I felt the small red glow of rage at his words, but I laughed it off. "I was strange to begin with, so I had the advantage." I thought a moment. "Hey, Paul—"

That's when he pulled me close and kissed me full on the lips.

The mind is a funny thing, isn't it? Well, at least mine is. I remember having an out-of-body moment then, half my mind saying, "Well, so *this* is how it feels to kiss him," while the other half said—

"No!"

I pushed him away with a violence that surprised us both. For a long moment, we stood squared off in embarrassed silence. Then he took a step toward me.

"Are you saying what I've felt between us from the beginning isn't there?"

I ran a hand through my wet-rat hair. "I . . . I don't know what I'm saying. I've felt something, too, but I never led you on. It doesn't feel right to kiss you. That's all."

"It's Strauss, isn't it?" he said flatly. "I sensed something there the other night. Some kind of history between you. Alison says you spend most of your time avoiding each other, but I think you're still carrying the torch for him."

When I didn't answer, he grabbed his coat off the chair and stalked out the front door. I heard it slam, then footsteps back toward the kitchen.

I turned and felt relief wash over me. Alison stood in the doorway.

"Thank God, you're home. I was worried."

She ignored me. "What the hell is the matter with Paul?"

I must have been red-faced and flustered. "Don't know. Think he's upset with his family history," I lied. I turned away, but her silence told me she wasn't buying it.

"Did something happen between you two just now?" Alison said in a low voice.

I sighed. "He kissed me, and I pushed him away. He's pissed off, and I'm confused. That's it."

As Alison changed into dry clothes, I decided to upgrade from tea to brandy. The sky grew dark as the sun set, the clouds making it seem to happen all at once. Instead of letting up, the rain grew stronger, beating on the windows while the trees swayed menacingly in time. The throbbing in my knee had upgraded itself from suggestion to statement that didn't bode well for the coming night.

"I think we're in for a serious blow," I said as Alison came out of her bedroom. I held up the bottle. "Pour you one to chase the chills from your walk?"

"I'll pass, thanks," she answered curtly.

I set the bottle down with a sigh. "Alison, if you're still mad from yesterday, I thought we straightened that out. I never thought your dad was on the take. We don't even know if anyone was. We just have to look at everything. I warned you this would be hard," I added, putting ice in the glass. "Sometimes the knowing is harder than the not knowing."

"I know you're a real piece of work."

"What?"

"You heard me. Poor Paul comes to you for help, and you fawn all over him. Then when he responds, you push him away. And you wonder why he's angry."

I almost spit out the brandy in my mouth.

"I did *what*?"

"You went after him. Not because you want him. Just like Strauss. You don't want them, just want them around. Following three feet behind you in case you get bored. A real chip off the old block."

The glowing ember of rage that Paul had ignited earlier reached full flame status.

"Are you referring to my mother? What the hell did she ever do to you?"

"You have no idea," she said flatly, and started to walk away.

I grabbed her by the good arm and pulled her around to face me. At that moment, I didn't give a goddamn if I were hurting her. I wanted to. "Oh, no. You don't make a statement like that and drop it. You started it, you finish it. What did my mother ever do to you?"

"She made me leave. She made me not say goodbye." Tears suddenly choked her, and she struggled to speak. "I left and never said goodbye to my father. And then he died."

"What the hell are you talking about?" I demanded, although suddenly I didn't want to hear the answer.

She shook her arm free. "Sometimes the knowing is harder than the not knowing. Right, Farran? Well, this is one of those times.

"You want to know the real reason I left without you for school the morning my father died? I'll tell you. Your mother was just like you. She went after men just to collect them, not to have them."

"No . . ."

"Dave Carlson. She dangled him along for months. He deserved better." Alison moved in closer, her face inches from mine. "*And my father.*"

"You're lying!" I shouted. I didn't back away.

"I found out the hard way," she said softly. I could barely hear her over the wind outside. "The morning of the shooting. I went early to pick you up and walked in on them in your kitchen."

Speechless, I shook my head. Somewhere outside, a branch crashed to the ground. The darkness was all around us, black as pitch, blurred by the downpour on the windows.

"I was fifteen years old. I didn't know what to do. I couldn't go home and tell my mother, and I sure as hell couldn't face you." Her voice began to rise hysterically. "So I left your house and went to school alone. I left. And I never said goodbye to my father."

Alison began to back away from me, tears streaming down her face.

"Do you understand what I'm saying, Farran?"

"No . . . Alison . . . No. It's not true . . . "

Alison ran to the back door and tore it open.

"*She was in his arms!*" she screamed, and disappeared into the storm.

Chapter ELEVEN: Rage

Without a thought, I followed her into the raging black.

The rain whipped into my eyes, blinding me for a moment. I could hear the trees on the lawn groaning as they battled the wind. Then lightning flashed, and I caught a glimpse of Alison ahead of me, stumbling toward the seething river.

"Alison!" The wind tore the word from me. I cupped my hands and tried again. "Alison! Stop!"

Alison didn't slow down, but the storm kept her speed with mine—her demons driving her on despite the pain of her injuries. Finally, she fell in the grass on her knees a few feet from where the water hurled itself against the shore.

"Alison." I caught up to her and put my arms around her. "Alison, we have to get back inside," I yelled over the storm.

"*I didn't say goodbye!*" she screamed into the night with a voice I didn't recognize. "I didn't say goodbye! Daddy, I'm so sorry. I didn't mean it. Please forgive me." Her voice broke into sobs that racked her body in my arms. "I'm so sorry, so sorry."

A growl of thunder shook the air and a branch from a big maple tree lost its fight, hitting the ground only a few feet away. I screamed and huddled with Alison, wondering how the hell to get us safely back into the house. I couldn't carry her, and she wasn't responding to me. I wondered if she knew I was there.

"Help!" I called stupidly into the tempest. "Someone help me!"

And then a miracle happened. Strong hands appeared out of the blackness to pull us to our feet. They grabbed Alison and picked her up to start back toward the house.

"Let's go, Mackenzie," ordered a voice I thanked God to hear.

I followed Jerry Strauss back through the dark to the lights of the house. He carried Alison right to her room and carefully laid her on the bed. After a quick check for injuries, he nodded to me and left me to it. I took Alison's wet things off her and threw a heavy quilt over her still form.

"Alison," I said softly. "It's Farran. I'm here. Everything's going to be all right."

I squeezed her hand, ice cold from the gale outside. She was still crying softly and didn't open her eyes. Again, I wasn't sure she knew I was there. I stroked the wet hair away from her face and tucked her in to sleep.

167

Strauss had poured a stiff brandy for me.

"Here," he said as I walked into the living room. "You need it."

I didn't argue, and he joined me. Then I got us each a towel to dry off, and we sat in silence for several minutes.

"Of course, you know she's close to a total collapse," he ventured finally. I said nothing. "And you don't look too good, either."

"I'm sorry to disappoint you, Jerry." I smiled grimly and got up to look out the patio door. It was useless. "I'm not going crazy. I crossed that line long ago."

"What happened?"

I felt my throat close up on me, and I struggled to speak. "We were arguing about the morning of her father's death, why she didn't pick me up for school. And then she started to cry that she hadn't told him goodbye that day and ran out into the storm."

Jerry instinctively picked up the important thread. "Why didn't she pick you up for school that day?"

I turned to face him. "Because she walked into my kitchen and caught my mother in her father's arms," I said brutally.

He looked at me for a full minute, then asked softly, "Do you believe it?"

"I don't know what I believe anymore," I faltered, and then lost it. I covered my face with my hands and turned away, embarrassed to cry in front of him. Embarrassed at how things were falling apart all around me.

I heard him get up off the couch and cross over to me. He didn't touch me, but handed me a handkerchief. "Here," he said awkwardly. "It's clean."

"A handkerchief?" I sniffed. "I didn't think anyone used these anymore."

Jerry shrugged. "I'm old."

I had to laugh at that, and wiped my eyes.

"Listen, Farran," he said, putting his hands in his pockets, "maybe it's time for Farran Mackenzie to start taking care of Farran Mackenzie."

"What do you mean?"

"I mean stop playing white knight to every person that comes along with a problem. You've got them lined up around the block."

"I do not." I handed back the handkerchief.

"Yes, you do. You're spread way too thin right now. It was only a year ago that you walked into a hornets' nest of your own.

"I can think of several good reasons why you should have backed away from this mess with Alison," he continued. "And now, on top of that, you're up to your ears in someone else's family skeletons.

Someone you barely know. And we need to talk about Sergeant Paul Vaughn. That's why I'm here."

"What about him?" I went into the kitchen to make coffee—and to get some space between Jerry and me. He followed.

"What do you know about him, Farran?"

On one hand, I was happy the "Farran" and "Jerry" days were back (for now). On the other, I didn't like where the conversation was headed.

"I know he's a sergeant with the St. John's Police Service in Newfoundland. I know his father was a friend of my father. And I know he's here to find out the truth about his parents—whatever it may be." I banged the cupboard door. "I know how that feels."

"Maybe that's what he's counted on," said Jerry ominously.

"What do you mean by that?" I stopped with the coffee scoop in mid air.

"After your dinner the other night, I ran a check on him."

"Why does that not surprise me?" I slapped the coffee filter in and turned to face him, arms crossed. "Let me guess. He's actually a serial killer wanted in three states."

Jerry gave me one of his looks.

"No, Vaughn is who he says he is. And he's had a good career. One of the best on the St. John's force. Until now. Did he tell you how his parents died?"

"How his parents died?" I echoed. "Yes, he did. They were killed last year in a head-on collision. Both died instantly."

"The other vehicle was a police car." The wind that had started to taper off now seemed to grow louder again. "Chasing an escaping suspect. The driver was Vaughn's best friend. He died, too." Jerry let this sink in. "Vaughn's not on holiday. He's on stress leave. The other officer was found not negligent, posthumously. Still, a few months ago, Vaughn started to crack up on the job." The silence was filled only by the hissing of the coffee machine. "I want you to be very, very careful around Sergeant Paul Vaughn."

I knew the advice was solid, but my lower lip came out anyway.

"I'm not a child, Inspector. I can handle myself. Besides, I've pretty much done what I can. Found the people he needed to see. Just helping out a friend."

"Are you sure that's all he is?"

The question slipped out, I sensed, and we froze. It lay between us, unwanted by both, and it wasn't going to go away. Paul's kiss that afternoon flashed through my mind.

"Fan?" I heard Alison faintly from the bedroom. When I made a move to go, Jerry put a hand on my arm.

"Let me talk to her."

He poured a brandy for her and walked to the bedroom. I watched him in surprise. Then I understood. Alison's demon had the same face Jerry's did for forty years—unfinished business with a dead father. Regrets and questions without answers.

The voices murmured on for a while. I'll never know what he said to her, but in retrospect I find peace that he did. As I listened to the storm, I suddenly realized my curious advantage over them both. In my case, there was no self-reproach possible. Someone had robbed me of my father before I was even born.

When the phone rang, I jumped. And I almost didn't recognize the agitated voice at the other end.

"Dr. Mackenzie? It's Sarah Hall," she said breathlessly. "I'm at work here at the Lodge and . . . and something's happened."

"Mila?" I sat in the chair by the phone, foreboding flooding over me. "Is she all right?"

"The doctor says so, but she's had a real bad night. I can't believe this has happened here. It's awful."

"What happened?" I demanded.

"Someone attacked Mila in her room about an hour ago."

"*What?*"

"The resident next door heard yelling and rang for us. The guy roughed her up a bit, I guess. Scared her badly. He ran out the fire entrance and that set off the alarm. She's sedated right now."

"Do you know who it was?"

"No. Mila just kept saying 'a bad man,' and the staff only saw him by emergency light. We lost power here around suppertime." Sarah paused for a moment. "You asked me to keep a close eye on Mila. I thought I should let you know."

"Thank you for calling me, Sarah. Are the police there?"

"Yes. The Cornwall police have sent one man. He's talking to the residents right now."

When I got off the phone, I pulled the paper with Paul's phone number on it out of my wallet. I tried both his cell and his room at the Ramada without success, but left him a message.

Jerry came out of the bedroom as I hung up.

"She's calmer now," he said. "I think she'll be able to sleep it off."

"That was Sarah Hall on the phone from the Glen-Stor-Dun Lodge." I gave it to him straight. "Mila Pierce was attacked tonight in her room at the Lodge by an unidentified man. She's fine, but not in great shape. The Cornwall police are there now. And," I admitted grudgingly, "I just tried Paul at the hotel and on his cell. He's not answering."

"Why does that not surprise me?" Jerry quickly put on his coat. "I tabbed him as a loose cannon the minute we met. Something just not quite right there."

"Is that a personal or professional opinion?"

"I'll answer that when you answer my question, Mackenzie." He strode off toward the door.

"Where are you going?"

"To find out what Sergeant Vaughn has been up to tonight."

"Why Paul? Why would he attack Mila?"

"Revenge. Or maybe he has his sights set on finding that necklace. As far as I can find out, it's never surfaced on the black market. It may still be here."

"He's not the only man involved with this." I stood between Jerry and the door to make my point. "Don't forget Frank Clifford."

Jerry firmly but gently moved me to one side.

"If Frank had a reason to attack Mila," he said, "why would he wait fifty years to do it? Don't open the door after I'm gone." Then he disappeared into the night.

Not trusting my knees, I sat down at the kitchen table. If Paul had a secret agenda, then I'd led him right to everything he needed. I was responsible for Mila's attack. Maybe he would have gotten there eventually, but I'd certainly made it easy for him.

My instincts had told me there was something deeper going on with Paul from the very beginning, but my ego distracted me. It was time to use my own advice: Get the job done. Put the emotions in a box until later.

Why would anyone kill Garnet Monroe? Freedom to marry? Money? The necklace? The robbery had been a clumsy affair at best, and if the necklace were the only thing stolen, why kill Monroe? And why not sell it?

If either Sheila or Charlie Vaughn had killed Monroe to marry the other, what was their son Paul capable of?

I sat at the kitchen table, focusing on Mille Roches. I didn't want to explore Alison's story—yet. But that life invoice would come due soon enough. My other gut feeling was that the truth about John Perry's death would be both personal and very, very frightening.

And at that kitchen table, with the storm giving me its last, I suddenly saw what Sheila Pierce Monroe had seen that day her husband died half a century ago.

"My God," I whispered hoarsely.

Then I was in sudden and total darkness.

"Ah, nuts." I got up and started pulling out drawers, feeling for something that resembled a flashlight. Then I heard Alison's door open.

"Fan?"

"I'm here, Alison. We've lost power. I'm trying to find a flashlight."

"I've got one in my tote bag," came her voice. "Hang on."

The halo of light came out of the room and over to me.

"How are you feeling?" I asked.

She stayed safely behind the flashlight's glow, so I couldn't read her face.

"I'm better," Alison said slowly. "I'm also sorry for that little scene, Fan. I . . . I—"

"Hold the light over the phone." I cut her off to change the subject. I wasn't ready to go over it all now.

"Who are you calling?"

"Someone I should have called back days ago. Sarah Hall's mother. Dorothy Baker?" I added when I heard the line pick up.

"Yes?"

"It's Farran Mackenzie calling. Are you all right in Long Sault? Have you lost power?"

"Yes, I'm afraid so. But I'm fine, thank you. Got lots of candles. Sarah is stayin' late at the Lodge. They're in a bit of an uproar over there."

"I know," I said. "She called to tell me."

"I hope the police catch whoever did that. What a terrible thing."

"Mrs. Baker, I need to ask you about something you said the other day, when you were talking about the days in Mille Roches."

"What's that, dear?"

"The day at your house when my father Hal was kidding Charlie Vaughn about a girl he liked. You warned them about girls getting themselves into trouble to get a husband. You said people with money could buy themselves out of that. And then you started to say a name." I paused. "Was that name Garnet Monroe?"

I heard a sigh at the other end. "It was a long time ago. And I only heard the rumour, never knew the truth of it."

"What was the rumour?"

"Garnet was home one summer from Queen's University. He was young, handsome and rich—and now a man of the city. Could have the pick of the local girls. One of them got pregnant, but his parents wouldn't stand for the marriage. So things got 'fixed up' as they used to say in my day. I believe the ugly word now is abortion."

"The Monroes paid for the abortion and paid off the family."

"That's how the story goes."

"Mrs. Baker, who was the girl involved?"

There was a long pause. "I suppose it can't hurt anythin' now," she said finally. "It's such ancient history. The girl was Mila Pierce."

I said goodbye and hung up the phone thoughtfully.

"Fan? What's going on?"

I looked at Alison over the flashlight's beam.

"I'll help you get dressed," I answered. "I have somewhere to go, and I can't leave you alone."

The farmhouse was in darkness like everything else, but I could see a small light where I remembered the dining room to be.

Ruth Hoffman's voice rang in my head from when I had dropped Alison off at the house in Ingleside shortly before.

"You shouldn't be driving out on the country roads on a night like this," she scolded when I told her my intentions.

"The rain's pretty well over, Ruth. Don't worry." I handed Alison over.

"It's still very windy and there are probably branches down all over the place. Alison," she added, "you talk to her."

"Off on another rescue mission, Mackenzie?" Carolyn's voice came from behind her mother. I wondered if she had been talking to Strauss.

"I won't be long," I said simply and left them there on the porch.

Now, with the wind blowing my hair in my eyes, I carefully climbed the steps to Frank Clifford's porch and knocked on the door. When there was no reply, I knocked harder.

"Frank? Frank, it's Farran Mackenzie. Please open up."

After forever, I heard footsteps over the sound of the trees and the door opened. In the shadow of the kerosene lamp, Frank Clifford looked much older than his age—such a contrast to this afternoon. Without a word, he turned and walked down the hall, leaving me on the doorstep. I followed. I found him in the dining room sitting at the table facing the portrait of Sheila Monroe. There was a decanter and a glass in front of him.

"Scotch, Dr. Mackenzie?" He waved at the buffet. "You'll find glasses in there."

"I'll pass, thanks." I slowly sat down at the table. It was still covered in newspapers, but the filing system was definitely gone. Stacks had been thrown in all directions, as though the gale outside had been allowed in.

"Are you all right, Frank?"

"No," he said simply and poured another drink. "It was all for nothing, you see."

"Killing Garnet Monroe?"

He looked at me and raised the glass as if in a toast.

"Very good. I pegged you as an intelligent woman. Are you sure you won't join me?"

"I'm trying to cut down," I said, and he nodded. "Why," I followed up, "was it for nothing?"

Frank Clifford looked into his glass. "I always say I've devoted my life to history. As you have, Doctor. Now I find I've given it away for the same reason."

With great willpower, I kept my mouth shut and let him speak.

"She said it would work out perfectly," he turned to me. "Just get Garnet out of the way. Then I would get everything I wanted, if I could be patient for a bit." He shot the drink back, and I wondered how many he'd had. "Then they left together. The necklace was gone."

"You wanted them both."

"Two things, beautiful and rare. Do you blame me?"

I had no answer to that. Frank raised his empty glass in another toast, this time to the portrait. "Ah, my lovely Sheila. You should never have married that brute. You were too good for him." He put the glass down and suddenly stood up.

"The phones are still working, Dr. Mackenzie. I presume you'll want to call the police. If you'll excuse me, there's something I have to do."

He walked out of the dining room and for a few minutes, I didn't move. Sheila looked down on me and I thought of Paul—Paul, his mother, her first marriage.

Then I smelled smoke.

I pulled open the dining room door to a hall filled with flames. Piles of newspapers were alight, the years being consumed before my eyes.

"Jesus Christ! Frank! Frank!" I stepped into the hall. "Frank, the house is on fire!"

The hall was quickly filling up with smoke. I started to cough and made my way toward what looked like the kitchen door. Someone grabbed me and pushed me into another room off the main hall, then locked the door. I pounded on it as I heard the footsteps run off to the front of the house and then back down the hall. Turning, I saw I was in a library, but instead of books, there were shelves and shelves of newspapers stacked to the ceiling. There were several piles on the floor already burning. I tried to put them out with my coat, but the heat was too much.

The smoke was building in the room, and my eyes blurred. Coughing, I tried to see where a window was to get out, but the light by the flames made it next to impossible.

I felt panic start to fill my gut, along with memories of another burning house two years ago—when I had lost everything that had mattered to me.

The swing door was hot to the touch,
but I pushed on it anyway.

"Okay," I told myself, "think.'

The heat hit me like a fist and drove me back into
the dining room.

"Find the window by feeling for it."

I paused for a second, then pushed through again.
The entire kitchen was in flames.

I tried not to gag and got down on my knees to breathe better.

I heard a second crash behind me and felt a sudden blast of heat. Turning, I saw that the fire had breached the swing door and was toasting the upper wall and ceiling of the dining room.

With a roar, the flames from the floor piles found those on the shelves. Through the smoke, I now saw a wall of fire.

Another soft moan reached my ears, followed by a sudden roar as the living room drapes went up. We were cut off from the front door.

Cold raw fear grabbed me by the scruff of the neck, jerking my head back.

I screamed.

Then, over the angry noise of the fire, a man's voice.

Fan . . . Fan . . . Over here . . .

With streaming eyes, I crawled toward the voice, straining my ears to catch it.

This way, Fan . . . the window is this way . . .

I found a place where there was smoke but no flames and put out my hands. Up, up, and glass. The window. Old, stuck tight. Standing, I felt around for a chair and hurled it through the glass. The sudden rush of wind doubled the inferno in seconds, and I dove through the frame, uncaring about the shards around me.

"Farran! Thank God!"

Gagging and coughing, I was dragged across the grass to a safe distance from the house. Sitting up and rubbing my eyes, I looked back. With the help of the wind, the whole farmhouse was ablaze, lighting up the entire property.

I looked up to see who my saviour was. Paul.

"What are you doing here?" I asked hoarsely. My throat stung from the smoke. "Not that I'm complaining."

"I got your message on my cell phone about Mila. I figured you'd come here to talk to Frank."

I swallowed carefully. "Frank killed Garnet Monroe."

Paul nodded. "When I heard about Mila, I thought that might be the case."

"He almost killed me, too," I said. "And he would have, if you hadn't helped me find the window. Thank you."

In the glow from the fire, I saw confusion on his face.

"What do you mean?"

"I couldn't see a thing in that room. I would never have found the window to get out if you hadn't called to me."

"I didn't call to you. I was outside, trying to find a way in. Frank locked all the doors and windows."

"Frank. Where is he?" I started to get up.

Paul turned to look at the burning house. "In there." He grabbed my arm when I made a move toward the house. "There's no way you're going back in there. When I got here, I was around back and Frank came running out with something large in his hands. I followed him to a shed behind the house where he left whatever it was and returned to the house. By the time I got to the back door, it was locked." He looked at me. "He never came back out, Farran. I'd say he's history."

Headlights and a flashing light cut our conversation short. We stood like deer in the beams while the car door opened.

"Farran, what the hell is going on?" Jerry's voice came from somewhere behind the lights. Then his body followed. "And here I thought Vaughn was the loose cannon. Where's Frank Clifford?"

"He's in the house. He must be dead," Paul answered flatly. "Frank set the house on fire and locked himself inside. Farran, too. She almost burned to death with him."

Jerry came up to look Paul in the eye. "How long have you been here, Vaughn?" he said quietly.

"How did you know where I'd gone?" I asked.

"Carolyn called me from her mother's house." Strauss turned to me, but kept his eyes on Paul. "Told me you were running off to do something crazy again. Are you all right?" In the distance came several sirens. "I have to see if I can find Frank."

"Jerry, you can't go in there," I called after him.

He was barely halfway across the lawn when the entire roof caved in, sending a volcanic blast of heat and embers out into the night. Then the Newington Volunteer Fire Department arrived.

When the paramedics brought up the rear, they tried to check me out. But I waved them off and headed for my car.

"Farran, wait. Let them look you over." Paul hurried after me. "You're cut and bleeding, and you've had smoke inhalation. Maybe you need to go to the Emergency."

"Mackenzie," shouted Strauss in a voice I didn't dare ignore. "Where the hell do you think you're going? You have to give me a statement."

"I will first thing in the morning. I have to get to town."

"Why?" Jerry countered. "Haven't you had enough for one night?"

"I have to talk to someone before it's too late."

"At this time of night?" Paul's voice was incredulous. "Who?"

I thought of all that had happened half a century ago.

"Iago," I said.

I must have looked like a crazy woman. Wild hair, black ash and smoke all over, cuts on my hands. That's probably why Sarah didn't argue.

The room was dark save for the soft glow from the emergency lights. I crossed the floor quietly, going around to the far side of the bed.

"She's been given a sedative," Sarah whispered. "She won't wake up till morning."

I gently laid my hand on the elderly one on the comforter. It was cold.

"Mila won't be waking up at all, Sarah," I said quietly. "She's dead."

The woman went into action. She felt Mila's hand, checked for a pulse, then went to press the alarm.

"It's turned off." Sarah turned horrified eyes to me. "I don't understand. I watched her take the sedative and left her when she slept. We had an attendant sitting at the door all evening, just in case."

"Is this the pill she was supposed to take?" I stooped down and picked up the waste can beside the bed. Something small rattled around inside. Sarah held out her hand, and I dumped the contents into it. Two pills, one pink and one blue.

"She didn't take the sedative," said Sarah slowly. "Or her heart medication this evening. Why would she risk her life like that?"

"Because Mila knew the secret was over. And in her heart she couldn't let it go."

Sarah left me alone with Mila to notify the powers that be. I sat on the bed beside the still form and gently stroked the pale face with the bright eyes that had gone out forever. Then I saw the doll wrapped tightly in her arms.

"She was your baby, wasn't she, Mila? The baby they took away from you. The child that never was." My eyes blurred for a moment. "I understand that much."

"Is she all right?" Paul's voice came from the doorway.

I didn't look up. "She's dead, Paul. I didn't figure it all out fast enough. She didn't take her medication this evening, turned off the alarm and waited for nature to take its course. With all the upset of Frank's attack, it probably didn't take too long."

"Why?" he asked, coming softly into the room. "You said something about Iago and took off before I could go with you."

"I didn't want to disturb your lovefest with Strauss," I said dryly.

"If Frank killed Garnet Monroe, why would Mila kill herself?"

"Because she put him up to it. Whispered in his ear. Convinced him he could have the woman he loved and the artifact that any historian would kill for. Kill Garnet, make it look like robbery or perhaps like Charlie Vaughn did it, marry Sheila and have the estate and the necklace that his wife would own."

"Except that my father had spent that morning with my mother and had an alibi," Paul nodded. "And she eventually left with him. What about the necklace?"

I looked at him then. "That was the key. That was why Frank went berserk and came after Mila tonight. Strauss said he would have done it years ago if he were guilty. But something changed today."

Paul thought for a moment. "Me?" he guessed.

"You," I agreed. "You—bringing the news that you knew nothing about the necklace until now. After fifty years, Frank hears the truth: *Sheila didn't take the necklace with her.* He'd been played for a fool."

"So who had the necklace?"

"Mila did. She took it the day of the murder, smuggling it out in a pitcher full of soap flakes."

"And she sold it for the money to live on." Paul sighed and came over to the bed.

"No. She didn't sell it. It was never about money. It was about having. And it was about revenge." I carefully slid the doll from Mila's cold embrace. The head and arms were china, the body stuffed cloth. Turning it over, I felt under the dress along the back. Sure enough, there was a raised seam, hand-stitched, as though someone had once opened the doll's body.

"Do you have something like a penknife?" I asked Paul. "You're the boy scout type."

He gave me a look, then handed over exactly that. I carefully slit open the stitches and put my fingers in the doll. Inside was a little cloth bag. It, too, was stitched up and there was something hard inside. I have to admit, my professional hands shook as I opened the bag. Gently, very, very gently, I emptied the contents into my hand.

"I think this belongs to you," I said and held it out.

Even in the low light, the silver necklace was breathtaking. The delicate hand-wrought filigree put the tarnish of the years to shame. For just a moment, I reached across the centuries and touched the hand of Paul Revere. Then I passed the piece to the other Paul, and the lights came on.

He took it carefully and held it up. "The diamond's gone," he said, disappointed.

"No, it's not." I got up, thinking of the blue light on the wall right in front of me the day before. Was it only a day? It felt like a lifetime.

I crossed over to the Victorian lamp with the two remaining dingle-dangles. Choosing the larger of the two, I unhooked it and held it up to the overhead light, admiring the blue fire that burns in the heart of a true diamond.

"No, Paul," I said quietly. "The eye of the god has been here all along."

"It was after you left my house tonight," I said to Jerry. "I sat at the kitchen table, thinking of Sheila and the day of the murder. I thought of her sitting alone in the kitchen of Monroe House, her husband dead in the front room and her cousin trying to take care of everything as usual. And then I realized the full import of what she saw that day at her own kitchen table all those years ago, the ugly truth that came to her as she sat waiting for Mila to come back downstairs."

It was well after midnight. We all sat around Ruth Hoffman's kitchen table back in Ingleside, food and coffee into their second rounds. I had returned with Paul after the Lodge took over with Mila. Jerry met us there shortly after with the news that the fire was out and nothing was left of Frank's house but the brick walls. They would search for his body in the morning. Alison sat with us, eating little, dark circles under her eyes. Carolyn helped Ruth in the kitchen. As for me, I'd had no supper and ate like a horse. Brushes with death seem to do that to me.

"What did you see?" Paul sat with his back to the kitchen, on the edge of his seat. He'd come in with me under duress and was now distinctly uncomfortable. I wondered why Jerry had that effect on him.

"Boxes of food," I replied. "Remember Mila said she pushed boxes of food off the kitchen table before she and Sheila sat down to think over what to do about finding Garnet dead? Now it might have been nothing, but this was fifty years ago. Meals didn't come out of a box like they do today. I realized those boxes were *groceries*. Frank was doing his deliveries all that morning, Mila said. It sounded like an alibi. But the boxes told me, as they did Sheila, that Frank had already been there that morning while she was out. Frank killed Garnet." I took another sip of my coffee. "It must have been a terrible moment for your mother. Sitting in that house with her husband dead in the next room, knowing that one of the two people she loved most was not to be trusted."

Jerry looked at me. "Do you think Sheila knew Mila was in on the murder?"

"I think that came to her later," I answered. "That's why there was no contact for fifty years. Why she broke down on the stand at the hearing about Mila having a good heart. Up until then, I think Sheila saw Mila as only stealing jewellery from the house. The small stuff that wouldn't be missed, and other pieces left where they could be

179

found to make old Mrs. Monroe look like she was going batty." I rubbed my eyes. "Sheila had time to think about everything while in jail. She had to face the fact that not only did Mila take the necklace that morning, but she also came prepared to do so. Mila knew that Garnet would be killed and it would be her one chance to take something so valuable right under everyone's nose."

"Prepared how?" This was the first time Alison had spoken since we'd arrived.

I looked at my old friend, the fatigue blending with the last of her cuts and bruises. The outside reflecting the inside. Despite the bombshell about my mother she'd dropped on me that evening, I felt the war was over.

"With the pitcher for soap flakes," I explained. "Frank Clifford said that wash day in Mille Roches was Monday, religiously. Wash in the morning; hang out on the lines in the afternoon. Garnet was murdered on Tuesday, March 26th. The day *after* washday. Why would Mila need soap then? She would have come on the Monday for it, when she needed it. And why come at all? Frank would have just put it on her tab at the store."

Ruth came in and set a plate of brownies in the middle of the table. Chocolate.

"Ruth, thanks so much." I took her hand for a moment. "Has anyone told you lately you're a saint?"

"No, actually, Mackenzie," Carolyn said pointedly, "they haven't." She whipped my plate away from under me, and I made a dive for the last of my sandwich.

"I'm just glad everyone is safe," Ruth shook her head. "You scared me running off like that into such a storm." She put a hand on Paul's shoulder. "Would you like more coffee, Sergeant Vaughn?"

Paul dropped his eyes to the table. "No, thank you, ma'am," he mumbled. "I should really be going, I think."

"I think not." Jerry took his spoon and started tapping it end over end on the tablecloth. "I have some questions for you, Vaughn."

Fatigue was starting to claim me, too. I zoned out of the coming jousting match and thought of Mila hoarding her treasure all those years.

"Poor Mila," I said.

"Poor Mila?" Paul got up from the table. "That woman almost sent my mother to the gallows. They were still hanging back then. How can you condone what she did?"

"I didn't say I condoned it," I looked up into his eyes. His eyes. Something there . . . "Paul, you and I will never know what it's like to grow up poor, to go through the Depression and come out with nothing, to have to live on the grace of family. To wonder where your next meal is coming from.

"Mila learned to survive the only way she knew how. No money for an education and too proud for menial work. When she couldn't marry money, she made damn sure your mother did—knowing that Sheila would always look out for her. Later probably, Garnet started tightening the purse strings on Sheila so Mila started stealing from Monroe House to pay her bills. Even now, I'll bet she was blackmailing Frank a little, making him cover her bills out of fear. The Glen-Stor-Dun Lodge is a quality nursing facility. Rooms there don't come cheap. I don't think our old age security would cover it. And the Lodge doesn't hand out real satin bed jackets to its clients, either.

I put my hand over Alison's. "I don't condone what Mila did. But I do understand it." I caught Alison's eye. "And understanding is the first step toward forgiveness."

Alison gave my hand a silent squeeze.

"So it's okay to orchestrate a murder to survive?" Paul shot back.

"She didn't do that to survive," I returned. "She did that for revenge. It was the doll that sent her over the edge."

"Why? My mother bought her that because she loved her. Because Mila couldn't have one when she was a girl."

"Things weren't going well leading up to that point." I put two brownies on a napkin. They were disappearing fast. "Look at it through Mila's eyes. It was an uncertain time for most people because of the upheaval of the Seaway project. No one was sure of their economic future, least of all Mila, who depended on Sheila and Frank's parents to get by. Sheila had met your father, and something was building between them as the Monroes' marriage disintegrated. Mila had made a huge personal sacrifice to put Sheila where she was, and it looked like Sheila was thinking of throwing that away. Now, Garnet insults Mila by suggesting she work as hired help—in a house that Mila should have been mistress of if she had been allowed to marry Garnet years ago. And for the Christmas of '56, Sheila gives Mila a china doll. It represents childhood, and the child Mila never had. Both were lost in situations where Mila Pierce had little choice."

I took a bite of my brownie, letting the taste of chocolate revive me.

"All around Mila," I continued, "people are taking care of themselves with no thought as to her feelings or needs. Everyone is getting off scot-free. Something deep inside Mila snaps and she decides to call in those debts. Destroy the father of her baby, the man who was a party to the murder of his own child. Use Frank and his unrequited feelings for Sheila. Get the estate from Sheila who didn't appreciate it, and live the life she should have had."

"The one I feel sorry for is Frank," said Alison unexpectedly.

"Frank Clifford killed a man," Jerry said curtly.

"Oh, I know. I know. But he loved Sheila his whole life and ended up with a portrait and memories to show for it." Alison took a second brownie. "It's terrible to love someone like that and not have them love you back."

I nodded slowly. "Mila probably told him that Sheila needed his help to get out of a bad marriage, then got Garnet all riled up one day and took him to the Cliffords' store to show Frank that Monroe was a violent man. Reminded Frank that Sheila would inherit clear title to the necklace as Garnet's wife. But Sheila already loved Charlie Vaughn. And Frank and Sheila grew up together. She would never see him as a lover, only as a brother."

I got up to stretch and headed toward the living room. I was suddenly very tired of death. It hung heavily on me like unwanted armour, both slowing me down and keeping me safely away from life.

"'Death is the brother of sleep, is he not?'" I murmured, quoting from a favourite childhood story.

I heard the back door open and Ruth call out in surprise.

"Lynn? What are you doing here at this hour?"

"Me?" Lynn Holmes stood in the kitchen, taking everyone in. "What's going on? A midnight coffee klatch?"

Everyone started talking at once, but somehow through years of practice as a journalist, Lynn got the gist of the story. She shook her head.

"I live in Ottawa, for Chrissakes, and the real action is always down here." She gave Ruth a hug. "Ruth, the storm was pretty much over by the time I finished work so I decided to drive down to see you. I got another e-mail from Steven, but . . . " Lynn shot a glance at Carolyn, who pretended oblivion. "I'm a little confused about it."

Alison shot a glance at me.

"Steven is . . . " I started, then stopped.

"Steven is a son I gave up for adoption years ago," Ruth said firmly, saving me as usual.

"Mom," Carolyn scowled. "It's a family matter."

"It won't be for long," her mother replied, forcing a smile. "We've made contact. Steven will come home soon."

Lynn came over to me and gave me a hug. "Fan, I'm glad to see you one more time before you head back to Cambridge."

I returned the hug. "Hi, Lynn. It's good to see you, too. I'm sorry we've been playing cat and mouse."

"That's okay," she laughed. "I tend to have that effect on people sometimes." She looked at Alison. "I'm Lynn Holmes from *The Ottawa Citizen*. Are you Alison Perry Standish?"

I held my breath. Alison slowly stood up, suddenly her old self. Her bruises seemed to fade and the fatigue vanished. I saw a new strength behind her eyes.

"I am," she said simply.

"I've been looking for you, Mrs. Standish. A lot of reporters have. I'm the editor of the national pages. Would you give me an interview tomorrow morning?"

"I would be happy to, Ms. Holmes. There is a lot that must be said."

"Call me Lynn. Any friend of Farran is a friend of mine." Lynn turned to Paul. "I'd like to talk to you, too, Sergeant Vaughn. That's if you wouldn't mind answering some questions about your trip here."

"You'll have to take a number on that, Lynnie." Jerry rose to his feet. "I have some questions for Sergeant Vaughn that can't wait."

"I'd love to hear them, Strauss." Paul came over to him and crossed his arms. "You're bound and determined I'm guilty of something."

"And you've been doing the dance around me since we met," said Jerry bluntly. "A major chip on your shoulder. I'm not a guy that needs to be liked, but I'm definitely wondering why."

I sought refuge in the living room. The picture of Harland Hoffman, Ruth's father, stood in its customary place on the mantelpiece. Her mother Alice's chair was still beside the window. These were the people, the neighbours, who took my mother in when she was left alone in the world as a young woman.

"Thank you," I whispered to both of them. "I never said thank you for taking care of my mother all those years ago."

"Maybe I have a problem with redneck country cops who run their space like it's the Old West." Paul's voice cut into my thoughts. "Maybe it's personal."

I could feel the back of my neck get warm.

"Hey," said Carolyn. "Aren't cops supposed to be brothers in arms or something? You're on the same team, you know."

"Well, Farran, looks like you've pulled it off again," said Lynn brightly—too brightly. "Solved another mystery in the past. You're one smart cookie. Isn't she, guys?"

"I'm not smart, Lynn," I said grimly over my shoulder. "I'm resilient. I have the strength to keep throwing myself into brick walls until something gives. If I were smart, Mila Pierce would still be alive. No," I added, taking Harland's picture in my hand, "I spend most of my life stumbling around half blind until I get lucky."

"You weren't lucky tonight, Farran," said Jerry. "You almost died in that fire. Vaughn, if I find out you had anything to do with that . . ."

Half blind.

"All I had to do with it was watch a distant relative lock himself in his burning house to die. I also pulled Farran to safety after she broke through the window," Paul shot back. "I'm sorry this wasn't your favourite scenario, Strauss: shoot first, ask questions later."

Colour-blind.

"What the hell are you talking about?"

Two cops. Two visions. Two truths.

"Boys, I won't have any fighting in my home," Ruth said firmly.

Beauty is truth, truth beauty. Who wrote that? I couldn't remember. But if beauty is in the eye of the beholder, so is truth. And as I looked into the eyes of Harland Hoffman in the photograph, I saw it.

. . . the truth is we tried for ten years. I can't have children. I think it was harder on Martin than he ever admitted . . .

. . . it's such ancient history. The girl was Mila Pierce . . .

And a kiss.

"Mackenzie," Jerry growled.

As if in a dream, I walked over to Ruth's oak desk and pulled out a folded sheet of paper. I opened it. Taking another paper out of my pocket, I held them together. I was suddenly very aware of my heart beating.

"Mackenzie, I'm through talking to this crazy man until later." Jerry's voice came through my fog. He started pulling on his jacket.

"It's all about revenge," I said softly. "All of it."

"He's your friend—you deal with him. Oh, and he says it's personal," Strauss added, turning to leave. "I'll let you call me about that."

"It's all about revenge," I said clearly.

Jerry grunted and started for the door. "Thanks for the hospitality, Ruth. I appreciate it."

"Freeze, Strauss!" I walked back into the kitchen. Jerry stood waiting by the back door with a crusty look on his face. I stopped beside Paul.

"I'd love to think you two were fighting about me, but that isn't what this is about." I turned to face Paul. "Is it?"

He ran his fingers through his hair, avoiding my eyes. "I should get going, too. It's late."

"It's about revenge," I persisted. "All of it."

"Frank and Mila?" asked Lynn.

"And this." I turned back to Jerry. "It's about revenge, or at least thinking about it. Paul can't handle being around you, Jerry, because . . . because . . . you killed his father."

Now Jerry looked at me as though I were the crazy person. I had a feeling he wasn't the only one at that moment.

"As a cop, he understands what you did," I continued. "Probably would have done the same. But as a son, he's having a hard time dealing with it. You closed the door to something important in his life."

"Mackenzie," Jerry growled, "I haven't seen Charlie Vaughn in fifty years—"

"Not Charlie Vaughn," I interrupted. "I'm talking about Paul's real father, his biological father. My Uncle Gordon. The man you killed last year to save my life."

With a pounding heart, I looked Paul Vaughn right in the eye. "Isn't that right . . . Steven Hoffman?"

It was so quiet in the room I don't think anyone was breathing. Certainly I wasn't. The shock about what I'd said paled in comparison to the fact that I'd said it at all. To a crowded room. I'd taken a terrible chance with Ruth's feelings, a woman I count as a dear friend. What was I thinking?

I waited for anger, for a demand for an explanation, for a silent exit. I got none of the above. Paul raised his eyes and looked at me. Then he turned to look at Ruth, who had crossed the kitchen floor and put out one hand to touch him gently, as though he were glass.

And finally, ever so slowly, after over forty years, Steven Hoffman reached out and held his mother's hand.

Chapter TWELVE: Forgiveness

The Robert H. Saunders - St. Lawrence Generating Station was opened on September 5, 1958 by the Hon. Leslie M. Frost, QC, LL.C., D.C.L, Prime Minister of Ontario.

Named to commemorate Robert H. Saunders, CBE, QC, Chairman of Ontario Hydro from 1948 until his death in 1955, for his effective contribution to the negotiations leading to the construction of this project.

These mighty works make manifest in enduring form the spirit of cooperation of the Hydro-Electric Power Commission of Ontario and the Power Authority of the State of New York.

The Hydro-Electric Power Commission of Ontario and all those associated with it are proud to have participated in this undertaking which brings to this province the benefits of a great natural resource.

James S Duncan, CMG, LL.D.
Chairman

Dedication, Front Entrance
The Robert H. Saunders Generating Station
Cornwall, Ontario

It was already September. The last of summer had slipped through my fingers here in the Seaway Valley.
The calm after the storm brought work to do. Clean up time, personally and professionally. At first glance, my list was short: one official letter to the University of Waterloo, a call to Gordon's former lawyer here to talk about handling Steven's claim to his father's estate, and an effort to end Alison's visit on a positive note.

Two things to avoid: my newly found cousin, and sleep.

I talked to Ruth every night on the phone, to keep tabs on how she was taking everything. Despite my cavalier handling of such a personal and emotional situation, Ruth still accepted my calls. She is a woman I can only hope to be someday. I'm not sure I would have done the same in her shoes.

Carolyn showed no signs of packing up and heading home to Brockville in time for her son's school year. Odd, but entirely her own business. I sure as hell wasn't going to ask her any personal questions at this point. But I did wonder how she was dealing with her long-lost brother—the one she hadn't wanted from the beginning.

Paul stayed on at the Ramada and started coming for visits to his mother's house. It was, at least, a beginning. All journeys have to start somewhere and finally Steven Hoffman had come home. With the mixed feelings I had for the man and the loaded history between his biological parents, I worried about how he might treat Ruth as time went on. To be honest, I was glad that Carolyn was on site for now, with her ever-present verbal boxing gloves ready to keep Paul/Steven in line.

And I didn't answer his calls.

Alison started by making up nice excuses when she'd pick up to his voice. Eventually, after haranguing me about giving the guy a chance, she started telling him the truth. I knew that sooner or later Paul Vaughn would pop up at my door, but felt I would deal with that when it happened.

As it happened, the other cop showed up first.

"You're going to have to talk to Vaughn sooner or later, Mackenzie." Jerry poured himself a coffee from the machine on my counter. He seemed more at home than usual, and I watched him as though for the first time. Except for one man, I've made it a rule to never take any male seriously. In terms of relationships, I've been a game player—using the excuse of privacy as a tool to deflect commitment.

But you just don't play games with Inspector Jerry Strauss, personally or professionally. He refuses to even sit at the table, except perhaps when officially closing in on his prey.

"Besides," Jerry handed me a mug, too. "You owe the guy a second chance."

"Christ, Jerry. You sound like Alison."

"She's right," he said simply and sat down. "The guy's family and that's not going to change. He had a lot of bad stuff to deal with in a short time. Give him a break. None of us have perfect track records, either."

"I thought you didn't like him," I said with surprise.

"I didn't like his attitude. Now I understand it. We'll certainly never be buddies or anything cozy like that, but I'll give him professional courtesy, at least. And you need to let him mend fences with you," Jerry added. "If you can't do it for yourself or for Vaughn, then do it for Ruth. She needs your support with this right now."

As usual, Strauss had put his finger on the priority in this situation. Sulking was a luxury I would have to indulge in on my own time. Paul was my cousin and Ruth's son. I needed to be with her during this emotional roller-coaster ride. It was time to take a grow-up pill.

That night I called Paul and told him to meet me the next day where it had all started—the St. Lawrence Valley Union Cemetery. For the first round, I didn't want to have to make nice with him under Ruth's eye. As Alison had put it to Lynn, there was a lot that must be said and I wanted room to take the gloves off.

The weather the following day co-operated, and Paul was there when I arrived. The fall wind was coming in off the river, making small whitecaps where Wales had once stood. Mercifully, the cemetery was deserted.

He was standing at my Uncle Gordon's grave, hands shoved in pockets, and I tried not to register how alone he looked at that moment. I approached as close as I dared to the tombstone I was actively avoiding and stopped. Paul looked up and saw me. After a few moments, he came over to where I stood. We didn't say anything for several minutes.

"How did you know?" he finally asked quietly.

"I think I knew who you were the first day we met," I answered. "But only at the subconscious level. I remember having a strong sense of déjà vu, as if I'd had that conversation with you about the cemeteries once before."

"And I was half right." I turned to face the St. Lawrence. "Last year, I stood here with my uncle—your father—Gordon Leonard. We talked about the villages a bit, and graves." I looked back at Paul. "You don't look like Gordon, but you act like him. You *seem* like him. It felt like being with him again."

Paul crossed his arms and glowered down at the grass—just as Gordon used to do. "That's not a lot to go on, Farran," he said. "And for the record, I didn't come here to pull a fast one on anybody; I just got caught by surprise when I realized how close I was to where Ruth lived. I covered my tracks as best I could and kept my mouth shut. I didn't think anyone would put two and two together. Where did I screw up?"

"You didn't screw up, except once. It was actually a lot of little things that started to add up."

"Such as?"

"Do you remember giving Alison and me your contact numbers that day at the power dam? You wrote them on a piece of paper. I looked at that and had a gut feeling it was the beginning of something. Your handwriting is quite distinctive. If I had been using my brains instead of my feelings, I would have realized there was something familiar about your handwriting. It matched the writing in Ruth's letter from Steven Hoffman."

"Your feelings?" Paul took a step toward me.

I moved away. "There were other things. You don't look like either of your parents. That night at Frank Clifford's farmhouse, I noticed there was no facial resemblance between you and Sheila in the portrait he had in the dining room. I assumed you took after your father, Charlie Vaughn. Then I remembered that wouldn't work, either. Mila Pierce had said at our visit that Charlie was good-looking, like you *only different*. Now that wasn't conclusive. Some people take after their grandparents—which is the truth in your case. You have Harland Hoffman's eyes.

"But I began to wonder if you were adopted when we talked to Frank. He said all the Pierce men were colour-blind. You're a cop, so you can't be colour-blind. But if you were Sheila's biological son, there was an extremely good chance you would be. Colour-blindness in the family isn't a guarantee that you'll get it. But it's a dominant trait and an interesting genetic weakness because it's a trait that usually only the men inherit—only through their mothers.

"Then there was something Al . . . a—a friend . . . said to me recently," I said evasively, thinking of Alison. "That she and her husband tried for the ten years they were married to have children, but they couldn't.

"Sheila and Garnet Monroe were married for over ten years, yet there were no children," I continued. "I'm sure there was pressure on Sheila to produce an heir to Monroe House, to keep the old family line going. So why no children? If Sheila were your real mother, then the fault lay with Garnet. But Dorothy Baker told me about Garnet's troubles when he was a young man about town. Remember that he got a local girl pregnant and his family paid hers for an abortion to 'fix things up' as Dorothy said it was called. If Garnet Monroe got a young Mila Pierce in trouble, then he wasn't the one who couldn't have children. It was Sheila."

I stopped there, where it was safe. I didn't want to mention the immediate connection I had felt between us, the feeling that he knew me, understood me and could sometimes look right through me. I was still angry with Paul on several counts and didn't feel like giving anything away.

"And in Ruth's living room," I finished, "when I realized who you could be, your attitude toward Jerry Strauss made perfect sense."

"I was also jealous, Farran." Paul laid a hand on my arm. "When I did the follow-up on you before coming here, I found out what Gordon did, what happened to him. But just before I left home, Ruth's letter arrived and it blew me away to realize that Gordon Leonard was my biological father.

"So I had to find you, and I did. I didn't tell you who I really was right away because I needed to find the truth about my parents' past. And I didn't think you would help the son of the man who killed your father.

"Then Inspector Jerry Strauss walked into your house that night I was there for supper, and I couldn't handle it. He'd gunned my father down. Maybe for all the right reasons, but he had. So that got us off on the wrong foot to start with. And that night at dinner, I read between the lines about you two and realized I was jealous."

"Bullshit," I said simply.

"Are you telling me that you didn't feel what passed between us when I kissed you?"

I pulled away my arm. I could feel my cheeks get hot.

"I'm telling you that your one screw-up about hiding your real identity happened the night you kissed me." I looked him straight in the eye. "We were talking about what I'd gone through last year, and you said, 'Stir in your uncle and a long-lost cousin.' The fact that Ruth had had a child by my uncle Gordon was never leaked to the press or put in the reports. It had no bearing on my father's murder or my uncle's death. The few people here that know aren't talking. So the only way you could have known is if you'd received Ruth's letter telling you about your parentage. If you were, in fact, Steven Hoffman.

"I started to ask you how you knew that. I think you realized the mistake as soon as you said it. So you thought fast and came up with a way to utterly change the subject and cut off any questions. That's why you kissed me," I ended bluntly. "Isn't it?"

Paul didn't answer. He also looked away, avoiding my eyes.

That's when I hit him.

I would like to be able to say now that it was a ladylike, Hollywood-type slap across the face. But it wasn't. I have my grandfather's temper, and my mother's skill with her fists.

I decked him.

Paul sat on the ground, rubbing his jaw. "I suppose I deserve that," he said quietly, still avoiding my eyes.

"Well, it sure as hell makes me feel better," I snapped. "First of all, Vaughn, that's for Ruth. How dare you come here and spend a couple of weeks prancing around the Seaway Valley without going to see a woman who has thought of you every day since she gave you up over forty years ago? The mother you said you would meet, then put on hold. Are you made of stone or just damned selfish?"

He opened his mouth to answer but I cut him off.

"And you didn't have to play games with me, either. I would have helped you work it out. God knows, I would understand how you feel. I've been there." I stood over him. "In case it hasn't occurred to you, Paul, on your father's side I'm all you have left. So you'd better behave around me." I put out a hand and helped him up. "Welcome to the family, Vaughn. I'll call you when I've finished cooling off."

The life invoices kept coming in for payment.

Lynn's article on Alison made the front page of *The Ottawa Citizen* and then my phone was ringing off the hook. The media found its way to Ault Island shortly after and we were temporarily under siege. Alison talked to them all, outlining her platform and the focus on keeping children safe from criminals like drug pushers. The media loved her and her image as the fierce but loving guardian of Ontario's innocent. Her record as mayor gave her promises the clout they needed. Before we knew it, she was on the national news. The pit bull of Cambridge was back—and bigger this time.

"So you're officially out of hiding, I take it?"

The call from retired police chief Brian Miller in Cambridge came on my house phone this time, during a rare quiet moment one afternoon.

"Yes, it would seem that way," I replied. "I think every reporter in the province has been here. I'm not sure I feel safe about that, but the cat's out of the bag now. But I guess if anyone wanted to keep Alison quiet, it's too late now. She's been singing like a bird to anybody with a microphone." Alison had gone for a walk, and I could talk freely. "Miller, I haven't heard anything on the news in the last week. What's going on up there?"

I could almost hear him smile over the phone.

"That's why I'm calling. Make sure you both watch the six o'clock news tonight. There's been an unexpected breakthrough, but from another investigation. It caught us all by surprise. But we're not complaining." He paused. "Tell Alison she can come home. It's over."

The call to have a police inquiry into the old shooting of Sergeant John Perry was cut short when a long-time Waterloo Regional investigation into a drug money laundering ring turned up the name of Mike Denny's son, the lawyer—including ties to organized crime figures that Alison had tangled with as mayor years ago. It all seemed to fall into place with what we'd been through. Alison and I watched the news cameras follow Denny Jr. and some of his associates as they were put into police cars leaving their arraignment at the courthouse, all loudly claiming their innocence. The poison-pen letters about John Perry's death had stopped. Miller had told me that none of the notes they had tested for fingerprints had offered any evidence. But it was only a matter of time before the police would build a connection between these arrests and the threats to Alison Perry's life. I knew the Waterloo Regional Police were out for blood because the attack on Alison had cost them one of their own.

"I'm so glad there's been a break in Alison's case." Gail Melvin called early one morning from her RCMP office overseas. "You both must be so relieved that it's almost over. I've been keeping tabs on all this from here. How have you been holding up?"

"It's been a bit of a wild ride, for sure," I answered. "But we're both okay. Alison's chomping at the bit to get back and take on the world—or at least the greater Kitchener–Waterloo region. I appreciate your keeping an eye on us, Gail."

"There's talk of a special police remembrance service for Dave Carlson, Farran. I may take a red-eye flight home for that. Will I see you both there?"

That caught me off guard, and I suddenly couldn't breathe. That night in Ruth's living room I had seen the truth about Paul Vaughn—and about Dave Carlson. The former had kept my mind busy for now, and where the latter was concerned, I was still emotionally holding the door shut on the rest of the truth of John Perry's shooting. As I had been from the first day Alison walked back into my life, I was afraid of the questions we had to ask and the answers they would bring.

"I—I know Alison will be there," I stammered. "I'm not sure when I'm going back to Cambridge. I have some personal things going on down here right now."

"I understand," came the reply. "I hope I'll see you there. I'm just glad it's over for you both."

I was acutely aware as I hung up that it was far from over.

"That means I'll be heading back to Cambridge soon."

Alison and I sat in the living room, with an early fire in the fireplace to ward off the September evening's chill. We had drinks, and I was matching hers two to one. If she noticed, she said nothing.

"I'm not going back." It was the first time I'd said the words out loud, even to myself.

"What do you mean, you're not going back? What about your job at the university? Your condo?"

"I told you that day you walked into my office that I was moving out," I replied. "I didn't mean to a new office. I meant out of the university entirely. And I'm putting the condo up for sale."

"Sounds like a big change for you," Alison said quietly, staring into her drink.

"It is. But that's what I need. A fresh start." I got up to refill my drink. "The person who lived that life is gone."

"I was . . . I . . . I guess I'm disappointed to hear that, Fan. I was hoping to . . . to spend time with you now and then. Do lunch, talk, that sort of thing. It's been crazy, but it's been good to see you again. I've realized how much I missed our friendship. How much I still do."

A thousand emotions must have crossed my face then. Thank God I had my back to her. And—also thank God—the phone rang.

Expecting another reporter, I let the machine pick it up. But after the beep came Paul's voice.

"Farran, I know you said you'd call me first, but I've had some calls about things with both Mila and Frank, and I thought you should know. We need to talk." He cleared his throat nervously. "Also, I'm . . . I'm finally going to Upper Canada Village to see Monroe House. It's time I did. I wondered if you would go with me. I could use the company. Uh . . . if you want to, I'm going tomorrow at ten."

Paul hung up, and the machine clicked off. When I turned around, Alison was giving me the eyeball.

"You will meet him there, won't you? How long are you going to hang him out to dry?"

"I'm not hanging him out to dry," I snapped.

"Yes, you are," Alison insisted. "He's apologized, and you two had it out the other day. Forgive and forget."

I put my drink down. The way this conversation was going, I'd had enough alcohol.

"Forgive and forget. What a stupid bloody saying that is." I stomped over to the patio window to avoid her look. "Forgiving takes a hell of a long time. And even if you can forgive, God knows you'll never forget. Never."

A heavy silence hung between us, like wet wash on the clothesline. And no breeze.

"Is this about Paul . . . or me?" Alison ventured finally.

"It's about a lot more than you," I admitted. "It's about Gordon taking my father away. It's about my mother never sharing the truth with me, even though she did it to keep me safe. Yes, it's about you and about Paul, too. But most of all," I hesitated, "it's about me."

"You?"

"Yes, me." I fell silent for a moment, struggling to put into words what I had spent twenty years trying to forget. "A long time ago, I did something I couldn't deal with. I had a baby then, too, and I gave her up for adoption to keep her safe from me." Tears threatened at the corners of my eyes, so I took a deep breath and let it go. "I couldn't forgive the girl I was. I couldn't forgive Fan Mackenzie, so I emotionally deserted her. Left her standing on the curb of life and drove away, never to look back. Now I can't forgive myself for that."

I heard Alison set her drink down and stand up.

"For what it's worth, Fan, we've all got something like that buried inside. And I have no answer to it. Real forgiveness is a divine quality, I think, and mere mortals like us don't do well with it. I know I haven't. The best I've been able to do is learn how to cope with it day to day."

We were deep in dangerous territory, and by tacit agreement explored no further that night.

The next morning found me under the large oak tree outside Monroe House in Upper Canada Village. I watched Paul go by, knowing the tree would keep me out of view. At the last moment, he turned once more at the door and our eyes met. He waited, and when I did not join him, he walked into the darkness of the old house.

I sat on the bench under the tree. The village was beautiful in its early autumn glory, the horses drawing the tour carriage slowly by. The drama that had happened there one year ago seemed like a movie I had seen once.

The drama of Monroe House and its fallout also seemed unreal to me as I looked at the old building, yellow and cheerful in the sunshine. I thought of Frank Clifford and his unrequited love for Sheila Monroe. Would he have let her go to the gallows in the end? Or admitted his guilt to save her life? I wondered if even Frank had known the answer to that question.

Finding the answers in life—finding yourself—is hard work. It's trial and error, and not for the faint of heart. I know that being a coward is easy. One size fits all. The only problem is that eventually you run out of places to hide.

So when Paul Vaughn walked out of Monroe House a little later that morning, he found me still sitting on the bench under the oak tree, waiting for him.

Sleep was terrible. I had awful dreams that would wake me in the middle of the night with a pounding heart, the bed soaked with sweat.

They were always about being chased by an unknown man. I began to sleep as little as possible, and took to my old habit of sitting out in the early morning. I had seen little of the beautiful St. Lawrence until then. It was good to lock into the moods of the river, and forget for a while. Even my old friend, the Great Blue Heron, was glad to see me back, I think.

By the second week of September, Alison felt well enough to plan a drive back to Cambridge without me. I was staying in the Seaway Valley for the time being, at least until I decided what my next step would be. I honestly didn't want to go back right then, but I also didn't want to face five hours in the car with my old best friend.

Her birthday fell on the day before she left. I had organized a little birthday/going-away party for her, and we'd made it to the car rental place in Cornwall so she'd be able to drive home. Although the cast on her wrist would not come off for another week, it was more of an annoyance than an injury. Alison refused my offer to take her to the train station, insisting that she preferred to drive and have her own wheels when she arrived in Cambridge.

"Is there anything I can help with, Alison?" I leaned on the doorframe to the bedroom that had been hers, having run out of busy work in the kitchen.

She turned from the suitcase she was packing. Her tote bag stood on the floor. "Actually, I was about to come out and ask you the same thing. People will be coming soon. Can I help you get ready?"

"Nope. Everything's done. I'm pretty basic with these things. No Martha Stewart in this house."

Alison smiled. "You didn't have to do this for me. It's very nice of you."

I shrugged. "I wanted to," I answered sincerely. "We've all been through a lot over the past month. Now that we've dealt with . . . with most things, we deserve a party."

"Most things? Not all things."

"No."

Alison sighed and sat on the bed. "Farran, I'm sorry about how I acted the night of the storm. About the things I said. I was very upset and emotionally drained. I shouldn't have taken it out on you."

"Upset because Paul kissed me?"

She turned a deep pink. "Yes. Can you believe that? How high school can you get?"

"So what you told me about my mother and your father wasn't true?" I crossed my arms.

Alison looked up at me, then rose. "Oh, it was true alright." She walked past me into the living room. "But at the time I think I read more into it than there was."

I followed her. "How so?"

"Well, that morning I panicked because I saw them together. But looking back, I don't think anything was inappropriate. They weren't kissing, Fan. Or even holding each other. Your mother was crying and my father had his arms around her, comforting her."

"My mother and I had a huge fight the night before about my father," I explained, "about knowing who he was. We still weren't speaking the next morning. That's why she was crying."

Alison looked out the patio doors to the river sparkling in the fall sunlight and shook her head.

"I assumed the worst. I left without you so I wouldn't have to face you. I didn't say goodbye to my dad. I was very upset. Christ, I was fifteen years old."

When will I ever learn to shut up? I know to this day if I had done so right then, things would be very different now. But I opened my mouth and the volatile words came out.

"You were also upset because you thought my mother was involved with your father—and had just accepted a date with the other man you loved. Dave Carlson."

Alison became very still, back to me.

"Yes," she said quietly. "I guess I was a little possessive of Dave. Maybe a little jealous that he was going out with Leslie. He was like a favourite uncle to me."

"You loved him as a woman loves a man, Al," I persisted. "I think I sensed it back then but never acknowledged it until now."

No response.

"A question I've asked myself for thirty years," I continued, "is why did our friendship die? It wasn't because you moved away. It had started long before then. And your father's sudden death should have brought us closer together. We were best friends since Grade Two. But instead of needing me then, you shut me out completely."

I sat down on the couch.

"Alison, what's the number one reason high school girls fall out of their friendships, even at a time in life when friendship is so crucial? A man. The boyfriend is the one thing that can come between them. And that's what happened to us."

"I didn't have a boyfriend, remember?" She turned to face me then. "Not a real one. I was stuck on David Cassidy. I had it so bad you guys used to make fun of me about it."

"That's right," I agreed, "until your fifteenth birthday. You had already started to change. To dress more maturely, to try to be grown up. Natural, I guess. But the weekend of your birthday, all the David Cassidy posters came down. And you cut your long hair into a shag, making you look older. We didn't do these things together like the old days. You did it on your own and I was left to catch up. You wanted to catch the eye of an older man, a real man—not a handsome face on a poster. Someone fairly young and attractive, with a cool job and a great red sports car. David Cassidy got dumped for Dave Carlson, and you didn't want me to know."

Alison shrugged and walked over to steal a chip from the bowl on the coffee table. "I had a bit of a crush on him. And you and I were growing apart. It happens, Farran."

"It was a lot more than just a crush, Al." I watched her closely but she focused on the chip bowl. "You loved him. I think your mother knew, and she was worried about it. How your father would feel if he found out. At the double birthday party, you were the one that gave him the gold watch. For a while, I wondered if it had been your mother and that was the cause of the black looks I remember between your parents. That maybe Jessica had feelings for Dave or something deeper. Gail Melvin said to me that your father was preoccupied with something in the weeks before his death. Something personal. She wondered if there were marital troubles at home, and assumed it was Jessica if there were.

"But you had spent your savings for our planned trip on a gold watch for Dave. That's why you started to fudge on something we'd planned for years. Something only a year away."

"My parents bought him that watch."

"You did. Your father looked surprised and upset. Your mother wasn't all that surprised, but she was concerned. And you read the inscription on the back without missing a beat."

"What?" She finally met my eyes.

"Alison, inscriptions on the backs of watches are very fine and hard to read. You have to hold them in the right light and bring them close. I remember how you just flipped that watch over and read it with a glance. That's because you didn't have to read it. You knew what it said. And you didn't include a birthday card. You wanted to give that to him later when you were alone and could tell him how you felt. And you did just that later that night outside the house when he was leaving. He bumped into me under our big elm and thought immediately it was you because you had already talked to him out in your yard."

"Where are we going with this, Farran?" Alison asked icily. "So what if I went overboard on a crush when I was fifteen years old? Get over it." She started to walk into the kitchen.

"I'm not the one who isn't over it," I returned, rising from my seat to face her. "I guess I'm running with this because of what you said about forgiveness, about having something buried inside you can't forgive yourself for, just like me." I jumped off the emotional cliff. "I want you to know something before you leave. It wasn't your fault that Dave Carlson shot and killed your father."

That blew the last of her cover, and she froze. For several minutes, she stood with her back to me. I wondered what was going through her head, if we would continue playing emotional poker with the past and just how far it would go. When she finally turned to face me, I could see the bullshit part was over. The old wound was still raw and in her eyes for all to see.

"It wasn't?" Alison whispered.

"No, it wasn't. I think you've always blamed yourself for that, believing that Dave shot your dad because they had quarrelled over you. Things were strained between them in the final days and seemed to come to a head the night of the birthday party. John and Dave had words after my mother and I left your house that night, and again the next morning before they got the call for the Regency garage. In your young and romantic mind, your love for Dave could be the only thing that might make two best friends and brothers in arms fall out like that. But it wasn't."

I came over and gently put my arms around her.

"You were right, but for the wrong reason, Alison. Dave Carlson did shoot his best friend John Perry, but it wasn't intentional. It was a terrible accident, a tragedy because it could have been avoided."

She looked at me, and her eyes were unfathomable.

"Alison, *Dave was already going blind.*"

And then the doorbell rang with the first of our guests. As usual, my timing was impeccable.

I have already said I give strange parties, and this was no exception. Everyone came—Ruth, Carolyn, Lynn, Jerry, even Paul with his tail between his legs. All were on their best behaviour, and it seemed as if they were actors in a movie I couldn't turn off. The strain of the past few weeks and all the water under the bridge were evident. Except in Carolyn's case. She just shoved a casserole dish at me when she came through the door and then retired to a corner of the living room.

I cashed in on the chatty atmosphere, saying little all evening but drinking well. Alison had her public persona switched on and was a brilliant conversationalist—but she drank well, too. Fortunately, both of us could hold our liquor (or do we always only *think* we do?), and no one was the wiser to the landmine we'd stepped into. Except maybe Jerry, who did give me a couple of looks over the course of the evening. But then he's always giving me the fish eye, so it probably meant nothing.

Ruth gave me a hug on her way out the door that night.

"Farran," she said quietly, "the rest of the family will be coming home next week to meet their brother for the first time. I'd like you to be there, too."

"Are you sure I won't be in the way?" I asked. "Maybe it should just be you and your children, Ruth."

Ruth shook her head. "Come. For me," she said as Carolyn came up to join her.

Ruth moved off to say goodbye to Alison, and Carolyn turned to me. "Will you be here for the family hoedown?" she asked grimly.

I put my hands up to ward off the comments.

"I think it should be just your family, but Ruth feels she needs me there."

"She does," Carolyn agreed, surprisingly. She looked over my shoulder at Paul, who was putting on his coat. "For that matter, so will he. Guaranteed—the natives won't be friendly."

Paul gave Alison a hug and then came up to me.

"I'm going to see Ruth . . . Mum . . . to her car," he called awkwardly to Carolyn as she headed for the door. "I'll just be a minute." He shoved his hands in his pockets, shot a glance at Jerry who was deep in conversation with Alison and then looked at me.

"I need a small favour from you, Farran."

"What's that?"

"Well, as Sheila Monroe's legal heir, I'm the only family left for both Frank's and Mila's estates, such as they are. Everything will be in probate for a while, and I have to legally file a claim to the estates, which I will do because there's no one else left."

I nodded. "That's what I did with my uncle."

"Well, the portrait of my mother didn't burn down in the house that night," he said. "Jerry told me they found the painting in the garden shed outside. That must have been what Frank had in his hands when he ran past me, before returning to lock himself in the house."

A brief flash of memory came to me from that night in the burning farmhouse: pounding uselessly on the locked door of the library, flames all around me, the sound of footsteps running into the house and back out to the back door.

"Frank couldn't let it burn," I said softly. "He was ready to destroy himself and his house, but he couldn't destroy the last piece of Sheila he had."

Paul nodded. "The favour I need is for you to store it here. It's still impounded, but I should have it by next week. I don't want to leave it in the hotel room. I'd feel better if it were here with you."

"Sure. I understand."

"Another thing is the necklace."

I put up my hands again. "Oh, I won't store that here. It's too valuable."

"No. No. That won't come to me for a while. I guess the old wills under both Garnet Monroe and his mother state the wife of the firstborn son inherits it outright. They need to have it appraised, and in order to do that the necklace's history has to be authenticated. I suggested talking to you about doing that. So they're going to call you." Paul sighed. "If the damned thing really is a Paul Revere piece, I want you to help me figure out what to do with it. After all," he added, "you found it."

Exhaustion and alcohol hit in equal force that night. With no strength or desire to open the can of worms we'd stepped into earlier, Alison and I fell into our beds without further talk.

I dreamed again. This time the shadowy man caught up with me, grabbing me by the arm. It was John Perry. He was in uniform, bleeding from the chest in two places. His mouth kept opening as he tried to tell me something. But, except for the words 'Stop' and 'Alison,' I couldn't make out the garbled sounds.

I woke up, my mouth open in a silent scream.

There was no sleep for me after that.

I got up and made myself a pot of tea, taking it and me out to the patio. Wrapped in a blanket, I sat in the silence particular to early autumn, waiting for the first rays of light to appear across the river.

It was September 10th. Thirty years ago, Sergeant John Perry had died, and so many lives had changed forever in the wake of it. In Alison's case, the fallout was still going on, and I didn't know when it would end—or if it would at all. Some wounds just never heal. Some things you just can't get over. Sometimes, all we can do is be human.

I thought of Dave Carlson, waking up thirty years ago to the horrible truth that he'd shot and killed his best friend. That his refusal to face what was happening to his vision had cost a human life when he had sworn to serve and protect. It must have been like a death sentence to a young man with an active life and full career ahead of him to realize he would soon be giving it all up to sit in the dark. I understood the fear and crushing sense of defeat that Dave must have been dealing with at the time, and why he had failed to see the tragedy that his denial could—and did—bring.

Then the years of denial and self-punishment for causing John's death. Would things have been different if Dave had confessed the truth at the time? Officially, extortionist, arsonist and murderer Mike Denny would have walked away a free man, at least on the charge of murder. Unofficially, a young woman would have been given what she needed back then to find closure and healing for a terrible loss in her life, instead of living for three decades with a burden of guilt that wasn't hers to carry. But Dave Carlson had failed to see that, too.

For her part, Alison had chosen to see what she wanted to see that summer—that Dave loved her as a woman, not as the child of a close friend, a kid he'd watch grow up. I thought of John and Jessica and my mother, and of the currents of life that had moved around me as a teenager. Youth had allowed me the luxury of seeing only what I chose to as well, of being asleep at the switch of my life.

Personally, I had carried that approach into adulthood and for far too long. Where the past was concerned, I wasn't a kid anymore. As the first rays of light cracked the early autumn gloom on the St. Lawrence, reality stood in front of me in its black shroud like the Ghost of Christmas Yet to Come, finger pointing ominously at the truth that had me cowering on my knees, face to the ground.

But, unlike Scrooge, the truth would not save me.

By the time Alison got out of bed, I had been up for several hours. We avoided talk until she had coffee, both of us hungover and uninterested in breakfast. She joined me out on the riverside patio when she'd showered and dressed. I was still in my housecoat and made no sudden moves to change that. We sat in absolute silence for what seemed a long time, watching the St. Lawrence constantly changing, yet staying the same through that very process of change.

"Thirty years, Fan," Alison broke the quiet. "Thirty years ago today my life changed forever."

"Things changed for a lot of us when your dad died, Al. He was that kind of man." I studied my tea cup. "All this upheaval of the past weeks did one thing for me—made me realize I never properly grieved for your dad. I couldn't handle it at the time, and locked it away until now."

"Many old wounds never healed. Like mine. Listen, Fan," she turned to face me, taking my hand. I didn't pull away. "I thought about what you told me yesterday. I understand what you're trying to do, and I appreciate it. You're right. I have carried a huge guilt that I helped cause my father's death. But what I've been able to realize over the last few weeks is that if Dave did shoot my father, he was an adult and made a choice to do so. I didn't tell him to do that and I didn't force him to, either. I've let it go."

"Dave didn't do it for you," I said quietly. "He was already going blind."

Alison shook her head and got up to walk to the edge of the patio.

"Al," I persisted, "it was right in front of us, and we didn't see it. I don't know what kind of visual degeneration was going on, and now we'll never know. But that's why Dave refused treatment after the shooting. He didn't want anyone to see the truth. And he wanted to pay for the death of his best friend in the only way he could handle."

"I don't see it now, Fan." She shook her head again.

"At Ruth's house, I told Lynn I was stumbling around half blind. And the word 'half-blind' hit me. That's what all the weird things with Dave had been about. The constant sunglasses to protect his sensitive eyes. Not driving his car at night. Putting that car, his baby, away for the winter in September—one of the best months for cruising the roads. Charming Gail Melvin into typing up his reports. Asking you to read the inscription on the watch. And the night of your party, when Dave ran into me outside my house and thought it was you, one big reason was his fading vision. I know you had been outside, too, but I was standing in the circle of light from the streetlamp. And you had just cut your hair short. There should have been no mistake. But these were the actions of a man half blind."

"My father would have known," she snapped. "We would have known."

"Your father did know." My voice was lifeless, as though someone else was talking through me. "And it must have terrible for him. Gail Melvin said in the weeks before his death, he was preoccupied with something she felt was personal. She said a curious thing: that he seemed even unhappy with his work, unhappy to be a police officer. Think about that. She didn't say he was frustrated or fed up. She chose her words carefully and said he was *unhappy*. That's why she assumed it was personal. But it affected his feelings about his work. What could possibly make John Perry, a man proud to be a cop, feel that way?"

I finally looked up at Alison. "Only one thing—the burden of being Dave's senior officer. A man who is responsible for the performance and safety of the officers under him. And John's best friend was going blind. It wasn't getting better. As each day passed, the chance of something going wrong on the job grew. Dave was virtually playing with other peoples' lives going out there with a visual impairment. But Dave loved his work, and his career was central to his life. A desk job of any sort was probably out. I think he dragged his heels, putting the onus on John to force the issue. Dave got along as long as he could. It strained the friendship to the breaking point. Things snapped the night of your party, and that's what the arguments were about. John said it was time for Dave to see Chief Miller and resign. They probably would have gone in that morning to do it, but then the call came over the radio and the tragedy unfolded."

I watched Alison carefully as she thought about this. She played nervously with the ties on her jacket and started to cry a little.

"Miller said my dad's gun was half empty when he walked into that garage," she shot back, her voice shaking. "You said there was a cop on the take who wanted my dad out of the way. Maybe that was Dave. My dad was set up."

"I think John forgot all about doing his gun the day before, as he usually did, because of what was on his mind. He knew that the following morning he would have to end his best friend's career. And he would have had spare ammunition on his belt. Why not check his gun before going into the Regency garage? God only knows what words passed between them that morning on the way there."

I stood up, and my knees didn't feel very good.

"If Denny's gang had someone on the take," I said gravely, "we'll never know. And it has no bearing on your father's death. Dave Carlson shot John Perry. And he didn't do it over you. He did it because he walked into that garage and couldn't see."

Alison looked at me, then away to the river. "You're saying this just to make me feel better, Farran. I appreciate the effort, but I've always wanted only the truth."

"I wish it would make you feel better, Alison," I said sincerely. I walked up behind her, crossing my arms to keep my hands from shaking. "But I know the truth will only make you feel worse. The way you looked at it before, I think it all kind of held together, made things clear and simple. The problem now is, you know you shouldn't have killed Dave."

Only the sound of the wind followed my statement. She stood with her back to me, and I waited. I had thought to leave it all alone, just let her leave with it all unanswered. It was mostly conjecture on my part, and I could have been very wrong. But her reply told me the truth of that.

"Accident or not," said Alison to the river, "he still killed my father. He deserved to die."

I closed my eyes. The shaking was moving down to my legs.

"Dave didn't deserve to die. And you don't deserve to be a killer."

I opened my eyes and she was facing me with an odd look on her face, the same one I'd seen on John Perry's face years ago when discussing the murdered Simser boy.

"Justice must be served," she said.

"And no mercy, even for someone who already gave up his life in payment for killing a friend?"

"Dave broke my heart. Destroyed my life. Killed the man I loved most in this world. Mercy?" She looked at me with flat eyes. "I think not."

The wind came in off the river with icy fingers, and I felt naked without the blanket wrapped around me. But I didn't move, facing her and reality, searching the face I had once known so well for something left I would recognize. "You've never wanted the truth, Alison. You already had your mind made up. The day you walked into my office at the university, you didn't say you needed to find out the truth—you started to say you needed to know if I could *figure out* the truth. Those two ideas are very different. I was the only person on earth with close to the same memories as you. You needed to know if I would be a danger to you."

"Sounds kind of calculating to me." Alison's voice was smooth and detached.

"It was. When you found the letter your mother got long ago, it confirmed your fear that you were partly responsible for your dad's death. That Dave had shot him when quarrelling with him about you. Getting the second one pushed you over the edge and drove you to exact revenge on the man who killed your father.

"So you came to me." My mouth became a grim line. "To see if I could figure it out or if you were safe. To give you an alibi at the cemetery. To stir up trouble with my amateur efforts at investigation and bring notice to the issue of your father's death. Just to make sure, you sent the anonymous letter to the newspaper."

"I didn't send the letters about my father," she said. "You just said the one I got pushed me over the edge. You're not making sense, Farran."

"Just the one to the media, Alison" I answered. "It arrived over a week after the others did. The originals were sent out all at the same time—by Dave Carlson. Except for the one your mother got. I think Dave sent her that when he heard she was dying. It was the closest he could bring himself to tell her the truth. This time, he'd been diagnosed with terminal cancer himself and wanted to atone for his guilt. He wanted someone to figure out the truth and let him off the hook emotionally. So he sent poison-pen letters with terrible whispers about the death of John Perry. The idea? It came from the Agatha Christie book that was sitting on the end table in his living room. *The Moving Finger*. It's one of her best. It's about the use of poison-pen letters in a village to create a stir as a cover-up for a well-planned murder. Because, as Agatha's characters say again and again, where there's smoke, there's fire."

"Where there's smoke, there's fire," she murmured.

I couldn't face her anymore and turned away.

"What did you do at the cemetery, Al?" I asked softly. "Tell Dave to turn on the engine to get warm while you went back for your purse?"

"Something like that. It worked."

"Your years overseas working in landmine removal and handling explosives with your husband came in handy, didn't they?"

"Yes. It seemed better that way, more appropriate. And, of course, more like a gangland hit."

"You set the wires before you left home, switched from a purse to a tote bag to carry the device in, connected the bomb while Dave was getting out of the car, and let him turn the key after. Of course, he wouldn't see it getting back in because he was blind. Have I got the general idea?"

"You're bang on as usual, Fan."

Hearing the old nickname made it hard for me to speak. So many years, so many conversations, so many secrets shared. But those secrets had brought us closer together. This one would tear us apart for good.

I turned and looked at Alison standing on my patio, the river behind her.

"You killed a man, Alison, and you used me to do it."

She sat back down in her chair and I waited for . . . for something. Anything to try to make it right. An explanation. An apology. Most of all, the words that would end the nightmare, tell me that I had it all wrong. What I got wasn't even close.

"Are you going to call Jerry when I'm gone?" she asked bluntly.

"I don't know," I answered honestly. "It's all guesswork. I can't prove any of it." I came to stand over her chair. "I'm going to take a shower now, but in case you're wondering, I don't think I'll ever feel clean again."

I took my time in the shower, thinking how I shouldn't think about anything at all. It was all like a dream I wanted desperately to wake up from. The hot water felt good on my chilled skin, but inside I was numb. Numb was better than nauseous, I figured, but when I got out and dried off, I was still shaking all over. Alison had packed her car and was waiting for me. I'd hoped that she'd be gone when I got out.

"I thought of leaving while you were in the shower, Fan, but I couldn't just go like that." She stood in the kitchen, her tote bag on the counter next to my car keys.

"You've done it before, Alison."

She nodded. "Not this time. A few things have to be said. Like thank you for helping me when I came to you. For trying to be a friend one last time. For being my best friend all those years. You know, Fan," she added, rubbing her hands together as though cold, "I have so many happy memories from my childhood, and you're in most of them. I'm glad I knew you." Her voice broke.

I sat down in a kitchen chair, not trusting my knees or my voice.

"Just go, Al," I whispered. "Just go."

And when I looked up, she was gone. I heard the door close and then the motor of the rental car start up. Fighting the tears, I noticed her tote bag was still on the counter beside my keys. I swallowed a hysterical giggle and was about to try to catch her when I heard the door open.

"I forgot my purse again," Alison said sheepishly. By this time, my eyes were blurred with tears and I didn't care. I just nodded. I couldn't speak. She grabbed the tote bag off the counter. "For the children, Fan," she said, and vanished again.

Then, through my tears, I saw something gold on the counter. Not the silver of my car keys, but the gold of a man's watch. I reached over to pick it up. It was Dave's watch. And my car keys were gone.

No.

I exploded from the chair, a tangle of limbs and panic.

No. No. No.

Shaking and stumbling, I ran down the hall and out the door to the porch overlooking the driveway. The rental car was idling away, but Alison sat behind the wheel of mine.

"No! Al! No!" I screamed.

John . . . John . . . I tried to stop her like you warned me to. I ran toward the car, calling her name. For one eternal second, I looked into the eyes I had once known, the eyes again filled with that pain so hard to see.

Then Alison turned the key.

A flash of light. A roar of thunder.

And the blast
body-slammed me
into the black.

PART FOUR: Light

At that moment a curious crack sounded inside the statue, as if something had broken. The fact is that the leaden heart had snapped right in two. It certainly was a dreadfully hard frost.

Oscar Wilde
The Happy Prince

Chapter THIRTEEN: The Hard Frost

Dark.
Light.
Grey sound.
She was both mine and the girl from Farran's Point.
"Mom?" I whispered.
Mist and distance, back again.
No, Fan. Go back. Not now . . .
My arms reached out vainly to hold her one more time and I cried.
Someone else. A man.
Haley . . .
I started to sob. "Mom, please."
Haley . . . Find her . . .
Tears filled my throat. "Come back," I pleaded.
I couldn't see her face now.
Trouble . . .
I opened my eyes and another face came into focus. It was Jerry, looking about a hundred years older than when I'd seen him last. He touched my cheek, and I felt it was wet.
"Farran," he asked softly. "Do you know me?"
"Jer," I said and closed my eyes.
"Farran," he said again, "wake up."
I opened my granite lids and looked at him. "Why?"
"You're in the hospital. You've been unconscious for several days."
I could hear other people in the room, but it was too much effort to look. And somewhere out of view, a machine beeped quietly.
"Water."
Jerry brought a glass to my lips and helped me take a drink. He said something to one of the people and I heard footsteps squeak out the door.
Trouble.
Sudden dread rushed over me. Something was wrong, something . . .
"There was a fire," I managed. "I was hurt in a fire?"
"No." Jerry looked grim. "Just rest now. We'll talk later."
"Paul was there. He's all right?"
"Rest, Farran," Jerry took my hand. "Paul's with Ruth. They've been waiting outside since you were brought in. They'll give Ruth a few minutes with you, okay?"

"Ruth." Ruth's house. All of us at the table. Something I said to Paul. Alison sitting there so tired . . .

Alison. Fire. A fireball.

My eyes flew open in terror. "Alison!" I cried out.

Then I heard a woman's voice screaming from somewhere beside me, and Jerry was holding me . . . people were moving . . . something was warm in my veins . . . I floated back into the grey . . .

Falling. Landing. I opened my eyes to focus on another face. Ruth was sitting holding my hand. She was crying silently.

"Have I died?" I whispered. "I'm sorry, Ruth."

"Oh, Fan. Fan." She stood up to kiss me on the forehead. "No, thank God. We still have you. You scared the hell out of us for a few minutes, but that's over now."

I tried to reach out to hug her, but only one arm seemed to work, so I touched her face to wipe the tears.

"Don't cry. I never meant to make you cry."

"Rest, Fan. Just rest," said Ruth softly. "Then I'll take you home."

The ICU at the Cornwall Community Hospital has no windows. I lost all sense of time. Wrapped in my cocoon of shock, I let hours slip by listening to the monitor in my room. I didn't think.

"You were very lucky, Ms. Mackenzie." Doctor Barkley stood over me, the man who had treated Gordon last year, the night we rushed him in. I remembered Barkley's dry sense of humour at the time, but now he was very serious with me. "The other car in the driveway partially shielded you from the explosion and the flying debris. If it hadn't, you'd be dead. Your left arm is broken from landing on it. You have several cracked ribs, but none of them punctured the lungs. There were some mild head injuries as well. We've been watching for reactions, but aside from a slight concussion, there's been nothing so far. That's the good news." He looked at me and his face grew graver, if that were possible. "We don't know why, perhaps due to severe shock, but you went into cardiac arrest while you were in triage. It took us over a minute to get you back. I'm telling you this for a reason. I want you to be very, very patient with yourself in the weeks ahead. You have a lot to come back from."

If he only knew about the rent in my heart. But I said nothing, keeping the harrowing secret deep inside.

I went into automatic. Ate what they brought me, took all the pills, moved up into Observation, then a private room. I had a police officer outside my door round the clock. Lynn came. Paul came. Detective Constable Jordan Wiley dropped by with Jerry to get a statement and left with an empty notepad. Flowers and messages began to arrive. I read them all. Nothing penetrated. I let them turn on the TV they brought me, but I didn't watch it. Turned it off when Alison's picture flashed on the news. Magazines I flipped through if anyone were watching and sidelined when alone.

But still, there were whispered discussions outside my door every day. Maybe because since I'd talked to Ruth, I had not uttered a single word.

On the fourth morning, Jerry came in to find me standing, my breakfast untouched. His glance took in my clothes on me, such as they were, and the lumpy cast stuck in my jacket. I held out a piece of paper.

"Gail Melvin's note says she's coming home for the memorial service for Alison in Cambridge," I said, breaking my silence. "It's scheduled for tomorrow. I'm going. Are you coming with me?"

Jerry opened his mouth and then closed it. We stood squared off for a few moments, silence restored. Then, he slowly held out his hand and helped me to the door.

I think the City of Cambridge shut down for that day.

Jerry and I arrived minutes before the service, in the big Lutheran church on King Street, in the former Preston area. Traffic was cordoned off for blocks, with security through the roof. There must have been over a thousand people in the church and down the sidewalk into the street, watching the service on monitors set up for them outside. Half the church inside was filled with police officers, most of them Waterloo Regional, but many from other services all over the province. Jerry had thought to stop for his uniform on the way out of the Seaway Valley and thankfully arrived in full dress. That fact and his ID badge got us through security into the church. Then, after a brief discussion with someone at the door, we were whisked up to one of the front pews, TV cameras following our every move. I know Jerry did that for me, thinking I wanted to be close. He had no idea that in fact he'd brought me up close and personal to hell itself.

The service seemed to go on forever. Everyone who was anyone in Cambridge had something to say. Retired police chief Brian Miller spoke about both Alison and Dave, and of course the late Sergeant John Perry. I thought about the day Alison and I visited the elderly man In his home to talk about the past. The frailty I'd seen slowly leave him that day was back with a vengeance.

"I will say on behalf of the Waterloo Regional Police Service that the investigation into these deaths is top priority," Miller finished. "We have leads, and they will be followed. We'll get whoever did this." Emotion struggled with self-control. "That's a promise for Dave and

Alison," he whispered, the microphone barely catching the words. "We won't rest until they rest."

I saw Gail Melvin in uniform several rows back, looking white as a ghost. And in the front pew on the other side of the church sat a man I recognized from the photographs I'd seen in Alison's bedroom a million years ago, the night I went to get her things and leave for the Seaway Valley. It was Martin Standish, her ex-husband, looking as though he'd finally stepped on one of those landmines he'd devoted years of his life to eradicate.

Even the Premier of Ontario was there, suitably grim and wrapped in bodyguards. He nodded in silent agreement throughout the final address, given by the Minister for Community and Social Services. References to Alison's career as mayor and the focus she had had on community building were stressed as proof she had been ahead of her time. "Alison Perry worked well with the tangibles," he said. "Economic development, strategic regional alliances, long-term planning. But she also kept a close rein on the intangibles, those things that mean so much to the quality of life for us all: community-building, recreation, library and resource services, history and cultural development. This she did for many reasons, but one above all. For the future. For the children of Cambridge."

For the children, Fan.

"All this Alison would have brought with her to Queen's Park, if fate had allowed her to do so," he continued. "Her energy, ethics and ideals would have been an important addition to the workings of the province. But we stand here today, instead. The death of Alison Perry Standish is an irreparable loss to her family and friends, and to the people of Cambridge. And I know it is also such a loss to the Province of Ontario, in particular to our children, for whom Alison believed that security and justice must be served."

Justice must be served.

"I have to get out of here," I whispered to Jerry, trying unsuccessfully to rise. He'd kept his arm wrapped tightly around my shoulders to hold me up since I'd stepped out of the car. That same arm now held me down.

"Don't move," Jerry whispered curtly. He held up a hand to block my protest. "I understand your feelings, but if you bolt right now the press will be on you like wolves the minute you reach the front steps. Our only chance to get out of here in one piece is with the crowd."

As usual, he was right. I stayed put and put my face in my hands to keep from screaming.

The next clear memory I have is being swept along with the crowd, moving out of the church's gloom toward the light. I deliberately kept my eyes to the ground and let Jerry steer me through the sea of people, avoiding any visual contact with Brian Miller or Gail Melvin. I couldn't face either of them at that point.

However, as Jerry stopped to talk with a few police cronies on the way to the car, I felt a hand on my arm.

"Aren't you Farran Mackenzie?" I heard an unfamiliar voice say.

I looked up into the eyes of Martin Standish, Alison's ex-husband.

"Yes," I whispered. I couldn't run away from him. He looked as bad as I felt.

"I recognize you from the newspapers. Alison often talked about you," Martin said, a sad smile moving on and off his face with equal speed. "I always hoped to meet you one day, Ms. Mackenzie, but never . . . never . . . " He broke off.

"No." I took his hand and squeezed it.

"I still loved her, you know. I wanted her to stay with me, where it was safe. I tried . . . "

I looked him square in the eye. "The Alison I knew and got to know again always made her own decisions," I could say honestly. "What happened is not your fault."

"Press," Jerry growled beside me.

I turned to see a swarm of microphones and cameras coming through the crowd toward us like fighter jets. Someone in military fatigues hauled Martin Standish off in one direction while Jerry steered me in the other. We made a beeline for the car, a circle of police uniforms falling in behind to buy us the time to escape.

After that, I didn't dare have Jerry drive me to my condo in Waterloo to pick up things I might need. Instead, as we headed slowly up King Street through the traffic toward Highway 401, I pointed with my good hand.

"Turn left before the bridge," I said.

Jerry did so without comment and we cruised down Chopin Drive, the former Water Street, stopping where Number 251 had once stood. The street was as quiet as a graveyard. I had not been there since I'd sold the lot after the fire that took the house of my childhood—and everything of that life with it. Someone was building on the old foundation and walls were taking shape. The old back shed was gone, as were the peony hedge and the vegetable garden Mom had worked on for so many years. There was a new swing on the tree in the backyard. And over it all towered the massive elm in the front yard, the tree I had been under when Dave Carlson came over from the Perrys' home and mistook me for Alison with his failing vision.

I inadvertently looked over at the former Perry house, the scene of such drama and tragedy all those years ago. It seemed little changed from those days, and I could almost see Alison flying out the front door as she so often did, calling me to come over and play.

Tears threatened.

"Let's go," I said quietly, firmly looking out the front window. I felt Jerry turn to me.

"I'll help you if you want to get out and walk around a bit," he offered.

"No, thank you." I put a hand on his arm. "Thank you for bringing me here, and to the funeral. I'd just rather go now. This isn't my neighbourhood anymore. I guess I just wanted to say goodbye."

It's hard to yell with cracked ribs.

"Quiet!" I carefully raised my good arm to wave at them. "Hey! Over here!"

Ruth, Lynn and Paul all stopped talking at once and looked at me. We were in Ruth's living room in Ingleside, with me propped up on the green-gold couch. Carolyn was conspicuously absent.

I had arrived there from the Cambridge shindig with Jerry the evening before. On my insistence, we'd driven straight through to the Seaway Valley after the funeral service and the pit stop on Water Street. I made it only because of the heavy painkillers Dr. Barkley had given me at the hospital. Going home to my uncle's empty house was strictly out for many obvious reasons, so Jerry delivered me to Ruth that night. Carolyn gave up her guest room, surprisingly without a grumble, and I'd fallen asleep when my head hit the pillow—with a vague sensation that Ruth was taking a strip out of Jerry for driving me halfway across the province in my condition.

Now we were having a huddle to discuss the care and keeping of one invalid Farran Mackenzie, soft in both body and mind.

"You'll stay here, Fan," Ruth repeated firmly. "It's that simple."

"I can't," I said again. "Carolyn and Tommy are here. They're your daughter and grandson. They have seniority. Carolyn can't keep sleeping on the couch for the next few weeks. Besides," I pointed out, "your other children are on their way here as we speak to meet their new brother. Am I right?"

"That's been postponed," Ruth said unexpectedly. I glanced at Paul, who looked secretly relieved.

"Why?" I asked.

"Because of what just happened with you," said Ruth, taking her mother Alice's chair by the window. "Carolyn said it would be too much for everyone with you in the hospital and with Alison . . . " The woman took a deep breath and let it out. "For once, I agreed with her and let her call her brothers and sister last week to cancel. We'll see how things are at the end of the month."

"Ruth, you have no idea how much I appreciate your generosity," I began, "but I have to get—"

"Back to the house on Ault Island," Lynn finished for me. "That's fine. I'll stay with you."

"You?" I said, brows raised. "Like you can walk away from your work at *The Citizen*. No. No, I can't—"

"I have sick leave coming," Lynn cut me off again triumphantly. "It'll be a chance to really visit. At least for a week or two. I could use a break from the grind."

"And about the house . . . "

"I want you to stay there," Paul stepped in. "I know it's part of my father's estate and everything, but I have no need for it right now. At least live in it till spring and give me a chance to decide about it."

I stopped speaking and looked at them, really looked at them. Three people I had never met two short years ago and here I was. I'd lost my share of battles, to be sure, but for the first time I felt that I was winning the war. And for once, I wasn't sitting on my tongue.

"I know you love me," I said softly. "I'm lucky you do. I love you, too. You're my family now, and I do need you. Dr. Barkley said I have a lot to come back from, and he's right. But it seems that every time I come here, I end up in pieces, and you have to put me back together again. Not this time. I need to know that I can come back on my own two feet. And what I need from you is the space and time to do it in. That," I added suddenly, "and one other thing."

I looked at Ruth and then at Lynn.

"Lynnie," I said, using Jerry's nickname for his old schoolfriend, "I need you to help me find my daughter. I need to find her soon."

Lynn smiled slowly and sat down beside me on the couch. "I thought you'd never ask, Fan."

"You have a daughter?" Paul took the footstool nearby.

"Yes." The secret that had stayed inside for so long was finally ready to come out—some of it, anyway. "When I was doing one of my degrees at Oxford in England, I got pregnant. Gave the baby up for adoption because . . . for a lot of reasons. I named her Haley after my father, Hal. She'd be a grown woman now." I turned to Lynn. "I registered with the national registry last year, but there's been nothing. I want to start my own search, and I hope you can tell me what to do. I . . . she's in trouble. I need to get started. I've put it off too long already."

"Why do you think she's in trouble?" Ruth spoke at last.

215

I looked at each of them, remembering my mother's voice coming to me wherever it was I had gone while unconscious—or dead.

Haley . . . Find her . . . Trouble . . .

I could tell from their faces if I shared that one it would be off to the psychiatrist for me after everything else.

"Let's just say I have a strong feeling about it," I said.

"That's good enough for me," Lynn patted my hand. "I'll get started Monday morning. If I don't call you here, where will you be?"

I smiled over at Ruth. "I'll stay a few more days and impose myself on Ruth until the house . . . until they . . . until the police are finished with everything at the house and it's all . . . it's . . . you know," I finished. "Then I'll take Paul's offer and move back for the winter. I'll have to get someone to come in for a few weeks to help me, but that's no big deal. As I've told you, I'm no longer at the university, and I'm not going back to Cambridge to live. The winter will give me time to think about what's next. If I stay here, I'll need to start looking for a place of my own."

"A lot of nice little spots around here," Paul remarked. "Anywhere special you're going to look?"

I thought a minute.

"I'm not sure," I said slowly, "but I have, as Hercule Poirot would say, a little idea."

OCTOBER

I stood on the yellow grass in front of the little brown cottage I had rented for my first visit a year before. It was just down the road from Gordon's house on Ault Island, and I had noticed a For Sale sign on it that summer with Alison.

My old friend was heavy on my mind that morning. A parcel had arrived from Cambridge, from her ex-husband Martin Standish. The letter inside said he'd been packing up her home and possessions and found something for me as a keepsake. To help keep the happy memories, he wrote. I'd torn off the wrapper to find the photograph from the wall of her bedroom, the one I'd taken years ago at Dave and Alison's birthday party one day before tragedy. I looked at the smiling faces, now all gone. The life long over.

Yet the parcel had not sent me into the tailspin it would have just a few weeks earlier. Lately I was feeling the curious sensation of silence in my head. I often found myself looking at me as though from a distance, watching . . . waiting.

Life and death.

It's really just that simple, isn't it? The two moments in the human experience when the universe stands still are when you hear you're going to have a baby and when you learn a loved one has died. Life had stopped for me for now, and I was in no hurry for the universe to start up again.

I looked at the little brown cottage and remembered Alison in all her ways. Some days that's all I could do to deal with the secret pain in my heart. I wondered about friendship, the second most important relationship in our lives. Why do we pick the friends we do? What is the underlying contract between us? What do our friends do to the patterns of our lives, the directions we move? Could I have done anything years ago, let alone now, to have stopped all this? Or did I blindly help to bring it about?

I felt the anger coming back. Using its strength and my good arm, I pulled the For Sale sign out of the ground and threw it down. It had a Sold banner across it, and I knowingly felt for a new ring of keys in my pocket. I crossed the yellow grass and unlocked the front door.

The inside was quiet and clean, and crowded with memories from my first visit: Lynn's cousin Meredith standing framed by the patio door talking of "wickedness," Lynn herself sitting out by the river with me saying how the new landscape of the St. Lawrence "wasn't real," and Jerry Strauss standing lost in my hallway at 3:00 a.m., dealing with the truth about his own father's tragic death forty years after the fact.

I looked at the bare walls. It was not so different from my condominium back home in Waterloo. Ten years of living, and it had taken only a day to reduce it to bare walls and packed boxes, as though I had never really moved in. An empty canvas like my life, as if everything that had gone before was for nothing.

"Well," I said to the empty cottage, "you're mine now. For better or worse. If I'm going to stay, I'll have to winterize you in the spring." My voice echoed in the silence. "I guess we both have a long way to go."

There is a legend that the tears of the phoenix bird can heal all wounds. Like the phoenix, my friendship with Alison Perry had risen briefly from its own ashes into a new life. But I had cried myself empty over the past few weeks since her death to no avail. Some wounds never heal and perhaps should not.

The not knowing is always worse than the knowing, Alison had said to me. And I had said the same thing to Ruth last year about needing the true story of my father and how he had died. But as I locked the door on my way out, I remembered that truth in life is only so when there is an exception to make the rule. And now I had lived mine.

"Mum's not here." Carolyn let me in the small hallway at Ruth's on a Friday afternoon. The smell of coffee greeted me. "She plays bridge till four."

"I know," I admitted. Warily, we both stayed standing in the hall. "I've come to see you."

"Me?" Now she really had her guard up. "What about?"

"I guess about everything that's gone on in the past few weeks. About you and me."

Carolyn flushed. "Listen, Mackenzie, I know I've been . . . well, difficult . . . with you and Stev—Paul . . . "

"Actually, Carolyn," I said quietly, "I've come to say thank you."

"You have? For what?"

"For being a friend." I looked at her a moment and then stumbled through it. "I don't know if you meant to or not, but you have been. You've always spoken your mind with me and kept to the straight and narrow. You even chased me to my car once to warn me about falling into the past again.

"And you're very good to your mother. Like making her postpone the family gathering when I was in the hospital. She wouldn't have done that for herself."

Carolyn shrugged. "I just didn't feel she was up for the Inquisition. Neither were you or Paul."

"Well, for what it's worth, that means a lot to me. I've grown to love your mom. I'm glad that you take care of her the way you do. I really value people who are upfront about all the bullshit that goes on in life. You're a lot like your grandmother, Alice, you know."

For the first time since we'd met, Carolyn was at a loss for words. We stood squared off in silence, our emotional weapons lowered. It was an odd moment.

"I miss Nan," she whispered.

"I do, too." I nodded slowly. "I'll get out of your hair, Carolyn," I added. "I just wanted to say thanks."

I turned to go and headed for the door.

"My husband and I are separated."

I stopped to look back. She looked at the floor.

"Things came apart this summer. We've filed for legal separation. It's been very hard for me, and for my son." Carolyn's eyes came up to meet mine. "If I've been upfront with you, a lot of it is just that my crap quotient is full at the moment. That's all."

"I understand," I said. Turning the knob, I pushed the front door open and stepped out onto the porch.

"Hey, Mackenzie," she called and then cleared her throat. "Um, I mean . . . Farran. I have a fresh pot of coffee on. Would you like some?"

I stood on the porch and looked at her standing there in the doorway.

"Yes," I smiled slowly, "I'd love some."

"Are you ready?"

This time, Paul stood on my porch and I was in the doorway. We were going together to Ruth's house to meet The Family.

"Absolutely," I answered, and moved back to let him in.

"Lucky you," he muttered. "I've changed three times. Feel like I'm going on my first date, for Christ's sake."

I had to laugh at that.

"Carolyn calls it the Inquisition," I said, closing the door. "But don't let that scare you."

"Carolyn scares me," he said, flinging himself down on my couch. I swear his lower lip stuck out.

"For your information," I shot back, "Carolyn is on our side. She told me to tell you that the other three are all bluff."

"She's on our side? No way."

"Yes way." I went into the bedroom to brush my hair. "I'll just be a moment."

A moment later, Paul appeared in the reflection of my dresser mirror standing behind me. He held out what looked like a blue velvet box in his hand.

"I brought something for you," he said.

I gingerly took the box and opened it. Inside was the Paul Revere necklace. Taking it out, I saw that the diamond was back on its setting and the whole piece had been cleaned. It was beautiful.

"Put it on, Farran," he said softly.

"I—I couldn't."

"Yes, you could. We wouldn't have it if it weren't for you." He took the piece out of my hands and placed it around my neck. I stood mesmerized by my reflection, one hand unconsciously touching the diamond where it lay on my skin. I thought of Sheila Monroe standing very like that in the portrait.

As if he heard my thoughts, Paul said, "The only one who looked more beautiful like that was my mother."

My cheeks felt warm and I took it off.

"It hasn't been a very lucky necklace for its owners," I mumbled.

"No," he agreed. "It hasn't. So many lives wasted for this bauble."

"Well, I wouldn't exactly call it a bauble."

The necklace lay warm and sparkling in my hands.

"No, but it is a thing, Farran. Only a thing. It's certainly not worth a life."

I held the necklace up, catching the light from my ceiling fixture in the god's eye. The blue fire flashed, winking in and out as the diamond moved.

The American Revolution. Young, star-crossed lovers trying to fight the tides of history just to be together. A secret hidden for generations in a family estate. Two other young and star-crossed lovers on opposite sides of marriage and the violent upheaval of a massive engineering project. A man willing to sell his soul to the devil for the sake of history and love. And a woman lost and alone, making a deadly choice for her life.

Winking in and winking out. A blink in the eye of God. Is that all our lives amount to in the end? Or maybe, if we're lucky, they hold a flash of brilliance in the moment we are given. And then we are gone.

"No," I agreed quietly and put the necklace back in its box. "I'll make some calls tomorrow and get going on this. I'll let you know who's going to take a look at it."

I returned to the living room to put the box away and Paul followed.

"Listen, Farran," he began. "I know things are . . . well, unsettled in your life right now. It's still the same for me . . . " He faltered to a halt.

I waited.

"My stress leave is almost over, unless I apply to renew it for another six months." Paul looked at me. "I thought about it a lot for the past week. I'm heading back to Newfoundland on Monday. It's time to get back in the saddle."

"I'm glad to hear that," I said sincerely. "I hope things settle down for you now."

He sighed. "Me, too. I can't go back to my life as the same person, but maybe I can start over somehow."

Impulsively, I hugged him. "I'm sure you'll find what you're looking for, cousin."

Paul held me at arm's length. "I did," he said softly, looking into my eyes. "But it's not the right time. I'm going back home, Farran Mackenzie, but I'm not disappearing from your life. You don't get rid of me that easily. Maybe when I come back . . . maybe next year . . . "

He stood there, looking so handsome. A good man who could see into my soul on a whim. A man most women would play dirty to get close to. But that small thing, that certain something so important between a man and a woman, curiously just wasn't there.

I think my silence spoke volumes. He dropped his arms.

"Well," Paul said grimly as he started to help me on with my coat, "I just hope the inspector really knows what the hell he's got."

NOVEMBER

I had not stayed so late here the last time. Day by day, I watched the beauty of fall slip away—here, and across the river. The strip of brilliant colour reflected in the waters of the great headpond slowly faded to a sad and quiet brown. The geese held their pre-flight meetings and eventually left. Mr. Heron called it a day for the winter, too. For the first time in my life, I was truly alone with no work to anaesthetize life's voice.

Paul held his own through the Inquisition, probably using the same approach to disarm his new siblings that he would to a criminal with a loaded gun. It was a huge relief for us both when it was over and that it had gone well for Ruth. One invoice paid in full.

He left us a week later in a hugging and crying session at Ruth's house. We didn't say goodbye alone and I appreciated that. I didn't have it in me at that point to handle any more emotional surfing. I was still on overload about Alison, with no one I could talk to about the horrible truth. I had lost her, physically and emotionally, just as I was starting to have her back. My heart was like lead and cracked in two, and I didn't have the foggiest idea how to continue on from there. I think Paul saw that in me—not the whole truth, but the fact that something more than bereavement was at work. After the initial shock of Alison's death, he studiously avoided talking about her with me, only asking how I was doing with it all.

And I had no answer to that, even for myself. I kept getting up in the morning, putting one foot in front of the other, eating and sleeping. Other than that, it was all safely just out of range.

Inspector Jerry Strauss was also safely out of range for the most part. He had been so there for me through the darkest days, but once I was all set up in the house on Ault Island again, he seemed to distance himself from me. Jerry called every day and stopped by at least twice a week to check in, but he kept me at arm's length on a personal level. I wondered why. Certainly, it could be chalked up to not wanting a girlfriend with all my head problems and emotional baggage, and the record for courting death on a regular basis. But I felt there was something else, something he was dealing with that would come out in its own good time.

"Just relax and have a good time," said Jerry one night as he drove us to the Wiley home. Detective Constable Jordan Wiley's wife Michelle had come by the house the week before with her daughter Diana to visit and invite me for the supper we'd discussed the day of my mother's service. Both she and Diana had insisted on the invitation and—emotional fatigue and personal cowardice aside—I had no real reason to refuse. And I would never hurt Diana's feelings that way by doing so.

"Oh, I will," I said. "I'm just not sure if I'll be great company, that's all."

"The Wileys know that, and they don't care. They're good people." He was silent a minute. "You need to get out again, start getting back into life."

"I don't know what that is, anymore," I replied, the darkness of the early evening giving me some personal space in the car with him. "That bomb blew away that last of my old life, whatever shreds were left after last summer."

Jerry fell into a heavy silence, as though I had said something wrong. I didn't pursue it, and we exchanged no more words until we pulled into the driveway on Kent Crescent in Long Sault.

The house had changed little since that summer day last year when I had arrived to return Jordan's book, *Voices from the Lost Villages*, and had ended up spending time with Diana—with almost deadly results. Michelle greeted us at the door and took my coat and bottle of wine.

"I'm so glad you feel up to coming, Dr. Mackenzie," she said softly. "Please make yourself at home."

"You're going to have start calling me Farran at some point, Michelle," I smiled.

"Fan, come and see my room," Diana said, carefully hauling me off down the hall to the bedrooms. It was typical of a twelve-year-old's room—with one glaring exception. Whereas Alison and I had covered our walls with David Cassidy and others, Diana's walls sported only a few pictures. But my trained eye saw the pinholes still there from recent posters.

"What happened to all those young heartthrobs you showed me last year?" I teased.

Diana coloured a little. "Oh, they're still hot, I guess. But I've moved on."

"What's his name?"

She flushed pink, opened her mouth to protest and then caught my eye. "You're awful, Fan," she blustered. "If you weren't still injured, I'd hit you with my pillow."

I had to laugh, then pulled her close with my good arm.

"Diana," I whispered, "promise me that you'll have a grand time as a teenager. Live it to the fullest. It comes only once."

"Come on out of there, girls." Jordan Wiley stuck his head in the door and smiled. "Time to join the grownups."

For a moment I was back thirty years ago to that day in Alison's room. But for only a moment. That was then and this was now.

"You heard the constable," I let Diana go. "Let's go."

"Actually, Fan," Diana said as her father retreated, "it's sergeant now. Dad just got promoted to detective sergeant. That's another reason we're having the dinner. To celebrate."

Celebrate we did. I relaxed and enjoyed myself. Michelle's supper was flawless, of course, and by dessert even Jerry seemed more his usual self. There was no mention of Alison, but Diana had read the papers and wanted to know all about the Monroe family and the famous Paul Revere necklace.

"Now, we don't know if it's real, yet," I explained over coffee. "I've sent it to a colleague with the Boston Museum of Fine Arts, and I haven't heard anything back so far."

"What do you think, Farran?" Michelle placed a snifter of brandy beside my cup without asking. I owed her one for that. "Do you think it's the real thing?"

"I don't know," I admitted. "Technically, it's not my background. But having seen the piece, having wor—held it . . . well, there's something about it. It certainly wouldn't surprise me to find out it actually was made by Paul Revere." I took a sip of brandy. "On any account, I'm going to ask Paul Vaughn if I can use the god's eye for a bit. I'd love to find out the true history of that diamond. According to the family story, it goes back much farther than the necklace itself."

"That's so exciting," Diana sighed. "A real mystery to solve."

"If Paul lets me research the diamond," I offered, "maybe you could help me with it."

"Only as long as there aren't any more burning buildings involved," said Jordan.

"Dad!" Diana rolled her eyes.

"No," I contemplated the bottom of my brandy, "no more burning buildings. It's all over." I looked up to see Michelle watching me closely. Protective mother, perhaps. Couldn't say as I'd blame her. "Anyway," I added, raising the snifter, "here's to your promotion, Detective Sergeant. To good changes."

After the toast, Jordan shot a look at Jerry.

"Speaking of changes, sir," he broached carefully, "there's a rumour at work that you're applying for early retirement. Is that true?"

We all turned to Jerry, who gave a short laugh. "You can tell everyone to stop crossing their fingers, Wiley. It's true. Or, at least," he added, the smile leaving his face, "I'm looking into it. I haven't made up my mind yet."

I opened my mouth and closed it again. Not now.

"Actually, sir," Jordan cleared his throat, "we'd all certainly wish you well if . . . if that's what you want. But for the record, for everybody at SD&G, I think I can say that . . . that it . . . well, it just wouldn't be the same at the detachment."

After a long pause, Jerry raised his eyes to meet Jordan's. "Thank you, Wiley," he said slowly, "I appreciate your saying that."

Later that evening as Michelle helped me on with my coat, she drew me aside.

"Farran, I want to talk to you about what you said tonight. About it all being over."

I looked at her for a moment, puzzled. Then comprehension cleared my face.

"Don't worry, Michelle. I know very well that it's far from over." I self-consciously jammed my good hand in my pocket, a habit I'd picked up from my cousin. "What happened with Alison will take a long time to get over, a long time to grieve." If only they knew. "I'll tread carefully around Diana. You have my word."

She shook her head, motherly buttoning up the top button of my jacket for me.

"That's not what I meant. I want to give you a piece of advice. When I was seventeen years old, my older sister was murdered. By a jealous boyfriend." There was a flash of the old pain in her calm brown eyes. "I can't tell you what that did to me. What it did to my family."

Unconsciously, I reached out to hold her hand.

"The man was tried and convicted. But it didn't help. It's just beginning for you, you see. The loss, the grief, yes, but that's natural. To be expected. We may not like it or handle it well, but we're comfortable with grief." Michelle squeezed my hand. "It's the rage, Farran," she whispered as Jerry came up to go. "Watch out for the rage."

Michelle had put her finger exactly on it. The rage. The internal fire that forgiveness struggles to put out. And its offspring: revenge and guilt. Frank Clifford and Mila Pierce in Mille Roches. Dave Carlson and Alison Perry in Cambridge. All consumed by it. All dead. And now, as Michelle had warned me, it was my turn. Revenge and guilt are the dark twins that come to sleep with us after tragedy strikes. And they offer us a deadly choice: Do we turn the knife on others— or on ourselves?

"Stay for a drink?"

Jerry and I had safely survived our small talk on the way back to my house from the dinner. He helped me take off my coat and was starting to shake his head. Then maybe he saw something in my eyes.

"Sure," he said briefly. "But let me bartend. I'm a lot faster than a one-armed bandit."

I waited until we both were armed with drinks, seated facing off on opposite chairs in the living room. Then I cut to the chase.

"Why are you taking early retirement? That's not like you."

He shrugged. "Maybe I've just had enough of the grind. Maybe I'm ready for something new."

"I don't believe it. You love your job, just like John Perry did. And you're damn good at it, just like he was. That's why none of your officers wants you to go." When he didn't reply, a thought occurred to me. "It's not because of health reasons, is it?" I asked.

"No." Jerry got up to avoid my eyes.

"Then what the hell is it?" I persisted.

"I can't do the job anymore," he said quietly.

"Bullshit." I rose from my chair to face him. "You're one of the best. Your officers respect you."

"I screwed up, Farran. I screwed up big time. And it cost a human life." He slowly turned to me, but didn't meet my eyes. "Alison's. Alison wouldn't have died if I hadn't screwed up."

"What the hell are you talking about?" I whispered.

"Your security. After we talked on the bike path that day, I had an officer posted outside your house for security. I took turns with it myself to stretch the manpower. SD&G is a big detachment. We never seem to have enough officers . . . " Jerry shot back his drink and put the glass down. Then he finally looked at me. "That's not an excuse. Just an explanation. When the news came about the arrests in Cambridge, I pulled the security detail off. I thought it would be safe, then, with Alison's story all over the wire. I should have known . . . " He struggled for a moment. "I let Alison down. I let you down. I'm sorry."

"No," I said through numb lips, "no, Jerry—"

"I should go," he said abruptly and headed for the door.

"The bomb wasn't meant for Alison. It was meant for me."

There. The ugly words were spoken. I'd finally said it out loud—to him and to myself. Jerry stopped dead in his tracks. I started to shake. He carefully turned to face me.

"What did you say?"

"I said the bomb was meant for me. Not for Alison. You couldn't have saved her if you'd tried." Seeing the look on his face, I began to babble it out. "Alison killed Dave Carlson for killing her father and once she knew I'd figured it out she planned to kill me, too."

"But that's imposs—"

"*I said it was meant for me!*" I screamed. The rage ignited. I turned and hurled my glass across the room. It hit a framed print on the far wall, glass meeting glass, exploding into a thousand fragments. The silence that followed was deafening.

Even the shaking inside me stopped.

"It's the rage, Jerry." I said finally. My voice was calm and detached, as though coming from somewhere else. "Gordon destroying my family, robbing me of my father, forcing my mother into a lifetime of hiding. And now this." I had my back to him, and I spoke over my shoulder. "Last year, you had to deal with finding out the truth about your father's death, and that the truth had been kept from you for over forty years by someone you considered a friend. Not to mention losing your dad when you were just a boy. I know how much that hurt you. So how did you do it?" I turned to him. "It's the rage that I can't deal with. I've tried to forgive and go on. How did you do it? How did you make it go away?"

Jerry slowly crossed the floor and looked me right in the eye.

"It doesn't go away, Farran. I'm afraid it's part of you, now. But," he cut off my protest, "it's like having an illness. You learn to live with it. Not by denial, or by being hard on yourself. By accepting it. Look it in the face. If you can see it for what it is—" Jerry put his hand under my chin to raise my face to his. "For *who* it is. That's when you start taking control back. Putting a name to the monster takes its power away." At the word "power," Jerry looked at the mess I had made.

"I know, I know. I'm a real head case." I muttered miserably.

"Head case?" Jerry nodded at the destruction and smiled at me. "For what it's worth, Mackenzie, welcome back to the land of the living."

I gave a weak smile in return, and he dropped his hand.

"Listen, about this story about Alison trying to kill you," he said grimly. "You don't have to make me feel better by—"

"I'm not." My hands started to shake again, and I rubbed them together as if to warm them. "God help me, it's the truth."

"Why on earth would Alison ever do anything like that?"

So I told him. Pacing the living room, I shivered and stammered and cried a little as it all came out. I didn't know where it would take us, but for once I didn't care. I needed to share it with someone I could trust absolutely.

When I finished, the grave look on Jerry's face told me I'd convinced him.

"Do you have any concrete evidence to back you up?"

"None." Except maybe . . .

"I can't pursue this without something to hang it all on," he explained.

"Why should we?" I asked. "It's over and done with."

"Not for the police," Jerry reminded me. "For the police and the politicians, it's just beginning. Special interest groups are picking up Alison's motto about it being for the children as their new battle cry. Standish, her ex, has a lot of friends in high places. The federal government is really going to feel the heat build now about better child protection laws and mandatory tougher sentences for sexual predators and criminals who use children, let alone murder them. I think Alison Perry is going to have more clout in death than she had in life."

"That doesn't sound so bad," I murmured.

"It is for a group of undesirables sitting in prison for fraud, knowing they're the target of a murder investigation. Your story might save their collective ass."

"Do you think anyone would believe me?"

"On the street? Probably chalk it up to mental stress. In court?" He shook his head. "It wouldn't hold up. Too many holes. Unless," he added carefully, "you had something tangible to show as proof."

I walked to the patio doors and the blackness beyond. I could see Jerry in the reflection of the living room, standing behind me.

"I guess it stays our secret, then." I put my hand on the coolness of the dark glass.

"Have you told anyone else? Does Ruth or . . . or Mr. Vaughn know?"

"No one."

Jerry slowly moved nearer.

"Then why would you tell me? Why not keep your secret safe?"

"I couldn't let you accept the guilt for Alison's death. You didn't screw up."

"And you wanted to save me from ten extra years on a golf course somewhere, right?"

He was close behind me now, both inches and emotional miles away. I struggled with the policy of a lifetime—and won.

"No," I turned to him. "I need you, Jerry. I can't bear this alone. And you . . . you are my best friend."

The grey eyes softened, the ones that had seemed so inscrutable the first day we met.

"I had a best friend once," Jerry said. "Only once. For years, we were inseparable. Then he went away." He gently pushed the hair away from my face, and smiled. "I waited three days in the hospital for you to wake up. I thought you never would. And when you did, do you remember what you called me?" When I shook my head silently, he said, "Jer."

"Jer? I called you that?"

"Yes. It startled me at the time. Only one person on earth ever called me by that name. But I guess it goes with being my best friend."

I laughed and started to cry. That's when he took me in his arms and held me close. Last year, when the pain from the past had been too much, Jerry Strauss had come to me. Now it was my turn. Through that long dark night, I put my head—and my world—on his shoulders, until the first rays of dawn broke through.

DECEMBER

"It's beautiful." Diana held the plate up to the light, admiring the delicate pattern of blue forget-me-nots on the white china.

"Yes, it is," I agreed. The set of dishes was spread out around us on the floor of the living room. "The set is quite old. My mother got the dishes from her mother. It was all she had left of my grandmother, and now it's all I have left of her."

"They weren't in your mom's house when it burnt down?"

"No. My mother didn't take them with her years ago when she left here to marry my dad. She couldn't." I smiled at Diana. "So Alice Hoffman, Ruth's mother, left them stored away at her place. Forgot about them. Ruth found them last year when she was cleaning out after Alice died and brought them to me. I'm very grateful to have them."

It was a wet and miserable Saturday, grey and cold with no sign of snow. Diana had come to spend the day and it turned out to be a pyjama party. I had moved the contents of my condo in Waterloo into storage down here for the winter the month before, but a few boxes of important items were still stacked in the extra bedroom. We'd decided to go through this one.

"What was your mother like?" Diana asked.

I thought about that for a moment.

"She was a good mother," I said simply. "And a special lady. Certainly beautiful. Also very strong. I know what my father saw in her." I set a cup and saucer down carefully. "And from what I've heard about my father, I know what she saw in him, too."

"Anything like what you see in Inspector Strauss?"

I saw the teasing in her eyes. "*Touché*, I guess," I admitted. "But be careful, Wiley. I'm not that injured anymore."

Diana grinned. "I'm glad you like him, Fan. I think he's nice. He might be The Bear at the station, but I think underneath all that he's a nice man."

"The Bear? As in Smokey the Bear?"

The girl coloured a little. "Uh, yah. The Big Bear. That's what my dad says they all call him around here because he runs a tight ship. Just don't say I told you, okay?" she added. "I'm not sure he knows."

I promised secrecy on that, with the thought running through the back of my mind that there was probably little happening around SD&G that Jerry wouldn't know about. The Bear. It fit. I filed that one away for the future and wondered what Jerry was thinking these days about early retirement. He hadn't said a word since the night of the Wileys' dinner.

"I'm getting seriously hungry," I changed the subject. "I think it's time for pizza, don't you?"

"Fan, can I ask you something?" Diana looked pensive. "I've been wanting to talk to you privately about it. I . . . I don't really know who else to ask."

I looked at her face and braced myself for a life issue, hopefully not one that would be Michelle's strict domain.

"Sure. Fire away."

Diana hedged for a minute, fussing with the china.

"Do you believe in ghosts?" she blurted out.

"Ghosts?" I echoed. Now that was one I didn't see coming.

"Yes, ghosts. I mean, well, with all the history work you do and old places you hang out in I thought . . . I thought you'd be the person to ask. Do ghosts exist?"

I unwrapped the old teapot and held it for a moment.

"If you had asked me that question even two years ago, I'd have said no. I've spent my adult life approaching history with the intent to capture the reality of it. Myths and legends are fine, but only as clues as to what the people were thinking and feeling at the time." I stopped.

"But," Diana prompted.

"But then I came here." I set the teapot down. "The Seaway Valley is the cradle of Upper Canada. They might have rearranged things here fifty years ago, but that fact remains. It's a very old part of the country, even going back beyond that with the native Mohawk and the Iroquois." I looked at Diana. "I've heard the voices from the Lost Villages."

"The ones that are supposed to come from the river?"

I nodded. "It's happened more than once. One time, it saved my life. I don't know why I hear them. Maybe it's as simple as I'm willing to listen. Now," I added, "why do you ask?"

"Well, I've been hearing about things from my friends."

"Things?"

"Things that are happening in some of the old houses. Things they see."

"Such as?"

"Children," came the unexpected reply.

The next night I took the portrait of Sheila Monroe out of the closet and set it on the couch for a good look. Ghosts. Frank Clifford had lived with the "ghost" of this young woman in his heart for fifty years, filling a house with history instead of a life. Perhaps that was the price you paid for what he did—all to have something that was never his to begin with. His act of self-destruction the night he burnt the farmhouse down had been only a token performance. Like Dave

Carlson sitting in physical exile or Mila Pierce living in constant fear of Sheila's return to expose her, Frank Clifford had been dead for years. God knows there are many ways to kill yourself in this world, physical annihilation being only one.

I knew that Paul Vaughn's life was filled with ghosts at this point. His parents, Sheila and Charles. His best friend that had died in the accident that claimed his parents' lives. The unknown father, my uncle Gordon Leonard. Even the ghost of his own past, his family history here, and all that might have been.

In the weeks following the "return" of Steven Hoffman, Paul and I had had many talks about his other identity. We'd banded together for the family showdown with Ruth's other children. We'd also talked a lot about Ruth.

But the issue of Gordon Leonard, of his character, of Paul's conception, of the tragedy committed in my own life, had remained untouched. And I had not pushed it. At this point in time, I knew Paul Vaughn had just enough to absorb and rework into his own mythology. That side of the new reality would wait until his return, and I wondered how he would cope with it until then.

I sighed and looked at Sheila Monroe, so young and so beautiful—and so alone.

"Don't worry, Sheila," I told her. "Your son is not alone. I'll be keeping a close eye on him."

And on me, for that matter. The inspector was right. It was time for Farran Mackenzie to look after Farran Mackenzie.

Jerry had told me to look rage in the face, to see not only what it really was, but also who. I knew what he was getting at. The most dangerous part of the rage is the inability to forgive ourselves whatever trespasses or failures, real or imagined, we have committed. It twists inside, strangling our hearts and minds, until we are only going through the motions of living. Living is replaced by surviving. And we have turned our backs on the one true friend we have in life—ourselves.

I had begun the slow process of re-entry into life. The new policy was to move toward whatever made the old cowardice kick in. Aside from the big job of finding and reconnecting with my daughter Haley—and dealing with whatever trouble she was in—I was cleaning house. Starting over. Making room for other people. Learning to be nice to myself. Building something real for the first time in my life. Because from here on in, I declared all life invoices paid in full.

All, that is, except one.

I stood on the dike overlooking Mille Roches, cold wind cutting through me like a scythe, the gold watch clenched tightly in my hand.

I was trespassing in a dangerous area, and I knew it. But I had to get to the River. And it had to be deep.

Alison had been on my mind ceaselessly since the weekend of Diana's visit and the talk of ghosts. The horror of her death and the nightmare of her actually setting the bomb to kill me continued to haunt me like a dream I couldn't wake from. Mercifully, there was one truth that offered salvation: the Alison I had loved and known all those years, who still lived and breathed somewhere beneath the hardened shell, had in the final moment been unable to go through with it—had, in fact, turned the knife away from me and back onto herself.

For weeks after her death, I couldn't shake the feeling that Alison was close by, waiting for me to do something. I chalked it up to the grieving process, until I brought my things back from Waterloo and started moving into the house for real. Then I found something I had almost forgotten—and I understood.

I took a moment to look out at the great headpond, thinking of all the lives whose stories now lay under its waters. Everywhere around me was brown and dry. Dead leaves danced down the dirt road behind me. Angry purple clouds gathered on the horizon. The River was a menacing grey, rolling and straining at the harness we'd given Her. Where the thriving community of Mille Roches had once stood, I felt like the last person on earth.

The old saying still lingers here in the Seaway Valley: Hydro is God. And on the surface it would seem so as they pull water levels up and down in their artificial lake. But the secret truth is that no one ever tells a river what to do—especially one the size and spirit of the St. Lawrence. With all their computers and gauges and concrete dams, at best what's been accomplished by Hydro in half a century is an uneasy compromise between the River and her keepers. At worst, it is a cold war. And not one local needs to place any bets on who's slowly winning.

I opened my fist and held up Dave Carlson's gold watch. The watch Alison had secretly bought him for his thirtieth birthday, paid for with the babysitting money she'd saved for our trip to Europe—and then with misplaced guilt for thirty years after that. A gift of time turned inside out. I carefully turned It over and read the real inscription on the back—quite different from what Alison had pretended to read the day of her birthday party.

To Dave. Happy 30th. All my love, your Alison.

Now I would have to decide what the final payment would be for this watch.

Jerry had said he would need something tangible, anything solid to prove my story and pursue revealing the truth. Otherwise, it was all conjecture and bringing it to light would only cause surface damage, changing nothing.

But what of coming forward with the watch? Would Dave's watch with the inscription, coupled with my story, hold any weight? And what would speaking up accomplish anyway? Tear down the reputation of a lifetime for someone who had already paid the highest price for her crime? Shut down the action groups working for the children in Alison's name? Turn the eye of government away again from the issues of protecting the unprotected, of replacing politics and bureaucracy with justice?

Justice must be served. Justice is based on truth, or at least that's what they say.

It is for a group of undesirables sitting in prison for fraud, knowing they're the target of a murder investigation. Your story might save their collective ass.

Jerry's words went through my mind like the brutal wind. Criminals or not, they had a right to a fair trial. The late Mike Denny was a murderer and an arsonist, a local terrorist in today's language, but he did not shoot Sergeant John Perry. His son had a right to know that. Everybody had rights.

Suddenly, the wind dropped, and I realized I was tired beyond fatigue. I couldn't think anymore. I closed my fist over the watch, took a last look at the River and turned away. Give the watch to Jerry and let the chips fall where they may.

Then . . . something softly caressed my face. I stopped, wondering. Snow. Looking back at the River, I saw She was quickly disappearing into a curtain of white. The snowflakes whirled around me in a dance. Ten, a hundred, a thousand. Each one unique, perfect in their imperfection, falling on my face, my hair, my hands, covering me like a benediction. I laughed and chased them with my tongue, feeling small and wonderful like a child.

And the face of a child came to me. The laughing face of an eight-year-old boy, the Simser boy. The face from the newspaper long ago, the face that had haunted John Perry right up to his death. The face that had had the right to laugh and live to celebrate his ninth birthday in peace. The face of a thousand others.

The watch felt sharp and cold in my hand, the exhaustion running grey through my veins. But I am Leslie Mackenzie's daughter.

"For the children, Al," I called to the River.

Pulling back into a windup my mother would have been proud of, I followed through and let the watch fly. It soared high, high, up above the breast of the St. Lawrence. Catching a maverick ray of the disappearing sun, the watch flashed brilliantly in the storm for just a moment.

And then was gone.

The Robertson House

The story of Monroe House is based in part on the actual history of the Robertson House in the Upper Canada Village heritage park in Morrisburg. The home originally stood near Robertson Creek in the former hamlet of Maple Grove, just west of Cornwall.

In 1784, this property was granted to Captain Jeremiah French of the King's Royal Regiment of New York for service rendered in the name of the king during the American Revolution. Twenty-eight years later in 1812, Captain French sold the house and property to his son-in-law, George Robertson.

Over the years, the house was enlarged and renovated many times into the neo-classic structure it now is. The oldest part of the house is the dining room, dating from 1790 and sporting original wallpaper from 1819.

The house was purchased in 1957 from Miss Lottie Robertson, great-great-granddaughter of George Robertson. Extremely difficult to move because of its length and weight (150 tons), the house posed a special problem for house mover William Hartshorne. Digging into his usual bag of tricks, the mover came up with ball bearings, tandem beams, sixteen extra dolly wheels and ball-joint couplings. One item, however, was a little unusual—the ball bearings were (honest) vintage 1812 cannon balls.

"The Cannonball Express," as the workers dubbed it, worked like a charm. The Robertson House was moved successfully to the historic village, where it now looks as though it has never known another home.

The Waterloo Regional Police Service

In 2003, the Waterloo Regional Police Service marked thirty years of policing in the Waterloo Region. Prior to amalgamation in 1973, the County of Waterloo was patrolled by a number of different police forces. The cities of Kitchener, Waterloo and Galt; the towns of Preston, Hespeler, Elmira and New Hamburg; the village of Bridgeport; and the township of Waterloo all had their own police forces. The townships of Woolrich, Wellesley, Wilmot and North Dumfries were patrolled by the Ontario Provincial Police.

With the formation of the Regional Municipality of Waterloo on January 1, 1973, eight municipal police forces amalgamated to form the Waterloo Regional Police Force. The following year, the WRPF assumed responsibility for policing the townships that had previously been served by the Ontario Provincial Police.

In 1973, the Waterloo Regional Police Force consisted of 330 officers and 48 civilian members, and policed a community of 265,273 people. The name was changed from Waterloo Regional Police "Force" to Waterloo Regional Police "Service" in 1991. Waterloo Regional Police currently number approximately 610 police officers and 220 civilians, policing a region of 1,382 square kilometres with a population of over 470,000.

In the thirty-year history of the service, only one officer has ever died on duty. In 1998, Constable Dave Nicholson drowned near the Parkhill Dam in Cambridge—trying to save the life of a child.

Reprinted with permission from the Waterloo Regional Police Web site (www.wrps.on.ca).

Resources

Denison, Merrill. *The People's Power: The History of Ontario Hydro.* McClelland & Stewart Limited, Toronto. 1960.

Emerson, J. Norman. *New Pages in History. 1957.* "Before the Flood." *Ontario History, Vol. L (1958) No. 1* (contributed).

Harkness, John Graham, KC. *Stormont, Dundas and Glengarry: A History, 1784-1945.* Mutual Press Limited, Ottawa. 1946.

Marin, Clive and Frances. *Stormont, Dundas and Glengarry: 1945-1978.* Mika Publishing Company, Belleville. 1982.

Rutley, Rosemary. *Voices from the Lost Villages.* Old Crone Publishing and Communications, Ingleside. 1998.

Interviews: Maple Grove, Milles Roches. 1977-78. Archive, The Lost Villages Historical Society.

Souvenir Cornwall: Inundation Program. City of Cornwall, Cornwall. 1958.

The Cornwall Standard Freeholder. 1954-58. Morgue files, Cornwall Public Library, Cornwall.

The Lost Villages Bus Tour. September 9, 2001 and August 24, 2003. Guided tour of the land of the Lost Villages. Tour guide: Mary Lynn Alguire.

Welcome to Cornwall, the Friendly Seaway City. Cornwall City Press. 1967.

About the Author

In the three years since the successful publication of her first novel, *A Violent End*, Maggie Wheeler has established herself in not one, but two, Canadian literary genres. By seamlessly merging the craft of the mystery novel with her passion for Canadian history, Maggie has become a prominent voice in the growing contemporary movement to preserve and celebrate the stories of this country.

As well as her literary endeavours, Maggie continues to travel and meet with people to talk about not only the novels and the writing process, but also the emotional and cultural cost of the St. Lawrence Seaway. Her classroom lectures, symposium presentations and media interviews have sharpened the focus on Canadian history in general and the Lost Villages in particular.

Maggie and her husband Robert Childerhose, a Seaway pilot, live on Ault Island, with their three daughters, ten-year-old Anna and eight-year-old twins Evan and Lindsay. They also share their home near Ingleside, Ontario, with Bagel the Beagle.

www.maggiewheeler.com

To order more copies of

The Brother of Sleep

Contact:
General Store Publishing House
499 O'Brien Road, Box 415
Renfrew, Ontario Canada K7V 4A6
Telephone: 1-800-465-6072
Fax: (613) 432-7184
www.gsph.com

VISA and MASTERCARD accepted.